Same Face Different Place

Beginnings

By Helen J. Christmas

To Linda, happy reading

xx

Dedications

To my sister Jocelyne, with love

INTRODUCTION

Same Face Different Place is a British mystery thriller. The saga begins with a political conspiracy followed a series of events, which inspires a group of characters to unite and create a strong community. Book 1 Beginnings is the first of a series of five books, set across four decades from the 1970s through to the start of the 2nd Millennium.

I have always been intrigued by the way in which the political and economic climate of each decade has shaped our nation and its people. Inspired by experiences in my own life, the idea for this story came to me whilst walking along the beach with my dog. I began to think about the way some people become victims; the extent to which their lives can be manipulated by shifting patterns of events and decisions made by those in power. Once I had planned an outline synopsis for this saga, I realised it was too big to be contained in a single novel! So the idea was to develop a series; one in which I would attempt to embellish each book with the different music, fashion and TV trends of the decade as well as the changing technology and socio-economic mood characteristic of its time.

Book 1 - Beginnings does not end quite as one might imagine it to but leaves a mystery begging to be solved. There is never any doubt, these same characters will meet again, under a completely different set of circumstances where the wrongs of the past must be addressed and the story will continue.

ACKNOWLEDGEMENTS

I would like to express my thanks to everyone who helped and inspired me, including photographer Ian Berry, Karen Walter of NME Magazine and Molly McHenry, my fellow writer friend in the USA. Special thanks go to photographer M C Morgan for kindly allowing me to use his photograph of a London landscape taken in the 1970s for the front cover design and to Jocelyne Gwilym and Susanna Curwen for taking the time and trouble to beta read my book and for their suggestions how I might improve it. I would also like to add that since editing this book in 2015, I received considerable help from the Grosvenor Hotel, London, especially Jack O Carroll, Relationship Manager. Last of all, a big thank you to Barbara Edwards for her scrupulous proofreading service.

CONTENTS

PART 1. ELEANOR

Chapter 1

I
July 1972

The day 16 year old Eleanor Chapman's father had to leave town was the day her life changed forever.

"Pack your things, love," he said softly, "it's time we made a move..."

She blinked, unable to believe what he had just said. Yet it took just one glance at his troubled face as he lingered outside her bedroom to realise something was not right. Eleanor had sensed it ever since she arrived home for the school holidays. She bit her lip.

"Has this got anything to do with Sammie?" she challenged him.

Oliver Chapman nodded. Eleanor couldn't ignore the torment that shadowed his expression.

"Sammie's gonna to explain everything," he replied, "but first we have to get ourselves away from here and then we'll go over and see him."

He disappeared right then. She heard his footsteps as they padded down the carpeted stairs, leaving her alone in the silent sanctuary of her bedroom. Now she thought about it, life had been anything but normal - a suspicion which had gradually emerged over time.

Sammie Maxwell was her father's boss, a powerful looking man who wore smart suits and drove around London in a beautiful, plum red, chauffeur-driven Jaguar.

Her father had restored it to mint condition. On the surface, Sammie appeared to be a very successful businessman; owner of the garage of which Ollie was manager, as well as the luxurious car showroom next door. He mainly operated in the East End, where he was reputed to run various snooker halls, a hotel and a casino. The diamond at the core of Sammie Maxwell's corporation however, was 'The Malibu,' a nightclub for which the East End was notorious. The building also served as his headquarters where he spent many long hours in the upstairs office, running his empire.

But nothing was as it seemed and as Eleanor grew older, rumours that Sammie was not exactly squeaky clean began to spread like ink stains on blotting paper. She could no longer ignore the idea that occasionally filtered through her mind that he was some sort of *crime boss*. Even more worrying, she sensed her father had been drawn into the avenues of a mysterious underworld known as 'Sammie's Patch.'

At times throughout her childhood, her father had been called away at very short notice; the hushed conversations - the assurances that *this business wouldn't take long* and as they hired a housekeeper, it wasn't as if she was ever left alone. She had grown used to the sinister phone calls. Ollie would close the door on her, or send her to her room upstairs. There were a few occasions when she had woken up to the sound of his car fading away in the middle of the night, only to return in the early hours before sunrise. But the reasons were never explained and Ollie remained tight lipped about it all.

So it would seem her father and his boss were no saints but this was the life she had grown used to. Other than that, they were comfortably well off and never seemed to go short of anything. As a teenager living in London in the 1970s, life was colourful. With the current craze being Glam Rock, youngsters flaunted sequinned outfits and beads; heavy platform shoes were all the rage,   accentuated by longer than average hairstyles and big afro perms...

The house they lived in was modern and spacious, north of the Thames and only 15 minutes from the centre of London by tube; never too far from the shops, cafés and cinemas. It was beautifully furnished too; soft carpets like sand, deep enough to sink her bare feet into, a suite upholstered in velvet and lots of polished dark wood furniture. They even had a colour TV. The lounge led into a dining room which was equally luxurious. Other than a place for dinner parties, her father often entertained friends with gambling games such as poker and backgammon.

Upstairs she had a big bedroom all to herself. But as Eleanor stood there numbly, she found herself drinking it all in, reluctant to leave and at the same time, wondering what could have happened...

Hugging her arms around herself, she felt a wave of unease. The memory of what she'd seen a couple of nights ago came back to haunt her - a creeping fear that Dad was up to no good, only this time it was serious.

At 2:00 in the morning, she had crept towards the top of the staircase in her pyjamas and peered over the bannister. The kitchen light was on. She could clearly see his reflection in the window glass as he leant over the kitchen sink. Pale and shaking, there had been traces of blood on his shirt. Eleanor watched in dread as he poured himself a glass of whisky and downed it in one.

Oliver remained in the lounge for now, slumped in one of the velvet armchairs.

Hands clasped, his eyes stared blankly into space as the darker memories began to pervade. What to do about Eleanor... and this troubled him more than anything. A sadness twisted his heart. Poor kid! What he was about to reveal was going to shake the very foundations of her world but she had to know the truth.

This was going to take some explanation. He had long sensed she had

2

cottoned onto Sammie's empire *but how much did she really know?* From her perspective, his mainstream job was in car maintenance; manager of Sammie's garage and showroom. What she probably didn't know was that showroom served as a respectable front for Sammie's darker enterprises; a covert channel for laundering hefty amounts of cash.

Sammie's real wealth came from organised crime; drugs, gambling and prostitution. Yet these were only the minor sidelines. At the heart of the Sammie's reign lurked his protection rackets and this was where Oliver's true role came into play.

Sammie had first spotted him when his favourite motor, an exquisite vintage 1940s Rolls Royce, had been in need of a makeover. Oliver Chapman was of gypsy heritage, a family in the South East who owned one of the largest scrap yards in the area.

His skill in handling motor cars had drawn him to work as a mechanic in London. A handsome man, Ollie possessed a set of hard, statuesque features but the one characteristic that captivated Sammie most was his eyes - such a unnaturally pale shade of amber, they came across as chilling. Sammie had recognised a degree of menace in the man and glimpsed his opportunity. Thus on the day Oliver had delivered his favourite motor, flawless, polished and good as new, he had made him a proposition. He wanted to hire him; initially to work on the motors and run the garage. But as time elapsed, Ollie's role changed; assisting Sammie with hired protection, that baleful stare of his came in very handy. People were petrified of him.

London was a violent city. Crowds flocked to the East End for a good night out and those who spent their lives running restaurants, pubs and cafés prospered well. But behind the exuberant party scene hid a world marred by thugs and rival gangs, all vying to make a mark on the neighbourhood. When legal business owners got any bother, it was Sammie's boys who sorted it out. It kept down the nastier waves of crime, which kept the police happy (many of whom were taking back-handers). So the wheels of the East End kept turning and everyone benefitted, just so long as Maxwell's boys received a lion's share of the pickings...

In the mid 50s, Oliver fell in love with Eleanor's mother, a beautiful nightclub singer who had arisen on the stage of the Malibu like a star; of mixed race, audiences likened her to Diana Ross. Martina's exotic looks combined coffee coloured skin with alluring dark eyes, her enchanting voice drawing crowds to Sammie's club like no other. She was a legend in her time and Ollie had eventually married her. With the birth of a baby daughter, never to forget Sammie's thriving business empire, he could not have reached greater heights of happiness.

If only tragedy hadn't intervened; that one dreadful event which had put an abrupt end to those golden years. Marti had been killed in a car accident. There were no suspicious circumstances. The driver had been drunk, that was all there was to it, a terrible and pointless theft of a human life. It threw Oliver into turmoil. A widower at 35 with an eight year old girl to bring up single handed, he dealt with his grief for the sake of all those around him... But inside he was a broken man, harbouring a pain which tore his very soul.

Gradually the pain healed, but layers of fury and bitterness formed like scabs over the surface. Oliver had never been quite the same. Losing his wife had turned him harder and more ruthless than anyone could have imagined, especially Sammie, to whom he had become a virtually indispensable asset.

In the years that followed, Oliver did not remarry. He dated women; some for a few months if they were lucky but not one of them came close to Marti. The minority who did hang around for long enough to get to know his daughter didn't fare well either. Eleanor gave them a hard time. She missed her real mother terribly and found it impossible to warm to these shallow dolly birds her father brought home.

By the time she had reached the age of 11, she was a bit of a handful - no longer oblivious to the secret meetings, nor the times when Ollie left home in the darker hours. It seemed only natural, she would start asking questions. The girl was growing up faster than he could handle her. She started her periods, suffered from mood swings and behaved badly at school.

Firm in the belief he was doing the right thing, Ollie had sent her to boarding school and not just to avoid the problems of parenting but to *shelter her* from the sleaze and danger which hovered in the environment, he and Sammie operated in. He needn't have worried. Eleanor loved boarding school and bonded well with the other girls.

Those were the sheltered years - the ones in which his daughter lived a life of blissful ignorance, unaware of new *faces* that were beginning to spring up in London. But all that was about to change. There was no point trying to hide it from her anymore. She had to know who their enemies were and who she needed to be afraid of...

Ollie bit his lip. He could hear her up there now, stamping around in her bedroom, the sound interrupted by the occasional bang of her wardrobe door or a drawer being slammed shut. Still, at least she was packing a case!

The next hurdle was to get to Sammie's club and hopefully without being seen. Old Maxwell was going to give her a resume of the situation they had landed themselves in and it was not going to be pleasant. Ollie knew he would have to explain a little to her himself, before they got there. It wouldn't do any good to have Eleanor exploding into hysterics in front of his boss.

He rose from his chair, restless. God, how could he relax knowing that somewhere out there, a rival gang had descended, wreaking havoc with the destructive power of an avalanche? Everyone had assumed *Sammie Maxwell* was the toughest man in the East End and no one dared touch him. A man in his 50s, grey haired, overweight and paunchy, maybe he was not the feared man he used to be; his leadership being challenged by younger gang leader by the name of Dominic Theakston.

Theakston was said to have risen from the slums of North London, which could never quite compete with the East End for organised crime. Rumours that his gang had starting infiltrating 'Sammie's Patch' had emerged over a period of several weeks now where regrettably, a number of businesses had already been taken over. He had been sneaking around his patch, operating like an underground sewer rat.

The first Sammie heard of it was from the owners of an Indian restaurant. The man himself was said to be a terrifying character who conveyed more power than Sammie's boys ever had. The owners had been presented with an 'alternative' contract for protection - shocked by the threats he levied should they refuse. The Indian family however, were not the first to voice their complaints and considered it to be Sammie's duty to protect them from this intrusion. On the day the penny dropped, it was said that Sammie's bellows of rage must have been heard across the whole Capital. But it served as a catalyst; one that ignited a fuse and set off a chain reaction of events, which would alter the future of many lives... From the moment, Sammie Maxwell declared a turf war, Oliver found himself caught right in the middle of it.

Thus came the fateful night when Eleanor had secretly witnessed his return.

Sammie had challenged their rivals to a fight near the docks at midnight.

The air had been damp and cold. With a light fog suspended over the river, Sammie's men had lingered, waiting for their rivals to appear. The silence had been eerie until finally, an army of Theakston's men emerged - dozens of them by the looks of it, maybe even a hundred. Sammie had held his best men back to begin with. Ollie could not help noticing how young some of the other gang members were and not particularly experienced fighters either, swinging their clubs around like toddlers in a play pen! Others wielded chains and knives. It was nasty. Ollie had long feared the carnage this battle would leave in its wake...

Then from the shadows he spotted Theakston's approach, recognising his distinctive looks in an instant. He appeared to be gripping a knife in one hand and a gun in the other. Ollie drew in his breath and sped across the ground, diving for cover in the shelter of a warehouse doorway. One final glance told him, the gang leader was just a few feet away and without delay, Ollie had aimed his own weapon and fired.

Regrettably, a man by the name of Giovanni Ponti had wandered into view and consequently taken the bullet; Theakston's right hand man. The shot pierced his gut yet turned out to be fatal. Ollie could barely recall what happened after that. The world seemed to stand still, men frozen on the spot, before a wail of police sirens rocked the upheaval.

For those final few seconds, Oliver and his rival had stared at each other; it was one of those rare moments where his life spun in a vortex and nothing would ever be the same again.

II

Eleanor stuffed her suitcase with as many clothes as she could fit in the gaps between her shoes, records and magazines. Their lovely house was about to be confined to the past, including all the magazine pin ups of David Bowie, T-Rex and Queen plastered on her walls.

Turning towards the door, she clocked her reflection captured in the full length mirror. Gracefully slim and athletic, she was dressed in faded flared denim jeans and a pretty embroidered artist's smock. Beads swayed from her neck, matched by the bangles on her wrists. With her father's arresting stare, coupled with her mother's feminine features and full lips, she possessed the type of looks that turned heads. Her long, dark hair hung in ripples beyond her shoulders, shimmering in the light. Her greatest asset however was her large, honey coloured eyes; they often took on a startled expression, conveying a look of vulnerability.

Dragging her feet slowly downstairs, she could hear hushed words emanating from the sitting room. Their housekeeper was fussing around - begging Ollie to re-let the house and let her stay on. With a profound look of sadness, he fished out a bundle of bank notes.

"I'm sorry, love, it's not safe for you to stay here. What if they turned up and started questioning you about my whereabouts? Ivy, you *know* what form that questioning would take. Just find yourself a new place..." He pressed the notes into her hand. "Make a new start and don't worry about us. I'll inform the letting agents we won't be renewing the rent."

Eleanor frowned and that's when they saw her. Ollie wore the same pained expression, as she emerged from the stairs. She gazed at him icily, daring him to explain; *like why was he ordering her to pack her bags so suddenly? Why they were leaving their home?*

"Cab's outside, sweetheart," he said softly. "All the best, Ivy and thanks for everything."

Kissing the middle-aged woman on the cheek, he grabbed Eleanor's suitcase before she too bid her farewell. Next thing she knew, they had crept outside to where a black cab awaited them.

Eleanor craned her neck in the direction of the house for the last time, reluctant to turn away until it had disappeared from sight. Her father was braced next to her in the back of the cab.

"OK, you deserve an explanation," he began. "So tell me - what do you really know about Sammie Maxwell, do you understand the type of man he is?"

"Is he a gangster?" Eleanor answered frankly.

Ollie let out a deep sigh. "If that's what you want to term it," he confessed. "So you appreciate that not everything Sammie does is legal, do you?"

"I suppose," Eleanor said. "It's not just the club and the showroom he runs is it? Does he pay you to frighten people?"

She saw the tension grip his face. Maybe under any other circumstances, he would have laughed at that statement yet she wasn't completely naive!

"Yeah," he sighed. "I guess… Little shops and restaurants round here get a bit of bother from time to time, so it's up to guys like Sammie and me to sort things out. But that is not what I'm trying to say, love. You must have realised that London's a very violent city. Even with Sammie as boss, things can go wrong...."

"Are you in trouble, Dad?" she whispered.

There was no denying the anxiety mapped on his face.

"There have always been gangs in the capital," Oliver said, "and every so often, men like us face a challenge. But this is something different. Right now we're in the middle of a turf war. Another gang are trying to take over Sammie's patch and they are the worst thugs we have *ever* had to deal with..."

"What's happened, Dad?" Eleanor pleaded.

He seemed to be struggling with his words now, snatching the occasional glance out of the cab window as if scouring the streets for something - *or someone.*

"I killed a man," Ollie whispered. "That's what."

Eleanor studied the chiselled outline of his profile and shivered.

The minutes ticked by. The cab travelled towards East London, the streets crowded with an assortment of buildings on different levels. Shabby pale apartment blocks reared up above rows of dark brick terraces; and above them, a multitude of high rise tower blocks. The disorganised roads accommodated clusters of shops and pubs where a few of the *finer* buildings prevailed. They were adorned with decorative pillars and balustrades though on the whole, the area came across as dark and claustrophobic, the streets narrow, buildings partly demolished...

Yet there in the distance, Sammie's club, the Malibu, rose like a jewel. A magnificent construction, three storeys high, it squatted proudly on the corner of two roads, a facade of multi-coloured brickwork. With dozens of windows retaining their original stone dressings, it seemed in tune with some of London's more traditional Victorian architecture.

Eleanor however, was reeling, having never guessed her father was about to reveal anything like this. In the time it took to complete their journey, he had recalled the grittier details of his story in as few words as possible; all that mattered to him was, their lives were in danger. They were about to be stalked by enemies so deadly they would stop at nothing to gain retribution...

"And that's why we've had to leave our home," he finished sadly. "It would only be a matter of time before we came under attack. I couldn't bear the thought of exposing you to that risk, I mean, what if I just happened to be out?"

Eleanor looked at him, wanting to forgive him but she said nothing.

The cab pulled up outside the club and with a furtive glance around the area, Ollie smuggled Eleanor through the door before returning to collect their belongings. Once inside, they were escorted up to the office suite on the third floor.

Like everything else Sammie owned, his office exuded masculinity and power - richly furnished with a brown leather Chesterfield suite and a magnificent board room table carved from mahogany.

Behind that table, lingered Sammie himself. Hands folded behind his back, he stood as still as a statue. He possessed one of those faces which looked as if it could have been hewn from rock; high cheekbones and large brown eyes, which were turned down slightly. He was visibly overweight with a double chin and a large protruding belly, his cropped hair completely grey.

Like a fine wine, Sammie had mellowed with age and in truth, he really didn't need a turf war at his time of life. The moment they arrived, he released a sniff. Head inclined, his eyes harboured regret.

"Ollie...." he sighed. "Glad you came. Sit down, please, both of you."

He turned to Eleanor before lowering his bulk into a chair.

"How are you, love?" he added softly. "Really sorry to 'ave to break this to you..."

"What?" Eleanor demanded. Her voice, light and soft, was prone to breaking huskily at times when she was afraid.

"Ain't you told 'er yet?" Sammie grunted, glancing at her father.

"I've explained as much as I can," Ollie said. "I told her about the turf war and the fight but as for the the rest... It's better coming from you."

"I see," Sammie replied. He looked grave, his fingers steepled together on the polished table top. He turned his eyes back to Eleanor. Tense with

8

anxiety by now, she sat very still, wondering what he was about to reveal...

"You know your ol' man shot someone then, do you?"

She nodded.

"Thing is, he's in serious trouble. Wanted man 'e is, by one of the most evil villains in the Capital. We can no longer guarantee your dad's safety any more, Eleanor, which is why he 'as to leave London."

"No!' Eleanor spluttered, clamping a hand over her mouth.

"Best 'e goes alone," Sammie continued, "we've decided it's in everyone's interests. Better for you to remain here under protection...."

"What?" Eleanor protested. "Dad, you can't leave me. I want to go with you..."

"Ssh, sweetheart," Oliver said, touching her hand. "Just hear Sammie out."

"I know this might seem 'ard," the other man pressed, "but it ain't that simple. Time I told you a little more about the man 'imself."

Sammie paused for a moment, as if wrestling with the words he was about to impart next.

"Thing is, Eleanor, this is one right nasty piece of work we're dealing with 'ere and we can't afford to take no risks. His name is Dominic Theakston - e's already made a name for himself in London as one of the most feared gang leaders around and believe me, people are scared of this man. You just don't mess with 'im. Those who do pay a savage price, which is how he earned himself a reputation... It's not money Theakston rules by, it's terror."

He paused again, allowing the words to sink in but Eleanor heard him loud and clear - guessing he was about to reveal something far worse.

"This brings us back to Ollie, sat 'ere," Sammie sighed. "Shot one of his top blokes, he did! Means he ain't happy and yer Dad's made a fatal enemy. Word's out, Theakston's already flashing 'is cash around, offering a reward for any information leading to a man named *Ollie Chapman!* Means he's out for revenge."

"What happens if he finds you, Dad?" Eleanor shivered.

Oliver did not speak. It was Sammie who just kept chipping away.

"Few years ago, a killing took place which sent ripples of shock through the ganglands of London. Rumoured Theakston was behind it - murdered a rival gang leader, 'e did but it was more of an *execution* than a simple bullet."

Eleanor turned cold.

"But it's *you* we're worried about, see," Maxwell pressed. His eyes bore into her, never wavering for a second. "Theakston's a master when it comes to taking revenge on 'is enemies. One of 'is particular specialities is hurting people's loved ones and making 'em watch. Even been known to film such events and posting the reels of film... He's a sadistic piece of scum!"

"I couldn't bear that," Ollie interrupted. "You have to promise me you'll keep her safe, Sammie, otherwise she's coming with me."

"Ollie you 'ave my word," Sammie insisted, leaning forward to catch his eye, "and this is why it 'as to be like this. If ever he did find you, it'd be bad for Eleanor, 'specially if he knew she was yer daughter. So now do you understand? We can keep you safe, Eleanor, just as long as he never finds out who you are..."

A dragging silence ensued. Oliver looked devastated, as if fearing every word could become a reality. This was the only reason he had agreed to go along with all this. Eleanor sensed his discomfort as she looked up, feeling the lump in her throat. There was no doubt in her mind that the trouble he had landed himself in was terrible - worse than she could have imagined. She watched numbly as Maxwell grabbed hold of a leather bound folder and lifted out a press cutting. Thrusting it across the table towards Eleanor, he urged her to take it.

"This is 'im. This is the man you 'ave to look out for..."

Eleanor stared at the black and white photo, absorbing every detail; a man who appeared as handsome as he did cocky. With his face turned to one side, he glanced up through narrow, dark eyes. They slanted as he smiled. Dressed in a black leather jacket, his long, dark blonde hair hung to his shoulders. Yet as she studied his face, she knew that looks could be deceptive. A cold shudder rose from deep within her body, the words Maxwell voiced still reverberating. Numbly, she handed the press clipping back to him.

"No, keep it," Sammie whispered.

"Okay," she said, "though it's hardly a face I'll forget. This man is out to kill Dad, right?"

"Yes," Sammie replied bluntly.

Ollie threw his boss a stony glare.

"Right, so what now? I've agreed to go into hiding but what exactly have you got in mind for my daughter, Sammie? Whose she gonna stay with?"

"Well, you know I'd let 'er live at my place," Sammie sighed, "but unfortunately, that in itself, could be risky! However, there's a married couple I know who handle my accounts and they've agreed to 'elp. Have you met the Mallorys?"

Both shook their heads.

"Got a house in a nice neighbourhood, they 'ave," Sammie smiled. "Toby and 'is wife Pauline. They ain't got no kids of their own, so they've agreed to let Eleanor stay with 'em for a bit."

Eleanor bridled. "Sammie, please! I'm not a baby! I don't want to move in with some couple I've never met. Why can't I just go back to boarding school, or get a little flat somewhere?"

"Eleanor, you need protection," Sammie pressed. He leaned forward and grasped her hand in both of his own, enveloping it in warmth. "All you 'ave to do is blend in and remain anonymous. It is the only way you'll be safe but here's a compromise. As it's the school 'olidays, you can come and work for me - do a bit of waitressing in my club and earn some money. As you know, there are plenty of geezers 'ere who'll look after you."

Eleanor turned and stared at her father.

"When do I next get to see you?" she demanded, a sob catching her throat.

"With any luck it shouldn't be long," Sammie assured her. "Just give us time to deal with Theakston then 'opefully everything will get back to normal."

Ollie returned her stare and smiled at her, his pale eyes filled with affection.

"See you soon, sweetheart," he whispered touching her cheek. Leaning down he took her face in both hands and gazed deep into her eyes.

"Dad," she whispered, "be careful... a-and please come back soon."

"Bye, my love," he replied and kissed her forehead.

Turning to his boss, he gave a nod. Eleanor watched in stunned silence as he left the room.

III

She gazed back at Sammie, her eyes swimming with tears. She could not believe the things she had learned in the last half hour! The finality of seeing her father walk away left her dazed and now she was about to meet her *new guardians*.

"Everything'll be okay, love," Sammie said softly. "I know 'ow much yer dad means to you and e's one of the best men I've 'ad working for me, I wouldn't wanna lose 'im for the world. So try not to cry, eh?"

His eyes emitted a little twinkle. Eleanor tried to smile but it was impossible. How could Sammie possibly understand how she felt, having known nothing about the violence that shook the edges of her world?

A knock on the door interrupted her reverie. There was no denying, she was nervous. This wasn't like *staying with friends* which would have at least been a bit more fun. These people were complete strangers and she didn't feel comfortable about it.

Pauline, at first glance, came across as a slender woman in her 30s with thick golden hair fixed in curls. Her face might have been attractive if it wasn't so hard; thin lips painted with red lipstick and small grey eyes, positioned too close above a slightly hooked nose. From the moment she saw

11

Eleanor, those crimson lips curved into a smile.

"Is this Eleanor?" Her voice betrayed both surprise and delight.

"Yes, Pauline," Sammie replied. "Ollie's daughter. Like I explained, she needs a safe place to stay for a while. She's still a schoolgirl so I want you to take extra special care of 'er. D'yer think you can do that for me?"

"Of course," the woman said silkily. "We'd be delighted. Such a pretty young thing..."

Eleanor winced. She loathed being referred to as 'pretty' and didn't really appreciate being called a schoolgirl either, even if Sammie *was* trying to be protective. "Look… I really appreciate what you're doing for me but I don't want to be any trouble..."

"Shush!" the woman insisted, raising a hand for silence. "We're honoured, Sammie has asked us to help, in fact we've already agreed to this. Our house has three rooms and plenty of space."

"Eleanor will have her own room, of course," piped up the husband, Toby.

Eleanor glanced at him, having paid little attention to him until now; a thin man whose face possessed a hungry look, he had slightly long hair and sideburns.

"We'll give her as much privacy as she wants, though she's welcome to join us for meals or a natter. Ain't that right, Pauline?"

Pauline smiled. "I am sure the three of us will all get along just fine."

Eleanor swallowed. This was happening too fast. She had only just said goodbye to her father yet the way these people were sweeping in to claim her felt strange; like rolling downhill with no brakes, she no longer had any control over her fate. *If only she could run away from all this.*

"What about the club?" she spluttered. "Is it still okay to come and work here?"

"I said so didn't I?" Sammie beamed. "From 6.00 in the evening, Eleanor's gonna be doing a bit of waitressing work, so if you wouldn't mind dropping 'er round, Toby..."

Toby gave a shrug. "Good excuse to get a drink down me neck!"

"Look," Sammie finished, "I'm happy for one of me boys to bring 'er home and save you the bother of collecting her but you both know 'ow dangerous it is for her out there..."

"Of course," Pauline murmured. "Poor Oliver! I heard about this new gang leader who's after him but I'm sure it'll get sorted... in the meantime, we'll take good care of you."

"Thank you,' Eleanor relented, "it's good of you to do this."

Pauline was still smiling yet her eyes concealed a granite hardness - there was something unnerving, almost predatory about her. Throughout the whole conversation, she sensed the woman's scrutiny, reminded of a hovering eagle ogling a baby bird. But what else was there to say? The decision had been made.

"Keep yer pecker up, love," Sammie finished, "I'll see you tomorrow evening for your first shift. Just be careful, eh?" He winked at her fondly.

Eleanor couldn't speak as they drove away from the East End. Staring out of the car window, she watched the chaotic tangle of streets and buildings fade from view. Her chest felt tight. At times, she had found it hard to breath in Sammie's office but who was she to complain? Like a leaf captured in a gale force wind, she had to go with the flow...

It seemed little time before the car turned into a side street. A row of smart houses swung into view. Modern and new, they were constructed in clean red brick with white painted doors and window frames. They stood regimentally behind a crisp communal lawn, guarded from the road by black railings. Toby lifted her suitcase out of the boot of the car while Pauline hastily unlocked the door, inviting her inside. The Mallorys seemed to be doing everything to make her feel welcome and within a few minutes they showed her the room they had prepared upstairs.

To her surprise, they didn't seem to expect anything of her, allowing her time to unpack.

Only a little later, did she venture downstairs to find the couple relaxing at their dining table playing cards. The news droned subliminally on the wireless. It took only a moment to study the interior, a lot smaller than her old home and decorated in a style that was prevalent of the 70s. Boldly patterned brown wallpaper clashed with a suite of bright orange furniture. Tall floor lamps with fringed shades stood in each corner and above the fireplace hung a familiar picture of a herd of elephants. They seemed to march right out of the frame.

There was a stereo and a television with teak effect casing. The only pleasing object which drew her eye was a lava lamp on top of the TV set. Sadly, it brought back memories of her old home; times where she had sat and stared at it, hypnotised by the writhing blobs of coloured oil.

On that very first evening, the Mallorys bought fish and chips in her honour and let her watch 'Top of the Pops.' Touched by their efforts to make her feel at home, she finally managed to relax a little. But deep below the surface, she was missing her real home. The absence of her father left a desolate ache; she wondered where he might be, horrified to imagine him on the run!

By the time she retired to bed, she could no longer stem the flood of tears that soaked her pillow and the first night was not an easy one. As the night wore on, not only was it her own sorrow plaguing her but a deeper, clawing anxiety. It related to all the warnings Sammie had voiced.

Every time she closed her eyes, an image of Theakston's smiling face flashed in her mind, causing her to grip the bed covers in terror.

Eleanor did her best to blend into her new environment. Her low mood left her quieter than normal but she managed a few pleasant words with her guardians, making every effort to socialise. She watched TV with them in the downstairs lounge and taking a leaf out of Ollie's book, taught them how to play dominoes. She also helped Pauline with household chores.

But the times she looked forward to most were the evenings when she worked at Sammie's club. Not only was the Malibu the most stylish place in the East End but the atmosphere was intoxicating. Music pulsated from speakers across a beautifully lit dance floor. The club often hosted shows, such as local tribute bands, singers and professional dancers. Downstairs the seating was cabaret style where guests could relax in chairs set around tables, to watch the show or dance. Upstairs, there were two neon lit bars; one at each end. They buzzed with activity. Some guests were happy to order their own drinks while others preferred waitress service.

Eleanor found herself gliding around the carpeted balcony which spanned the perimeter of the lower floor, drawn to guests whenever they caught her eye to order drinks. A polished wooden rail enabled her to steal an occasional glance at the ballroom, to observe the effervescent party scene below. Paid by the hour, the real bonus was the tips, especially in the later hours as punters became more merry. In fact, she was earning plenty - enjoying herself and feeling very much a part of Sammie's club. Soon, she might even have enough money saved to afford a flat of her own.

Eleanor shuddered with excitement, just thinking about it.

IV

One morning, it dawned on her that she had been living with the Mallorys for an entire week, amazed she'd survived it without agonising about her father too much.

But in the back of her mind, she sensed that things were not right in Sammie's world. On the few occasions she had caught sight of him, she couldn't help noticing the furrows that pinched his face. He lacked the effervescence people knew him for.

Right now she was getting ready to begin her shift. Brushing the tangles from her hair, she coiled it into a French pleat, before slipping into her uniform black dress and grabbing her handbag. Only as she wandered into the lounge did she notice Pauline hovering.

"You look smart," she smirked, "but you don't make nearly enough of your looks, love!"

Eleanor snapped to a halt.

"What you need is a bit of makeup," she added, creeping towards her. "Something to bring out those lovely eyes..."

"It's okay," Eleanor muttered uncomfortably. "I'm not into wearing makeup. Dad says I don't need it and it'd only make me look tarty."

"Nonsense!" Pauline argued. "He just doesn't want to see his little girl looking all grown up, a typical father being overprotective."

She was about to open her mouth to protest but refrained. Pauline waved her hand towards the table, a chair already pulled out and waiting for her.

"Sit down," she ordered, tugging a black leather case out of her handbag.

With some reluctance, Eleanor obeyed. There seemed no point arguing. Like a bird of prey Pauline swooped; she was stood so close, Eleanor wished she could escape but no sooner was she hit by that thought when Pauline took her chin and tilted her face back. She closed her eyes.

Something greasy was smeared over her face. She imagined it must be foundation but it didn't end there. After puffing her face all over with powder, she applied eyeliner and then shadow. Eleanor nearly shuddered, dreading what looked like. Pauline's face was set in a mask of intent as she started applying mascara; two coats of the thick black stuff!

"Just a little lipstick and we're done." She fished out a startling shade of red.

Eleanor baulked. "Not that bright!" she gasped.

To her relief, Pauline relented, choosing a softer, rosier shade.

"Thanks," Eleanor mumbled, gazing up at her without expression.

She found herself propelled towards a mirror where the vision that loomed in front of her alarmed her. Her painted face looked *hideous*.

"You're 16, Eleanor," Pauline said fixing her with that same predatory smile. "Time to take an interest in your looks. We must take you out shopping and get you some trendy clothes. Mini dresses are all the rage now, worn with shiny, high heeled boots..."

"I like fashion," Eleanor enthused, turning away from her ghastly reflection. "We studied it at school. I wouldn't mind going into fashion design as a career."

The smile on Pauline's face turned flat - almost a grimace.

"I have to start thinking about my future," Eleanor pressed, sensing her disapproval. "I can't wait until Dad comes back, so we can discuss it."

"Of course," Pauline snapped, "but for now, why not live a little. You're still young, you need to have fun, enjoy yourself, visit a few more clubs... You haven't even got a boyfriend."

Eleanor suppressed a sigh, unsure what it was about that sentence that irritated her. Right now, she wasn't interested in any of those things. The only boys she had met were immature. Some of the men at the club were more presentable but probably too old. *No, she had far too many important things on her mind right now.*

"I've got to go," she huffed. "My shift starts soon..."

"Toby will give you a lift," Pauline answered, mercifully packing away all her crayons, tubes and makeup pots. "He's seeing Sammie himself later and needs to take the books over."

"My word!" a male voice resounded from the doorway.

Toby sauntered into the room, dressed in a dark blue suit, hair brushed, sideboards sticking out from his thin face. He had long front teeth like a rabbit, whistling as he drew in his breath.

"Looks a star doesn't she," Pauline said smugly and taking her jacket from the coat rack, she held it out for her. "Go knock 'em dead, darling. The punters are going to love you."

"Yeah, thanks," she said hastily, shrugging into the jacket. "See you later."

Escaping from the house, she felt herself cringing. Toby stepped around the passenger side and opened the car door for her. The couple then grinned at each other. Eleanor froze, unsure why it made her feel uneasy; it was as if they had been *plotting something*. They were only supposed to be looking after her for a *week or two* so why did they care what she looked like or what she chose to do with her life?

For the first time since meeting them, Eleanor wondered if they had other ideas. It seemed the Mallorys wanted to control her life just a bit too much. She would speak to Sammie tonight and relay her fears.

They drove in silence, just as a news bulletin was breaking on the radio.

A grave voice reported the atrocity of a car bomb in a quiet Surrey village... Eleanor turned rigid as the next words chilled her. A prominent MP, Albert Enfield, had been celebrating his 40th birthday with friends and family, before they had boarded a mini-bus bound for home; the horrific explosion had erupted seconds later, killing everyone inside. Early spectators suggested, the IRA were responsible.

"Oh my God," Eleanor shivered, "wasn't he about to be the next Prime Minister?"

Toby glanced sideways as if surprised. "Didn't know you were interested in politics, love, but yeah... He was a popular chap. Most people seemed to like him."

Enfield was rumoured to be a front-runner for the leadership of the Labour party. It had also been predicted that with this man at the helm, Labour would achieve a landslide victory against the Tories, whose current prime minister, Ted Heath, had led the country since 1970.

"Do you think he might have changed anything?" Eleanor murmured, thinking out loud. "Why would anyone want to kill him?"

"Dunno," Toby remarked. "I guess, being British didn't help, especially if he was set to run the country. Can't say I know much else other than that. Why?"

"Just wondering," Eleanor responded numbly.

Toby gave her a sly grin as they pulled up outside the club, the news bulletin forgotten...

"You go on in, love. I'll park me car an' see you soon!"

"Bye, Toby," Eleanor replied politely and with a smile, she stepped from the car towards the steps of the Malibu.

Right in front of the building, hovered the bouncer, Harvey, a huge West Indian man over six foot tall. Heavily built, he possessed a shiny, brown complexion and sombre face, although as soon as saw Eleanor, his face opened into a wide, toothy smile.

"Eleanor..." he grinned, holding the door open, "you look different tonight, baby. You okay?"

"I'm fine, Harvey," Eleanor said, "just worried about Dad! I don't suppose you've heard anything have you?"

"I wish I had some news," Harvey muttered, ushering her into the hallway. "But there's been no word! If I did hear anythin', you'd be the first to know."

Eleanor offered him a grateful smile as she walked through the hallway. A huge crystal chandelier cast a pool of soft white light across the carpeted floor. She approached the bar - about to ask for a glass of lemonade when she was halted by a tall, powerful looking man. Middle-aged, dressed in a smart grey suit, there was something nasty about the way he leered at her.

"Well, well," he muttered. "You're a pretty little thing. You new?"

"Just a waitress!" Eleanor snapped, turning away.

"Let me buy you a drink," he drawled, "and soon as you've finished for the night, come back and find me. I'll make it worth your while..."

Something hidden in his tone turned her stomach. She spun away without another word.

Only now, did she feel nervous. There was no denying, the atmosphere was different. On previous nights, customers hardly noticed her, other than to order drinks. She just blended into the background. Yet from every direction, men seemed to be ogling her. They stared unashamedly, greedy eyes devouring her, sizing her up as if she was put on this earth for their pleasure.

It had to be the make up. With a sob, Eleanor almost fell into the lavatories. Concealed from public scrutiny, she turned on the taps, drenching her hands with water and soap, to scrub the makeup off. Gradually it began to slide away, exposing her flawless complexion. She closed her eyes, feeling cleansed and breathed deeply. Now to get back to her job...

Toby had finished his meeting with Sammie. Having 'gone through the books' he was making his way back to the bar. He wore a smug smile, remembering the second reason he was here; very soon he would be engaged in another meeting, only this time with Pauline's kid brother. He spotted Sadie walking past, a voluptuous blonde who was a friend of theirs. Manageress of the club, her job was to supervise the staff, including Sammie's newest recruit, Eleanor.

"Hi Toby," she smiled, "just seen your Eleanor!"

"Oh yeah?" Toby smirked. "Looks good tonight, don't she?"

"Well, she did a minute ago," Sadie blurted thoughtlessly. "Last time I saw her, she was in the lavatories, scrubbing all her makeup off!"

Toby felt the grin slide off his face. Sadie on the other hand, simply shrugged. He watched her go plodding down the hallway, moments before Eleanor appeared as described; her youthful face was completely clear of makeup. He felt his jaw clench.

Unable to hold back, he strode over to her. The club was still quiet, lacking the usual swell of customers; dark enough for him to snatch her arm and tug her away from the balcony.

"What the hell do you think you're playing at?" he hissed.

"What?"

"My wife took the time and trouble to make you look more grownup tonight," Toby said quietly. "You've washed it all off haven't you! What's the hell is wrong with you?"

Eleanor stared at him in shock. "I'm sixteen!" she gasped. "I don't want to look grownup. I'm sorry, Toby, but she made me up like a tart!"

"She did not," Toby whispered, "she made you look beautiful."

"Well, I hated it," Eleanor retorted, "and I didn't much like all the men leering at me either. I'm not your property, so leave me alone!"

"Is there a problem here?" a third voice resounded silkily from behind.

Both of them whirled around.

"Terry!" Eleanor gasped in relief and turning back to Toby, she smiled apologetically. "Look, I know your wife meant well but don't be cross with me. It was all a bit much!"

"It's alright," Toby sighed. Eyes narrowing, he seemed to be scrutinising the man who had approached her. "You know this guy?"

"He's been a mate of my dad's since I was little, isn't that right, Terry?" She was smiling now, thankful to see a friendly face.

"That's okay then," Toby finished, a shifty look creeping onto his thin face. "I'll be off then and grab meself a beer. Let us know when you're done, love, and I'll take you home."

"Thanks, Toby," Eleanor sighed, "and don't be offended..."

Watching him wander down the passageway, she waited until he was some distance before turning back to her dad's old friend.

"Eleanor," Terry fretted, "are you sure everything's okay? I've been away, see. Only just heard about the trouble Ollie's in..."

Gazing back at him sadly, a lifetime of memories flooded her mind. Terry often came round to their house; times when she had been a little girl, usually curled up on a sofa reading comics, while Terry and her Dad played snooker in the lounge. Sometimes they went for a drive or a trip to the pub, where he would treat her to a glass of coca cola and crisps. Terry was heavily built with a round face, a head as bald as a billiard ball, although he always managed to find a few spare strands to comb over it. He had warm brown eyes that twinkled when he smiled. Eleanor smiled back; their families always got together at Christmas. With a couple of kids of his own, she enjoyed playing games with them, while the adults consumed cigarettes and liqueurs.

"... so what the hell are you doing, hanging out with that sleaze bag?" Terry finished.

"Who, Toby?" she frowned, tugged back to the present. "I'm just lodging with them for a bit, that's all, while Dad's in hiding. Sammie organised it."

"Go on."

Eleanor shrugged. "He said they were a nice couple. No kids of their own but they seem happy enough to look after me for a while. Why? Is there something I should know about them?"

Terry lit a cigarette and inhaled deeply. The club was starting to fill up with revellers now. Some would stay the whole evening while others would drift away after an hour or two. She spotted Toby again on the opposite side of the balcony. Gazing across the rail, staring at her, he appeared to be in conversation with a blonde man whose face was masked in shadow. Something about their sneaky glances suggested they were talking about her.

A familiar apprehension nagged her senses. "What up, Terry?" she urged. "Tell me!"

"It'll keep," he said softly, "but I'll be having words with Sammie later. Believe me, those two are not trustworthy, sweetheart. He should never have left you in their care. I may be wrong but if I were you, I wouldn't get too close to them..."

Eleanor bit her lip, knowing there was an element of truth in his words. She had never felt entirely comfortable in Pauline's presence, a fear, she wanted to possess her...

"Any other news?" she whispered, changing the subject. "Has Sammie seen off this rival gang leader yet?"

"No," Terry said gravely, stubbing out his cigarette. "Things are not good, Eleanor. Two of our best men went down last night..."

"What, you mean, killed?" Eleanor gasped.

"Shh," he urged her, "but yes, killed. This Theakston bastard's been sneaking about, throwing his weight around and he doesn't operate alone. He's got some seriously nasty thugs working for him. Do you know Big Al, who runs the snooker hall? Place got torched last night! Three days before that, Johnnie Mason, another mate of yer Dad's was knifed in an alleyway. The fact is, we're losing ground. Chances are, we might all have to go on the run soon and that includes you and me."

"Don't say that," she shuddered, "Sammie's tougher than that, surely?"

Terry raised his eyebrows.

"Isn't he?"

"People are saying Sammie's lost touch," Terry admitted, "he hasn't kept his finger on the pulse, which is the reason these bastards moved in so quickly. Police are staying well out of it. Gang politics ain't got nothing to do with them apparently! So unless Sammie cranks up the pressure, we're all gonna end up working for Theakston or *dead*."

"Which means Dad'll never be able to come back," Eleanor said huskily, feeling the trap closing in. "Oh God, Terry..."

Terry reached into his wallet and pulled out a business card.

"Call me," he said in a voice of stone. "Mallory's giving you a lift later, I heard him say that... But the first opportunity you can get to a phone, give me a bell."

"Of course!" she sighed back. "It's good to see you, Terry, and best of luck with your meeting. Pass on my best wishes to Sammie, will you? He's not been looking good lately and I'm worried about him..."

V

A heated meeting took place in Sammie's boardroom on the top floor. It was attended by several men, including Terry. Yet by the time Eleanor left the club, they were still in heavy discussion.

Recent events had left 'Sammie's Patch' in turmoil; employees had been called away at short notice to deal with a spate of burglaries and arson attacks, while various packs of thugs took it in turns to jump on the *smaller* establishments.

Such incidents proved to be a distraction. Only when Sammie's best men were diverted, did the rival gang see an opportunity to launch their most offensive tactics.

One example took place in a brothel in Whitechapel, run by a husband and wife. On the night the husband was called away to deal with the latest scam, the wife had been left on her own with the girls; a time when Dominic Theakston had paid them a personal visit.

The husband had returned to find his wife handcuffed to a chair. Worse than anything, he was confronted by the sight of Theakston himself with a knife at her throat. He had brutally informed them that *he would be taking over their place from now on* whether they liked it or not. The poor man really had no choice in the end.

By the end of the week, three quarters of the brothels under Sammie's rule, had been taken over by Theakston.

Sammie Maxwell ended the meeting bitterly upset, reluctant to face the fact that he was losing ground. Yet how could he give in? Having successfully run his patch for almost 30 years, he had never once lost a battle. He had always managed to crush his rivals. But even his own employees were beginning to see that Sammie couldn't fight a gang leader as determined as this man...

"Time we killed the bastard!" he managed to splutter as he sagged in his boardroom chair.

"Rumours out, Theakston's living in Whitechapel now," one of his men advised. "Renting some scummy apartment! Suits 'im, if you ask me!"

"I don't care 'ow you do it," Sammie sighed, "you can sort this out amongst yourselves or you can 'ire a contract killer... Just as long as you get 'im off my patch!"

No one failed to notice how pale he looked.

On the one hand, he was right; the only way to claw back their territory was to take out the main man himself. Thus it was agreed, they would choose a hit man of the highest calibre and this is how he closed the meeting.

Terry Williams was left floundering. The gravity of the turf war had completely swallowed up the evening, leaving him no opportunity to voice his concerns about Eleanor. Furthermore, she would have left with that slug, Toby Mallory, by now. The very thought left him cold.

All he could pray, was that she would phone him; the safest option was to whisk her up to the West Midlands and move her into their family home, away from London and its prevailing dangers. He was surprised Sammie hadn't thought of it in the first place and together they might be able to trace her old man. But best get her away from that pair of predators before it was too late. If he didn't hear from her by tomorrow, he'd be calling round there himself.

On the very same night however, Sammie suffered a massive heart attack. Too many years of indulgent living, drinking and smoking had finally caught up with him; all that combined with the overwhelming stress of the last week proved to be fatal. He was rushed to hospital by ambulance but the consensus was, *he was unlikely to survive.*

Toby turned his car into the neighbourhood and pulled up sharply. With Eleanor braced in the passenger seat, it had been a tense journey where neither of them spoke.

Next, she was going to have to face Pauline, her nerves taut, having already prepared herself for the altercation yet to take place.

Predictably, Pauline awaited her in the lounge. Her face was set like concrete, thin lips pressed together in a crimson line. *She knew.* Toby must have telephoned her from the club.

"So," she began in a cold, clipped voice. "You scrubbed it all off. I wasted my time and my makeup trying to turn you into a sophisticated young lady..."

Tears sprung to Eleanor's eyes. "No!" she sobbed. "You made me up like a tart! And that's exactly how the men at the club treated me! It was horrible!"

She was horrified to clock the triumphant glitter in the other woman's eyes.

"You've got no right to be angry with me," she gasped. "If anything I'm the one who should be upset. What do you care what I look like anyway, you're not my mother!"

"Too right, I'm not," Pauline said, sipping her gin and tonic. "Thank God!"

"Shut up, you stupid bitch!" Toby intervened nastily. "What's the point of being angry? It's too sodding late for that, just leave it..."

He turned back to Eleanor with a look of icy disdain.

"Go upstairs and pack your bags," he said curtly.

"What?" Eleanor frowned.

"Go on," he insisted. "This ain't working. I think it's time you moved on."

"But I don't understand," she faltered. "Where am I supposed to go?"

"Your old friend, Terry Williams, seemed desperate enough to get you away from us," Toby sneered. "I saw him give you his card..."

Glancing at him nervously, the words brought a bubble of hope. "W-well, I have known Terry since I was little," she faltered.

"Best you get in touch with him then," Toby finished

Pouring himself a shot of Martini from the drinks cabinet, he wasn't even looking at her now. Eleanor backed numbly from the lounge towards the stairs. Their simmering fury repelled her but more than anything, she couldn't wait to put some distance between them...

Wasting no time, she hauled her suitcase from under the bed.

She snatched a furtive glance over her shoulder as she unfastened the latches, half expecting Pauline to be lurking there, observing her. The case

22

had never been fully unpacked, where half her belongings still nestled at the bottom. It took only seconds to grab her few remaining clothes and underwear from the wardrobe.

Swiftly discarding her waitress's uniform, she squeezed into a pair of flares and dragged a t-shirt over her head. Finally, she headed towards the bathroom to pack her wash bag.

Downstairs, she could hear a murmur of conversation. The Mallorys spoke in hushed tones and were no doubt discussing her. In truth, she was stunned by their reaction; *all this hostility over a stupid bit of makeup.* It just didn't make sense! She slipped her feet into her platform mules and made her way downstairs, the case bouncing noisily with each step.

Plonking the case down by the door, she grabbed her coat from the bannister. The Mallorys turned. For a brief moment their faces looked smug. Maybe they were as pleased to be rid of her, as she was to be leaving...

"Might as well go then," Toby said.

"Shouldn't we phone Terry first?" Eleanor protested.

"Terry's still at the club," Toby snapped at her. "There's some big meeting going on up there! In fact, we may as well let Sammie know an' all. He ain't gonna like it if he suddenly finds out you're not lodging with us no more..."

"Okay," Eleanor nodded.

By the time they left it was nearly 11.00 at night. There was an icy stillness to the air as the darkness closed in; nothing but an echo of footsteps from the neighbouring paths and a distant hum of traffic. Eleanor did not look back at the house. She had no desire to.

Toby drove. A frosty silence hung between them, just as before. Eleanor sat perched in the back where an atmosphere of tension strained between them like a tightrope. There was something very sudden about their decision and she had only just realised it. On the one hand, she was relieved to be leaving but on the other... everything was happening too fast again. Eleanor recalled the same apprehension as she had on the day of her arrival.

The streets as well as the surrounding buildings had become so familiar by now. Any moment, Toby would turn right, towards a busy main road which led to the club in the heart of the East End. Eleanor braced herself. Except Toby turned left, heading in completely the wrong direction...

"Where are we going?" Eleanor piped up. "Club's back that way."

Pauline glanced around. Peering up from below her eyebrows, her eyes seemed even colder.

"Time to call in on my brother," she said. "Little bit of business... shouldn't take long."

Eleanor fell silent. *Couldn't they have at least dropped her off at the club first?* Robbed of all speech, she glanced from side to side, drinking in her environment. The streets were less crowded, in fact, the whole area possessed an air of neglect; roads hemmed in by high, brick buildings. They passed under a railway bridge. Piles of bricks, broken walls and plaster lay crumbling beyond a chicken wire fence, a sign that demolition work was taking place on a larger scale here. A couple of women tottered along a dingy, litter strewn pavement, in short skirts and very high heels. A man lounged in the doorway of a scruffy pub, smoking a cigarette, his eyes following them.

Toby turned into a narrow side street which led to a very different neighbourhood.

Eleanor held her breath. He paused on the corner of two roads, glancing towards a tall, detached house bordered by a high wall. Finally, she observed the house; a very large house, three storeys high, lined with windows. The curtains were drawn. Stranger still, was the pinkish glow that seemed to emanate from behind them.

The Mallorys slid out of the car. Without warning, Pauline wrenched the back door open where Eleanor remained frozen. She experienced a wave of fear - especially when the woman seized her arm and hauled her off the back seat.

"What are you doing?" she squeaked. Her voice sounded hollow, drained of strength.

In the next instant, she was shocked to feel the iron grip of *Toby's* hand close around her other arm. Together, they yanked her towards the house.

The front door swung wide open, sending a river of crimson light spilling across the driveway. A tall blonde man stood in its frame, hands on hips, glaring at them. Yet he was flanked by two other men, both black...

"Move!" Toby snarled, thrusting her roughly forwards.

Eleanor struggled in terror but the adults were too strong.

The blonde man smiled down at her, stepping aside as the Mallorys forced her into the house. The next thing she heard was the crash of the front door as it closed behind her.

Her world was turning black; all hopes of seeing Terry or returning to the club fluttering away like ashes. Stepping shakily into a large lounge, Eleanor absorbed her surroundings.

The pinkish light came from the lamps positioned around the room; with drooping shades hung with beads, it was the painted bulbs that emitted that rosy glow.

The furniture appeared elegant; gold chairs with spidery legs, a velvet chaise longue and a deep settee, piled with cushions. It seemed unnaturally luxurious, given the neighbourhood, from the white fur rugs to a multitude of little tables, cloaked in cloths for drinks and ashtrays.

A thin veil of smoke hung suspended in the air where two heavily made-up girls stood in the corner, chatting. Their eyes flickered over her. Yet some signal from the blonde man compelled them to leave. Eleanor felt a horror tear her senses; she had already guessed the type of place this was. She looked at her former 'guardians' in shock. Toby looked a little sheepish; Pauline on the other hand, was smirking.

"What the hell is going on?" she whispered.

Pauline embraced the blonde man. "Hello again, Mickey." She turned back to Eleanor, her hard grey eyes finally emitting the malice that had been hidden there all along. "Meet Mickey Clark, my brother!" she announced. "But you can call him Clark, everyone else does. You're working for him now, sweetheart, he's gonna be your pimp."

"What?" Eleanor shouted. "No! No, he isn't! You bastards! This was what you had planned all along wasn't it? You never intended to keep your word to Sammie!"

"Maxwell's finished," Toby intervened. "He's already lost this battle and I'm betting yer old man won't be coming back either, so we can do what we like. Sorry, kid, but you ain't got no choice."

"The deal's done," Pauline jeered. She beamed at her husband. "You wanted to get onto a career path, well this is it. Get used to it."

"How can you do this?" Eleanor whimpered, releasing a sob.

She glanced up at the blonde man. Young, maybe in his mid-twenties, he was as lean and hard-faced as his sister; yet those same features mapped on a man's face seemed even more cutting. He too had thin lips. They were pulled tightly back across his gritted white teeth.

"So, you're Eleanor Chapman, are you?" he hissed evilly.

"Please," she whimpered. "Don't make me do this."

"What? Turn down a pretty girl like you?" he reacted. "Forget it! You're working for me now and you'll do exactly as I say! Now what did we agree, Pauline?"

"Two hundred," the woman snapped in a manner that was almost business-like. "She's very young, only sixteen and like you say, pretty - most likely a virgin too. Some of your punters would pay a fortune to be her first. You'll get your investment back in no time!"

"Fine," Clark snapped.

The scenario turned ever darker. Clark snapped open his wallet and counted out a wad of notes. Pauline smiled again, her predatory face betraying nothing.

Eleanor was too enraged to speak, her mind spinning as she stared from one to the other, taking in the whole sordid scene; her fate bartered away like a prize cow in an auction. *This could not be happening.* A hastily muttered conversation hovered above her head until finally, the Mallorys moved towards the door, ready to leave.

"You can't do this to me," she bleated surging forwards.

One of Clark's henchmen seized her arm pulling her back.

"You bastards!" she sobbed in fury. "You bloody bastards! Sammie trusted you!"

The men in the room started laughing, at which point Eleanor collapsed onto one of the settees and burst into tears.

Chapter 2

I

Eleanor couldn't move. In just over a week her life had been thrown into chaos but now it was about to change beyond recognition. *A prostitute.* How could anyone expect her to cope with this awful turn of events?

An attractive young black woman sauntered over and offered her a drink. She had a halo of afro hair and delicate features; high cheekbones, full lips enhanced by luscious dark lipstick.

She introduced herself as Della.

"I've worked here a couple of years now," she smiled as if it was just some passing conversation. "Clark ain't that bad. Just don't try an' double cross him."

Eleanor sipped her drink. Guessing it to be some sort of cocktail, the taste of tropical fruit disguised an underlying flavour of alcohol.

"The other guys are bodyguards: Clive and Leroy. We get the occasional 'rogue punter' an' if things get rough, the boys sort 'em out..."

"I see," Eleanor whispered. She gave Della a long and searching look. "Listen, I can't work here, okay? What those bastards did is evil. How dare they dump me in a whorehouse. No one can force a girl to do this!"

Della gave a sigh. There was a glint of sympathy in her eyes.

"It ain't a bad life," she counselled. "All the girls here are quite happy... I guess this is happening a bit too fast but try not to worry. It's just sex, sweetheart."

"How can I not worry?" Eleanor protested. She drew her head closer. "Della, I've never ever done it before! They were right about that part. I was hoping, I'd lose my virginity with someone I loved, not some punter..." She fought back another sob. "How could my dad and for that matter, Sammie, trust such a pair of scum bags?"

"What, you think anyone in this world can be trusted?" Della chuckled. "Get real, love!"

"What?" Eleanor croaked, feeling the rise of tears again.

"Face facts, sweetie, we are all low life! Not just the Mallorys... This is the criminal underworld and there ain't no nice people in it."

Eleanor shook her head as Della relayed the stark reality.

"Have you absolutely no idea what kind of guy Sammie Maxwell is?"

"I-I know he's no saint," Eleanor faltered. "I've only just learned a bit about his business but he's still my father's boss... He's always been good to me."

"Yeah," Della added, "'cept his business includes casinos and whorehouses, hard drugs and hired muscle! Up until now, Sammie's been everyone's boss!"

"So what else do you know?" Eleanor pressed.

Della took her hand. "You're asking about your dad, ain't you? We all knew Ollie. One of Sammie's top hard men. He ran that garage and car lot... Well for a start, the place was a money laundering front. Apart from that, he assisted Sammie with all sorts of stuff, mainly in the protection rackets. Sammie liked Ollie 'cos he looked mean. Had them eyes that made you go cold all over!"

Eleanor gazed back blankly when in truth, she felt stunned.

"When Clark told us, Ollie's girl was bein' brought here, we were expecting some tough chick. Where's he been hidin' you all this time?"

Eleanor's frown deepened. "He sent me to boarding school, away from all this criminal stuff."

"Explains a lot," Della relented and letting go of Eleanor's hand, she lounged in her seat. "Look I don't mean to upset you and you're right, you probably don't belong here. What Clark's sister did ain't right though don't tell him I said that. Just try to understand that nobody in this game can be trusted. You might wanna remember that in future..."

She rose to her feet.

"C'mon, I'll take you to your room. Clark agreed to let you have your first night off so make the most of it. He ain't usually so considerate."

Coaxed from the lounge, Eleanor allowed herself to be led dreamily upstairs. *Two flights.* She wished she could close her ears to the sounds of obvious sexual activity emanating from all corners of the house. Exhaustion was beginning to sink in now. It must have been very late and her head felt heavy. She wondered if her drink contained some sort of sedative, though under the circumstances, she really didn't care...

Her room was small. At first glance, she clocked a single bed with a leopard skin effect cover, her coat and suitcase resting on top. The lighting like everywhere else in the house was very soft and similar to the glow of candlelight. Yet she felt too drowsy to take any more in.

"Get some sleep," Della sighed. "I got work to do now, so I'll leave you to settle in. Bathroom's on the right... Oh and you may as well know, this is the attic floor and we lock it at night, so don't go getting no fantasies about escapin.' Sorry this has been a shock but you'll get used to it..."

Eleanor slept heavily. By the time she awoke, she kept her eyes closed at first then gradually prised them open. Dismayed to discover her situation hadn't changed, she had almost clung to the hope, it would be a dream...

The anguish of her situation jolted her, the tears surfacing yet again. She rummaged through her coat pocket to find Terry's card, dismayed to discover it missing. She half expected it. One of the Mallorys must have taken it, while her coat was dangling from the bannister. Only now, did it seem obvious why the makeup had been such a big deal. She had seen the blonde man at the club with Toby, no doubt intent on showing her off... The abrupt appearance of Terry had forestalled him, compelling them to rush ahead with their plan anyway, before he had a chance to interfere.

Hot tears streamed down her cheeks. Right from the start she had known there was something predatory about the Mallorys and she had let them take control. She should have done a runner at the first chance, away from them, away from Sammie and away from London. Somehow, she could not get her head around the mess she had ended up in and with no clue as to where her father was, nor any means of getting hold of Terry. That left only one other avenue: Sammie. Even Terry had voiced some concern that he was losing the battle. So where did this leave her?

Her hands shook, as she started delving through the drawers of her beside cabinet. Other than skimpy underwear and stockings, she discovered perfume and makeup. Further down, she was even more revolted to discover porn magazines, condoms and lubricants; *this was a world that was completely alien to her.*

Wiping the tears away savagely, Eleanor knew she was well and truly on her own now. She was either going to have to find a way of coping - or escape - and to hell with what Della warned her.

As the morning unfolded, she showered, dressed and was eventually coaxed downstairs to join the others for breakfast. She assisted Della in clearing up; collecting empty glasses, wiping the tables and emptying ashtrays... Other girls began to emerge, yawning. They looked dishevelled in their bathrobes and slippers, hair tousled, faces still dirty from last night's makeup. Clark had six girls in addition to Della and ultimately, Eleanor.

An enormous sprawling house, the ground floor comprised the main lounge and bar, a kitchen and three bedrooms. The second storey accommodated four more bedrooms and a games room; there were three extra rooms on the attic floor, Eleanor's being the only one occupied. Clark and his henchmen slept in a ground floor annexe.

As the day wore on, Eleanor remained silent and sulky, taking every opportunity to study the layout of the house. It would help if she knew which direction it faced, so when one of the girls offered to take the rubbish out, she immediately volunteered to help.

A cluster of metal bins stood outside the back door. Eleanor studied the tiny lawn; a tall horse chestnut tree stood in one corner where a second brick wall backed onto a road. Okay, so escaping from this side of the garden would be complicated... *unless she could climb that tree.* Cautiously turning to the other girl, she introduced herself; horrified to learn that she too had been manipulated by the Mallorys.

"I had no idea they were traffickers!" the girl known as Libby confessed.

Having escaped from a violent home, they had taken her under their wing, using the same compelling charm Eleanor knew so well; a few nights sleeping in a soft bed, good food... she had entrusted them to deliver her to a new home, which of course turned out to be this place!

"I swear I am going to have those bastards one day," Eleanor snarled to herself.

At around 12.00 noon, Clark appeared, announcing the house open for business. According to Della, they worked alternative shifts. Anyone who worked the night shift could do as they pleased for now, whilst those remaining were available to any men calling in the daytime. It was decided, Eleanor would work the day shift until she became more experienced in her trade. *Night time pulled in more punters.* Della explained this, along with other rules; no one minded the girls drinking alcohol, so long as they didn't get reckless. Drugs were available too...

"I've never touched drugs in my life," Eleanor sniffed, "not even a joint."

"Maybe you've never needed to," Della said quietly, "but if they help...."

Clark was strutting around, making calls. Tall and muscular in a sleeveless black vest and jeans, her old school friends might have described him as *hunky*... if only he wasn't some cold blooded East End pimp, hankering to get his money's worth out of her. Eleanor took a deep breath, running her fingers through her hair. Determined to appear a little braver, she ambled into the lounge. Leroy seemed the more laid back out of the trio, his slightly longer hair braided into corn rows. Loitering behind the bar in flared jeans with a gold chain draped around his neck, he grinned at her before offering to mix her a cocktail.

Eleanor felt a smile lift her face. "Are you from the Caribbean?" she enquired.

"Yeah," he said, his voice smooth and rich. "Been living here five years now, earned myself some real good money and without doing none of the shit jobs, us coloureds get recruited for." He was stirring a tall glass, spooning in ice cubes and topping it up with pineapple juice.

"This good Jamaican white rum and coconut. We call it a Pina colada. Enjoy!"

Eleanor took the glass and sipped it gratefully. "Thank you," she said. "It's nice."

The place was imbibed with a light, party-like atmosphere. Jazz music could be heard from an old cassette player as the girls began to appear, hair coiffured, makeup perfect, dressed in clothes which were undeniably sexy. Eleanor took it all in. If nothing else, this was an establishment where people had fun. Yet at the same time, she felt hollow; she didn't belong here.

Clark seemed restless. Eleanor decided to pluck up the courage and talk to him. Strolling over to where he stood, she found herself trailing her fingers through her hair again.

"Look," she murmured, "I know you paid a lot of money for me but I'm really not cut out for this! Why don't you let me talk to Sammie... insist he pays you back, just to let me go?"

His eyes crawled over her - a smile dancing around his mouth.

"Forget it, darling," Clark snapped. "You're one of the hottest girls I've seen in a while and the punters are gonna pay good money. So I think I'll stick to me investment and screw Sammie!"

"But I am only sixteen!" Eleanor protested.

"Makes no difference to me," Clark smirked, "and frankly, I couldn't give a shit! There's plenty of girls younger than you go on the streets..."

"Yeah and your sister puts them there doesn't she!" Eleanor retorted, turning away.

Clark gripped her arm, making her wince. "Don't you disrespect my sister," he spat. "Times have been hard, you've got no idea how hard. You're just some spoiled little girl and you haven't a clue about real life! Well, I have and me sister's been good to me. Just you remember that!"

"I'm s-sorry," Eleanor faltered. "I'm just begging you... I'm not a whore!"

"We'll see about that," Clark finished, releasing her arm. "Now finish your drink. You've got a punter in about half an hour and Della's gonna get you ready."

The next hour passed in a blur, gradually descending into a nightmare...

Her first punter was a teacher in a secondary school who had a fetish for teenage girls, especially virgins. Eleanor sat shakily on the bed, while Della explained - selecting a pair of black stockings for her to wear, just visible beneath the hem of a gym slip, along with a school tie... Sweeping a little pink blusher onto her cheeks she braided her hair in plaits.

"There!" she smiled, standing back to look at her. "You look so cute!"

Eleanor closed her eyes, hands clasped to stop them shaking.

"At least he's a gentleman," Della smiled. "Just be nice to him."

A few moments later, there was a knock on the door. The man might have been presentable in his expensive looking suit and trench coat. But all she took in were his small, greedy eyes behind a pair of rimless spectacles. Eleanor shuddered. Bald with greasy brown hair, he was older than her father!

"You're quite lovely aren't you? Let's have a look at you..."

Tucking a finger under her chin, she felt her face being tilted back.

"I teach a classroom full of girls around your age," he kept drawling. His voice had the slow creeping quality of an oil slick. "Have you any idea how much I desire them?"

Pervert. The thought made her feel sick, already he disgusted her. He was still looking at her, running his tongue over his fat wet lips. Eleanor shrank as far back into the wall as she was able.

His hand fiddled with his flies. "This is your first time isn't it?" he smiled, leaning over her. "You're going to be my special pupil... and this is lesson one..."

Eleanor's heart started pounding. Looming right over her, one hand gripped her shoulder, the other tugging his zip. It took one glimpse of his flaccid pink organ before she let out a shriek.

"You dirty old bastard!" she screamed, pushing him away. "Don't touch me! And if that thing comes anywhere near me, I'll bite it off!"

The man looked startled. He moved away, leaving her huddled against the wall.

"If you don't want me to do this, I won't force you," he said and turning away, he grabbed his coat and fled from the room.

Eleanor could not stop trembling. *There had been teachers his age at her school* where the thought of having sex with them horrified her.

Yet she had turned away a punter. She chewed her lip, struck by the notion that Clark was not going to be happy...

She wasn't wrong. The minutes dragged by painfully, the rise of angry voices just discernible from below, until finally Della came back for her.

"Della! Get Eleanor down here, now!" Clark roared from the stairwell.

Escorting her downstairs, Della's face wore a pained expression.

Eleanor on the other hand, felt nothing but defiance as she glared at Clark. His eyes flashed dangerously before he stepped forward.

Before Della could stop him, he hit her across the face with the back of his hand. With a cry, she staggered backwards.

"You bitch!" he bellowed.

Before she had time to react, his fist swung, delivering a brutal punch into her stomach. Winded, she collapsed to her knees. Yet it seemed, he hadn't finished... His movements were fast as he swung his foot, kicking her thigh. Eleanor screamed, gripping her leg in agony but he kicked her again, right in the backside, jarring her.

"Stop! Stop it!" Della shrieked. "Are you mad?"

Clark was insane with rage, teeth bared, out of control and ready to do more damage. Assisted by Leroy, Della managed to seize his arms, pulling him back.

"Leave it out man!" she cried, "don't bruise her. You know it's bad for business, calm down!"

"Stupid bitch lost me fifty quid!" Clark kept spitting. "Cross me again,

32

Eleanor, and I'll take a blade to you next time!"

"Don't be crazy, man!" Leroy sighed.

"There's plenty who would," Clark snarled. "I'm not putting up with this shit! You work for me, girl, you do as I say and you never refuse a punter!"

The savage threats rained down. Eleanor lay curled up on the floor, eyes closed unable to stop sobbing. She could not believe what had just happened, her body throbbing. Only now did the reality come clear; the very thought of succumbing to that school teacher had repulsed her but there would be others. She had one choice and that was to run...

She opened her eyes gradually and stared at the door. The argument was still in full throttle; a chorus of ranting voices, the open space ahead beckoning. Contemplating her next move carefully, she took a deep breath then rolled across the floor. Seconds later, she had staggered to her feet and like an athlete reaching the finishing line, she made it to the front door.

She wrenched on the handle and for a moment, felt a blissful waft of cool air from outside.

Then all gravity was lost as she hit the floor face down.

One of them had tripped her up. Hit with a sense of devastation, Clark's second henchman, Clive, stood smirking above. He must have emerged from the toilet...

"Right, that's it!" Clark shouted as the others filled the hallway. "Time we got her doped up before there's any more trouble."

At first Eleanor didn't understand. Clive and Clark gripped her arms, hauling her to her feet.

Bundling her into the annexe, they forced her into a chair. Next thing she knew, Della had reappeared with Leroy. She saw the leather case he dropped onto the table and then the syringe. A heavy black cord was bound tightly around her arm. She could feel a thick pulse beating in her arm as Clark deftly swiped the syringe from his partner's hand and pushed it into her vein. A sharp sting followed - a sense of despair.

"No," she whispered, her voice husky. "Not this....."

The effects were sweet while they lasted. Her mind filled with clouds and she became oblivious to everything, her limbs like liquid as they took her upstairs and locked her up again. Eleanor sensed she was in her room, lying on the bed, covered in a blanket. The lamp was still on, casting a pretty pink haze around the walls; the noises around her distant, fading in and out subliminally as she hovered on the edge of sleep. She seemed to be floating...

Engulfed in softness, she felt as if a layer of cotton wool had been wrapped around her. Her mind started swimming - gentle memories. She could picture her mother with her soft brown eyes and warm smile, the chime of her voice as she sang along to songs on the radio. There were times, she had kissed her and tucked her in at bedtime with her teddy bear.

The next memories conveyed the protective presence of her father; days when he took her to the park to swirl her around on the roundabout or push her on the swings - a trip to Southend-on-Sea with rides at the fairground and ice creams. Like episodes in a TV drama she let the memories run on. She felt as if she was re-living her childhood, with the knowledge that she could never have those days again...

Newer, nastier memories attempted to encroach on the happy ones but Eleanor pushed them away. Then as time drifted on, she began to focus on her current surroundings.

Something seemed to shift within the house; another new episode but this one bore an element of danger. She could no longer ignore the unnatural noises interrupting this timeless loop... These were not the normal nocturnal sounds of adult voices, laughter, creaking stairs and bedsprings but something far more sinister...

She picked up a slam of car doors and muffled shouts from outside, sounds of violence and fear. A low rumbling arose from deep in the nucleus of the house; an eerie thumping as if a heavy object was being dragged down a staircase. A metallic clang followed and then an abrupt empty silence. She sensed it was very late. She even wondered if she had awoken in the early hours. Despite the mind altering drugs they had administered, she felt scared, knowing that something had happened here tonight. Her mind battled to piece it all together, until gradually sleep overwhelmed her and she sank once more into the darkness...

II

It was almost mid-morning when she awoke. She dragged herself slowly out of bed, stretching her arms. Her whole body felt stiff, her head groggy. Stumbling into the bathroom, the first thing she caught sight of was her reflection. Her huge eyes bore dark circles. The natural golden hue of her skin appeared almost grey, like a dishcloth that had been through the wash too often

At least they allowed her a bath. Melting into hot water piled high with bubbles felt like pure bliss. Apart from an angry purple bruise on her thigh, there were few traces of Clark's violence, other than a tenderness in her body. The warmth of the water caressed her aching limbs. She washed her hair and scrubbed her face until her skin glowed. Once she was back in her room, she even applied a little makeup. Eleanor crept downstairs, wearing a simple black dress and high heels. With her freshly washed hair gleaming, it hung loose down her back in ripples.

Today a lavish spread of food appeared in the kitchen - one of the girls celebrating her birthday. Eleanor hungrily tucked into quiche lorraine, coleslaw and potato crisps, unable to resist a slice of chocolate cake. The after effects of the drugs had left her not only weary but ravenous.

The instant she emerged in the lounge, Clark and his men eyed her with amusement.

"Make yourself at home," Clark remarked. "Hope you're gonna *behave yourself* today."

"I'm sorry I tried to escape," Eleanor mumbled, "but you-you h-hurt me..."

Clark surveyed her with a cocky smile. In a strange way, he seemed to be warming to her, as adult men usually did after a while. Eleanor had spent her whole life socialising with her father's colleagues and had developed a natural rapport.

"You might wanna see this," he said, holding out a polaroid. "One for the portfolio. Some punters like to take a look at our girls before they choose..."

Eleanor stared at the glossy black and white picture as if in a dream. They must have taken it while she was drugged. Soft shadows pooled in the contours of her face and made her look beautiful. The school uniform captured her fragile youth. Only her eyes looked strange; wide and without expression, their golden colour accentuated. Uneasy about such a photo being included in their portfolio, she nevertheless had no choice but to nod.

"Nice photo," she murmured.

Trying to fight them was impossible and she had only just started to accept this. Not only were they stronger, but kept a close eye on her. If she really wanted to find a way out, it was essential to gain their trust. Soon, she would be faced with another punter. She had to find a way of coping, even if it meant a few of Leroy's cocktails to numb her senses. Maybe with enough alcohol, the true, sleazy nature of this trade might elude her in the end.

The thought of more drugs was horrifying. Her body felt defiled. Della had already warned her that Clark would resort to the same tactic, if she continued to cause trouble; and with frequent use, she would develop a dependency. It wasn't uncommon for pimps to use drugs to control their women... The concept chilled her, forcing her to accept her fate; there was no way she would give them the excuse to inject her ever again.

Feeling a little more in tune with her environment, Eleanor helped clear away the food and the plates. On the two occasions the doorbell rang, it was a couple of regular businessmen with top city jobs. Nothing worked off managerial stress better than a screw with their favourite girl. For the time being, Eleanor was spared - free to settle down and relax in the lounge with the others.

Sipping her coffee, she flipped through a glossy fashion magazine. At times she joined in the chatter with some of the girls and of course, the mellow natured Leroy.

At 4.00 in the afternoon a long black car pulled into the driveway. At first no one could see the occupants. They were hidden behind blacked out windows. Della bit her lip, then rose.

"Oh shit," Eleanor heard Leroy mutter from behind the bar.

Even Clark looked anxious. "What the hell are they doing here?" he hissed.

Eleanor felt a shift in the atmosphere. For some reason, she was remembering the ominous sounds she had picked up the previous night, knowing they were not a product of her imagination. She stood up to peer through the window, curious to know what could cause such a reaction. Oddly enough, so did the others, as if joined by a thread. The doorbell rang. Clark gave Della a nod to answer it and within seconds, the door of the lounge swung open.

Eleanor watched the scene unfurl as three men sauntered into the lounge but her eyes were fixed on just one of them, recognising the straight, dark blonde hair which hung to his broad shoulders. She clocked the evil slant of his eyes; remembering the newspaper clipping Sammie had showed her. There was no mistaking, this man was *Dominic Theakston*.

He was tailed by two tough looking men and together they exuded an air of menace. Apart from his distinctive looks, there was something else. It was the way he moved; slowly but with flashes of sudden animation. He possessed the prowl of a tiger. His height too, surprised her. Considerably taller than the others, he was powerfully built with a muscular torso, which could only have been sculpted from working out with weights...

"Hello folks," he said softly. His voice rang with a sinister echo. "Surprised to see me again so soon?"

"What can I do for you?" Clark asked.

Eleanor was shocked to hear how nervous he sounded. Theakston looked as if he was enjoying himself as he swaggered from one end of the room to the other, almost revelling in the effect he was having on the residents. She remained where she stood, rigid as a statue. Was it possible, Clark's brothel had been taken over, by now?

"Oh, there's been another development, Mickey!" he piped up. "But you needn't be worried. Might not affect you but then again, maybe it will..."

"Go on," Clark pressed, "what development?"

Theakston offered him a broad smile. "We closed the Malibu down earlier! Thought you might like to know that."

Eleanor let out a little gasp although no one appeared to notice.

"Oh and news is out, Maxwell's finally snuffed it!"

"What?" shrieked Della. She fired Eleanor a warning look, compelling her to stay quiet. "When did this happen?"

Dominic turned and gave her a long, appraising look. His smile deepened, carving identical crescent-shaped curves in the sides of his mouth.

"Wednesday night as it happens. Had a coronary. They tried to hush it all up but nothing gets past me, so yeah, Maxwell had a heart attack! Fat slob obviously couldn't cut it any more."

Eleanor pressed her eyes shut, suppressing tears. *Sammie! Dead! It was impossible!*

"I see," Della said gently. "Well, sorry to hear it, Mr Theakston, that's sad news. Sammie's been pretty good to us over the years."

As the dialogue took place, Eleanor's mind started racing; *Wednesday night.* That was the last time she had worked at the Malibu, before the Mallorys had brought her to this place. Of course, she had no idea what had been happening behind the scenes. News of Sammie's death shocked her deeply, though instinct compelled her to stay quiet. There was no way she could risk drawing attention to herself...

Regrettably, something about Theakston's conduct as he paced the room, suggested there was more to come. His smile faded as his eyes swept around the room, gazing at every one of them in turn. Everyone was waiting for the bomb to drop, the room charged with tension.

"So," he murmured dangerously, "only a few more scores left to settle, which brings me here. We asked a few questions in the Malibu, see, mainly concerning the whereabouts of that cock sucker, Ollie Chapman..."

Eleanor froze, hardly daring to breath.

"Funny how a cash reward can loosen people's tongues," he went on. Turning slowly away from Clark, his eyes fell to the floor. He wandered past Clive and Della - past the other two prostitutes in the room until eventually he reached the silent corner where Eleanor stood. "I hear you've got a new recruit, Clark."

He looked up and stared straight into Eleanor's eyes.

"This one, yeah?" he questioned, keeping his tone soft.

Eleanor could not move. With the room already spinning, she felt giddy.

Theakston spun back around to Clark and Leroy.

"Well?" he barked. The crescendo in his voice made Della jump.

"Yeah, she's my newest," Clark admitted reluctantly. "Joined us a couple of days ago, why?"

"Little bird told me she's Chapman's daughter," Dominic said in a voice of ice and he turned back to her. "Eleanor, is it?"

She hugged her arms around herself in fear. *He knew.* With a sinking heart, Eleanor realised that *she* was the reason he was here.

"Yes," she whispered huskily.

His stare didn't waver, his eyes narrowing. "Like I say, no one can hide the truth from me. Fifty quid bought us all the information we needed..."

"Who told you?" Eleanor whimpered. "Was it the Mallorys?"

Dominic Theakston let out a harsh laugh.

"I visited them later!" Addressing the whole group again, he reached into his pocket and flicked out a metal tin, took a cigarette and lit it. With a deep draw of smoke he exhaled with a satisfied sigh. "That ponce nearly shit his pants when we turned up at his door! Cow faced wife didn't look too happy either!"

Eleanor couldn't fail to notice the flash in Clark's eyes. He didn't like hearing people bad-mouth his sister.

"Didn't have a lot to say as it happened," he finished. "But then again, I found out everything I needed at that club... Some girl leaked it. Blonde, fat chick by the name of Sadie! Led me upstairs to Sammie's office, opened his safe and I hooked out Chapman's file. There was a photo of you in there, love! Didn't know Ollie had such a horny daughter!"

Eleanor stared at him, speechless.

"Turned out to be a hot tip, so I paid her off. She also let slip, the Mallory couple dumped you round here, at Mickey Clark's knocking shop. Lucky me! What I call a good morning's work. Shame, you didn't think to tell me though, Clark..."

"Didn't think it mattered," Clark said quickly. "She's just a girl, she's nothing to you..."

"Oh, now there you are wrong!" Dominic replied, a sinister tone creeping into his voice again. "This is the daughter of a piece of shit who killed my best friend. Believe me, she is everything to me! So, moving on, has she pulled a punter yet?"

"Not yet," Clark replied. "I told you, she's only been with us for about a day..."

"So how much are you charging for her?" Dominic pressed. "How much, to turn a trick?"

"Fifty quid," Clark said curtly, "for a first shot..." He looked devastated.

"Seems a lot!" Dominic snorted. Surveying her again, his expression turned to one of intrigue. "Don't tell me she's a *virgin*."

An uncomfortable silence hung thickly. Nobody dared say a word, which pretty much confirmed the truth. Dominic stubbed out his cigarette in one of the ashtrays. Eleanor flinched. There was little doubt, what he was thinking. His oak brown eyes gleamed as they swept over her from head to toe. They rose to her face, impaling her where she stood.

"Okay you've got a deal," he said. "Fifty pounds it is, Clark, I'm gonna be her first punter."

"No!" Eleanor gasped, backing into the wall.

He took a couple of steps forward, drawing himself close.

"Oh, we are going to have fun with you, baby," his voice was a hiss. "Yeah, me and a couple of me boys... Give you a night to remember."

Eleanor pressed her eyes shut, unable to believe what she was hearing. She felt sick.

"And another thing," Dominic added. "I want a decent size room, Clark, so we can set up some filming equipment..."

"No!" Eleanor whimpered in terror. "Please, no..."

With increasing horror, she knew where this was leading. Everything Sammie had uttered a week ago was materialising into a brutal reality: *we can keep you safe, Eleanor - just as long as he never finds out who you are.* Eleanor felt her whole world crumbling right where she stood.

Theakston took hold of her chin, tilting her face up so she was forced to look at him. She was so scared, she wanted to die.

"See - this'd make a really good film," his soft voice mocked. "One we'll make sure your dad hears about before we find a way of getting it to him! We know he's in hiding. 'Spect he's down in the Costa del Sol but I'm guessing, as soon as he gets news of this little blue movie, we'll have him flushed out of that hole like a rat out of a drain pipe!"

Her bottom lip trembled, a single tear rolling from her eye. Dominic stroked it away from her cheek with his thumb, a gesture which was almost tender.

"So do we have a deal?" he murmured, flicking another sideways glance at Clark.

"Do I have a choice?" Clark snapped.

Eleanor glanced at him, her eyes pleading, but it was Della who spoke up.

"Aw, come on, this ain't fair!" she protested. "Don't hurt her, *please* Mr Theakston, she's just a baby. We're sorry you lost your friend but *you know*, it ain't Eleanor's fault!"

"Life's not fair," Dominic said, "but this is the way I operate. Everyone knows that and I'm not about to turn soft now..." Returning his gaze to Eleanor he gave a cruel smile. "Fact is, she's working here as a whore, you said her fee was £50 and I've agreed to pay you that."

With no choice but to agree, Clark could no longer look at her. With a nod, he turned away.

"Right, I'll be back in a few hours," Dominic said. "Got another bit of business to tend to but make sure there's a room ready... and keep her under lock and key! You'd better not let this *baby* escape or I'll hold you responsible, Clark; you and the black tart!"

Eleanor glimpsed the outrage on Della's face, loathing the feel of his hand locked around her chin. A sharp tinge of nicotine mingled with the acrid scent of his aftershave. Worse than anything was the look of lust simmering in his eyes. She felt like a rabbit in a trap.

"Don't do this," she croaked. "Please - I'm not your enemy."

"Deal's done," he smiled back at her, "and besides... I'm looking forward to our date!"

His grip on her chin tightened before he kissed her. His lips dragged down hard over hers. Eleanor could barely struggle, he was way too strong; this was a gesture of pure domination, a final reminder of the power he held over her. She staggered backward in the moment he let go.

With a snigger, the three men finally sauntered from the lounge and left the house.

III

Dominic slumped in the passenger seat and lit another cigarette, as his driver revved the engine. He glared back at the house while they backed from the driveway - seeing the shadows looming in the windows. *Yet he was buzzing...* Never in his whole life had he felt so powerful as he did now; it charged through his blood like a drug. To think how *quickly* his gang had dominated Sammie's Patch. Like a plague, they had taken over so many businesses and finally seen off the old man himself. It made him want to laugh out loud.

But the globe kept on spinning and right now, he had a far more serious meeting to attend; the only reason this was a flying visit. He had got what he had wanted. Finding the Chapman girl had been a dream where nothing fuelled his ambition more than the thought of drawing her father out of hiding.

As for Eleanor... even he never expected to find such a beauty. He had known who she was from the moment they entered the room, of course - recognising her from that photo. *Oh, how she had cowered in the corner of Clark's lounge trying to be invisible.* He had enjoyed playing with them but what turned him on more than anything was her fear - this was going to be so sweet! The vision of her terror-filled eyes and the way her lip trembled practically gave him a hard on. He could not wait to return. But the filming was important and not just for the purpose of tormenting Chapman. In truth, he yearned for a copy himself just to savour the moment again and again...

For the rest of the journey, he said little more.

In the back of his mind rested the other matter; a meeting which involved a contract killing for which he had been offered a fortune. He really needed to focus.

But every so often, his thoughts were drawn back to Eleanor, delivering wave after wave of euphoria. He felt like a king. He had conquered Sammie's Patch and in a couple of hours he was going to deflower Chapman's ravishing daughter.

40

This, he decided, was about to be the best day of his life.

Back in Clark's brothel, the atmosphere was very different. Only Clark remained in the lounge, flanked by his two men, Della and Eleanor, all reeling in the aftermath of what had occurred.

"Shit, man," Clive spluttered.

"I can't believe it," Della muttered under her breath. Her eyes danced from Eleanor back to Clark. "It ain't right!"

"Too fucking right, it ain't!" Clark bellowed. He began to pace the room, fists clenched, about to do some damage, then pounded the back of the sofa. "Fuck!"

"Is that all you can say!" Della shrieked at him.

"What else is there to say?" Clark shouted. "That piece of scum comes here, strutting around likes he owns the fucking joint, insults me sister, calls one of me girls a black tart..." his words tailed off, reluctant to mention the more sinister threat towards Eleanor.

But they looked at her now. She hadn't moved since Theakston had left; pressed in the same corner, quaking with fear. No sooner had Della turned to her when she finally let go of her emotions. She started sobbing hysterically.

"This is way out of line," Leroy snapped. "You can't let him loose on her, man, he's an animal!"

"What, you think I had a choice?" Clark shouted back. "You don't mess with him, Leroy. Double cross him and he's the type of man who'd rip your fucking bollocks off!"

"Can't sit here and do nothin'," Leroy argued. "I'm getting quite attached to this girl!"

"Yeah, and I'm quite attached to my bollocks!" Clark argued, lighting a cigarette. "There ain't nothing we can do!"

From the other side of the room, Eleanor could no longer hold back the sobs bursting out of her. Della gathered her in her arms, distraught at the sounds of her torment. There was no doubt that everyone had been shocked by this awful turn of events.

"For what it's worth," Clark said, "I'm sorry, kid. I never meant for this to happen..."

Eleanor felt chilled to the core as Della led her gently back up the stairs to the attic floor. Unlocking the door with a sigh, she coaxed her inside. Eleanor slumped on the bed, her head in her hands. Della lowered herself down next to her. She was stroking her shoulders in an attempt to comfort her and although her tears had subsided she couldn't quite ward off the tremors emanating from deep within her body.

"Hey!" Della whispered, her voice soft as velvet. "C'mon baby, calm down now."

"I can't believe this is happening to me," Eleanor shivered.

She turned to her friend in fear. It took one glance at her kind face to feel the onset of tears again. She looked so much like her mother, a sight that immediately brought back memories of the night she had been drugged; the smooth brown skin and big eyes. Perhaps it had been Della all along.

"What the hell am I going to do?" she said, her voice breaking huskily.

"I'm sorry," Della sighed. "I wish I could help. But you must know the type of man Theakston is and why everyone's so shit-scared of him. Didn't Sammie give you any idea at all?"

Eleanor nodded. "Yes, he did," she said shakily, "but even I never imagined he would be so evil! Della, I can't go through with this. I'd sooner die!"

An image of his face burned in her mind. The original newspaper clipping had done nothing to convey the power of his presence nor the menace he breathed into that room. Every word he spoke had been poison. He had stalked her like a predator.

"The thought of what he's going to do to me!" she whimpered. "He mentioned other men! This is my first time, Della and it is going to be a nightmare!"

"Ssh," Della said. "So maybe things could get a bit rough but you're just gonna have to play the game, sweetheart..."

Eleanor pulled herself up sharply. "W-what?" she stammered. "You mean just go along with this? I-I can't!"

"Yes you can," Della sighed. "At the end of the day, he's a man and men are simple creatures, 'specially in the hands of a seductive woman. Treat 'em right, they turn to putty!"

She spoke slowly, gazing deeply into her eyes.

"This needn't be as bad as you think and if you're frightened he's gonna hurt you then anythin's worth a shot! Clark'll let you have a few drinks to calm your nerves. So just be nice to him. I'll make you look real pretty too, might turn him on a bit."

"Della, he is going to rape me!" Eleanor sobbed. "You heard the things he called my father... He isn't doing this because he *fancies me*, he is doing this to get back at him!"

"What if you're wrong?" Della protested. "It's just sex, Eleanor."

"Sex with a man who wants revenge," Eleanor shuddered, hugging herself in horror. "Can't any of you understand how I feel about this?"

"Sure," Della said. "We're as pissed off about it as you are. I'm just tryin' to make the best out of a bad situation. We'll do whatever it takes to help you get through this."

Her arm coiled around Eleanor's shoulder.

"Do you know what I feel sad about? That Sammie didn't protect you better. He should never have trusted them Mallorys. I'm shocked Theakston could just wander into Sammie's office and look at your dad's file! What kind of security is that?"

"Sammie's dead," Eleanor said sadly. Another tear tumbled down her cheek. How could she forget the hateful way he had sneered about it? "Theakston's boss now but none of it matters. It's Dad I'm worried about. You heard what he said about the filming, the sick bastard."

"Yeah, even I gotta admit, that's nasty," Della relented.

"So why can't we run away?" Eleanor said quickly. She grasped Della's hands, staring into her eyes. "Why don't we both just sneak out of here before anyone notices."

"What about Clark?" Della said tightly.

"Isn't Clark tough enough to handle this by himself?" Eleanor pressed. "How come no one is standing up to this bastard?"

Della's eyes turned hard. She pulled her hands away, causing Eleanor to frown.

"You just don't get it, do you," she said harshly. "D'you know how many men Theakston's got? He spent the last few years takin' over every gang in London, north and south, before he came here. That's how he made a name for himself - someone to be feared. What's more, he's got some of the nastiest thugs workin' for him now an' not only do these guys outnumber us but a lot of men who were on Sammie's team jumped ship. We can't win! If we let you escape, Eleanor, Clark'll most likely end up beaten to death!"

Eleanor gave a shudder though it seemed, Della hadn't quite finished. Her eyes blazed.

"As for me... It's not just me I'm worried about, I gotta little girl..."

"What?" Eleanor gasped.

"She lives a few streets away with my Ma! The ol' lady's disabled. She helps looks after my kid while I earn the money that pays for their food and rent. Fact is, Theakston makes it his business to know these things about people. So I hope you won't mind me saying that I ain't gonna do nothing that'll put my baby in danger."

"No," Eleanor said, feeling sudden defeat, "of course not. I'm sorry." She wiped the tear from her face. "Have you ever thought about getting out of prostitution?" she added naively.

Della laughed but it was a mirthless sound.

"You mean, get a proper job? Me? Like work in a factory twelve hours a day stickin' lids on biscuit tins for piss all? I earn ten times more money working for Clark and besides... what do I care about turning tricks for a living? Men have been shafting me since I was nipper in a care home, love, so a few more don't make no difference to me."

Eleanor couldn't speak - shocked by such revelations.

"Like I say," Della finished gently, "don't go thinking none of us care about you, babe, 'cos we do." She offered her a smile and stroked her hair away from her face. "Sorry, I can't get you out of this. I'm gonna talk to Clark now but I'll be back soon to help you prepare. Try not to worry too much, it may not be as bad as you think..."

Eleanor closed her eyes. Trying to convince Della had been useless, leaving her no other choice than to wait for the ordeal to begin...

IV

She heard the rattle of a key as Della locked the attic door, trapping her inside. Yet their conversation left her dazed. Half of her wanted to accept her fate. Maybe Della was right; enough booze would blot out the whole sordid business but there was more to it than that.

The thought of the filming turned her cold. She knew her father. He would walk bare foot across red hot coals to rescue her if he knew of the situation she was in now. If he even got wind of such a scenario, he would rush back to London and straight into a trap.

Eleanor rose. Sammie had already hinted that Theakston was planning a brutal murder; she had to find a way of thwarting him.

Breathing deeply to steady her nerves, she could barely think straight. She rummaged through the drawers of her bedside cabinet, hoping to find something useful; something she might use as a weapon but there was nothing.

Her reflection caught her eye. The short black dress she wore looked alluring enough not to raise suspicion; simple and practical if she succeeded in her escape. She kicked off her shoes and delving into the wardrobe, found a pair of knee-length black boots. With smaller two inch heels, it wasn't impossible to run in them.

Time was racing by. One glance at her watch suggested, she might only have an hour before Theakston's dreaded return. She raked her fingers through her hair in despair, forcing her mind to go blank again. If she could only get out of this damned attic...

Before she knew it, the click of Della's footsteps resounded from the stairs, yanking her out of her reverie. Feeling the bitterness of defeat, Eleanor slumped down on the bed again.

Della appeared in the doorway as expected, only this time she carried a shoulder bag. She wasn't smiling any more, Eleanor noticed.

"I've been speakin' to Clark," she began. "Chin up, Eleanor, he's agreed to let you get drunk. That's something at least, so I got something for you!" She opened up the bag and pulled out a bottle of vodka. "Where's your glass?"

"Vodka?" Eleanor frowned.

"Yeah and not just vodka, babe," Della whispered as if about to share a secret. "I got you these!"

She dug into the pocket of her hot pants and pulled out a packet of pills...

"It's Valium," she explained, "a strong sedative. Now get a glass of vodka down, let that sink in and take the pills. You need to get 'em down before they come back then I swear, whatever happens tonight, you ain't gonna know a thing about it."

"Right," Eleanor muttered. She was studying her expression - trying to imagine what she and Clark might have been talking about.

Della forced a wide smile. "Anyway, I'll help you get ready and then you may as well join us in the lounge, so we can keep an eye on you."

Eleanor's heart sank. They were obviously taking no chances. She glanced at the vodka bottle then back at Della. Reaching for her glass, she unscrewed the cap, sloshed out a huge measure and took a gulp. With a shudder of disgust she screwed up her face. "Ugh!"

"Good girl," Della said bluntly. "You'll feel better in a second. Now about your face..."

Eleanor guessed she looked awful, her cheeks blotchy from layers of salty tears.

"Anyone can see you been cryin.' Best not let Mr Theakston see you like that..."

"What, you think he's going to care?" Eleanor spat in disbelief.

"It's not that," Della sighed, trailing a finger over her cheek. "You just don't wanna be lookin' all tearful, like some frightened little girl. Best never show fear... Brings out the nastier side of powerful men like him."

Eleanor gulped back her fear. So she wasn't talking about seduction techniques any more.

"Let's start by making you look a little more glamourous."

Della fished out a case and placed the shoulder bag on the floor to make room.

Positioned cross legged at one end of the bed, Eleanor sat at the other. She tilted her head so she was facing her, ready to be made up. Della dabbed a little cold cream onto her face, smoothing it over her skin before brushing on a light powder. Eleanor opened her eyes and stared at her. Strangely enough the vodka *was* beginning to work, a warm sensation which dissolved her inner anxiety. With her inhibitions fading, she allowed her mind to wander...

No sooner had Della applied a warm peach blusher when she started on her eyes. Sweeping on a little smoky grey eye shadow and mascara, she asked her to open them. Eleanor stole a sideways glance in the mirror. The shadow was subtle, making her honey toned eyes look beautiful. Last, she selected lipstick; a terracotta shade that enhanced her soft, full lips followed by a slick of gloss to make them shine.

"You look sensational," Della smiled. "No man'd wanna hurt you now! Drink up!"

Eleanor wasn't sure she could handle another mouthful of vodka. Even the first swig had gone to her head. She nevertheless drained her glass and topped it up again - offering the bottle to Della.

"Won't you have some?" she said, her voice a monotone.

With a shrug, Della accepted the bottle and took a swig.

"You'll be fine," she murmured as if thinking aloud. "Sorry things turned out like this but at least, you've got us to look after you. Best take your pills and go with the flow..."

Eleanor's eyes felt glazed as she attempted to make sense of it all. The whole scene turned surreal, as if she had reached a turning point. A hazy idea wove its threads around her mind as she hovered on the brink of a decision...

"What do think's going to happen?" she whispered. "What about afterwards?"

For a moment, Della looked uncomfortable. "I'm not sure," she answered gravely. "We're hopin' it won't last too long... Clark said there was another reason Theakston was coming here; some other business besides his appointment with you..."

Eleanor stared at the floor, her face rigid. "Go on," she urged her.

"Clark's gonna give you another shot of morphine, soon as it's over," Della let slip carelessly. "I hope they don't hurt you. But if they do..."

The words hit Eleanor with shocking impact and finally she knew what she had to do.

She watched carefully as Della closed her makeup case. Turning her back for a moment, she dropped it into her shoulder bag as it slouched on the floor.

Within a flash, Eleanor grasped the vodka bottle and raising it high above her head, she belted it down across Della's head.

The bottle smashed. Della crumpled to the floor without a sound, her head rolling sideways. Eleanor dropped to her side feeling a bolt of panic. *What had she done?* She had never meant to hit her so hard! She sank her fingers into a ball of afro hair, horrified to feel the wetness of blood. Broken glass lay everywhere coupled with an overpowering smell of vodka. Eleanor started trembling, unable to believe her own actions. Stroking Della's face, she was relieved to feel a flutter of breath against her skin. She was going to be okay; maybe out cold, at least for now...

Wasting no time, she rummaged through the shoulder bag. Sure enough, there was a flick knife in there and a bunch of keys. Feeling a surge of hope,

Eleanor grabbed her denim blazer from the wardrobe, pocketing the knife along with some cash.

Without delay, she crept away, leaving Della unconscious on the floor. Finally she slipped out of the room. Clark would find Della soon, but for now, this was her only chance to find to a way out of here.

She tried the keys one by one until at last, she found one that fitted the attic door. Mercifully the door swung open. Having taken her first steps towards freedom, she paused at the top of the staircase - listening for any sounds, which might indicate the presence of someone nearby. A continual shift of movement rose from all corners of the house; doors opening and closing, voices drifting up from the lower floors. She could even hear a faint trickle of music from the lounge.

Waiting for a lull of stillness, she began to tiptoe down the staircase towards the second floor. She paused half way - satisfied there was no sign of anyone - then completed her descent, her heart pounding in her ribcage.

By now the vodka had rushed to her brain, making her giddy. Yet that subtle inebriated feeling boosted her confidence and this was the thing that kept driving her. She had not been lying when she told Della she would rather die than allow Theakston to carry out his hateful plan. Now all she had to do was find a way out of here...

Eleanor pressed her body against the wall. She took a sideways step, paused and took another. She knew there were five rooms on this floor, four of which were occupied by the prostitutes. She passed the first room. But for some reason she was drawn to the largest one lingering at the end of the corridor.

She slid a little further along the wall before a loud, ecstatic groan resounded from behind the second door, startling her. She froze. It had to be a punter of course, being pleasured by one of the girls. A tinkle of female laughter followed it. No sooner had she recovered her composure, Eleanor began to move again, hoping that whoever was inside the room would be too preoccupied to notice any disturbance.

To her horror, she heard the sound of a door knob being turned from the opposite end of the corridor. Eleanor flung herself towards the final door and wrenched it open. She leapt inside.

Easing it closed, just as a flurry of voices emerged in the hallway, she finally let go of her breath, then stared at the room's interior.

Observing her new surroundings, she gave an unexpected gasp, unable to believe what she was seeing...

Chapter 3

I

This had to be the games room. A large round table lingered under a canopy of spotlights. It reminded her of her old home; Dad had set up the dining room like this for his poker games. So this establishment was not just a brothel. Men could come here and gamble too. There was a leather sofa stretching along the length of one wall and a giant drinks cabinet opposite. A few more side tables were dotted around the room, topped with lamps and ash trays.

Eleanor's eyes shot to the far end of the room, seeing large double windows dressed in heavy drapes. To her increasing delight, they were tied back from the windows with cords; woven and robust, they might even be strong enough to use as a rope, offering an instant solution to her predicament. She would have to climb down from the window but this was perhaps the only way to escape undetected. At last she felt a surge of hope... until another sound made her jump.

A metallic clang echoed deep underground. Eleanor froze again, knowing she had heard the sound before; the night she had been drugged. She remembered how deeply the sound had troubled her, at which point she noticed another door.

Eleanor frowned. Positioned next to the drinks cabinet, it would be easy to miss it at first. It looked as if it might lead to another room, or maybe it was a storeroom.

Next came the sound of footsteps, slow and heavy from somewhere below; yet they definitely materialised from behind that door. It sounded as if a couple of people were ascending a flight of steps. Eleanor tensed, unable to ignore the fact that the footsteps were getting closer; that whoever it was, they would walk into this room at any moment.

She snapped out of her trance, filled with a sudden urge to hide.

Her eyes completed another circuit, searching... Opting for the long leather settee, she crouched low, crawling into the space behind it.

Finally she heard voices; a series of alternating murmurs rising up from the secret passageway. Eleanor braced herself, her breath suspended. The door clicked open.

Two sets of footsteps clomped across the floor boards and in the same instant, the conversation boomed into the room.

".....this is a fucking joke!" She recognised Clark's voice.

"I don't like it any more than you do..." a second voice pulsated: *Clive's, she was sure of it.* "But don't worry, man, he'll be out of here tonight. Theakston promised!"

"Yeah, well I'll be pissed off if I have to shut my games room for a third night on the trot! Holding the kid is one thing, but as for having to check up on him every few hours..."

"He said 24 hours, right?" Clive assured him. "Theakston wants him despatched and disposed of. This time tomorrow, that kid's gonna be dead, man!"

"Hope he does it some place else," Clark hissed, "I'm fucked if I want any of this pinned on us, especially if the cops come sniffing round. I want this over tonight but it depends on how long he's gonna be with the girl..."

The silence turned heavy as Eleanor digested those words. This was a conversation no one was meant to hear. At last their footsteps were resumed, retreating towards the exit.

"I'm not bleedin' happy, Clive," Clark muttered. "Eleanor's my best girl. I was saving her for some of our more exclusive clients... Theakston's a cunt!"

"Where is she now?" Clive asked him gravely.

"Della's with her," Clark sighed, "getting her drunk to mellow her out a bit."

"Best way, man," Clive's voice echoed and they were gone.

Eleanor could not move, stunned by what she had overheard; those last damning sentences concerning her own fate didn't bother so much as the earlier part of the conversation... *'Holding the kid is one thing ... 24 hours... despatched and disposed of...'* The words encircled her mind like a tape being replayed.

They had been discussing someone about to be killed.

II

Eleanor hauled herself out of her hiding place and stared at the door. With no hesitation, she wandered right up to it. Forgetting the importance of her own escape, she had to know who was being kept down there. Only now did she understand the implications of the sounds she had heard last night. First came the slam of car doors, the muffled shouts... Words fell into place now, sharp and defined; a voice which had yelped out, *'help me somebody, help me!'*

Next there had been a rumbling noise, a series of bangs as if a heavy object was being dragged downstairs *or a person.*

Last of all, she had detected a metallic clang, identical to the sound she had just heard; a metal door closing as if shutting someone in, *someone kept down there as a prisoner.* It had been followed by an abrupt silence.

Nervous of what she might find, Eleanor opened the door and stepped onto a cold, draughty landing. Sure enough there *was* a staircase, a little like

49

a fire escape. It descended downwards. She hesitated, wondering if it was wise to go any further. The truth was, she didn't know what she was getting herself into yet the thought that someone might die tonight, tore her conscience...

Eleanor darted down the staircase as it turned around one corner after another, leading her deeper into the unknown. The walls were of bare brick - a smell of damp concrete wafting into the chilly passageway, as if the construction was fairly new. But she kept going until she reached the bottom, abruptly coming face to face with yet another door.

This was the one; this was the source of that sinister clanging sound. She guessed it would be made of metal.

Staring at the bars, she clocked the heavy bolt that secured it. She took a deep swallow, her throat dry with fear, realising what this was. She had discovered an underground dungeon.

Without thinking, she drew back the bolt, staring through the bars and into the basement. She searched for a light source, discovering a switch. Her fingers trailed over the surface; dreading what was about to face her in the claustrophobic darkness, she flicked the switch.

The basement was illuminated by a single bare bulb suspended from the ceiling.

It threw a pool of yellow light into the centre of the room, the corners dark with shadow. But in one of those corners, a figure emerged; someone who appeared to be slumped against the wall.

The shadowy figure glanced up and then she saw him; a young man, possibly in his twenties and of slim build. Perched on a mattress with his arms pinned behind his back, his very posture indicated that his hands were tied - and he was also gagged - a strip of duct tape plastered across his mouth, his eyes wide with terror.

"Oh my God!" Eleanor whispered.

He looked so fragile and vulnerable, as much a victim as she was. There was no way she could just leave him...

Hurrying across, she felt for his hands - shocked to discover the nylon cords that bound them. The concept of what she was getting herself into horrified her. It seemed unreal. With increasing dread, Eleanor wondered how much deeper into the criminal underworld she was being drawn.

At the same time, she remembered the flick knife she had stolen from Della's bag. Heart thumping, she began to saw through the ropes as carefully as possible, although it was as if they were made of steel. She cut harder, relieved when they ultimately began to fray and separate. The second his hands were freed, the man pulled the tape from his mouth. Visibly shaken, he somehow managed to struggle to his feet, leaning against the wall for support. His face appeared pale, almost luminous in the gloom of the basement.

"Th-thanks," he muttered wearily.

"Come on," Eleanor whispered, charged with a growing panic. Turning, she headed back through the metal door. "Let's just get out of this place - quickly!"

Wasting no time, they scuttled up the stairs and into the games room. Thankfully it was still empty, which meant that no one could have heard them. All the same, Eleanor glanced at her watch, shocked to discover they had about ten minutes...

She stared out of the window then froze.

There was a man standing on the corner of the road, right outside the house.

He stared up at the window and met her gaze. With a gasp, Eleanor backed away. She did not recognise him but one glance suggested he was respectable. Smartly dressed in a suit, he seemed quite young; dark haired with pale skin and light blue eyes... yet he had been looking at the house, looking straight up at this room, which made her wonder if he was in any way tied to this boy's fate. She waited, aware of the minutes ticking by - shy of the risk they were about to take next.

"We need to untie one of the curtain cords," she whispered. "We're a long way up..."

"Okay," the boy agreed and with long, deft fingers, he unfastened one of the cords. His movements were quick and graceful. Eleanor felt sure she had done the right thing in setting him free and it felt good to have an ally. The next time she moved up to the window, she was relieved to see, the stranger outside had completely vanished.

"Let's go," she said quickly. "I'm as desperate to get out of here as you are..."

Stealing another hasty glance at each other, her ally looped the curtain cord around the window stay. He passed the other end to Eleanor.

"Thanks for helping me," he said to her. "You saved my life. My name is Jake..."

"Jake," she repeated, hearing the word roll off her tongue.

There was something a little strange about his voice, slurry and slightly musical, with the hint of a foreign accent.

"Actually - would you mind going first?" she added. "I'm a bit scared."

"Okay," he said, "but first, will you tell me *your* name?"

"Eleanor," she replied. "Now just go!"

There was no time to argue. Jake hauled himself onto the window sill and climbed over the edge. Gripping the cord in both hands, he gave it a tug to

51

test its strength then slowly started to lower himself. Eleanor watched him go. *He made it look so easy.* He had reached the bottom in no time, dropping gently to the ground.

He beckoned her with his hand. With a swallow, Eleanor copied, grabbing the cord before she could stop herself. Moments later, she also managed to ease herself down the wall.

Just a small stretch of lawn rolled out between them and the boundary wall, their only escape route. It was Jake who encouraged her; his fingers light on her arm, encouraging her to keep moving. Taking their chances, they raced across to the tree in the corner...

The brick wall in front of them towered about six foot, a little too high to run up and vault over. Jake speedily offered her a leg up so she could reach the lower branches.

Hugging the branch tightly, she clambered higher. At the same time, she couldn't resist a glance at the house; it wouldn't be impossible to be spotted from Clark's lounge. She paused, her heart pounding faster, her earlier fear taking root again. Jake kept going and despite his time in captivity, he displayed incredible strength and grace. Leaping up even higher, he swung his long legs over the branches.

"Keep going!" he urged her. "Come on, it is just a wall!"

He took a long step from the higher branch, planting one foot on the wall followed by the other. For a second he just crouched there. He possessed the agility of a cat, both hands in front to steady him. Yet all the while he was drinking in his surroundings, Eleanor saw his expression change. A look of fear crossed his face and she followed his gaze.

There was a large, dark blue transit van in the driveway.

"It's them," he gasped with a shiver, "the men who brought me here. Come, quickly!" He stretched his hand out towards her.

The words hit her like a bucket of ice, bringing back the echo of Clive's words; *Theakston wants him despatched and disposed of.*

She leapt wildly. With one hand clinging to the tree branch, her booted feet skidded onto the wall. Perched and ready to jump, she was relieved to see Jake land safely.

Everything would have been perfect if it hadn't been for the car lurching around the corner. Long, black, undeniably sinister, this was the *same car* she had seen in Clark's drive, a few hours ago. Only this time it screeched to a halt, parking in a careless lop-sided fashion.

The passenger door flew open.

Eleanor could not move. She saw the flash of a black leather coat before a man jumped out. Dominic Theakston materialised right in front of her. Every muscle in his body seemed to be braced; a coiled snake ready to strike. His eyes glared back at her, insane with rage.

"Eleanor!" Jake hissed.

At this point, Dominic noticed him too. His narrow eyes shifted to the exact spot where he cowered in the shadow of the wall. Jake's hand shook as he reached towards her.

"What the fuck?" they heard Dominic shout.

"Run!" Eleanor whimpered, her voice a squeak.

"Not without you," Jake snapped and snatching her hand, he yanked her from the wall.

The instant her boots struck the pavement, Dominic surged forwards with the velocity of a tiger. But Jake and Eleanor were running too. No sooner had he made a grab for Eleanor, she hurtled out of his reach just in time.

"Get them!" he roared to the driver. "Turn the fucking car round, now!"

Eleanor did not look back. She had never run so fast in her life...

Reminded of a hare trying to outrun a pack of hounds, she charged ahead, leaving the house behind. But the hunt was on. She heard the car turn, a squeal of tyres on the road. Another car honked its horn; next came a roar of acceleration as the driver rammed his foot down hard.

Eleanor did not dare look around. Dominic was still hammering along the pavement after them where the road stretched for miles. How could they ever hope to reach the end without being caught, especially now a car was involved?

Impossible though it seemed, they *were* gaining ground. Eleanor had been good at sports; her long limbs leant themselves to superior running ability on the athletics track.

Jake too was fast, being of such thin, light build.

Dominic on the other hand was running out of breath as the gap stretched between them.

They continued to charge up the road, glancing from left to right, desperate to seek an escape route; a side street, an alleyway or any type of diversion but the road seemed to go on and on. Houses were packed along its entire length; towering, brick buildings, high walls but with no gaps between them.

Dominic had leapt back into the car by now. It screeched to a halt just ahead of them in an attempt to block their escape. The blacked out windows concealed the men inside.

Eleanor and Jake paused, fearing the moment the occupants of the car would spring out and grab them. So they changed direction. The car, now facing the wrong way, would be forced to turn around again.

It turned out to be a good plan. In the time it took for Theakston's driver to complete another three point turn, they had almost re-run the entire distance back to Clark's brothel. Positioned on the corner of two roads, a right turn would take them along another road just like this one; a road that stretched endlessly into the unknown. But to the left, they could see a road ahead, blocked by three black bollards, preventing vehicle access. Eleanor and Jake did not hesitate. Almost skipping through the bollards, they passed under a bridge, where a further road lay in shadow.

As the car reached the same junction, the passengers immediately saw where the couple were heading. Dominic clenched his teeth.

"I'm gonna kill those two!" he snarled, jumping out of the car for a third time.

Spotting a bright red telephone box on the opposite side of the road, he charged towards it, not caring that there were a couple of kids in there making a phone call. He grabbed them both by their collars and forcefully hauled them out of the booth.

"Hey, hang on!" one of them protested.

"Fuck off!" Dominic hissed.

One look at his slanted, hate-filled eyes prompted the boy to raise his hands and back away, his friend rapidly following suit.

Next he made his call.

"Need a motorbike over here quickly!" he barked into the receiver. "We're on the corner of Newton Road, near Clark's place. The boy's escaped along with Chapman's daughter! Can't get the car through from this end so we need back up and fast!"

He did not wait for a reply. He had issued his orders and expected his contact to execute them without question; although he had a rough idea where this road led. Instructing his driver to turn the car yet again, it was time to take a detour. One right hand turn would bring them to the other end of Newton Road, the very side street Jake and Eleanor were tackling right now...

III

Jake and Eleanor slowed to a light jog but they didn't stop running.

This road was quieter than the last, devoid of the main drag of traffic. Narrow and paved with grey brick, it was lined with Victorian terraced houses. They opened directly onto the pavement, guarded by wrought iron railings - there were no gardens but another row of railings stood opposite. They enclosed an area of trees, Eleanor identified as the edges of a park.

The few cars in the area were facing towards them, as if to indicate that this was a one way street. Eleanor was panting heavily from exhaustion - guessing, it would only be a matter of time before their pursuers caught up with them. She didn't want to even consider what would happen if Theakston and his men got their hands on them. So she forced herself to keep moving with Jake by her side. Guessing the relentless chase wasn't over, she began to study him more closely.

His face was slim and chiselled with high cheekbones and a wide flat forehead. He possessed a certain beauty; his complexion pale, his green eyes sharp and alert as he scanned the area for an escape route. There was something slightly hippie-like about the way he dressed; a collar-less striped shirt, jeans and a fringed, brown suede jacket. Eleanor couldn't help but savour the shine of his dark, auburn hair, worn long in a ponytail. Nor did she fail to spot the pendant around his neck; dangling from a single leather thong, it bore the appearance of stone. She took it all in, sensing a gentle nature and a pure heart... Why anyone would want to kill him remained a mystery.

As they darted along the street, people began to materialise as daytime filtered into evening. The sun appeared hazy as it hung low in the sky, casting shadows across the pavements. They passed a few more houses and a high rise blocks of flats, then finally reached a point where the railings ended; an opening into the park...

The park too, had been gradually filling up with people, some walking, others resting on a park bench enjoying the summer evening - a few drunks lay under the trees, oblivious to everything around them. This restful place seemed to offer a perfect sanctuary. They afforded each other another glance and with a mutual nod, slipped through the opening.

From the moment they entered the park, they proceeded to sprint across the grass, away from the paths. Fringed with trees, a mixture of beeches and elms were dotted among the smaller silver birch saplings. Close to the boundary railings, grew a dense thicket of laurels and rhododendrons. They noticed that some paths branched off in places, offering a choice of escape routes in case their enemies caught up with them. But for now, they moved in a straight line; one which trailed diagonally across the park towards an exit.

They were about 50 yards away when the sound of an engine rumbled close by. Eleanor tensed. Seconds later, she saw a motorbike materialise out of nowhere. Large and powerfully built, it paused by the exit, engine revving like a warning. Eleanor felt a creeping fear, sensing its purpose. No sooner had she thought it when she heard a squeal of tyres, which sounded horribly familiar.

Sure enough, the long black car had arrived at the same exit. She could see it through the railings as it lurched to a halt.

Feeling her chest constrict, her exhausted heart crashed against her ribcage.

"They've found us!" she gasped.

Jake said nothing. Gripping her hand, he pulled her in another direction, choosing a different path. All plans of reaching that exit had to be abandoned. She nevertheless swivelled her head, where she couldn't fail to spot the terrifying figure of Theakston again, as he bounded into the park on foot. Leaping onto the back of the motorbike, he was ready to join the chase.

With a final blast of the engine, they surged forwards. Eleanor felt all hopes of escape crumbling, almost ready to face the consequences. There was no way they could outrun a motorbike.

The powerful Honda sped across the grass, accelerating wildly and already gaining ground. Onlookers stared in disbelief. It seemed insane. Children were screaming; several dogs started barking and the peaceful sanctuary of the park had been transformed into chaos.

It appeared Theakston and his men would stop at nothing to catch up with them.

But Jake was not about to give up. He switched paths again; one that dipped downwards, weaving its way through an avenue of bushes and trees on the edge of the park. His grasp on Eleanor's hand was tight as he hauled her around each twist and turn, bringing them face to face with a metal gate. Without hesitation, he flicked up the latch, pushing her through.

He too passed through to the other side. Slamming the latch down, they were on the other side of the railings again; it was the motorcycle riders who would have to dismount if they intended to follow. The tables had turned again...

Yet the bike was right behind them. Bit by bit, it lurched around each corner until it had also reached the gate.

Dominic jumped from the bike and strode up to the gate. He stared into Eleanor's eyes.

In that brief second of eye contact, he not only unlatched the gate. He dug inside his leather coat and grabbed something from his belt. Time seemed to stand still as he unsheathed a lethal looking knife. The blade shimmered as it caught the last of the sunlight, more curved and sharp than Eleanor could have imagined... and as he brandished the blade, his teeth flashed, his expression one of pure hatred.

Eleanor broke into a sprint again, powered by the force of her own terror. They had emerged onto another busy main road. Cars, black cabs and red double decker London buses surged up and down in both directions and somewhere close by, rose the wail of a police siren. Being a commercial area, it was lined with towering office blocks and shops. Other establishments such as cafes, restaurants and hotels were only just coming to life.

More people filled the streets. They had either just finished work or were venturing out for a night's entertainment. Smartly suited men and women donning jackets with summer dresses, mixed with young revellers - girls in short mini-dresses and platform shoes - young men who wore their hair long, fashionably dressed in tailored jackets with wide ties and flares. The second they reached a zebra crossing, they joined the mass of people crossing the main road, weaving in and out of them as briskly as possible to get to the other side. It was clear the hunt wasn't over, especially now Theakston had launched his new and deadly threat.

"He's going to kill us both!" Eleanor gasped as they fought their way through the crowd.

"He can't run down a street full of pedestrians!" Jake shouted. His gaze shot from left to right. "Just keep moving!"

If only they could have blended into the heaving mass of people but all eyes were drawn to Eleanor. Her short black dress and knee length boots didn't fail to draw attention to her figure and long legs. Men paused to stare at her. She was panting heavily, releasing huge gasps of breath. Her long, dark hair flowed out behind her as she ran, her face glistening with sweat. She could not have looked more alluring and he was certain Theakston must have noticed her too. There was a stark finality to the way he had drawn his knife, perhaps sensing the end of the chase was within his reach.

As they charged along the pavement, he noticed a hotel. It lay a little way back from the road, only accessible via a wide flight of steps leading to the entrance. With a surge of hope, he started to bound up the steps, Eleanor close behind. He knew the steps would create another barrier between them and the motorbike, making it impossible for them to follow. Luck was on their side, it seemed. They were still in with a chance...

They slid through the revolving doors and into reception where a crowd of people hovered inside. They were smartly dressed too; men in dress suits, women in long evening gowns. Jake was instantly rocked by the exuberant beat of 'Tumbling Dice' by the Rolling Stones as it drifted from the bar, guessing this to be some sort of party.

In an attempt to be inconspicuous, they slid surreptitiously around the back of the group, to discover a corridor leading to the rear of the building. This in turn opened up into a dining room. It was already set up with round tables topped with white cloths, glasses, vases of flowers and baskets of bread rolls. They spotted the double patio doors at the end.

Jake turned to Eleanor and beckoning her to follow, he darted through the tables to get to the doors. It was perfect. As soon as he pulled them open, he could see the beer garden - a few patio tables nestling on an island of crazy paving - an ornamental path crossing a lawn.

This in turn led towards a low wall and a gate, where another street lay beyond.

As they stepped into the shade and onto the path, the shadows loomed longer. Eleanor was finally beginning to recapture her breath, a welcome reprieve from all that running.

At last they passed through the gate into an unknown street at the back of the hotel, safely concealed from view. The street lay parallel to the busier, more commercial one. It took them past warehouses, car parks and the backyards of several businesses, including a printing works.

Only now, did it make sense to hide...

There was no sign of Theakston's men anywhere. Maybe they hadn't yet arrived but neither could be sure if they had been spotted entering the hotel. The notion, they might eventually be drawn here, ready to spring an attack, could not be overruled.

Jake took another glance at his surroundings and came to a decision. His eyes met Eleanor's and convinced there was no one around, he seized his chance. He dashed into the yard behind the printers. Several skips stood in ranks against a high brick wall, filled with cardboard, paper and plastic wrapping.

"I cannot think of a better place to hide, can you?" he said to her.

She looked back at him, clearly dazed by recent events. Yet she gave him a nod.

She turned and gripped the top of the skip, accepting another leg up, so she could jump inside. He leapt in after her. They arranged the huge sheets of cardboard to cover themselves and once entombed in the darkness, they adjusted their position to make themselves comfortable. Now all they had to do was lie still for a while.

They closed their eyes, grateful for a chance to recover from the relentless chase but yet to be convinced, it was over.

"Why don't we just rest for a bit," Eleanor whispered. "It will be dark soon and when it is, we need to start moving again - get ourselves right away from this area..."

The traffic droned in the distance but the familiar squeal of tyres was strangely absent.

Luck on the other hand, did not appear to be on Dominic's side.

In the moment they forced their way through the park exit, they had been about to resume the chase. Except a police car had pulled up right outside, blocking access. Two regular policemen, clad in dark blue uniforms and hats had leapt out and stopped them in their tracks. Threatening arrest, vital seconds ticked by as they questioned them... It transpired, someone had used a call box to make a 999 call and with several people having witnessed the motorbike speeding through the park like a maniac, *did they have any idea of the bedlam they had caused?*

Dominic was fuming, wary this was swallowing up precious time. At one point, he thought he caught a glimpse of them again, the slim figure of the girl… Just the briefest flicker of black mingled amongst the crowd of people crossing the busy main road. He even clocked the distinctive auburn gleam of Jake's hair as it was caught in the low sunlight.

"Look! Is it possible, we could get going?" he urged the police officer. "We're actually trying to tail someone..."

Narrowing his eyes, he studied the face of the officer, choosing his next words carefully.

"Check with Inspector Hargreaves if you don't believe me. He'll vouch for me."

"I beg your pardon?" the officer demanded. "In what way are you connected to Inspector Hargreaves?"

"That my friend, is confidential," Dominic said, "but feel free to contact him. Pretty sure he won't be happy about you lot holding us up like this. Go on, I dare you..."

The police officer looked anxious now, unsure whether to believe him. One glance might have suggested he was some sort of villain. Yet at the same time, he exuded such confidence.

"This had better not be bullshit," he muttered. "For your information, we've got details of your vehicles and your number plates."

The next time he caught up with his driver, Dominic's fury rose again like thunder. He had not been bluffing when he had mentioned the *police inspector*; this regrettable turn of events was about to have serious implications...

"Lost 'em," he said coldly, sparking up a cigarette, "but we're not giving up. Monty, I want you to phone around, get some more blokes over this way now! I want a man stationed outside every fucking tube station, just in case they try that tack!"

"This is seriously bad shit, Dominic," the other man in the car sighed.

Tall and thin with hawk like features, his icy blue eyes skewered into him. His name was Dan Levy and he was one of Dominic's more senior deputies. "How the 'ell did that kid escape? And I'm guessing he rescued the Chapman girl..."

With those words, Theakston felt a second surge of outrage.

"Other way round," he whispered evilly, "but we'll find her. We're gonna track the pair of them down before the night's out, I swear..."

PART 2. JAKE

Chapter 4

I

Jake and Eleanor lay huddled in the skip for over an hour. The last of the daylight had drained from the sky, leaving them in total darkness. But as the shadows stretched, the air became chilly. Eleanor started shivering.

By the time they emerged from their hiding place, the noise of traffic had died down. With considerably fewer cars around, the onset of danger seemed to have subsided. A drumbeat of music emanated from the distance in waves, probably from the hotel they had passed through. Other than that, the area had lapsed into an era of tranquillity. It seemed a good time to move on...

A clear night, the stars shone brightly, casting a watery glow across the streets. They moved with increasing stealth as the area turned more residential; rows of tightly packed streets closing in on them. They had absolutely no idea where they were or where they were heading but it made sense to keep moving north, right away from the area of Poplar and the house they had escaped from. Eleanor was convinced that Theakston would still have men scouting around the area. Her voice lowered to a whisper as she conveyed the truth to Jake; he was rumoured to have an army of thugs working for him.

After what seemed like an eternity of relentless walking, the houses gradually thinned out.

They seemed to be moving out of the maze of dingy streets; now hovering on the edge of a very different area. Barren and industrial with an expanse of wasteland, they found themselves surrounded by building sites with chicken wire fencing. Taking no chances, they darted across the exposed area with haste, footsteps soft on the earth. The road ultimately led to a railway tunnel flanked by steep, grassy banks. Wandering up to the embankment, they were curious to know what lay on the other side...

Jake drew a finger to his lips, certain that he could hear footsteps. The roll of a tin can echoed from deep within the tunnel before the eerie silence was resumed.

"It could just be some drunks," Eleanor whispered.

"I'm not sure I want to take my chances," Jake replied. Something about the dark yawning tunnel unnerved him. "Let's go up the bank..."

Their eyes scanned the area. The stillness of the environment was quite unsettling with nothing but the sound of distant lorries moving around. Convinced they were alone, it seemed safe. So they proceeded to clamber up the slope towards the top of the embankment, clinging to the long grass for support. No sooner had they made it to the top when they saw a single set of tracks gleaming under the stars. It didn't appear to be a major railway line. Given the type of area they were in, it seemed far more likely, it was used for industrial freight.

Yet they felt exposed; two distinct silhouettes lingering at the top of the slope.

Wary of the advent of danger, they scuttled a little further along the track to distance themselves from the tunnel. Within another fifty yards, they noticed a disused carriage. Jake took a deep breath and tip-toed across to it, careful to avoid the rails. Without comment, Eleanor followed him. Once they were on the other side of the line, they slipped into the carriage and lowered themselves into a sitting position.

For the first few minutes, they rested in silence where Jake finally let go of his tension a little. Gazing across at Eleanor, he could just about make out her features in the glimmer of moonlight. With her face half masked in shadow, her eyes widened. Shining in the little bit of light there was, they appeared almost luminous. She looked very young, possibly a teenager. He had already began to wonder what might have happened to her in all the time they had been running... *Why would a girl like Eleanor be kept in the same house where he had ended up a prisoner?* Right now she was trembling all over. Maybe it was delayed shock in the aftermath of their escape; but deep down he feared that she had been about to face her own ordeal.

"Hey," he murmured, leaning towards her. "Are you okay?"

She let out a sob. Jake hesitated for a second, then slowly moved across to sit with her. Pausing again, he finally summoned up the courage to wrap a protective arm around her. He pressed her shuddering body close to his own, wishing for nothing but to comfort her. He could only imagine the depth of her distress...

"Sorry," she sighed, wiping the tear from her face. "I don't think I've ever been so frightened in my life. I can't believe we escaped!"

"No," he answered gently. "They came very close, especially in the park. Who was that man? Do you know him?"

He felt her brace sharply beneath the protective canopy of his arm.

"Yes," she whispered. "His name is Dominic Theakston. He's the most dangerous gang leader in London and now I know why."

Jake was silent for a moment, taking this all in before he lapsed into troubled thoughts of his own. He had spent the last 24 hours discarded in that basement with his hands tied and his mouth taped over, thinking the nightmare was never going to end. Yet that was nothing, compared to the day of his capture; a day where one minute he had felt safe and the next, he had ended up in a most dreadful place, his fate in the hands of men who were dangerous and evil. A ripple of cold ran over him, forcing him to push the memory aside. No, he didn't want to dwell on that right now. He instead directed his focus on Eleanor.

"So, he was after you too?"

"Yes," she shivered. "I'd never even met him before today though I was warned about him…"

Over the next few minutes, she whispered out her story; so her father had worked for a man named Sammie Maxwell, a well known figure in the East End… She tried to explain a little about the turf war; the ever present threat as a newer gang had been encroaching on Sammie's territory, leading to the terrible fight at the Docks...

"One of Theakston's men got shot... unfortunately my dad did it!"

Jake shook his head in disbelief. "Unbelievable," he murmured, "go on..."

Eleanor took a lung full of air as if building up to something worse. With some difficulty she finally described her own situation; the manner by which she had ended up in that brothel, right up until the moment Theakston had claimed her.

"I'm guessing he would have hurt you," Jake said bitterly.

Eleanor gave a nod, her eyes glittering - he could see she was on the brink of tears again.

"C'mon," Jake urged, "you can tell me."

"H-he threatened to film me. This is the one thing Sammie warned me about, it's what he specialises in. Theakston wanted to be my first; a bit of fun, he said, for him and his men… His plan was to avenge my dad and lure him out of hiding..."

"Bastard," Jake gasped. What she was describing seemed monstrous!

He had seen the man clearly in the instant he'd pulled her from the wall; his towering height, threatening stance, never to forget the insane fury in his eyes. *How anyone could even think to do that to Eleanor, fragile as a flower by comparison?* His grip around her shoulder tightened.

"At least we escaped," Eleanor finished, taking another deep breath.

A long silence stretched between them. Jake glanced out of the carriage and into the draughty night air whilst considering their fate. Maybe they should start walking again. The railway carriage offered no shelter from the cold, the floor rock hard against their weary bones. It seemed a safe enough bolt hole when they had stumbled across it. Though he was unsure as to whether he wanted to spend the whole night here. Even with a jacket on, he was freezing!

Eventually he broke the silence. "We should take a look around and see if there is anywhere else we can go. I don't like it here, do you?"

"Not really," Eleanor replied. He could see that she too, was shivering.

"Why don't I look?" Jake nodded. "You stay and get some rest. I'll only be gone a while and I will come back, I promise. At least you are well hidden..."

The moment he said it, he understood the risk he was taking yet it didn't deter him. He rose shakily to his feet, watching her carefully. Her expression had turned blank.

"Go on then," she relented softly. "Just don't be long. I couldn't bear it if they captured you again, not after we've walked all this way."

"Just a few minutes," he reassured her. "Let me see if there is a better place to hide."

Jake crept along the embankment, his senses sharp as radar.

Alerted to the sounds penetrating the night sky, he froze every time a car door slammed or a gleam of headlights swept past his vision. He could hear the rumble of a train in the distance but sensed it was too far away to be heading for these tracks. Gazing over the the bank from where they had emerged, the familiar scenes of heavy construction prevailed; warehouses, factories and cranes towered as far as the eye could see. In the distance, he could just about make out the shape of gas cylinders squatting in the darkness.

Peering across to the other side, he observed a housing estate. It seemed unlike any other neighbourhood he had seen recently. For a start, there was an element of green space and as he moved along the bank, the houses began to thin out a little.

The hedge running along the top of the embankment eventually opened into a little footpath. It twisted down towards the houses. Jake glanced back. He could still see the railway carriage, tiny in the distance. He did not want to lose sight of it yet he decided to venture down the footpath, to see where it would lead him.

The footpath veered left. Running parallel to the embankment, a boundary hedge shielded him from the gardens of yet more houses. The first house appeared to be modern; a long, neatly tended garden and a small orchard, dotted with fruit trees. The lights were on in the upstairs windows, despite the lateness of the hour. He could hear the sound of car engines bursting to life; dinner guests maybe, just leaving.

Sneaking a little further, he spotted another distinctive house. This one was also detached but older with large sash windows built into its grey walls. There were ledges sculpted between the floors and huge brick chimneys on either side of the roof. Its long, wild back garden reached right up to the hedge as he stood, silently observing it.

What compelled him to study this house more than anything was the windows. There were no lights on yet the curtains had been left wide open.

The grass in the garden stood about a foot tall. In fact, it looked as if it might be abandoned...

Jake bit his lip. Glancing to check if the coast was clear, he came to a decision. Squeezing through the hedge, he slipped down the garden path, right up to the house itself. As he crept up to the back door, he noted the wine rack filled with dusty bottles. There were several flower pots overflowing with dead plants but they hadn't been watered for weeks.

He could see right into the kitchen now, which lay masked in shadow. It would appear the house was open plan as if a wall had been knocked out between kitchen and lounge. The window at the far end looked out onto a street, where the lighting provided enough illumination to reveal the interior. Jake felt along the window ledge, wondering if he would find anything - a loose brick for example - any type of cavity that might conceal a key... He did not want to leave Eleanor for too long but on the other hand, he was desperate to find a way in.

Crouching to his knees, he searched beneath the flower pots. Next, he poked inside the wine rack, feeling under the rows of bottles. Then at last, he found something. His fingertips bumped against a glass jam jar at the base of the rack. He heard a clink of metal against glass.

Ever hopeful, he extracted it. The rusty lid was intact but inside rattled a key. It was a small Yale key and fitted the back door perfectly. Jake felt a surge of excitement. It turned easily in the lock and the door pushed inwards, emitting a slight creak. The second he peered around the door, he acknowledged a damp and slightly fusty smell; the kitchen felt cool. His first instinct had been correct. No-one had lived in this house for a while.

Jake sped back to the railway carriage to find Eleanor gently dozing on the floor.

Within minutes, the two of them stood inside the kitchen of the abandoned house, gazing at their surroundings in wonder.

"I can't believe it," Eleanor whispered. "This is like a dream! Maybe it's a holiday home but what a piece of luck..."

Jake closed the living room curtains. The embroidered fabric felt heavy in his hands but he didn't dare turn a light on. According to Eleanor's watch, it was gone 1:00 in the morning so he lit a candle instead, hoping that any light in the room would be invisible from the outside. As the warm glow spread across the walls, the interior of the house was revealed.

"Oh wow," Eleanor gasped.

It was like nothing she had ever seen, stark in comparison to the gaudy decor which typified the 70s. The wooden floorboards were bare with just a faded Turkish rug thrown over them. None of the furniture matched. There was a big baggy sofa pressed against one wall and a tall wing-backed armchair in the corner next to it. Opposite that stood a stripped pine cupboard and a smaller leather tub chair. It clashed with a solid oak bureau in another corner, bearing a cane lamp and a stereo. The shelves and bookcase were crammed with books, some of which looked ancient.

Obviously, the house still had an owner, their personality stamped all over it but there was no denying, it felt safe.

"I think we should stay here, even if it is just for a night," Jake said. "It's perfect! So long as we keep ourselves hidden - make sure none of the neighbours see us."

Eleanor sank herself down on the settee and let her head roll back.

"Great plan," she murmured, "and well done for finding this place. It's a gift from the gods."

Jake lowered himself down into the larger of the two chairs. For now the hunt was over. He could relax and allow his mind to settle at last. But as his tension began to release itself, he could no longer ignore his own fate. The memories were starting to filter through again, hazy and almost dreamlike...

He remembered the men who last visited him, moments before Eleanor had arrived; the hours of sitting in that cellar, hands bound, his shoulders stiff with cramp, just waiting to die.

He knew the place was a brothel, they had said so. He also knew those men were being paid to hold him captive in their underground dungeon. Every few hours they had checked up on him yet he had never even learned their names... *24 hours.* Those were the words his original captors used on the night they had dragged him there; their goal, *to keep him out of sight.* They had left with the lingering promise, *they would be back to finish this business...*

Jake felt his stomach knot. If it hadn't been for Eleanor, his life would be over now. He allowed his eyes to wander to the settee where she was resting.

Staring deep into her eyes, he managed a smile.

"Are you okay?" she asked him.

Jake rose to his feet. "I am starving," he replied. "I wonder if there is any food in here."

Ambling back towards the kitchen, he observed a set of painted blue cupboards. The fridge was switched off but rummaging through the cupboards, he discovered a muddle of glasses. As well as being hungry he was hit with a clawing thirst. Running the cold tap, he filled two glasses with water, gulped one down and offered the second to Eleanor.

"Oh, thanks," she sighed, dragging herself to her feet again.

She sipped her water as Jake continued to search the cupboards. He discovered boxes of muesli and a few jars filled with a medley of foods such as rice, pasta, beans and lentils. But none of it looked particularly appetising.

"Rabbit food," Jake muttered. "These people must be health freaks..."

"Oh well," Eleanor smiled back. "I guess we could always buy a few things."

A vegetable rack at the bottom contained a bag of green potatoes, spouting shoots - a few onions and some ancient looking carrots.

"Fancy a carrot?" Jake smiled holding one up. It looked so wizened and leathery, even a rabbit would turn its nose up. Eleanor giggled but Jake kept on looking until he eventually found a tin of plain crackers and to his further delight, a jar of peanut butter.

He found plates in the higher cupboards before delving into the drawers for cutlery. Removing a stack of crackers from the tin, he spread them with peanut butter. The first he passed to Eleanor but she shook her head.

"It's okay," she smiled. "You have it... I still feel a little queasy."

Jake wolfed down the cracker as her words rolled in his mind. She was not only brave but gifted with a clear head. He couldn't stop thinking about the things she had told him about her father. Not only did he work for some crime boss but he had killed a man. Eleanor had been dragged deeper and deeper into a dangerous criminal underworld and not only that. She had been left at the mercy of her father's enemies who had claimed her as bait!

Jake bit into a second cracker. He followed it with a swallow of water to wash down the crumbs. Eleanor seemed too delicate to be part of that world yet despite her predicament, she had stuck her neck out for him. Only now, was he swayed by a decision. He would do whatever it took to protect her from this gang leader.

"How long since you've eaten?" Eleanor asked, interrupting his train of thoughts.

Jake gave a shrug. Struggling to swallow the dry crackers, he took another gulp of water.

"I lost track of time. They offered me cake - a few hours before you found me..."

"What?" Eleanor gasped.

Jake shrugged again. "They knew I wasn't going to be alive for much longer." A sense of fear churned in him and he could no longer suppress it.

He could feel Eleanor's stare. Her honey coloured eyes were like orbs in the candlelight and they penetrated his very soul.

"Jake, why were they going to kill you?" she demanded. "I have to know!"

"You are right," he sighed. "It is time I told you my story...."

Wandering back into the sitting room, he selected the same wing backed chair. Elbows on knees, he stared blankly into space, wondering where to begin.

"You *did* save my life," he added. "I cannot thank you enough for that and you are right... They were going to kill me."

"I'm pleased I found you," Eleanor pressed, "but you still haven't told me why. What on earth did you do to offend them, Jake?"

"Nothing!" he snapped. "There is someone else who wants me dead. Those thugs were hired to get rid of me. You see, one minute I was at Scotland Yard, giving evidence about a car bomb but when I left, there was a van hanging about, just waiting for me."

Jake closed his eyes. He let the memories drift into his mind, allowing the pieces to fuse together and so he began his story...

II

He had left Scotland Yard, his mind reeling from the interrogative nature of the questioning he had been put through. As if the car bomb had not been horrifying enough... Yet what happened next had launched a turning point in his life; a split second when two strong men had seized his arms and literally thrown him in the back of a van. The doors slammed shut to imprison him, a sack forced over his head. He breathed in dust, coughed and tried to shout out before the van surged into motion. He was flung backwards with the momentum of it.

He tried to stagger upwards yet immediately felt the grip of fists on his arms again, shoving him to the floor.

"Get your hands off me!" Jake screamed.

"Shut the fuck up!" a male voice growled.

Pain shot through his ribs as someone kicked him. Defenceless and beaten, Jake lay slumped on the floor of the van. They drove fast, obviously keen to get away from the police headquarters. The van surged down one street after another and with every turn, he rolled from side to side, bashing against the steel panels. He knew someone was in the back with him where any attempt to escape would likely earn him another kick in the ribs. So he closed his eyes, utterly helpless, just waiting for the nightmare to end.

It seemed a good twenty minutes before the van finally lurched to a halt.

Heavy boots thudded onto concrete. He heard a loud rumble as the doors were wrenched open, the familiar grasp of hands before he was yanked from the van. Whoever his captors were, they were dragging him towards a building. Jake tried to make sense of his surroundings but the sack on his head obscured his vision. It sounded like a rough neighbourhood; noisy and chaotic with the crash of dustbin lids, men shouting abuse... He flinched to the roar of a motorbike engine and could hear several dogs barking. Someone opened the door of what he guessed to be a house and he was shoved inside.

Forcing him into a chair, they pulled his arms behind his back and snapped on a pair of handcuffs. Jake started trembling, his heart pounding so fast, he couldn't speak. He sensed they were in a kitchen - the overpowering smell of cooking fat and fried onions making him feel nauseous. Then finally a man spoke, a soft, slightly sing song voice with a strong cockney accent.

"Take that sack off 'is head for Christ's sake. Let the kid breath!"

Sure enough the sack was removed, allowing him the briefest glimpse of the man stood in front of him. The image was almost subliminal; a man who appeared tall and thin with receding dark hair. But no sooner had the noose come off when it was replaced by a blind fold, plunging him into darkness again.

"So, you're Jake Jansen," the man muttered.

"What the hell is going on?" Jake gasped. "Why am I here?"

"You've been telling stories, son!" the man said. "Things people don't want no one to know. Sad fact is, someone out there wants rid of you and we've been assigned to deal with it."

"What stories?" Jake demanded.

"That ain't for us to say," the man said and Jake could almost hear the smile in his voice. "As soon as the boss comes back, we're taking you some place else. Somewhere a bit more secret where no one knows you exist..."

So that was it. They were not going to tell him anything. He had been left in the kitchen for the interim; blindfolded, handcuffed and completely powerless to do a thing about it.

Time ticked by. He was unsure how much time, minutes, maybe hours... The worst horror was the complete lack of understanding as to why this was happening to him. Was it possible they had got him mixed up with someone else?

Eventually voices emerged from the front of the house. He heard the door open, guessing several more men had arrived. Jake froze as they stepped into the kitchen.

"Is this him?" he heard a voice sneer - a different voice - mid-range, slightly husky containing an undertone of pure malice.

"Yeah," replied another voice; the first one he had heard. "The boys snatched 'im as instructed. Now all we have to do is hide 'im for a bit..."

He picked up the flow of conversation. They mentioned the *East End*, the possibility of finding a house with a secret room; places where a man could hide or be hidden. A number of such places existed apparently, yet they needed to find one quickly. One of the men left to make a phone call. Just a couple of minutes later, he returned.

"Did you manage to find one?"

"Yeah, I did as it 'appens," sounded the familiar cockney lilt of the first man.

"Go on..."

"Brothel near Newton Road, run by a guy named Mickey Clark. 'Eard of him?"

"I know Mickey Clark," rose the second, more chilling voice. "Got a record of all them knocking shops round Sammie's patch. I took that one over a week ago. So is he gonna help us or not?"

"You know 'e will," the first man said. "I told 'im who he's dealing with and he ain't got no choice..."

"Fair enough," the other man responded.

For all the while they were talking, Jake could sense him pacing around. Every so often he would pause, turn and pace in another direction. He heard the flick of a lighter, followed by the smell of cigarette smoke.

"Tell Clark to expect us after midnight. Lock him in one of the bedrooms for now and guard him well. We'll wait 'til after dark before we move him..."

The man seemed to draw close. Jake felt the warmth of his breath flutter against his face, carrying a wisp of cigarette smoke.

"Shame, really," the man murmured. "Handsome kid! Can't imagine why anyone would want to kill him, but a job's a job. I ain't about to turn down a few grand out of pity. Doesn't say much though, does he?"

"What is there to say?" Jake relented sadly. "You've said you're going to kill me. Though, I wish I knew why. I'm a musician from the Netherlands and of no threat to anyone..."

And such was the truth; Jake *was* a touring musician, engaged in his own rock band.

Having completed a brief tour of the UK and Holland, their group had been hired to provide entertainment for a very special birthday party. More specifically, this garden party had been organised in a remote country hotel.

This was a day that had descended into horror; a day, a fatal car bomb had exploded and destroyed a number of lives...

"Oh my God," Eleanor gasped. "It was on the news! Something to do with an MP celebrating his birthday party?"

"That was the one," Jake said curtly, lost in his painful memories.

"I heard about it a few days ago," Eleanor spluttered. "Albert Enfield."

"Yes, that was the time it broke the news," Jake sighed. "They feared there would be wide spread panic among the public if I remember. But yes, Eleanor, I was at that party."

She was staring at him wide eyed.

As if that news item alone wasn't scandalous enough. Jake had actually been there. He had witnessed the whole shocking event. The next question begging to be asked was who could have engineered such a plot?

"Did you say you were from Holland, Jake?" Eleanor asked him gently.

"You're Dutch?"

He allowed himself a brief smile. "Yes. My father is Dutch. I have lived in the Netherlands for most of my life. Mother is from England. She never really wanted to leave her homeland, so I've spent time in both countries. I am half Dutch."

"I thought your accent sounded a bit different," Eleanor added. "It's the way you pronounce your vowels. Your accent sounds soft, a little like French. Whereabouts in Holland do you live?"

"Nijmegen," Jake replied, closing his eyes. "It's a beautiful town and I cannot wait to go back there. I expect my friends must be missing me..."

He allowed his mind to drift - imagining the town with its wide river spanned by the arches of a graceful steel bridge; the tall, ornate buildings sculpted in a mosaic of brickwork - the wide roads, the ever moving tide of cyclists. Nijmegen was one of the oldest cities in the Netherlands. He allowed the memories to pass before he opened his eyes. He saw Eleanor braced in front of him as if waiting for him to continue.

"So what did happen?" she whispered. "Before you were captured, I mean... What do you actually remember about that party and the bomb? Can you tell me?"

"Of course," Jake replied, wrenching his mind away from his home town; back to the dramatic events which lingered in the current loop of time...

He fell silent, eyes cast down as he tried to piece it all together again. The ordeal of the last two days had left him so traumatised, some of the finer details had become muddled and confused. In some way, he was pleased to recollect it again; to finally tell someone of this momentous incident that had changed his life...

It had been a beautiful day and he was enjoying the party with his friends.

Set in the grounds of a splendid country house, he could picture the walls of faded tawny brick. The garden outside was filled with ornamental statues and urns, set amongst circular beds of flowers. A gentle breeze ferried the perfume of roses and honeysuckle across the immaculate lawns, where guests congregated and mingled.

An area in the grounds had been set up with tables and chairs, along with a small marquee bedecked with red and white balloons. It enclosed a stage with speakers and microphones, ready for toasts and of course, the gig Jake's band were scheduled to perform.

Jake and his friends had managed to smuggle a bottle of champagne out. Concealed from view behind the tall conifers, they were taking it in turns to swig from the bottle.

He loved his music. At the times when he was playing, he felt most alive and he cherished the company of his band members; Matthias the drummer,

Andries the bass player and Youf on saxophone. Jake played lead guitar and was the main vocalist. His band 'Free Spirit' had grown in popularity throughout the early part of the summer. Touring the clubs and taverns of Amsterdam and Rotterdam they had also attended various music festivals; but what a privilege to be invited to play at this party. Apparently, Albert Enfield was a big fan of rock music. Just at the time, his family had been planning his 40th birthday party, 'Free Spirit' came highly recommended from friends who had visited Nijmegen recently. They had heard them playing live in one of the bustling bars and on discovering they were planning to tour Britain, they had taken one of their leaflets.

Earlier that day, Jake had met Albert Enfield in person. Intrigued by his politics, he had asked him what he believed in.

"To pull the people together as a nation, Jake," the man answered him simply. "I want to establish a society which is fairer. I don't believe people should work so hard for so little, while another sector of society hoard more wealth than they need. British culture is controlled by the greed of the ruling elite. My aim is to improve the workplace for the average British employee but through parliamentary reform, not trade union pressure. I'll campaign for decent wages and strive to keep jobs secure - boost our economy and turn us back into a nation of proud citizens..."

Yet it seemed, Albert's company was in high demand. Others seemed desperate to grab him. He had politely ended his chat and once Jake had shaken his hand and wished him the best of luck, as well a happy birthday, he did not converse with him any further.

For now they remained in the garden, warmed by the sun and lounging around together, drinking from the champagne bottle. There were about 55 people here in total; not a huge party, but Albert liked to keep things low key. By all accounts, he loathed huge, ostentatious affairs that other public figures were renowned for.

Guests enjoyed a simple buffet of crisps and sandwiches. A little later, they would sing happy birthday and bring out an impressive cake decorated with red rosettes and silver candles.

Jake knew that this was their cue to get the band set up and tuned for their performance. After a brief interlude, the entertainment would begin. He planned to start with a popular number, something lively enough to get people tapping their feet or even dancing. Hit with a wave of excitement, he took a last gulp of champagne. He passed the bottle to Matthias, who was smoking a cigarette.

"Hey! Did you remember to bring the spare amp?" he called across to Youf. He was strolling past the flower beds, munching a handful of crisps.

"No," Youf replied, mid mouthful. "Did you?"

Jake grinned. "I'll get it!" he volunteered. "Back of the van is it? Where are the keys?"

Youf delved into the pocket of his jeans, pulled out a set of car keys and tossed them to him. Jake caught them in one hand.

"See you in a second," he said.

Passing through the estate, Jake wandered beyond the grounds. He had been heading towards the lane where their camper was parked. The main guests already filled the hotel car park.

Pausing for a moment, he gazed into the hazy sky, where a cool breeze caressed his face. He took a deep breath and proceeded to wander down the path towards the lane. Bordered by neat hedges, bushes of lavender sent a heavenly fragrance wafting upwards. Bees danced among the blooms. His head swam with the effects of the champagne, bringing a rush of euphoria. He remembered feeling happy and carefree - excited to be getting up on stage to play.

Unlocking the back of the camper, he noted how tranquil an area this was. He could just about hear the sounds of the party resonating in the distance, the chink of glasses mixed with adult voices and laughter. Yet out here, the atmosphere lay still, the country lane devoid of traffic.

He saw the spare amp buried among their rucksacks and sleeping bags. At the same time, a peculiar smell wafted in the breeze - sweet, slightly perfumed, the unmistakable aroma of cigar smoke. Jake raised his head, searching for the source.

His eyes were drawn to a solitary black car lingering in the distance.

Pausing where he stood, he couldn't miss the way it gleamed in the sunshine. Flashes of light were reflected in the chrome bumper and hub caps before he recognised it as a Classic Daimler. Somehow, it didn't look out of place. He noticed a window wound down and then a man resting inside. A trail of smoke wafted from an open window. For a second, Jake studied him.

From that very first glance, the man appeared to be blonde and stocky. Dressed in a suit, he exuded an air of authority, lounging in his car seat, puffing on his cigar. The only feature Jake couldn't make out was his eyes - they were concealed behind mirror sunglasses.

Dropping his gaze, he secretly wondered if he was MI5 or something. Why else would some powerful looking figure be lurking here? Was he keeping tabs on things? He knew Albert Enfield's politics were contentious among some sectors of British society and besides... if he was a guest wouldn't he have parked his posh motor car in the car park with the others? Why would he choose some quiet little lane in the middle of nowhere?

He hauled the amp from the van and hugged it against his body. He used his foot to push the back door shut. The man was still there, observing something directly opposite. Without thinking, Jake followed his gaze.

He spotted a sturdy 12-seater minibus parked a few yards away. Positioned behind the camper, he attempted to lock the back door while at the same time, clinging to the amp.

Yet his head shot up again. It was like a *deja vu*; something kicked at his senses, compelling him to look at the minibus again or more to the point, a pair of legs sticking out underneath. Jake released a sigh. Judging from the dark overalls, he wondered if he was seeing a mechanic. Pushing the thought aside, he yanked the keys from the van door and stuffed them into his pocket.

He had been about to return to the hotel when he felt a sudden pin-prick of eyes.

He stole a backward glance but on this occasion, the man in the car seemed to be staring at him. His dead pan face was reflected in the driver side mirror so he couldn't be sure... Head lowered, Jake behaved as if he hadn't even noticed him and swinging onto the path, he strode back into the grounds to rejoin the party.

The rest of the afternoon passed in a blur of music, laughter and jollification. Guests danced by the stage. Couples wandered hand in hand, strolling around the lovely garden while others rested at tables, chatting and sipping champagne.

Albert too appeared to be enjoying himself as he merged with the crowd.

At one point, he was seen at the back of the garden with a couple of allies. They lingered in the shade of the conifers, engrossed in conversation; perhaps something more political seeing as he had momentarily detached himself from the crowd. Within a comparatively short time however, the discussion had broken up. With a devious smile, Enfield shook the hands of both his colleagues before immersing himself back into the party.

By late afternoon, staff began clearing away the litter of empty bottles - the wreckage of the birthday cake, which was starting to attract wasps. Jake threw on his brown suede jacket, picking up his guitar, ready to make a move. The band's performance had been outstanding and already, guests were enquiring as to whether they had produced any records.

Albert and his group were congregated at the front of the hotel, jackets slung over their arms. They too appeared to be leaving. A river of people could be seen spilling out onto the path just as the clouds were gathering in the sky. The air seemed chilly. Jake shivered, watching the cars crawl slowly from the car park. It seemed as if everyone was leaving en masse.

Albert and his group had hurried into the lane before them, clambering on board the minibus. Several people wandered after them, wanting to wave them off. They included Jake and his band.

No sooner had the doors clanged shut when the engine hummed to life. The minibus pulled away. They watched as it began to cruise along the lane, away from the tranquility of the hotel. Yet it barely reached the road junction.

The earth was rocked by a massive explosion. Onlookers watched in horror as the vehicle was consumed in a writhing ball of flame. Cars pulled up sharply and people jumped out, the group swelling larger, attracting more attention. What they were seeing could not be real. Then all pandemonium broke out and people started screaming.

"Shit!" Andries gasped, clutching Jake's arm.

"Car bomb!" someone shouted from nearby. "Call the police!"

Jake stood frozen, finally understanding the implications of what he had seen earlier; that mystery pair of feet he had so casually dismissed as a mechanic when the truth of it was, someone had been planting an *explosive device*.

By the time the police arrived, the entire road had to be cordoned off. Fire engines arrived, along with an ambulance but it was no use. Everyone on board the minibus was dead, including the driver. Back at the hotel, there was a tense and chilling atmosphere. Some sat in stunned silence; others paced restlessly. Men smoked cigarettes and from another corner of the reception area, a girl was sobbing, head buried in the comforting arms of a man. Yet no one was permitted to leave.

Two men in suits lingered, a third donning the uniform of a senior police officer. They were here to question the guests and staff. Other than the explosion, few people had witnessed anything suspicious. But then it was Jake's turn...

Spluttering out the details of the scene he had witnessed, he held nothing back; from the mysterious man in the black Daimler, to the mini-bus and the faceless person stretched flat underneath it... All of this had occurred at around 3.30 while guests were preoccupied in the rear garden, waiting for the cake to be wheeled out. There was some suspicion as to why Jake had *broken away* from the party. Yet on explaining the situation with the missing amp, the other three band members confirmed this.

As the interview ensued, Jake was certain of one thing; whoever these people were, he wanted to see them caught and brought to justice. He stared deep into the police officer's eyes as he voiced this, when in reality, he felt devastated.

By early evening, people were finally beginning to disperse. Before they left however, the same senior police officer approached the band. He asked them where they were heading, keen to *book them into a hotel in London*. As a matter of utmost security, an instruction had been issued from Scotland Yard, the notion that Jake was required to face further questioning.

"This is the specialist operation which deals with counter terrorism," the man insisted. "The atrocity was caused by a car bomb. Your evidence may be vital to catching those responsible."

So naturally, Jake agreed. He had no reason to refuse, glad to be of assistance. The following morning, he had made his way to the police headquarters, abandoning his friends to enjoy an extra day in London.

The moment he arrived, the same police officer had taken him aside, ushering him into a room to be photographed. Jake felt uneasy about this. It wasn't as if he was a suspect. The man had quickly explained, it was just procedure.

After being left in a waiting area for over half an hour, he was subjected to a barrage of questioning more thorough than he could have imagined. Forced to comb his mind, he recaptured every detail. He had to confess, he hadn't spotted the number plate of the suspicious black car in the lane. Nor could he accurately describe the driver, other than a head of blonde hair and a slightly stocky build. His eyes had been disguised behind those sunglasses.

The police officer took rigorous notes then escorted Jake back to the waiting room. Once again, he was abandoned; the excuse being, it was necessary to consult with someone else...

Eventually the man returned, where just at the point Jake thought he had completely ransacked his memory, the same questions were repeated again. The inspector probed for details of even finer precision. Jake felt exhausted. There was little else he could tell him and as the day wore on, he grew to dislike this man.

His name was Inspector Hargreaves; thick set, hard faced, he scrutinised him through piercing blue eyes. Jake was beginning to from the impression, he was being interrogated. He seemed courteous to begin with yet in the last hour, his manner had changed. Jake found himself being treated with a manner of a contempt which seemed almost sinister.

"You are absolutely certain the car was a Daimler?" Hargreaves snapped. "An expert in classic cars are we? Is it not possible you may have made a mistake, Mr Jansen?"

Jake felt his cheeks flush. "I know what I saw. Why don't you believe me?"

"It's not that I don't believe you," the man answered frostily, "but I must urge you to be absolutely sure in your convictions. Such vital evidence, in the wake of a terrorist attack, is always treated with some suspicion..."

By late afternoon, after a second period of detention, Jake was allowed to leave.

He felt tired and drained as he wandered through the double glass doors - dazed by the whole experience. He knew the investigation was far from over. The next time they met, he would be giving evidence in a court of law. But for now, he yearned to get back to his friends.

Jake sauntered along the road for a few more yards. Oblivious to his destiny, he approached the spot where a dark blue transit van was waiting in the shadows.

"Which is the point those men grabbed you," Eleanor finished.

Jake nodded. He was no longer looking at her, his eyes cast downwards as the horror of his experience caught up with him.

He never did get to return to the hotel, nor see his friends again. He felt sure that by now, they would have returned to the Netherlands, thinking he had abandoned them.

The aftermath of the explosion had left him reeling. He had mourned the death of Albert Enfield, his family and colleagues, never able to understand why anyone would carry out such a callous attack.

He had barely been able to get his head around it before he was seized by those men and the second ordeal had begun; 48 hours spent in fear, perplexed by the ever shifting path of his fate. Something about his evidence had been incriminating. The man he described conveyed power. It wouldn't be impossible for him to hire someone to kill him.

"Jake, this is horrible," Eleanor said, rising.

Without knowing what else to say, she filled the kettle to make some tea.

She spotted some mugs on the sideboard and ceramic jars containing tea, coffee and sugar. There was no milk except for a powdered variety. Eleanor persevered; stirring the powder to dissolve it, where it inevitably settled in tiny white lumps on the surface.

She took the mugs of tea through to the lounge and placed them on the bureau.

Jake had not moved. The sky outside was beginning to lighten now, revealing the silhouettes of bushes and trees. It would be dawn soon, a tunnel of time where day and night had merged into one, the earth completing its orbit, another day about to begin...

Neither knew what the future held but for now, they needed rest, drained by what had happened to them. Maybe they could even afford the luxury of a little sleep. Jake sipped his tea and gazed up at her. He looked exhausted with dark shadows beneath his green eyes.

"I will settle down here on the sofa," he yawned. "Why don't you see if you can find a bed upstairs. But don't switch any lights on. We're not meant to be here, remember..."

"Okay, I won't," Eleanor sighed as she finished her tea. "I hope you sleep well."

And this was how it ended; two young people in hiding with no alternative than to lie low. Eleanor did not even want to speculate what Theakston would do to them if they were captured. She recalled the moment he had drawn his knife and the vision turned her cold.

Tumbling into one of the beds in this strange house, she closed her eyes. Yet deep down she was plagued with the feeling, she had made her deadliest enemy.

III

Dominic Theakston didn't sleep much either.

Forced to abandon the chase left him livid. The last time he had seen Jake and Eleanor was the moment they had crossed that main road, after the police had halted him. Yet even with some hefty reinforcements, it was impossible to track them down again. Darkness had descended and they had disappeared without a trace.

He had sent Dan Levy back to Clark's place to question the residents, in too much of a rage to do so himself. Later that night, he was astounded to hear that not only had Eleanor smashed a bottle over the black girl's head, but had crept downstairs and escaped through the window of the games room. *Even he had to admit that took balls...* Yet she had gone one step further and let that kid out of the basement.

It was gone midnight before he let himself into his apartment.

Breathing heavily, his hands shook as he turned the key in the lock. The day had turned into a disaster and even Dominic could not believe how badly things had gone wrong. As he stepped into his lounge, his eyes were drawn to a mirror on the wall. Someone had scrawled the word *'bastard'* in red lipstick as if to aggravate him further. He ground his teeth, knowing this was none other than the work of *Christine*, the girl who had shared his bed two nights ago. He hadn't been back to his apartment since and obviously she hadn't taken it too well. Not that he cared. He didn't want to be in a relationship right now, he had far too much on his plate.

A larger part of him still hungered for the girlish body of Eleanor Chapman and to be denied such a prize only exacerbated his filthy mood.

According to Dan's version of events, her escape had been spurned by a terror beyond reason. It made him wonder if he had perhaps gone a little too far. Yet it was her fear that had turned him on in the first place and he enjoyed playing on it. Dominic ruled by fear and this was his style. Maybe he shouldn't have mentioned the filming...

There was no denying, he had found the perfect means of tormenting Oliver Chapman and in a way that was meant to be psychological. Ollie was the type of man who would be driven insane by the notion of his daughter being screwed by his arch enemy. He longed to taunt him, having never actually planned to harm the girl... But he had wanted her. He would have screwed the pants off her even if she wasn't Ollie Chapman's daughter. The fact that she *was* Chapman's daughter, that he could enjoy her at an agreed price, all the while she was trapped in that brothel... it thrilled him beyond his dreams.

And now she had vanished, leaving him floundering in a sea of conflicting emotions. On the one hand, he had never lusted for anyone more.

But another part of him could quite happily plunge a knife into her heart.

She had intervened in his business in a way any lesser man would die for. The fact was, that kid she had rescued from the basement was wanted *dead* by some very important people. He had only just accepted a contract to carry out the murder. Those at the top meanwhile, would demand an explanation as to why Jake was *still very much alive*; and this in turn, could yield disastrous consequences for him.

Knowing it was his job to find them again, his mood turned ever blacker. For now, he poured himself a whisky and rolled a joint, desperate to try and calm himself.

Tomorrow he would be speaking with Inspector Hargreaves.

He had met some bent cops in his life but none came more corrupt than he did. He was beginning to wish, he had never taken on this job. Yet Hargreaves had hand-picked him for it and was as deeply immersed in the conspiracy as he was. Two young people couldn't hide forever, especially with the police on their tail. He pulled on the joint, packed with good Moroccan dope. It eased his troubled mind yet his thirst for violence simmered on.

The following day, London buzzed with crowds as people flocked to the Capital. The sun shone down warmly, reflected in the windows of the Police headquarters.

From one of those windows, Inspector Norman Hargreaves gazed down from his office. A typical Saturday, the streets were busy but it was also the school holidays, which attracted hundreds of tourists. Hargreaves fanned himself with a clipboard to ward off the heat. The windows were open which at least allowed some of the cool air to waft in. Yet with it rose the intrusion of traffic noise, jarring his concentration. Barely able to hear himself think, he was not in the best of moods as it was.

One call from the switchboard would indicate the arrival of his visitor. He craved some time alone to clear his head. For a start, the papers were full of dark murmurings, suggesting the nature of crime had changed recently, particularly in East London. Not that he didn't already know this. In the last few weeks, Sammie Maxwell's patch had been terrorised; assaults, arson attacks, followed by that riot at the docks and a few suspect killings... All had been symptoms of a swelling tide of gang warfare which had finally seen off Sammie Maxwell.

But this had also paved the path for Dominic Theakston.

Some were saying, the police were not doing enough to stem the violence. But none of it mattered any more. Hargreaves was secretly delighted to be rid of Maxwell.

As if the man hadn't caused him enough problems in his time. Not only did he run the criminal underworld but discovered the darker secrets of those in authority. Whether one fiddled their taxes, accepted backhanders or emerged as a closet homosexual with a string of rent boys linked to their name, Maxwell got wind of it. *He was a crafty sod.* Not only did he have the East End in his back pocket but virtually the entire establishment rolling around in his palm like a juggling ball.

Many years ago, Norman's own personal life had been exhumed. Maxwell had discovered his shameful past as a wife beater. His first wife had ended up in hospital on so many occasions, Maxwell had become suspicious - to a degree where Norman divorced her.

His second wife, Felicity, had been a blonde and graceful young woman.

How regrettable, Maxwell was well connected with her father; landlord of a traditional London pub, not far from the Malibu, where he was known to enjoy an occasional pint.

On one such occasion, Maxwell had caught a glance of Felicity; her blacked eye and split lip had spoken volumes... Not only did Maxwell confront him and call him every name under the sun but arranged a safe passage for her abroad where she had remained in hiding ever since. That irked him! Maxwell had no right to interfere and as a result, Norman had never remarried; he poured his heart and soul into his career.

So for all this time, he had been awaiting an opportunity to get back at him. At least Maxwell was history now. Theakston had moved in, cleaned up and claimed Sammie's territory as his own. The greatest secret of all was, Norman had helped him do it.

With his attention drawn to the activities of this violent young gang leader, Norman had turned a blind eye. He couldn't care less what methods Theakston used to infiltrate Sammie's Patch, delighted to pave the way for him. Theakston's style was impressive. The man was cold, calculating and brutally efficient. He left no trail and dealt with his enemies without mercy. In the early days, Sammie Maxwell had been feared but one whisper of the name *Theakston* and people virtually 'shat themselves.' He instilled terror to such a degree that no one dared double cross him.

At the same time, Norman had become deeply enmeshed in a conspiracy.

His hunger for power had attracted him to a sinister political adviser who knew how corruptible he was; one who's single aim was to end the progressive victory of Albert Enfield. The car bomb had been perfect in its execution. The IRA had already crossed the line earlier that year; they had delivered a wave of terror that had people quaking. For this reason alone, they seemed the most obvious scapegoat for the atrocity about to take place. Unfortunately, someone had witnessed the man in the black car; a seemingly naive rock musician by the name of Jake Jansen.

Norman had been particularly calculating to seize the boy for an interview and before anyone else heard a whisper of what he knew. Jake's evidence had been potentially damaging, which meant he had to disappear along with his statement. Hargreaves had identified Dominic Theakston as the perfect killer; a decision supported by his fellow conspirators.

Yet to his utter disgust, he had only just learned that Theakston had failed!

The ring of his telephone seemed to mock him. Hargreaves grabbed it, ready to consult his visitor for an explanation. Throwing on his jacket he marched downstairs. He had already booked an interview room, which was of course soundproof. No sooner had he stepped inside when the sight of Theakston swam right in front of him. Hargreaves closed the door and locked it, having insisted on *no interruptions*.

Eyes pinned to him, he took a chair opposite. "So," he began in a low voice, "you screwed up."

Dominic raised his head and glared at him.

"I thought it was perfectly simple," Norman whispered. "You had the boy locked up, well concealed and all you had to do was to finish the job. And now I hear, he's escaped. So the first thing I want to know, Theakston, is how the hell did this happen?"

"Got a smoke?" Dominic retorted coldly.

Clenching his teeth in frustration, Norman tossed a pack of cigarettes across the table. Dominic calmly helped himself from the box, twiddled the cigarette between his fingers, then lit it. He inhaled deeply, fixing him with his deadpan stare and blew out a smoke ring. He almost seemed to be revelling in this...

"Well," he began. "Hate to tell you this, Mr Hargreaves, but someone let him out; a young girl as it happens."

"You what?" Norman murmured dangerously.

"You heard," Dominic snapped. "Clark and his boys swore he'd be locked up. So the last thing we expected was for someone to go snooping around. But someone did and the two of them did a runner..."

"Who was she?" Norman barked.

Dominic took a deep breath. "Not your average whore. She was brought in from the outside by some couple who worked for Maxwell - well known for dumping girls in Clark's brothel. Only, this one was a girl named Eleanor Chapman..."

"Chapman," Norman echoed. He steepled his fingers together on the table top, the cogs in his mind turning. "Anything to do with *Oliver Chapman?*"

"Yeah," Dominic said. "She's his daughter! Course, I had to go round and check it out. As I'm sure you understand, this girl was of huge interest to me..."

"Don't tell me you're still out to avenge Oliver Chapman!" Norman interrupted angrily. "Isn't it about time you let all that go?"

"Why should I?" Dominic snapped. "After what he did to Giovanni?"

Hargreaves saw the hatred which darkened his eyes.

"Good God, you're obsessed!" he gasped in disbelief. "You were engaged in a turf war, Dominic. People get shot and die - goes with the territory! So one of your men took a bullet yet it could have easily been the other way round. Just get over it!"

"Wouldn't expect you to understand," Dominic snapped back coldly. "You weren't there. But let's just say there was a little bit more to it than you think..."

Dominic was lost in his thoughts. *No, Hargreaves couldn't possibly understand...* More had taken place on the docks than just a simple shooting. He would never forget the moment Giovanni had fallen. It had been a chilly night, overcast, dark, with fog rising from the Thames in wisps. The fight itself had been a particularly vicious one. He was banking on the hope that few of Maxwell's men would stick it, given their superior numbers...

Hidden in the shadows, he had been watching from the other side of a warehouse.

The two of them crept around the corner, weapons drawn. Out of nowhere, they heard a shot. Shock pounded into him like a sledge hammer as Giovanni collapsed to the ground. Without another thought, Dominic had dropped to his knees, crouching over him.

He touched his forehead. Giovanni's eyes were blank, veiled with the darkness of death as they stared up into the heavens - his shirt bore a spreading dark stain.

In the same moment, Oliver Chapman stepped out of the mist, arm extended and a gun pointed at him. He absorbed the sight of his face. His eyes were like glowing orbs, pinning him where he crouched. Then last of all, he cocked the trigger. *The next bullet had been for him.*

Instinct compelled him to dive for cover. Breathing heavily, he could not believe what had happened! Next came the wail of sirens. It was no use. The fight was over at least, for now. A wave of grief consumed him followed by a hatred so powerful, he knew it would haunt him forever.

Who was this man? This cold-faced arrogant bastard? Dominic was used to seeing his victims cower in fear but this one showed no emotion; he had balls of steel. He had calmly shot Giovanni but what galled him more than anything was the notion, he could have happily killed him too!

He had finally met his match that night and now he wanted to destroy him.

Dominic could feel the same hatred twisting inside him. He would never give up looking for Chapman and as for his girl... He needed to find her too. She was the catalyst for rooting out his enemy but in the meantime, she had complicated matters.

He struggled to find the words to explain this. Hargreaves narrowed his eyes.

"So," he muttered frostily. "Putting your little vendetta aside, what happened next?"

"Chased them for miles," Dominic hissed, "both her and that fucking kid! We had the car, the van and a bike. Nearly caught up with them too. Shame, some of your boys in blue gave us a bit of bother and that's how they got away. Pity! See, I enjoy a good hunt but I expect to win. Never thought they'd actually get away..."

Hargreaves took this in, his mind spinning. So it would seem that Jake Jansen and the Chapman girl were in this together now.

"Find them," he ordered coldly, "especially the Jansen boy. If word ever gets out of what he knows, it will be the end for both of us!"

"Why do you want the boy?" Dominic sprung on him.

"You don't need to know that," Norman answered. "All you need to do is to kill him."

"Right," Dominic said, "and what about Eleanor?"

"What about her?" Norman smirked. "Let me think... she was in that brothel wasn't she? Did she distract you from what you were there to do, Dominic?"

For a split second, he looked a little furtive.

"Oh, I see," Norman sighed. "Thinking about your dick were you? So *this* is the reason you fucked up? Go on, spit it out!"

"It wasn't like that!" Dominic snarled. "So I admit, I went round there! I knew who she was and what's more, she was a real looker! I saw an opportunity..."

"To get back at her father!" Hargreaves finished.

"Yeah, if you like," Dominic said evilly. "She was a ravishing teenage virgin, what would you have done, Norman? I wanted to be her first! I was even thinking about letting a few of my boys join in. Best of all, I wanted old Chapman to see it. I was hoping to record it on film..."

82

"God, you're an evil bastard, Theakston," Norman growled.

Dominic reached into his top pocket and revealed a photograph.

"This is her," he pressed, ignoring that last remark.

Hargreaves stared at the Polaroid of Eleanor; one that had been taken at Clark's brothel. Dan Levy had snatched it, the previous night. Her dark hair hung in tresses around her shoulders, her eyes wide and dreamy, never mind the subtle glow to her skin.

"Unusual colouring," Norman remarked.

"Mixed race," Dominic said, enjoying the reaction his words would provoke. *He already knew Hargreaves was a racist bastard.* "Mother was West Indian. Don't tell me you've never heard of Martina Chapman? She was a singer - found that out from Chapman's file."

Hargreaves smiled nastily, probably a lot more motivated to track her down now...

"Well returning to the matter in hand," he muttered, "it's imperative, we find these kids before they cause any more trouble."

"We will," Dominic said with conviction. "We'll comb the area where they were last seen. Is there any way you could use your police force? Double our efforts."

"I've already thought about this," Hargreaves said and for a second, it was as if a truce had been met. "Jake's from Holland. I took the liberty of getting hold of his photo. He's got long hair and he looks like a hippy! Suppose he was involved in a bit of drug dealing? Pissed off some of the big boys out there, such as your lot and was ultimately shot as a result? It would solve all our problems in one go."

Dominic smiled icily. "And you call *me* an evil bastard..."

"That's not the point!" Norman snarled. "That boy has got to be dealt with and fast. So next time you catch up with him, just get rid of him. Cock this up again and we are finished. I can say goodbye to any promotion as well as my entire career and you can forget about being the next crime boss. In fact, we've got enough shit on you to put you behind bars - including all those recent killings, never mind the torching of that snooker hall! You might want to remember that..."

"I'm touched by your concern," Dominic drawled, helping himself to another cigarette.

"If you want my advice," Hargreaves continued, "I would tone things down from now on. You've got what you wanted and you are about to receive a substantial pay packet if all goes to plan. In the meantime, let's have no more excessive violence, no more arson attacks and no more threats towards family members."

"Okay, you've got yourself a deal," Dominic said, taking a deep drag of smoke, "but I want to make a condition of my own."

"What?" Norman snapped.

"I'm talking about the Chapman girl... Never did give me an answer the first time round."

"Tricky one," Norman replied, rubbing his fists against his temples. "Of course, the man who stands to lose the most in all this will probably want her dealt with too."

"She's not your problem, she's mine," Dominic said. "I'll take out the boy but you have to give me Eleanor in return."

"Why?" Norman demanded.

"Isn't it obvious," Dominic muttered, unable to disguise the menace that tolled in his voice like a bell. "This whole sorry mess is down to *her*. She broke every unwritten rule. Fact is, when you stumble across someone in captivity, you leave well alone. You don't interfere and you certainly don't help them escape. I'm sorry, Norman, but this girl needs to be taught a lesson..."

Hargreaves nodded in agreement. He didn't really care, just as long as they completed their mission to get rid of Jake.

"Fine," he said softly. "Just try not to go too far..."

Chapter 5

I

Sunshine streamed through the bedroom window as Eleanor was gradually teased out of sleep. She awoke feeling disorientated, the fragments of memory fusing together. She sat bolt upright, taking it all in - seeing the interior of the room, remembering the strange house...

She was still wearing the short black dress from Clark's brothel. Was it only a few hours ago she had escaped from that place? Her heart started to pound. She couldn't help wondering what had happened to Della. She had no idea how badly she might have injured her when she had hit her with the bottle. If only her situation hadn't been so desperate. Surely Theakston wouldn't hold her responsible for her escape - would he?

Eleanor clutched the bedspread, filling her hands with fabric that was silky and intricately embroidered. All the fabrics in this house were beautiful, she noticed; nothing synthetic like the quilted polyesters she was used to. The furnishings looked handcrafted and were possibly ethnic in origin, suggesting the owners had travelled a bit. It was the same with the cushion covers, spun in bright fabrics and decorated with sequins and beads.

This room belonged to another teenage girl, she was sure of it. The distinctive faces of Marc Bolan and David Bowie gazed down from glossy posters on the wall. A round paper lampshade dangled from the ceiling and in another corner, she could see an old fashioned rail hung with clothes, as well as a dressing table. Cluttered with photo albums, brushes, combs and strings of beads, everything seemed feminine and dainty.

Unable to hold back her curiosity, Eleanor rose and started thumbing through one of the photo albums. Theatre programmes and leaflets advertising different plays had been stuck on the pages. Eleanor's eyes drifted to the rail, seeing clothes which were anything but conventional; a satin gown, a shawl and even a grey wig fixed into a bun... She allowed herself a smile. Was it possible, the owner of this room could be an actress?

Her eyes were drawn to a framed photograph. It showed a family; a middle-aged couple with two teenage boys and a blonde-haired girl. Both parents appeared hippie-like; the woman wearing an orange kaftan and a string of beads. She possessed a powerful, almost masculine face and rippling silver hair. The man lounged against a VW camper van, his lined face partly concealed by a dark beard and moustache. Yet something about the photograph comforted her. These people were anything but conformist. Eleanor had little doubt that this was their house.

Snatching a glance out of the window, she could clearly see the garden now; a greenhouse, a vegetable patch scattered with weeds and an old caravan squatting in a sea of long grass. She wondered how long they had been away. The house was clearly lived in and filled with their belongings but when were they due to return?

She toyed with the idea of finding some different clothes. Sifting tentatively through the wardrobe, she discovered an assortment; from flowery mini-dresses and platform shoes, to flared jeans and halter necks. She stumbled across two lovely dresses, one white, the other deep blue. Both had long skirts and embroidered bodices so she slipped into the blue one. It felt practical and cool, if not a little loose on her. She also found a pair of sandals, fraying at the edges, yet their flatness was comforting. Her feet throbbed from the hours of walking in those boots. Finally, she dragged a comb through her hair, teasing out the knots, brushing it until it gleamed.

She raised her head, stretching out the tension in her neck, now hit with a clawing thirst. It was time to venture downstairs for a cup of tea, lumpy powered milk or not. She was craving an opportunity to sneak out and find a shop. With a few spare pounds in the pocket of her denim blazer, it would be enough to afford some basic provisions...

She wandered quietly into the sitting room where Jake snoozed on the sofa.

Eleanor gazed across fondly. He lay on his side, his eyes closed, an arm wrapped around his head as if to ward off an unseen attacker. He looked so peaceful, Eleanor took a moment to study him; the beautiful bone structure, the gentle curve to his mouth and his skin was so very fair. It looked almost luminous in the subdued light, the first shadow of stubble evident on his chin. His hair, free from its ponytail, fell to one side like a shining dark curtain. For a second, she yearned to stroke it. She turned away to make the tea.

The next time she looked at him, Jake was beginning to awaken. Rolling over onto his back, he stretched his arms above his head and opened his eyes.

"Good sleep?" Eleanor asked and placing a mug of tea beside him, she sat settled herself into the little leather tub chair.

"Not bad," Jake muttered. "It took me a while to fall asleep. How about you?"

"Went out like a light," Eleanor sighed.

They sipped their tea in silence. It was not an awkward silence; rather, a tranquil moment where two people could share the same space without the need for conversation.

Eleanor continued to absorb the house and its contents, noticing little details she had been too tired to take in the previous night. The shelves were filled with ornaments, from figurines to ceramic vases and pots. There were candles everywhere. A bowl of pot pourri wafted a floral scent, which mingled with a faint whiff of incense. On one wall hung a massive star chart, on another, a most unusual picture; it depicted the human form divided into bands colour. Eleanor stood up and peered at it closely, reading the columns of text - a spectrum of colours referred to as *Chakras*.

"Strange," she said softly. "Do you have any idea what it means?"

Jake too stared at it, pondering for a moment. "Perhaps it has something to do with *yoga*. I saw a picture like this at a music festival..." He gave a little grin. "I wonder if these people are Spiritualists. Look at the books..."

Eleanor gazed at the shelves, observing the columns of titles. She had already figured, the residents were intelligent, educated people. But these books were different to anything she had ever come across. Her dad was never really one for books. Only in the homes of friends had she spotted the usual bestsellers, manuals on DIY, gardening and travel - but none quite like these. They covered a myriad of subjects from palmistry and astrology, to religion and philosophy.

In fact, she was intrigued. "Incredible," she sighed, "I guess we won't be bored. This place is amazing! I don't know any of this stuff."

"How old are you, Eleanor?" Jake piped up.

"Sixteen," she replied sadly. "I've only just left school. I sat my O level exams last month but I'm not sure if I've even passed them. I don't suppose I'll ever know now. Other things got in the way..." she looked deep into his eyes, "like trying to survive!"

"Oh, Eleanor," Jake whispered. Sympathy shone in his eyes as he patted the side of the sofa. "Come - sit down - finish your story. You told me *a little* last night about your father. But there is a lot more, isn't there?"

"Yes," Eleanor whispered, lowering herself down next to him. "There is..."

She bit her lip, wondering where to start. *The day when her father had announced they were about to leave home?* Yes, that seemed to be the point where her life had taken a dramatically different twist.

In the moment she started talking, it came rushing back to her in waves, from the day she had left with the Mallorys, to the dark place she had ended up, cornered in Clark's lounge under the searing gaze of Dominic Theakston. Like a dam bursting, her story came pouring out and she did not hold anything back...

As the conversation flowed, so did the hours. By midday, they had finished the crackers in the cupboard and a tin of tomato soup. Left with little else to devour other than rice and pasta, it made sense to top up their supplies, though it would inevitably mean leaving the house at some point.

Eleanor's story however, left Jake numb.

For a girl so young, it seemed impossible to imagine how she had felt over the departure of her father. She clearly loved him. Yet to be betrayed on top and forced into prostitution... He didn't really want to dwell on the rest.

Powerless to wonder what lay in store for them, the conversation moved on. They had been discussing their enemies. Jake had presented an accurate description of the men in the kitchen, starting with the tall one and his musical cockney accent. The second man had been even more distinguishable; the pacing, the smoking, the impulsive flashes of movement, never to forget that soft, menacing voice...

"Theakston," Eleanor shivered. "It's got to be! He reminded me of a tiger... You do realise what this means? We're on the run from the same people."

"Hmm," Jake pondered, "then he must know, it was *you* who helped me."

"Yes," she whispered, clutching herself in fear.

"So what does this mean for you, Eleanor?" he pressed. "What if he finds you? Things could be bad, very bad. I wish you'd never got yourself involved in all this..."

"It's too late now," she said fearfully, "and what does it matter? They were going to kill you. I don't see how our situation could get much worse."

Jake nodded. If he was true to himself, he felt a lot more concerned about Eleanor. Theakston might not kill her, but he dreaded the fate that lay in store for her.

"It is essential we stay hidden," he concluded, "which reminds me... Did you see the calendar on the kitchen door?"

Eleanor looked at him with a frown.

"Come and take a look," he said gently, rising to his feet.

She followed him into the kitchen where sure enough, a calendar had been pinned to the door. The month of July was displayed. Yet someone had drawn a squiggle of red pen across the weeks, from the beginning of the month to the end...

"Ibiza!" Eleanor murmured, pronouncing it all wrong.

She lifted the page. The word was repeated at the beginning of August, followed by the same flowing pattern of pen... and again for September, right through to the 18th.

"They're away for the whole summer?" she whispered in hope.

"I imagine so," Jake nodded. "Have you heard of Ibiza? A part of the Balearic Islands, which are Spanish. I've often heard it described as a hippy retreat..."

"That figures," Eleanor sighed. "I found a photo upstairs. It's probably them, Jake, you should come up and take a look."

"Okay," Jake consented, "and I see you found some clothes. Maybe I could find something too and we can disguise ourselves..."

The relief Eleanor felt from looking at that calendar... Heart racing, she skipped up the stairs to the first floor: *September*. It meant they could quite feasibly hide here for almost two months if they needed to, which would be a dream! She had fallen in love with this house and its every characteristic. If they exercised enough caution, no one would even know they were here.

Wandering into the familiar bedroom with Jake in tow, she lifted the photo from the dressing table. Jake took a moment to study the family.

"I see what you mean... Bohemian is the word I would use."

Their eyes met with a smile. Curious to explore the rest of the house, they crossed the landing to discover a larger, master bedroom. Like the sitting room, it was embellished with the same artistic flair; wooden floor boards covered in rugs, a printed throw on the bed and lots of colourful cushions, adorned with beads. The bathroom Eleanor had used earlier lingered on the same floor while at the end of the corridor, another flight of stairs awaited them.

Jake peered up the stairwell to the attic floor. Wasting no time, he bounded up the stairs.

He paused on threshold to discover two smaller bedrooms; one tidy with black and white movie posters on the wall, the bed neatly made, the book shelf stacked in an orderly manner.

The other room could not be more of a contrast. Untidy and disorganised, clothes lay crumpled on the floor. One wall appeared to be plastered with photos and postcards, pages torn from old magazines - they had been arranged into some sort of collage. Eleanor remembered the boys in the photo who were clearly brothers. Guessing these to be their rooms, she clocked a music stand in the corner as well as a guitar propped against the wall...

"Here is someone after my own heart," Jake smiled.

"What?" Eleanor said. "You mean you're also this untidy?"

He released a little laugh and wandering into the corner, picked up the guitar. He lowered himself onto the bed. Eleanor was still leaning against the door frame, watching, as he plucked the strings. Adjusting the pegs to tune the instrument, he seemed to be enjoying himself.

His long fingers were positioned over the frets as he strummed the instrument with his other hand. A chord of the most haunting beauty rang into the air. Eleanor felt the hairs on the back of her neck stand on end and suddenly his fingers were flying over the strings. She recognised the opening notes of 'House of the Rising Sun' as they rippled from the guitar.

Closing her eyes for a moment, she allowed the music to caress her senses. The sound was so lovely, she could have easily cast aside her worries.

"Wow!" she gasped as the notes petered out. "You really are talented!"

He lowered the guitar to the floor with a mirthless smile, but Eleanor witnessed the shadow pass across his face. Perhaps he had been reminded of his friends and his band.

He gave a deep sigh and stood up. "Thanks."

"I mean it," Eleanor replied. "I'd love you to play more... maybe later?"

"Okay," Jake replied. "But do you think they will mind if I borrow a few of their clothes? I've been wearing these for about three days now, they must stink!"

Sifting through the drawers he found mostly T-shirts in loud, psychedelic patterns.

"Try the other room," Eleanor suggested.

Sure enough, the wardrobe in the first room contained a tidy array of garments. This, she presumed, belonged to the more conservative of the two brothers. There was something well organised and methodical about his living space that the other lacked. Furthermore, the clothes were less conspicuous. Jake picked out a grey shirt, jeans and a cotton pin-striped jacket. He also stumbled across a trilby hat and a pair of sunglasses.

"Perfect," he announced. "I'll have a wash and get changed."

Following him downstairs, Eleanor wandered back into the room she had slept in. She could hear the rush of water from the bathroom taps and closed her eyes. The house brought a familiar sense of comfort. It smelled musty from the owners' absence yet its ambience reminded her of her old home.

This in turn, stirred up memories of her father.

She felt a prickle of tears. Only now, did she wonder where he had been for the last few days. An image of his face sprung to her mind; his gentle smile, the moment they had said good-bye at Sammie's club. It seemed a lifetime ago but where was he? Had he managed to find somewhere to lie low or was he on the run still? Eleanor couldn't help wondering if there was any way she could find out. The most obvious source would be Sammie's club, the Malibu, except deep in her heart, she knew how dangerous that was. To think, it was one of Sammie's employees who had shopped her to Theakston...

Struggling to her feet, she proceeded towards the stairs but as she passed the bathroom door, she paused. Jake stood with his back to her. He had changed into the jeans, his torso bare, yet Eleanor could not take her eyes off him. His upper body resembled a sculpture; slim waisted and wide shouldered. He might be as thin and graceful as a cat but his arms and shoulders were corded with long, sleek muscles, his skin pale as marble. Transfixed, as he splashed cold water over his face, she couldn't fail to notice a crimson slash on his left shoulder. He spun around suddenly. Eleanor looked away - her cheeks turning warm.

"What happened to your shoulder?" she said, embarrassed to be caught staring at him.

"I had almost forgot," he muttered as he shrugged into the shirt. "It happened, the night they delivered me to that house. We were in a neighbourhood so I shouted for help. I thought maybe someone would hear me... But it was late and very dark - one of the men had a razor."

Eleanor winced.

"He c-cut me," Jake added shakily. "They really were a most terrible bunch of thugs..."

Eleanor shuddered, remembering the sound of his scream, the night she lay drugged. "I think we should put a bandage on it."

As soon as they were downstairs, Jake put his shoes on. He faced the mirror in the sitting room and grabbing his ponytail, poked it under the rim of the trilby hat. Jake's hair was particularly distinctive; blessed with a reddish brown shine of chestnuts laying in the sun

The dark glasses, he handed to her. "You wear them," he insisted. "If my biggest give-away is my hair then yours is your eyes. I've been wanting to say this, Eleanor, but you have the most amazing eyes. Such a beautiful colour..."

She felt a twitch of pleasure, trying not to smile. Accepting the sunglasses anyway, she wound a chiffon scarf around her hair, twisting it at the back and draping the other end over her shoulder. The two of them faced one another.

"Okay?" Eleanor whispered. "Do you think we're well enough disguised now?"

"I hope so," Jake said. "We will have to see. It is time we stepped out into the world again."

They crept out of the back door and across the garden to the gap in the hedge.

Once on the footpath, they followed it to the end until it eventually led to a set of crossroads. Rows of Victorian terraced houses stood to the left and right but directly ahead, they saw a post office; it marked the focal point of what appeared to be a parade of shops.

Jake and Eleanor wandered slowly into the light, then hurried across the road. The first of the shops included a hardware shop and a café; the next displayed mannequins draped in summer frocks. The area had a certain *class* about it - a profusion of window boxes overflowing with flowers, the tiny gardens which the residents kept so neat.

Within a few seconds, they found a grocery store and slipped through the doors.

Eleanor grabbed a basket. They had counted the money they had, which added up to nearly £20. Spent carefully, it could stretch to several weeks. So they picked out their purchases with this in mind; a loaf of bread, a few tins and seasonal produce such as potatoes and carrots. Jake reached out to pick up a box of eggs. Eleanor offered him a nod. He could not see her eyes through the glasses but sensed the merriment in them. Lowering them inside the basket, his fingers brushed momentarily against her own.

"Do you think this will do for now?" she murmured softly.

"We could get some milk," Jake suggested, remembering the clumpy powdered variety.

Eleanor smiled.

As if to reassure them, their shopping only came to a few pounds. How they would continue once the money had run out... they would cross that bridge when they came to it. Right at this moment, Eleanor felt the warmth of contentment spread through her heart. They had food to eat, a house to hide in and no one suspect had spotted them. Slipping back onto the path they vanished into the shadows where the surrounding bushes swallowed them. She stole another glance at Jake, pleased to have him ambling along by her side. His gentle, carefree mood lifted her spirits and within minutes they had returned to the house.

As day slipped into evening the shadows began to stretch across the lawn. Eleanor started to chop up an onion. Filled with the excitement of cooking their first meal, she placed a saucepan of water on the stove to simmer.

Jake meanwhile was rummaging around in the pine cupboard, reaching towards the back.

"I knew it!" he announced.

He pulled out a wine bottle. Dark green in colour, it was coated in a film of dust, the cork rammed down firmly.

"Jake!" Eleanor gasped. "Don't you think that's a bit cheeky? When the owners come back, they don't want to find half their stuff missing..."

"Rubbish," Jake snorted, "it is home-made. They won't miss a bottle or two..."

Eleanor raised her hands in mock defeat, unable to hold back her smile. *Dinner together and wine...* It felt so grown up! She grabbed a handful of spaghetti, missing the irony that this was also part of the owner's inventory. Within a very short time, she had sautéed the vegetables, added a tin of tomatoes, meatballs and last of all, crumbled up an Oxo cube to create a tasty Bolognese sauce.

No sooner were they seated at the pine kitchen table when Jake poured the wine; burgundy red in colour it looked slightly cloudy. They tapped glassed and their eyes locked. Jake had also stumbled across a candle rammed into an old bottle, thick with a coating of wax rivulets.

"Nice," Eleanor sighed, sipping her wine. She picked up her knife and fork. "This seems strange, doesn't it? Given what happened to us yesterday..."

Jake took her wrist, peering at her watch. His thumb and forefinger felt light on her skin as he turned it, observing the time.

"6:30," he murmured. "I was in the basement..."

"Yes," Eleanor whispered fearfully. Dropping her gaze, she began to wind the pasta around her fork.

Despite the beautiful ambience they had created, the reality of their situation loomed darkly, refusing to go away. Jake could quite easily have been dead by now; *despatched and disposed of.*

As for herself... Eleanor felt a painful tug in her stomach as an image of Theakston's face rose to haunt her again, wondering how she would have survived his assault on her body. He was out there right now, probably turning London on its head looking for them.

Pushing the thought aside she raised her head, watching with pleasure as Jake feasted on the meal she had cooked. Grateful of his company, it was a joy to share this magical evening.

II

It didn't pay to speculate. As Eleanor slept, her body writhed from side to side, the nightmares beginning to encroach. *They were back in the labyrinth of streets, weaving their way through East London. The shadow of a black car with sinister blacked out windows was never far behind. The tyres squealed as it reared up behind them. They had arrived at this house, having only just made it. Yet in a flash, Theakston and his men were in there too, sauntering across the lounge.*

Eleanor backed as far into the room as possible; the face of the man she feared illuminated in the candle light. He walked slowly towards her, trapping her deeper and deeper into the shadows. His dark eyes narrowed. He pulled out the knife. She tried to scream, before glancing around in panic. Where was Jake?

Lying on the sofa, as she had seen him earlier, his arm shielded his head - but something was different. His eyes were as blank as a waxwork - a gaping bullet hole in his forehead.

With a helpless moan of terror, Eleanor glanced around again. Her enemy lurked close, flanked by his men. He gave her a chilling smile and seized her chin - pushed her head back as the blade crept remorselessly towards her throat...

Eleanor awoke with such a jolt, she thought she had suffered an electric shock. Her heart started thumping as she gripped the bed spread; a dream. That's all it was *just a dream* but her fear was so very real. She let out a sob.

Rising shakily from the bed, she glanced through the window, thankful to see the garden basking in the hazy early morning light. According to her watch it was 7.30.

Her sleep had been a restful one until that dream had intruded. Yet it served as a reminder. They could *never* be too complacent. Theakston was still out there and would never give up hunting them. For a few minutes, she sat in silence, allowing the dream to dissolve and her heart to slow down. She could hear birds singing outside; the atmosphere so peaceful and still. Relishing the ambience, Eleanor rose, dressed, then tip-toed downstairs.

Jake had moved from the sofa into the tidier of the two attic rooms. At least he was sleeping in a proper bed now. Comforted by that thought, she poured herself a glass of water, imagining him in slumber as she stood by the kitchen window, gazing out into the garden. She so much wanted to go outside, craving the fresh air and the solitude. Restless as ever, she unlocked the back door, careful not to make a sound as she stepped into the hazy sunlight.

At first, she stood very still, savouring the ring of birdsong. Her senses were sharp as she tuned into her surroundings, listening for any sound which would indicate someone's presence.

Yet the area was reassuringly quiet, prompting her to wander further; slowly up the path where it meandered its way to the end. The grass might have been long but the garden possessed a certain beauty. Terracotta pots stood in clusters - borders filled with colourful flowers with the occasional urn or a statue nestling among them.

The caravan held its position on the dead grass, the windows dusty. It probably hadn't been used in months. Then finally, she reached the greenhouse. The plants inside had died but right at the front, almost hidden in the grass, she spotted a stone sink overflowing with strawberry plants. Peering a little closer, she noticed a number of bright red fruits glistening and with a smile of delight, grabbed a flower pot to collect a few.

Somewhere in the distance came a toll of church bells. The sound soothed her as it broke the silence. Yet in another way, those chimes were *her cue* to get back inside before the neighbours arose. Reluctant to leave the garden but with no desire to be spotted here, Eleanor jumped to her feet and disappeared into the house.

Safely hidden in the kitchen, she filled the kettle. She had found an old copy of *Paris Match* magazine, instantly recognising Jane Fonda on the cover. Yet as time ticked by, she gradually became aware of movement in the house; a creak of footsteps on the stairs that indicated Jake was awake. He appeared before her, smiling sleepily before making some tea.

"Hi," he murmured drowsily. "Good sleep?"

"Okay," Eleanor lied, with no wish to tell him about the nightmare. "You?"

"Not bad," he confessed. "It took a while to fall asleep again... I must try to read one of their big books tonight. It may take my mind off things..."

Sipping his tea he gazed out at the garden. The light was clearer now, enhancing the shimmer of grass and the colourful flower borders.

"I was out there earlier," Eleanor confessed. "Such a lovely garden. I needed some air..."

"Hmm," Jake nodded, "no one saw you, did they?"

"No, it was too early," she replied.

He rolled his head to ease the stiffness from his neck. But in the instant, he stretched his arms above his head, he gave a sudden wince.

"Your shoulder!" Eleanor gasped. "How is it feeling?"

"It hurts," Jake muttered. "I don't remember how long it is since that happened. What day is it?"

"Sunday," Eleanor replied. "C'mon, take your shirt off. Let me look at it."

His green eyes revealed a hint of unease as if fearing what she might find. Then slowly, he began to unbutton his shirt. Eleanor stood up and moved to his side, watching him peel back the fabric. She gasped before she could stop herself.

"Is it bad?" Jake asked her.

Her eyes were drawn to the long slash cleaved into his shoulder. At least six inches long, it was encrusted with dried blood by now. But the lower half didn't seem to be healing, the edges open, the surrounding area flushed with inflammation.

"It might be infected," she whimpered. "I wonder if I can find something to put on it."

She momentarily left to search the bathroom cabinet yet found nothing.

"Maybe they took their medicines away with them," she mumbled.

"It doesn't matter," Jake sighed, fastening his shirt buttons.

"Jake, it *does* matter," Eleanor insisted. "At least let me get some ointment from the corner shop. It's open until noon. I need shampoo anyway and the loo paper's nearly run out..."

"Okay," Jake sighed in defeat, "but please don't worry. Drink your tea and I'll make us a nice breakfast..."

A smile lit up her face. "I picked some strawberries!"

"Sounds great," he muttered, smiling back at her and for a second, his eyes never left her.

With a nervous gulp, he looked away again.

Was she imagining things or did he seem a little awkward with her today? In the last 24 hours, they had bonded like friends; hardly surprising given the shocking events that had thrown them together in the first place.

Yet Eleanor couldn't help wondering how this would pan out. She adored his company but to what extent did those feelings stem from the terror they had endured? More to the point, how long would it last? She had already started to question if he would return to his homeland; and what of *her* fate? She knew she needed to find her father.

"I've been thinking," she offloaded, "at some point, I wouldn't mind visiting the Malibu... Find out what the status quo is, now Sammie's gone."

"No!" Jake blustered. "Eleanor, that is too dangerous!"

"So I'll go in disguise," she pressed. "I need to know where the land lies. Sammie's employees are my last and only link to Dad."

"And just the type of place, Theakston will come looking for you," Jake persisted.

"Don't think I haven't thought of that?" Eleanor snapped. "If it makes you feel any better, I can phone first and arrange to meet someone."

Jake shook his head. "Don't go, Eleanor. I couldn't bear it if anything happened to you."

She let out a sigh, frustrated by the tightrope tension that dictated their lives. Yet the tenderness of his words touched her - a tiny place in her heart she never knew existed.

As soon as they had eaten breakfast, Eleanor slipped on the sunglasses and scarf, ready to revisit the shop. They had decided to take it in turns now. As a couple they stood out but as individuals it was easier to remain inconspicuous. Following the footpath, she marched up to the crossroads then hurried across the road to the shop.

Wasting no time, she grabbed a bottle of shampoo from one shelf, lavatory rolls, and a tube of antiseptic cream. Once at the checkout, she was served by the same girl as before; an attractive young Asian woman in a long, floating gown and matching headscarf.

"Hello," she greeted her. "Are you new in the neighbourhood?"

Eleanor braced herself. "Just visiting friends. Have you lived here long?"

"Six months," the girl said. "We used to live in the East End. We ran a shop there..."

"Really?" Eleanor smiled, cautious not to reveal she was familiar with the area.

"My father was targeted by criminals," the girl added sadly. "Horrid racist graffiti was daubed on our door; *Pakis go home...* Another night, someone threw a brick through our window."

"That's awful," Eleanor responded with genuine feeling. "Wasn't there anything you could do? Like talk to the police or something?"

She shook her head. "Police aren't interested in racist attacks. Then a gang visited us, offering protection... but they wanted money. Daddy said *he would rather die* than give in to protection rackets. We decided to move instead..."

Eleanor remained silent. It might have been her own father who had made that visit.

"That will be £1.20 please."

Eleanor reached into her pocket but as she did so, her eyes fell to a stack of newspapers by the till. The Evening Standard covered the news around London. Yet her eyes were drawn to a headline; *Violence in the city on the increase again. Horrific attack on young woman.*

Eleanor took one. "This t-too please," she said, fighting to disguise the tremor in her voice.

Returning to the footpath, Eleanor gaped at the front page. There was a picture beneath the headline, where one glance portrayed a horrific truth... The victim had been Della.

She could no longer hold back her tears. Jake had been leafing through a book but dropped it in the moment he saw her. He sprung to his feet.

"What is it? What is wrong, Eleanor?"

"This!" she shrieked, slapping the newspaper down on the kitchen table. "Read it!"

Jake frowned. "A prostitute from Poplar who was viciously attacked, is said to be recovering in London Royal Hospital. It is alleged the brothel, based in the Dockland area, was visited by a gang in the early hours, sometime between Saturday and Sunday where the attack took place..." He paused and swallowed deeply.

"What?" Eleanor cried. "What happened to her?"

She snatched the paper. Jake watched cautiously, as if dreading her reaction.

"Oh my God!" Eleanor whispered. "It says *the brothel owners were beaten up and they slashed Della's arm with a razor.* Jake, this is horrible!"

"Bastards!" Jake hissed. "I guess this is their way, using razors on people..."

"How could they blame her for my escape?" Eleanor whispered, another tear cascading down her cheek. "I smashed a vodka bottle over her head!"

Sadness clenched her heart. Della was one of the few people in that brothel who had shown her any kindness. She would never forget how traumatised she felt, the night she had been dumped there. Della had taken her under her wing. She would never forget her sweet face and now she had been hospitalised!

"This is my fault!" Eleanor whimpered.

"Eleanor, none of this is your fault," Jake argued and snatching the paper from her hands, he dropped it onto the table. "It is a very violent world out there, we both know that."

"You don't understand," Eleanor protested, "I bet the only reason this was done to her, was because of my escape... Theakston threatened them, especially Della!"

How could she forget his nasty words? Jake gazed at her with sympathy then gradually coiled his arm around her shoulders.

"Don't cry," he whispered. "Sit down..."

Without waiting for an answer, he guided her towards the sofa.

"Listen... These people sold you to your father's worst enemy! The place was a brothel, Eleanor, they were not the nicest of people. They knew you were frightened yet they were still prepared to take his money - allow him to do what he liked to you..."

Eleanor took a deep breath. "They didn't agree lightly, Jake. Theakston rules by fear and Della was genuinely scared..."

Slowly, he withdrew his arm and looked at her.

"So maybe you are right," he relented, "but think of the alternative. What would have happened if you hadn't escaped?"

Eleanor lowered her eyes; this was something she didn't want to think about right now.

"You escaped because you were desperate," Jake pressed, "and you took a huge risk. Don't think I don't care about what happened to this girl.." he pointed a finger at the paper. "I just don't think you should be feeling guilty about it."

"Maybe I could visit her," Eleanor said dreamily. The image of Della's face haunted her.

"No!" Jake snapped. "You mustn't!"

She gaped at him in confusion "But she's been hurt! It's what anyone would do..."

"Which is just what they expect you to do..." Looking at her intensely, a sudden power rose in his voice. "For a start, why is this reported? There have been many attacks across London, you told me! What if Theakston's gang did this to get at you? They attack the girl, put her in hospital and inform the local newspaper. I think we were meant to see this headline and if you go running into that hospital, Theakston's men will be waiting for you. It's a trap, Eleanor!"

"Perhaps," Eleanor whispered, turning the facts over in her head again. "Della might not want to see me anyway... and what if Theakston did turn up?"

"So you promise you won't go?" Jake whispered.

"Yes, alright Jake, I promise," Eleanor sighed, unable to stop another tear escaping her eye.

For the rest of the day she was subdued. After washing her hair, she liberally smothered Jake's wound with antiseptic cream, before covering up it with a bandage. She was clearly devastated about Della and Jake could understand that. She was that type of person. What Theakston's men had done chilled him; further proof that he was prepared to go to any lengths to entrap them.

But as evening approached, Eleanor remembered the strawberries, which seemed to lift her out of her melancholy. Drifting over to the kitchen sink, she began to rinse them - using a fruit knife to slice them into halves, dropping them into bowls.

Jake couldn't resist wandering into the kitchen to watch her. He leaned across to glance over her shoulder.

"English strawberries," he sighed. "The sweetest in the world..."

She felt his breath waft against her neck and her stomach gave the strangest flutter. For those few seconds she was lost for words, scouring her mind for something to say. Unable to stop herself, she spun around to face him and popped one of the strawberries into his mouth. He let out a murmur of delight and closed his eyes.

"Delicious... and you say you found these growing in the garden?"

"Yes," she smiled. "Some are not even ripe yet, so there'll be more..."

He was staring into her eyes in the most searching way and she couldn't seem to pull her gaze away. Some undefined emotion flickered from their intense green depths. She studied his irises; the dark rims encircling them, the tiny flecks of blue and gold; details she had never noticed but then again, he had never stood this close before...

He closed his eyes, lowering his head at the same time. She encountered the velvety softness of his lips as they brushed against her own.

Such a sensation released a wave of desire and with little hesitation, she kissed him back. She could taste the tang of strawberries. Reaching up, she slid her fingertips over his face, stroking his hair where at last, she savoured its silkiness. As his tongue slipped inside her mouth, her stomach did another little somersault, same as before.

It only lasted a second. Jake broke away, the breath on his lips shaking.

"Oh wow," Eleanor gasped.

"I'm sorry," he whispered, lowering his eyes.

"Why?" Eleanor protested. "It was nice..."

"You are so very young, Eleanor," Jake said, a sadness in his tone. "I mustn't take advantage."

Wandering away from the kitchen he sat down, letting his head droop into his hands.

"We have been through a nightmare," he continued. "It's bound to mess with our heads. So let's take things slowly. We have plenty of time to discover how we really feel."

Eleanor was stunned. She didn't want to take things slowly, she wanted him to kiss her again. Her lips tingled from the delightful sensations he had evoked and she longed for more. Yet he had backed off; there was no point trying to force things. Frustrated beyond belief, Eleanor brought the strawberries to the table and sat down opposite. She gave a tight smile.

"Enjoy your strawberries," she said through gritted teeth, "and for God's sake stop worrying about my age. I've grown up a hell of a lot in the last few days. It was only a kiss!"

III

In the meantime, Theakston was becoming impatient. Two days had elapsed since Jake and Eleanor had last been spotted and the trail was beginning to turn cold.

He had groups of men posted in all corners of East London now and constantly on the lookout, especially around the tube stations. Each had been furnished with copies of the photos so they had a better idea of who they were looking for. They were ordered to question anyone who may have spotted them recently.

His own party kicked off their search in Commercial Road, Poplar. Not only was this the neighbourhood closest to Clark's brothel, but the area where the chase had to be terminated. Combing the surrounding streets, Dominic had finally picked up a lead from a hotel. There had been a private party. One of the waiters distinctly remembered the two people as described racing through the corridor. They appeared to be completely out of breath before sneaking into the dining room. He had been about to shout out to demand what they were up to, but lost his chance in the moment they escaped through the patio doors. The garden gate lingered just yards away...

Dominic, accompanied by three men, followed the same path. Stepping into the dingy back streets, it seemed obvious why they had lost them. *If only that business with the police hadn't stalled them.* They too would have followed them here, instead of pursuing their fruitless search along the main road.

The back streets were quiet and secluded with less people around; perfect for a young couple to lie low. There were still a few shops nestled in among the tightly packed houses - smaller establishments where Dominic began his questioning unnoticed. On this occasion, he chose a newsagent. Luckily the shop was empty. Sauntering inside, tailed by his colleagues, one of them quickly reversed the door sign, indicating the shop was closed.

Lurking by the door to fend off any customers, Dominic and the other two made their way to the end of the shop where the owners sat in silence.

The man slouched behind the counter was engrossed in his newspaper; maybe in his sixties, he appeared to be round and fat with a pasty white complexion. A woman of the same age flipped through a sales ledger, ticking off orders. The man glanced up briefly, scowled and chose to ignore them. Dominic took the paper from him, folded it shut then placed it back on the counter. He drew his face close.

"Just a quiet word, old man," he began icily.

The wife glanced up with a look of fear that etched extra lines into her complexion.

"George!" she said in a stage whisper.

"What d'you want?" George grunted.

"I'm looking for someone," Dominic snapped.

"Aren't we all!" the man retorted. He had a surly manner and Dominic was starting to feel irritated.

"Not being very helpful are you?" he said softly, "and I don't like your attitude. Now we'll start again shall we? Have you seen either of these youngsters?"

The man next to him stepped forwards, slapping the photographs onto the desk right under his nose. Although he barely even glanced at them.

"I ain't seen no one," he muttered, "not sure I'd tell you anthin' if I did!"

Dominic clenched his teeth, though it seemed, he hadn't quite finished.

"You see, I know who you punks are! You might 'ave terrorised every other business in the neighbourhood but you don't frighten me!"

"Really?" Dominic sneered. "Well let's see... fucking lot of paper in this place ain't there?"

Reaching into his pocket, he fished out a lighter and ignited the flame. For several seconds, the flame hovered in front of the man's eyes. Dominic kept talking.

"Just imagine... this place'd go up like a bonfire! Thing is, when I ask for help I expect some co-operation but you are starting to get on my wick!"

"Are you threatening me?" George bellowed, staggering to his feet.

"What if I am?" Dominic hissed back. "Might teach you some respect!"

"Oh, you think you deserve respect, do yer?" the man kept ranting. "Well let me tell you somethin,' Son! People round 'ere preferred it when *Sammie* was runnin' things! At least 'e was reasonable. 'E didn't just go pickin' on folk when 'e felt like it. If you want respect, you earn it! Now get out of my shop!"

Dominic shook his his head; he felt murderous. "You're pushing your luck, you old fool! Now have you seen these kids or not?"

"No, I ain't!" George shouted and turning on his heel, he plodded into the back room and slammed the door.

His poor wife looked terrified.

"I'm sorry about me 'usband," she whimpered. "Don't take it personally. E's not in a good way, see, got a bad 'eart. Doctor's only given 'im about six months to live."

Dominic flicked his head towards his men to indicate they were leaving.

Finally, he glared at the old lady. "If he ever speaks to me like that again, he'll be lucky if he gets *that*," he shocked her by saying before they marched their way out of the shop.

The instant they were outside, Dominic exhaled a sigh. His face was drawn tight with fury as he dug for his cigarettes. Dan Levy offered him a light but as he held the cigarette to his mouth his hands were shaking violently.

"Hey!" Dan said. "You okay, Dominic?"

He took a deep drag on his cigarette.

"Get a grip, mate," Dan reassured him. "What I can't understand is why you didn't break that old bastard's face!"

"I wanted to," Dominic shuddered, "but you weren't at the pig shop yesterday! Been ordered to cool things down a bit, so no more random acts of violence..."

"What pissing use is that?" Dan spluttered. "Can't run the East End without fear!"

"Hargreaves thinks we've been throwing our weight around too much," Dominic sighed. "He's getting it in the neck from his superiors. Papers are saying, the police can't control us any more and if Hargreaves gets the boot, things could get heavy! Can't you see that?"

His eyes glinted like flints as he sucked on his cigarette. His hands had not lost their tremor, Dan noticed, a sign that his boss was stressed to buggery!

"Look," he said coolly. "Hargreaves knows that if we're gonna run this patch the way 'e wants, we can't show no mercy - especially not now!"

"Yeah," Dominic sneered, "'cept he also laid it on the line, if we go too far and I mean really too far like in the early days, we could end up in jail. Not that I'm bothered. Been there before! But think... we've worked fucking hard to get this patch and I don't wanna give it up just yet!"

"Fair enough," Dan snorted.

Having more or less taken over from Giovanni as Dominic's right hand man, he was enjoying the sense of superiority. He possessed a cool, clear head which made him perfect for the job. He wasn't prone to the unpredictable rages his boss suffered from.

All the same, he could understand how hard this was. Dominic was no stranger to violence. This was possibly the only language he understood and bore the battle scars to prove it.

Having grown up in the worst slum in North London, the gang life became a means of survival for him. Throughout his youth, he had frequently clashed with rivals, suffering some pretty nasty injuries as a result. These included being slashed, stabbed, shot and on one occasion, even tortured by a rival gang leader. Yet bitterness burned like salt in wounds. Such hatred had shaped him into the ruthless gang leader he was today and he was not going to back down...

Over the course of ten years, he had rampaged his way across London, terrorising every gang who dared cross his path. But after serving two years for manslaughter, he had made the most of his time in jail. He had built up his strength through weight-lifting as well as being educated by the more experienced inmates, to emerge as a professional criminal...

He quickly discovered that the only way to challenge enemies was to find ways of being nastier and more sadistic, which was how he had earned himself a reputation as *a man to be feared*. At the age of 27 Dominic was in his prime; confident to take on a well-established crime boss like Maxwell and with Hargreaves on board to pave the path for him, the battle had been won. He was determined to hang onto that status, even if it did involve a degree of self-control.

"Right so what now?" Dan piped up, changing the subject. "Where does this dump lead?"

The old fellow in the newsagent was long forgotten.

"Not sure," another of Theakston's men said. "My hunch is, if they were trying to avoid attention, they'd carry on moving North, maybe into the industrial estates. There ain't much else over that way."

"Then let's take the car and have a look," Dominic snapped. "These kids are clever! They're obviously avoiding the built-up areas, otherwise more folk would have seen 'em. Maybe it's time we cast our net a bit wider."

He glared ahead, where the back streets trailed into the distance. Packed with seedy rows of houses, he could almost imagine them running this way. Suddenly he was intrigued to know what lay beyond the maze, drawn in the same direction Jake and Eleanor had chosen two nights ago.

IV

The following evening, Eleanor lay on the floor of the lounge, engrossed in a book on herbal medicine. Thick and heavy with a leather bound cover, it was beautifully illustrated with photos and drawings. These books had opened her mind.

Over the last two days they had continued to share their respective life stories. The eldest of two siblings, Jake told her about his life growing up in Holland - the times he had spent in England, travelling around Europe, right up until the year they had established their rock band.

Eleanor entertained him with stories about life in boarding school. Only now did she realise, her father must have sent her there to *protect her* from the dangerous criminal underworld he inhabited under Sammie's rule.

Tonight, Jake had agreed to cook. He had chopped up the last of the onions and mushrooms, along with some potatoes, having promised to make a Spanish Omelette.

Earlier, he had discovered another door attached to the kitchen. Hidden in the shadows to the right of the back door, a tiny utility room lingered on the other side. It contained a chest freezer and a washing machine but not only that... a row of glass demijohns stood along a high shelf, filled with this season's wine. Jake found two wooden racks containing at least three dozen bottles. The plum wine they had opened on their second night had lasted two days but for tonight, he chose a different variety labelled 'gooseberry.'

The sun was beginning to fade. Eleanor rose, stepping into the encroaching shadows. She had picked a few flowers and arranged them in a vase with sprigs of lavender; though right now, she was hankering for a few more strawberries. Once outside, she breathed deeply, letting the cool air fill her lungs. She knew she was living in a fantasy world but if only time could stand still, so she could remain here forever... It would be nice not to worry about their fate, nor even consider the day they would be forced to leave this peaceful sanctuary. She basked in a moment of silence, broken only briefly by the melodic flute of bird song, then reluctantly made her way back indoors.

Jake had poured out two glasses of wine, golden and gleaming as it absorbed the candlelight. He had brought down the guitar from the other boy's bedroom where it took its rightful place by his side. In fact, he was playing it right now, strumming a sequence of familiar rifts. They echoed around the walls and he started singing...

"I've been through the desert on a horse with no name, it felt good to be out of the rain.

In the desert you can remember your name, 'cause there ain't no one for to give you no pain."

His voice was gentle and soft around the edges. Every so often it released a husky break, not dissimilar to David Bowie's. Eleanor was almost moved to tears, recognising the melody of a 'Horse With No Name' by the band, America. It had topped the charts, that very same year.

Eventually they settled down together to enjoy Jake's omelette; delicate in flavour, accompanied by a leafy green salad. The wine was smooth and syrupy like sherry, possibly a lot more mature than the last. Pleasantly sweet, it was also considerably stronger. After just one glass, Eleanor could feel her head swimming.

"This is lovely," she said as Jake lit a few more candles.

And there were so many candles. They had discovered a healthy stock pile of boxes at the back of the cupboards. Eleanor was beginning to recall the many power cuts they had suffered the previous winter, due to industrial disputes and strikes. Even her father had kept a stash.

As evening tipped into nightfall, the darkness began to spread. It enhanced the glow of candle light as it danced around the walls. She closed her eyes, cherishing the moment. Jake turned back towards the table and as he did so, he allowed his hand to wander to her neck, fingers lightly brushing her skin. Her stomach did a little leap.

"If there was anything you could wish for, what would it be?" he said.

"Anything?" she sighed, keeping her eyes closed. "Hmm - in that case, all I could wish for right now is that you would kiss me again!"

She opened her eyes to find him gazing at her warmly.

"Unless of course, you find me repulsive..." she added. Laughter sprung from her voice.

"Oh Eleanor!" Jake replied, releasing a little laugh of his own. "That is ridiculous! Of course I don't find you repulsive. I think you are beautiful."

"I wouldn't go that far..." she murmured, feeling her cheeks flush.

"But you are," Jake whispered. "I guessed you were mixed race. How else would you have that lovely colouring, such dark hair... and as for your eyes?"

"People in our neighbourhood used to call me 'a nigger brat,'" she said softly. Eyes lowering, she immediately regretted her choice of words.

"Those people were idiots," Jake sighed, folding his hand over his own.

His touch was so comforting and warm, Eleanor stared up at him, giddy with emotion.

"Didn't you say, your mother was a singer?" he added. "It is very sad what you told me about the car crash..."

"I was eight," Eleanor murmured. "It broke my heart. We missed her so much, though it crucified my dad. There were nights I used to hear him crying..."

A solitary tear ran down her face. It seemed to stir some reaction in Jake.

Eyes locked, she could feel the tenderness in his expression until at last, he leant forwards. He kissed her gently. The moment their lips made contact, Eleanor knew that any doubts about his feelings were groundless; the sensation of his mouth moving over hers so pleasurable she didn't want it to end. She struggled to her feet, clinging to his shoulders as she did so.

Jake grasped her hand, displaying a sudden strength as he pulled her away from the table. She did not protest as he guided her out of the kitchen and into the lounge; nor when he eased her gently onto the sofa. Lowering himself down next to her, Jake pushed a cushion behind her head to make her more comfortable. He smiled down. Shadows flickered in the contours of his face as he smoothed her hair away from her face and they resumed their kiss.

This time, it seemed to last forever. He held her face between his palms, kissing her over and over again, their lips parting until at last their tongues made contact, drawing them to the next level of intimacy. It felt almost magical.

Eventually they eased themselves apart, if not just to rise for air... Jake held her close, snuggling her into an embrace. It afforded her a sense of security; as if the strength of his arms alone could protect her from the spiralling dangers outside. *And there was danger.* She could sense it like a fog rising off the river Thames, relentlessly spreading itself over London.

Pondering over their situation, she let out a lengthy sigh...

"Jake," she whispered, trailing her fingertips over his cheek bone.

"What is it?"

"Do you think we will ever be safe again? I mean, what if we eventually did manage to escape from London? Then what?"

"I could take you to the Netherlands with me," he suggested. "We would be a lot safer over there and I'd love you to meet my family..."

"But what about that awful business with the car bomb?" she added. "The people who were behind it must know you're from Holland. Don't you think they might follow us?"

"There may be someone we can contact," Jake said. "An Embassy, some organisation who can protect us. I wish we could contact the police but I don't trust them..."

"No," Eleanor sighed. "Nor me. Not after what you told me. That blue van hanging around by the police headquarters... they must have known you were about to leave."

"Yes," Jake agreed. "I am sure someone set me up - someone inside the police force..."

Eleanor saw the fear cloud his eyes. She could almost imagine his thoughts. Whoever was behind that car bomb had liaised with some corrupt police officer. Their attempt to recruit a criminal gang to get rid of him had failed, so they were bound to be on the look out for him. With a sinking heart, Eleanor realised there was no one they could turn to. They were trapped.

"This can't be real," she shivered. "Your life has been threatened. We were chased across London by a gang of thugs. Don't you think the police should be protecting us? We shouldn't have to go into hiding like this."

"No," Jake said softly. "We shouldn't."

Lowering his head, he began to kiss her again and for a while, she savoured the sweetness of it. *If only she could forget her fears.* Yet she felt uneasy. Something else was troubling her and it kept tugging at her mind, refusing to go away. If anything, her anxiety was growing deeper, as she clung to him, kissing him with an even fiercer intensity. The next time they broke their kiss, she wriggled her way off the sofa and stood up.

"Jake," she said softly. "I want you to take me to bed..."

At first, he didn't react - smiling back through eyes that swam with affection.

"You have drunk too much wine," he teased.

"No, I haven't, Jake," she protested. "I'm scared, we may not survive this; that the day we leave this place, Theakston's men are going to close in on us like a pack of wolves. We might even end up dead!"

"Don't say that, Eleanor, please!" Jake argued. "There was a time when I thought I would be dead but you found me! And now we are here, still alive!" He prodded his arm as if to illustrate the point.

"But what are the odds?" Eleanor whispered, hugging herself in fear. "What if Theakston's got men all over London looking for us? If we go to the police, you might end up back in their hands anyway!"

"It does not mean we don't have a chance," Jake assured her.

Eleanor shook her head. "But it's such a slim chance. Please let's not waste any more time..."

She stood up. Her long blue dress hung in gentle folds, emphasising her slender body, her dark hair cascading down her back.

Jake took another glance into her eyes, as if seeking reassurance before he too, rose to his feet.

Without delay, he seized her hand and pulled her towards the staircase.

They raced up to the bedrooms. There was a sudden urgency in their quest, now the decision had been made. Jake coaxed her into the master bedroom and lay her down on the bed. Finding more candles, he arranged them around the bedside and started to light a few.

"You're so lovely," he whispered. "I want to to look at you..."

He took off his shirt and Eleanor stared at his pale torso. It so much reminded her of a sculpture; as if every smooth contour had been honed from marble. She could not deny, she was a little nervous about this. Yet if she was going to lose her virginity, she could not imagine anyone she would rather lose it to than Jake. Running her hands over his shoulders, she relished the feel of his hard and shapely muscles.

Settling down beside her, he lowered his head to kiss her again. His hand brushed her breast, sending quivers through her. She released a sigh but sank back down again, willing him to continue. The touch of his fingertips on her nipples sent the strangest currents through her body; warm, tingling feelings, almost like electricity.

He started to undo the buttons on the bodice of the dress, revealing a light bra, easing the fabric away from her shoulders so her upper body was exposed. Without thinking Eleanor reached around the back of her bra and unhooked it, slipping her shoulders through the straps. The next time, his warm hand closed around her breast, she stretched her entire body like a cat basking in sunshine. Gradually she shrugged out of the dress and let it fall to the floor.

Looking at him now, his eyes resembled dark pools in the candlelight. She ran her fingers over his lean body, from the plane of his stomach to the outline of his collar bone. They did not rush things, their movements slow, as they explored and stroked every inch of each other. Every so often their lips would join; it was as if their first experimental kiss had never quite ended... Only when Jake grasped the elastic of her knickers, pulling them down, she felt slightly nervous again.

This was it, there was no turning back...

As he removed the rest of his clothes, she began to wonder how many girls Jake had made love to. At the age of 22 he wouldn't be without experience. Finally, they slid into each other's arms, completely naked. Eleanor's heart started racing yet her limbs felt like liquid. She sensed his arousal, her hand on his manhood. Easing himself up onto one elbow, he pressed the palm of his hand against her inner thigh and pushed it out to one side. He then rose and knelt between her parted legs. Eleanor closed her eyes.

Surprised, he didn't enter her right away, his hand slid towards some secret place between her thighs where he began to stroke her intimately. Waves of delicious pleasure consumed her. She had never experienced anything like this, driven to soaring new heights of sensation. Like a wave rolling towards a seashore, something inside her erupted - the wave crashed, sending her entire body into a spasm. Eleanor cried out.

In the same moment, Jake eased himself inside her. She felt a tiny snap of pain as her virginity was lost, so swept up in her climax, it didn't phase her. His movements were slow but powerful and she relished the sensation, wrapping her arms around his neck, her legs around his narrow waist as they journeyed together in synchrony. His breath came faster, as he too rose to a climax and eventually they lay still. No sooner had the moment passed, he raised his face and kissed her with such passion, she could have wept... The experience had been little short of magical.

They lay together in silence but the next time Jake stared at her she knew a bridge had been crossed and nothing would ever be the same ever again.

They were in love. They did not even need to say the words, *they just knew.*

Chapter 6

I

The weather changed that night. Clouds gathered in the sky, drawing themselves over the stars like a veil, the barren area cloaked in darkness. A pair of tramps settled down on the ground on top of their blankets. They were huddled around a tiny bonfire, the surrounding area remote and under-populated, which suited them fine; fewer people around to bother them...

A light breeze gently shook the flames. It disturbed an empty beer can as it rattled around in the mouth of the railway tunnel. One of them glanced up suddenly.

Another sound had materialised out of nowhere and seemed to be getting closer; footsteps by the sound of it - several of them advancing across the ground from the distance.

"Cops?" one of the tramps muttered.

"Not sure," said his friend.

By now he could distinguish the silhouettes of four men as they marched in their direction.

Only as they drew close, did they glance from side to side - perhaps checking if the coast was clear before they approached them. The man felt nervous, fearing an attack was imminent. He nevertheless remained transfixed, bracing himself for whatever was about to happen. One of the strangers flicked on a torch. Its beam speared through the darkness, illuminating their patch. The man shielded his eyes.

"Who's there?" he called out.

"Your worst nightmare," a soft, but chilling voice rose up from behind the torch. "Unless you've got anything useful you can tell us..."

The man known as 'Old Harry' squinted as he peered upwards, gripped by a sudden fear. The towering shadow loomed over him - the other four men positioned on all sides, trapping them in a square. Harry swallowed nervously.

"What can I tell you then?" he surrendered in an equally soft voice. "I have no secrets." He possessed the voice of a man who was educated and with no hint of any accent.

He pronounced each word clearly. Face captured in the yellow beam, he conveyed an air of wisdom, his senses sharp.

"Friday night," echoed the voice of Dominic Theakston, "two young people came running this way... a girl and a young man. Just wanted to know if you saw anyone..."

"Oh, I saw them, alright," Harry answered. "Running like the wind, they were!" He inclined his head as he said it, shoulders braced as if proud to be of help.

"Keep talking," Dominic pressed, drawing himself another step closer.

"Thought they were going to slip through that tunnel, I did," Harry said, "but they didn't. They paused by the entrance and that's when I saw them. She was a real stunner... looked scared though. They climbed up the bank to the top. I watched them for a while as they stood there. You could see them clearly but then it was a clear night, not like tonight..."

"And then what?" Dominic said coldly.

"They wandered across to the other side of the tracks," Harry finished. "It's a bit more residential over there. There's a footpath a little further up, so I suspect they headed down that way and into the village."

He gave a satisfied smile and breathed deeply. He had nothing more to say though in the tense lull of silence, he felt obliged to keep rambling.

"Girlfriend of yours was she? Do I take it she ran off with this other fellow?"

"Nothing to concern yourself with," Dominic said gently.

He reached into his coat pocket. The old tramp froze, fearing he might draw a weapon. To his surprise, he unfolded a £10 note and passed it to him. Harry's face broke into a broad smile as he snatched it gratefully.

"God bless you, Son!" he blustered.

"Don't mention it," Dominic muttered, "but if you see them around here again, I want you to get a message to me. Just call in at the 'Dog and Duck' in Whitechapel. Ask for *Theakston*. I'll make it worth your while..."

Signalling to his men to follow, he turned from the tramps and headed into the tunnel, curious to explore the residential area which hid on the other side...

Dominic allowed himself a transitory smile, as the darkness of the tunnel enclosed him.

Once he had reached the other side, he drank in the neighbourhood; the green space, the wider roads and finally, the larger houses spread over a sparsely populated area. Like the tramp had indicated, this place looked more like a village.

He had no idea if Jake and Eleanor were still on the run or not but it wouldn't be impossible for them to be holed up somewhere, just waiting for the chase to die down. And this seemed the perfect place; a quieter area, far from the hub of the city, where two young people might easily hide...

It was too dark now and past midnight; too late to start searching the place or ask any further questions. But tomorrow he would return.

For the third day running, Jake and Eleanor woke up in the same bed. They had been in the house for almost a week now and the last few days had been a dream. On the night they had started their love affair, they had talked for much of the night, in between sipping wine and twice more making love.

Night and day seemed to merge into one now. There was no clear divide between the two. They cherished each other's company; taking it in turns to create meals from their last remaining ingredients and indulging in their newly discovered passion at every opportunity...

Eleanor went with the flow. Savouring the hours, she feared this blissful snatch of a romance might only be temporary. She had not been bluffing when she had voiced her fears; terrified, they may not survive... So they needed to plan their next move carefully.

Ever determined to risk the journey to Sammie's old club, the Malibu, a convincing disguise was essential. But it would be so worthwhile if they could find someone to help them.

Right now, she lay on her back, gazing up at the ceiling. Jake traced the contours of her face. It was a face he said, he loved - reminiscent of a Greek Goddess, from the tilt of her chin to the tiny curve at the top of her nose.

"It's a typical Chapman nose," she said with a smile, closing her eyes. "Dad's is just the same - he clearly passed it on to me..."

Jake laughed. Propping himself up onto one elbow, he tickled her under the arms until she wriggled and squealed for him to stop. As her eyes flew open, she caught the way he was staring at her with such tenderness... It made her heart swell.

"I love you, Eleanor," he whispered. "I felt something, the moment we escaped out of that window together."

"It seems such a long time ago now," Eleanor sighed. "I felt the same way too - as soon as we stepped into the park... and who could forget that chase? There are times I cannot believe we got away. On some nights, I have nightmares that we didn't..."

He leant towards her, stalling her words with another kiss and as she wound her arms around his shoulders, she just knew she wasn't going to step out of this bed for a while yet. Their time together was too precious. Besides, what did they have to get up for anyway? They were in the safest place they could possibly be and there seemed no reason to apply any brakes. Snuggled up in bed, they savoured the touch of each other's warm skin, before their bodies merged together and once again became entwined...

Hunger and thirst could not be ignored forever, as was evident when Eleanor's stomach let out a loud rumble. Reluctantly, Jake pulled himself out of the bed. He grabbed his clothes from the chair, unable to escape the inevitable. They had almost run out of food, so it was time to venture down to the shop again.

At least, they had used their money wisely, although it was gradually going down.

Fortunately, Jake had already planned for this, conscious of an extra stash he kept hidden. No one could have known of the secret cavity he had carved into the heel of his shoe. Stuffed with a tiny plastic bag, it concealed a £20 note. This had become something of a habit, especially at music festivals. It made no sense to carry large quantities of cash, in case it got stolen. So on the day their money ran out, he would dig into the rubber heel with a penknife to extract it.

Throwing on a dark blue T-shirt and his freshly washed jeans, he gradually became aware of the air temperature. It felt a lot cooler today, the skies covered in a blanket of cloud. With a shiver, Jake borrowed a leather jacket. Despite the gloom, he was compelled to wear the dark glasses and bunching up his ponytail, he secured it beneath the hat.

He could still hear Eleanor moving around in the bathroom.

"I'm just going to the shops!" he hollered up the stairs.

"Okay," her voice rang from above. "See you in a bit and don't be too long!"

Jake followed the usual routine, starting with a careful glance out of the window to check no one was watching. He dashed across the lawn and slipped through the gap in the hedge like a shadow. Keeping his head down, he strode along the path until he reached the crossroads. A few seconds later he was inside the grocery store.

It didn't take long to fill up a basket. Jake navigated his way around the shop in an orderly manner, choosing a variety of tinned foods, fresh produce, a bottle of orange squash and some bread. He joined the queue, clocking the mixture of people; teenagers, elderly folk who had just drawn their weekly pension. Being a Thursday, the store seemed busier than normal.

Jake stood very still, hoping no one would notice him. Within five minutes, he had reached the front of the queue where the same Asian girl, known as Daliya, awaited him.

An older woman, engrossed in unpacking cases of cigarettes, was stacking them on a shelf behind the counter. She too was dressed in Asian attire; perhaps she was Daliya's mother.

"Hello, again," the girl said quietly as Jake lowered his basket. "How are you today?"

"Okay, thank you," Jake replied. He momentarily took off his sunglasses, just to see better. Arranging his groceries into a brown paper bag, the interior of the store was quite dark.

Yet the girl seemed to be scrutinising him. Every time she rang an item through the till, she glanced up, her gaze lingering. Jake gave a nervous smile.

"Is something wrong?" he murmured.

Daliya flicked her eyes towards the other woman, still engrossed in stacking cigarettes.

"I need to talk to you," she said. "But not here. That will be £2.90 please."

Jake frowned. Already he felt uneasy. No sooner had he paid for his shopping, when Daliya turned to her mother before muttering something in Urdu. Without a word, the older woman stepped away from the cigarette shelf and took her place behind the till. Daliya slipped out from behind the counter and moved gingerly towards the back of the shop, beckoning Jake to follow.

Lingering in a corridor which led to the stockroom, they were momentarily hidden from sight and well out of earshot.

"What is wrong?" Jake whispered.

"I feel I should warn you," Daliya said darkly. "There were some men in here a few days ago, asking questions. Questions about you *and* your girlfriend."

Jake turned completely cold.

"What sort of men?"

"Bad men," the girl whispered anxiously. "I was frightened of them. First, they made us close the shop. I don't understand why they did that... but next, they got out some photographs. They wanted to know if anyone had seen you."

For a second Jake held his breath.

"Don't worry," she spluttered. "I didn't say anything..."

"Thank you," Jake nodded gratefully. "Can you remember what they looked like?"

A veil of fear passed over her face.

"They looked evil," she shivered, "especially the leader. He was tall and blonde, his hair quite long. He wore a black leather coat. They all looked mean... I think they might have been gangsters."

Jake closed his eyes in dread. He knew exactly who she was describing. To think, Theakston had actually been right here in this shop, snooping around, asking questions.

"What about the photos?" he pressed.

"They were black and white," she said. "My parents didn't recognise you but I did. Don't worry, we hate gangsters... You two seem like nice people so I didn't tell them anything."

"Thank you!" Jake sighed, laying a soothing hand on her arm. "Did they threaten you?"

Daliya took a deep breath. "Actually, they were offering money..."

"What?" Jake whispered, shocked by this revelation.

Daliya gave a brisk shake of her head. "I am not going to turn you in," she insisted, "but I must ask, why are they looking for you? Are you in some sort of trouble?"

"Yes," Jake said miserably. "This is a gang who took over the East End from a well-known business man. My girlfriend and I were on the wrong side... the losing side." He stared deep into her eyes. "They are our enemies. Thanks so much for keeping quiet about us."

A minute later, he crept from the shop, his heart pounding. *How the hell had they come so close?* He was convinced that for all the while they were hidden in the village, Theakston's gang would never find them. Obviously, he had cast his net wider, picking up other leads where the trail had led him here. How merciful Daliya had kept quiet although it went without saying, there were others in the neighbourhood who might not be so decent.

He paused outside the back door before opening it. For a few seconds he couldn't move; Daliya's confession had left him numb.

"What's wrong?" Eleanor's voice echoed from the lounge.

"Bad news," was all he could say to begin with

Rising slowly, she began to glide across to him. Yet he could no longer ignore the bewilderment on her face. He had to tell her.

"Theakston's been here! The girl in the shop told me, they came looking for us."

"No!" Eleanor whimpered, clutching his arms.

The truth of the situation hit them like an avalanche.

"That's it," Eleanor breathed. "I am going to the club, Jake. There could be news about my dad and let's face it, we need help... We can't handle this on our own any more, Theakston is way too powerful."

II

By Saturday, the cloudy wet weather had passed, leaving the streets of London cleansed before a welcome glow of sunshine warmed them. The Malibu Club hovered on the skyline, still a significant landmark. Since Sammie's demise, it had virtually closed down with just a handful of staff to maintain it. The bar stayed open in the daytime for the benefit of regulars who enjoyed a drink at lunchtime. Although it no longer opened at night.

Among the skeleton staff loomed Harvey, the bouncer. His role to provide security hadn't changed. Vigilant as ever, he continued to guard the club door; more to prevent Theakston's thugs from intruding and intimidating Sammie's customers. His giant shape towered prominently as he glared out onto the streets, scanning the area for potential trouble makers. A slight figure shuffled out of nowhere. Harvey braced himself. Although as the figure moved close, he saw it was just some old bag lady. Nothing unusual. London was full of homeless folk.

This one was wearing a dark blue dress, an old macintosh and socks over her stockings. Her face looked dirty, barely distinguishable beneath her wiry grey hair and head scarf. She plodded along with slow, painful steps, weighed down with two old carrier bags filled with rags. Harvey did not move. He waited at the entrance with a bemused expression, guessing she would be no trouble.

"Can you spare us a cup of tea, dearie?" sounded a soft, slightly husky girl's voice.

Harvey almost choked. Not only did her voice startle him *but her eyes...* none other than the honey gold eyes of Eleanor Chapman. Without a word, he stepped back from the doorway to allow her through; lingering for a moment as he completed his surveillance.

Fortuitously the coast was clear.

Concealed in the club foyer, his eyes turned to the silent figure hunched by the cloakroom. He pointed to a secluded hallway, where several dressing rooms lay beyond. They offered a place of privacy where one could engage in a quiet chat.

"Eleanor!" he breathed, the moment they were hidden in one of the rooms.

"Hello, Harvey," Eleanor smiled. She tugged off her headscarf and macintosh. "It's good to see you again. How are things?"

Harvey did not smile back. "Terrible, if you must know. Have you any idea of the risk you're takin'? I mean, I'm glad you came but Jesus... We're gonna have to be so careful, baby. Now, can I get you a drink?"

"I'm fine," Eleanor said, "and I know this is risky, which is why I phoned. I was desperate to talk to someone. You're one of the few people I can trust, Harvey."

She eased off the wig. Her rich dark hair had been pinned to her head and apart from the dirt on her face, she was beginning to emerge as the real Eleanor. Harvey stared at her as her vulnerable beauty was revealed.

At the same time, Eleanor studied him. His sombre face disguised an expression of worry, she had never before witnessed.

"What is it, Harvey?" she said, lowering herself into a dainty velvet chair.

Harvey shook his head sadly. "Eleanor, what the hell did you do to upset Theakston? You do know he's on your case don't you?"

"Yes," Eleanor whispered. "This is why I've been in hiding all week..."

"Well best you stay in hidin' for now," Harvey sighed. Slanting his tall body forwards, he rested his elbows on his knees to bring his eyes level with hers. "That man is obsessed with findin' you. He's got men crawlin' all over London. He's been putting pressure on Sammie's employees too, convinced one of us is hiding you. So what's goin' on, love? Rumour's out, he had you cornered at one point... Is that true?"

Eleanor bit her lip, unsure how much to tell him.

"Yes, he found me," she shivered. "You know the Mallorys dumped me in a brothel do you? Run by a pimp named Mickey Clark, Pauline's brother..."

"We found that out from Sadie," Harvey snapped. "Makes me sick to think how those bastards betrayed you, 'specially after Sammie trusted 'em. Oh, sweetheart, if only we'd known! One of us would have been over there like a shot, to spring you out of that place!"

"I know," Eleanor answered. She released a sad smile. "Theakston came here too, didn't he? Not long after Sammie passed away..."

She saw the cloud pass over his face.

"I'm afraid so. Bad day that was. We were just trying to deal with the news about Sammie, when he came stormin' in!" He pressed his eyes shut, the truth torturing him. "Even I couldn't stop 'em. At least half a dozen of Theakston's men grabbed me and threatened to cut my throat unless I gave 'em access. Swore they'd planted explosives, the night before... and if we didn't send the punters home, the place'd be blown to kingdom come!"

"Explosives?" Eleanor breathed.

Harvey shook his head. "Turned out to be a crock of bullshit! Just a ruse to get the staff to empty the club and close it down. The bastard!"

"So what happened next?" Eleanor pressed.

"I guess you must know, he came lookin' for Ollie!" Harvey spat. "That was the real purpose of his visit but there's no loyalty in this world, sweetheart. First came the death threats, then came the bribes! That stupid bitch, Sadie took him straight up to Sammie's office and opened the safe where he kept his most confidential documents..."

Eleanor felt a spark of anger.

"Yes, I know about that too," she snapped. "That's how Theakston found me. He came straight over to the brothel to check it out. I recognised him, as soon as he walked through the door. "

Harvey was shaking his head again, fearing what was coming.

"He had me right where he wanted me, Harvey... told the others to keep me under lock and key until he came back. I have never been so terrified in my life..."

"Eleanor," Harvey whispered, taking her hand. "What did he do?"

Eleanor lowered her eyes. She didn't want to recall the details of that terrible evening but Harvey needed to hear it. Rushing ahead with her story, she described the way he had cornered her, claiming her for his pleasure; the sinister threat of a film, another method of forcing her father out of hiding... It never failed to turn her cold.

"That was the worst thing," she shivered, "it was just like Sammie warned!"

"Sweet Jesus!" Harvey muttered. "Please don't tell me, he did this to you."

"No!" Eleanor added quickly. "I escaped and that's why I'm in hiding."

She saw the relief pass over his face

"Piece of scum!" he hissed to himself. "But tell me... is this is the only reason he's after you? See, I'm sat here thinking there must be something else."

"I'll come to that in a minute," Eleanor sighed. "This is only the first part of my story. So what happened this end? You say he's been back? Looking for me?"

"You bet!" Harvey said with a tiny grin. "One minute, we heard he had you cornered and the next, you went missing. Terry Williams was doing his nut! He'd already given the Mallorys some grief. Don't know what was said but they skedaddled out of London not long after. He called in at Mickey Clark's place too but you were long gone! Not one of us knew where you were and you may as well know something else... Ollie came back."

"What?" Eleanor gasped, her eyes widening.

"Yeah! The moment word got out, you were in Theakston's hands!"

Eleanor stared at him. Already she felt a sting of tears.

"He's been holed up in one of Sammie's villas," Harvey continued. "Reckon he drove the entire length of Spain in a single night and flew back to London to find you. He got here Saturday evening, hung around until Monday, but like I say, you'd disappeared... No one knew where to find you. Theakston didn't have a clue either so we urged Ollie to leave. Last I knew, he was off to suss out a new hideout... but we ain't heard from him since!"

"If only I'd known," Eleanor said. She sensed the wobble in her lip as if a river had burst its banks; a flood of suppressed emotion. Most painful of all was the memory of her father, the day he had kissed her goodbye. *But where was he now?*

"Hey!" Harvey murmured. "Don't cry, sweetheart. Best thing you did was keep your head down!" He leant close, his voice brushing across her ears like velvet.

"N-none of this should have happened," Eleanor sobbed.

"Damn right it shouldn't," Harvey continued to soothe her. "We all knew Ollie was puttin' his neck on the line but Theakston was too distracted in his search to find you. You see, some folks kept us well informed - folks like big George who runs a newsagent in Poplar. That bastard went round there showin' photos and asking questions about you and some guy. George didn't actually have anything to tell him but he told us about the visit and he was none too happy about the threats!"

"He paid a visit to our neighbourhood too," Eleanor shuddered, remembering Daliya's story. "Oh, Harvey I wish I knew what to do. You're right! He must have men everywhere!"

She gave a loud sniff. Harvey handed her a hankie and she blew her nose but at least, she had stopped crying...

"So are you gonna tell me what this is about?" Harvey probed her gently. "Cos I ain't seen no-one more demented than Theakston lately! He's offering a substantial reward to anyone who can provide a lead but there's a downside. If he finds out anyone's been helpin' you..."

He broke off with a shudder and suddenly, he couldn't look at her.

"Go on," Eleanor insisted. "Tell me!"

"They're dead meat!" Harvey spluttered, "and we all know he's a man with no mercy, 'specially when he starts swinging that little sack of stones of his. You heard about that?"

"No," Eleanor said fearfully.

"I'm talkin' about a bag like the ones the banks use for stashin' notes... filled with pebbles! Does serious damage! Victim ends up black and blue or worse - bones get shattered. People can even die! Please don't make me say any more..."

"And this is how he's been threatening people?" Eleanor gasped. "Oh God!"

She lowered her eyes, gripping her hands together in fear. So this was what was happening behind the scenes; not just the interrogation of shopkeepers but something far worse. Who was going to want to help them now?

"I should leave," Eleanor said abruptly. "I couldn't bear it if they hurt you!"

Harvey raised his head. "Hey, I didn't mean to frighten you, baby, but it's the truth. He's a violent guy when he's trying to find someone and he's obsessed with finding you! So c'mon, what did you do, Eleanor? And is there someone else involved?"

"Yes," Eleanor whispered, squeezing her hands together even tighter. "A young man. Someone Theakston and his gang were planning to kill."

"Yeah?" Harvey pressed her. "Go on..."

"I found him locked in Clark's basement," she continued, "on the day I escaped... Well, I couldn't just leave him..."

Harvey's eyes bulged in their sockets.

"What, you mean you let this guy go?"

"Yes," Eleanor replied. "Of course I did. We escaped together."

"Oh shit, Eleanor," Harvey breathed. "Was this a contract killing? 'Cos if it was, baby, you shouldn't have interfered. Not when someone like Theakston's involved. You do realise he could kill you for this? You *and* the guy you've just saved..."

Eleanor stared back at him in disbelief. Going by his face, she feared something ominous; something she wasn't sure she wanted to acknowledge... The horror in his expression suggested that she and Jake were condemned and there was nothing anyone could do about.

"We've reached the end of the line, haven't we," she said bitterly, "and you're right, I don't expect any of you to stick your necks out for me but I'm scared, Harvey. We've managed to stay hidden so far, but it's only a matter of time before he finds us. I feel like we're trapped in London. Is there any possible way we could get out?"

"Darling, I wish I could do more to help you," Harvey sighed, "but I'm leaving tomorrow."

"You are?" Eleanor whimpered. "But why?"

"Theakston's the boss, now," he said sadly, "and he's delivered an ultimatum. You either work for him or you get the hell out. There's no choice in between. No one knows where Terry is, nor Ollie. We've been scattered in all directions by this bastard."

"So where will you go?" Eleanor said huskily. She sensed her final hopes swirling away like water down a plug hole.

"Trinidad," Harvey replied. "It's my home. Ain't no way I'm gonna to stay here and work for that piece of shit, not after what he's done..."

Eleanor bowed her head.

"But don't look so glum," Harvey continued. He patted her hand. "You still gotta lifeline, which is why I'm glad you came. A group of us attended Sammie's funeral. We were called to a meeting afterwards with some solicitor 'bout his will. Seems Sammie left every one of us a legacy..."

He paused, as if waiting for a reaction.

"Including you," he finished.

Eleanor stared at him, unsure she had even heard him right.

"Sammie wanted you to be provided for, in case Ollie got killed. So take this card, Eleanor and wherever you are hiding, stay there! Wait for the dust to settle. Theakston can't keep up this search forever, so when the time is right, go and see this firm. This could be your way out."

He handed her the card; a cream-coloured business card with fine gold lettering.

"Simpson and Sharp Solicitors," she read aloud. "Oh God bless you, Sammie! I wish he was still around. London isn't a very nice place any more."

"And how are you managing for cash?" Harvey questioned.

"Okay," Eleanor shrugged, too proud to admit, they were almost broke.

"Here," Harvey grinned and fishing into his pocket, he pulled out some notes.

119

Eleanor blinked; a ten and a twenty? Pressing the notes into her hand, he covered them with his own warm brown fingers.

"Take it," he insisted. "This is the best I can do. If all else fails, use it for a taxi to get right out of the Capital. I had a great deal of respect for Ollie and I'm pretty fond of you too, doll. Now go! And good luck!"

"Thank you so much, Harvey," she whispered, "and I hope you get to Trinidad safely."

III

A short tube journey delivered her safely back to her own neighbourhood. No one appeared to notice her but then why would they? As a dishevelled old bag lady, people seemed to shy away from her. The disguise had been successful in that respect but at the same time, she felt a tug of sadness. *It was unlikely, she would ever return to the Malibu again.* The door had closed on her that day like the end of a final chapter.

She shuffled up the path, eyes roaming, to make sure she wasn't being followed. How could she suppress the tide of worrying thoughts that consumed her? It wasn't just the terror Theakston injected into the East London community but his obsession with finding them. She wondered how much this had to do with Jake. Harvey's reaction to the mere mention of a contract killing had charged her with anxiety.

At last, she reached the gap in the hedge and pushed her way through. Ever thankful to see the house again, she dreaded the day Theakston's men might discover it. Yet several days had elapsed since his visit to the store and with no imminent signs of danger.

She flitted across the garden and through the back door. At least she had made it back here, overjoyed to catch sight of Jake in the lounge. He rose the instant he saw her, his face animated with delight.

"Eleanor," he gasped.

For the first few seconds, they clung to each other as if afraid to let go. Eleanor pulled away first, laughing as she did so.

"At least let me get out of all this garb," she smiled.

She yanked off the mac, the scarf and finally the wig, massaging her hair with her fingertips as she did so. Jake watched her. A smile spread lazily across his face as her true character began to reveal itself. She kicked off the sandals then carefully peeled off each sock. It was the few stones buried in her socks which had enabled her to limp so convincingly.

"I have been so worried," Jake murmured in his gentle lilt. "The hours you've been away were hell. I have never known time pass so slowly."

"Well, I'm back now," Eleanor sighed, "and I've got loads to tell you."

120

Leaning back against the sofa, she closed her eyes. There was no denying, she looked exhausted. With some difficulty, she appeared to swallow. Jake, watching carefully, recognised the signs; especially the way she caressed her throat... He wandered into the kitchen and made her a mug of tea. Searching for a clean cloth, he dampened it with water. Once he was settled down next to her, he gently took her chin. Using the cloth, he proceeded to wipe the dirt from her face, never failing to miss the salty tear trails.

"You've been crying?" he whispered.

"A bit," she mumbled. "I heard a lot of bad things today. Sounds like Sammie's whole empire has crumbled since Theakston took over. He's been scouting around, dishing out some very nasty threats, which doesn't put *us* in a good situation."

"I'm not really that surprised," Jake muttered, lowering the cloth. He handed her the tea which she gratefully accepted. "I always guessed that the Malibu would be the most obvious place he would come looking for you..."

"It's like you said," Eleanor shivered, "he's offering a reward for any information which might lead to us - but those who choose to stay quiet - or help us in any way... they're being threatened with the most awful violence."

A look of dread sprung from her eyes as she stared at him.

"They could be beaten to a pulp, Jake. I might have landed Harvey in danger just for agreeing to meet me today. He's flying off to Trinidad tomorrow to get right away from here but supposing they get to him first?"

"Try not to worry," Jake said, slipping an arm around her shoulder. "No one could have seen through that disguise. I'm sure Harvey is quite safe..."

"I hope so," Eleanor said, sipping her tea.

"So what else did you find out?" Jake pressed her.

Her story unfolded piece by piece; first the news of her father rushing back to London... To think, Theakston needn't have bothered with his hateful film. Just the rumour *that he had her cornered* was enough to draw him out of hiding. She was touched by that. It served as a gentle reminder of how deeply her father cared for her, to have taken such a risk.

But now he had vanished again. *Last I knew, he was off to figure out a new hideout...* According to Harvey, he had slipped through the net, before his enemies were even aware of his presence. Now if only there was a way to contact him.

Her second piece of news concerned the legacy Sammie had left her and maybe this was their lifeline. She could not help but feel humbled by Harvey's disclosure. How could she forget how ill Sammie had looked on the final night she had caught a glimpse of him? He must have organised all his legal affairs, despite the turmoil his world had been thrown in.

Eleanor blinked back the tears. All they had to do now was to visit this solicitor; though given their circumstances, it might have to wait a while...

Last of all, she extracted the notes Harvey had pressed into her hand. Jake gaped back at her with raised eyebrows.

"That is very generous," he whistled. "Just think, it would be enough to pay for a train journey to Dover... but that is not all we have. I found something else."

He gave a secretive smile before scooping his shoe from the floor. Eleanor stared at the crater in the sole - it was as if he had carved a great chunk out of it.

"This is where I keep my secret stash," he divulged. "I was saving it for when our money ran out. My friends and I always hid cash in our clothes, especially during the festivals. But there is more than I thought." He delved into his top pocket to reveal a five and a twenty pound note.

"Brilliant!" Eleanor gasped, stroking the notes. "So we've got no more money worries..."

She broke off for a second, pondering their situation.

"Harvey did say that if we'd found a good place to hide, we should stay put for a while. No one knows what will happen in East London, now Theakston is boss. But we're safe here. We don't need to take any unnecessary risks, at least not yet..."

"I agree," Jake said. "You took a big enough risk today. I nearly went out of my mind with worry and I don't want you to put yourself in danger like that again."

Folding up the notes, he returned them to his pocket before resting his head against the sofa cushions.

"So it is not all bad news," he pondered, sliding his hand into her own. "I am pleased you heard something about your father. Let us hope we can make contact soon. We've got cash, you've been remembered in Sammie's will and for now, we have a lovely place to hide..."

Eleanor nodded as she absorbed her surroundings, warmed by the honey-toned gleam of the floorboards. This was a house that seemed to draw in the light from outside. Sunshine spread into every corner, illuminating the furnishings; its very ambience enveloped her with a sense of security.

Jake turned to her and his green eyes flickered with merriment. Yet he seemed to be holding something back, a smile dancing around his mouth...

"What is it?" Eleanor questioned.

"Don't be angry," he said, "but I went for a walk myself..."

"Jake, you promised you would stay here!" Eleanor protested. "There's no point both of us putting our necks on the line!"

"I couldn't resist it," Jake grinned at her. "It was hell sitting here on my own. So I found another wig and wore the sunglasses. Did you know there was a little market here today? There were some lovely stalls and I-I bought something..."

He delved into his back pocket and extracted a slim paper bag. With the same suppressed smile, he lifted her hand, turned it and tipped the contents into her palm. A small glinting object dropped into her hand: a ring.

Eleanor released a gasp. Picking it up carefully, she held it to the light.

Beautifully crafted from silver, the ring comprised two slim bands arching over the top, each embedded with a stone; one a clear golden amber.

"It is the same colour as your eyes," Jake whispered, pointing to the top stone. "Amber. The other is tourmaline. Don't worry, it wasn't expensive..."

Scrutinising the second stone, Eleanor was struck by its delicate green glow. As she tilted it sideways, the colour deepened slightly, reflecting the natural verdancy of a leaf.

"The other stone is the same colour as yours," she said numbly. "Jake, it's beautiful."

"Try it on," he insisted. "Here... let me."

Plucking the ring from her hand, he encircled it in his fingers and slid it carefully onto her third. It fitted perfectly. Eleanor could not stop staring at it. She raised her head and gazed at Jake in confusion, trying to read the expression in his eyes.

"Where did you find it?" she mumbled.

"I think it found *me*," Jake answered, his smile dreamy. "I wandered around the market, right past the jewellery stall but something made me want to go back... and that is when I saw it. Don't you think this ring was made just for us? It is like fate."

"Yes," Eleanor said dazedly. She could not take her eyes off it.

Neither did she fail to notice, he had slipped it onto her engagement finger. She trailed her fingertips over the stones, feeling a glossy smoothness. Her glance switched to Jake again.

"Yes, it is an engagement ring, Eleanor," he said gently. "One day, I want to marry you."

Eleanor froze. For a few seconds, she wasn't sure what to say, even though the answer was teetering on her tongue. Tears swam in her eyes as the vision of Jake shone before her. The nod of her head sent a single tear plummeting down her face.

"We may not have known each other for long," Jake whispered, "but enough to know, it would be nice spend the rest of our lives together..."

"Yes," Eleanor's voice resounded shakily.

She kissed him with renewed passion, driving the last fragments of their troubled conversation as far from her mind as possible.

PART 3. CAT AND MOUSE

Chapter 7

I
September 1972

The last weeks of summer drifted by in a blur of happiness yet as they moved into September, time seemed to accelerate. They had tumbled into the third week sooner than expected, fully aware the owners were due to return soon.

Having completed several circuits of the house, they gave each room a final dust and sweep, leaving the linen freshly laundered. Mindful of leaving it as they had found it, it was impossible to disguise *every trace* of their presence. The owners would know that someone had been here from the missing food and wine. But they clung to the hope their attempts to leave it clean and tidy would soften the blow...

Guiltily they had kept a few clothes too, though the one possession Jake was loathe to part with most was the guitar. For this reason, he felt a hankering to borrow it. He knew it belonged to one of the boys. Recent photos displayed the teenager holding a much newer instrument, which he must have taken to Ibiza. Going by his cool smile and laid-back hippy demeanour, Jake sensed he wouldn't mind... just as long as he brought it back one day, which he secretly planned to do.

He paused, unsure when *that day* would be.

They had been living on a knife edge for the past few weeks, drifting from one day to the next, unsure where fate would eventually land them. Hovering on the divide of an uncertain future, two distinct paths lay ahead of them; one that would guide them away from the Capital and on a ferry bound for the Netherlands. Whereas a worse scenario lingered; one that might throw them straight back into the path of their enemies. It felt a little like flipping a coin.

Leaving was hard but there was no other choice. The beautiful old house nestling in the suburb known as *Forest Haven* was about to be confined to the past. They had loved it here; a remote and secret pocket of London which had escaped the progressive spread of urban development. Cut off from the main through fare of traffic, the air smelt clean, people kept tidy gardens and the birds enchanted the atmosphere with their song.

And in the course of their fleeting life here, something else magical had happened.

Eleanor was pregnant. She seemed a little nervous when she had made the discovery, unsure as to how he would take it. A month after they had slipped into their wonderful love affair, she realised, she hadn't had a period since she had lived with the Mallorys. One visit to a nearby clinic for a pregnancy test confirmed the truth. But she needn't have worried.

Jake was delighted. Consumed with such waves of happiness allowed him to forget about the horrors he had endured. Despite the car bomb, not to mention the terror of his abduction, nothing like this would have happened if it hadn't been for that chance meeting with Eleanor. This entire sequence of events had changed his future; brought him face to face with a girl he knew he would love forever and now he was going to be a father.

Jake silently prayed for their freedom. If they could just get themselves on board a train now, one that would take them directly to Dover...

They left the next day. Being a mild September, they selected clothes which were light and cool. Eleanor packed the dark blue dress, along with the boots she had worn on the night of her escape, jeans and a warm cardigan. Today, she wore a dress purchased on one of the market days. A long garment made from white cheesecloth, it had half-length sleeves and crochet on the bodice. The light material floated around her slender figure in a way that was flattering yet in the advancing months of her pregnancy, would still be loose enough to be comfortable. She had braided her long dark hair into several plaits and wound them around her head, pinning them in place.

Slipping on her old denim blazer, she picked up a small holdall then stepped out into the garden. The long grass lay flat on the ground, yellow as corn, the strawberry plants reduced to a heap of dry leaves. A low, hazy sun warmed the air where everything seemed to shimmer with a coating of dew. She gazed at it sadly as Jake locked the back door. As a final gesture of goodwill, he dropped the key into the jam jar where he had found it.

Moving to her side, he slid a protective arm around her shoulder and coaxed her away from the house. She seemed reluctant to leave. Though he too, felt a prick of tears as they tip-toed down the garden path together.

"We have got to come back here, one day," Eleanor whispered, a sob slipping into her voice. "I would love to meet the Merriman family..."

Inspired by the people who owned this house, they had discovered their names as soon as the post began to pile up on the doormat. Most of it was addressed to a Mrs. R. Merriman. She would appear to be the main householder but somehow the name suited them.

"We will," Jake reassured her. "I have to bring back the boy's guitar. I feel bad enough taking it but I cannot seem to let go of it right now... It will be useful, Eleanor. I'll be able to do some busking and earn a little extra money. We have a long journey ahead of us..."

Eleanor did not smile back, displaying further resistance when they reached the gap in the hedge. Jake held her arm and attempted to pull her through. Her lips were tight.

"C'mon," he whispered. "You knew we had to leave. Let us just hold onto the memories."

Finally they reached the crossroads, the parade of shops lingering close to the bus stop. Jake hurried across the road with Eleanor trailing behind. Unfortunately, they had missed the last bus which meant a twenty minute wait before the next one. Jake glanced towards the café just around the corner. At least they could sit down to enjoy a last coffee...

From another side of the road, a figure emerged from the shadows but they did not see him.

Old Harry, as he was known, could not believe what he was seeing. He would have never recognised the girl from her appearance but the way she moved... Such a vision sent his mind whirling back to the night he had spotted them by the railway tunnel; that same flowing grace, every gesture refined and feminine. She did not walk, she seemed to glide. Reminded of a swan, the memory had stuck somehow.

Right now, he couldn't take his eyes off her; all that dark hair wound up in plaits like a Polish folk dancer... It emphasised her graceful neck.

Glancing at the boy, he must have cut his hair recently. He distinctly remembered it being long, tied in a ponytail. Yet he also couldn't fail to notice the way they looked at each other and Old Harry knew love when he saw it. The question was, what to do...?

He crossed the road, mesmerised. He had seen them wander into the café, waiting a few more minutes before he followed them. Only then did he ease himself into a corner seat.

The boy was hovering by the counter. He could clearly see his face reflected in the shine of a stainless steel tea urn. A sweet-faced, dumpy little woman in a pink checked pinafore was already placing cups and saucers onto a tray.

Harry grabbed a newspaper someone had left on the table, brushing aside pots of salt, pepper and vinegar. Spreading the pages wide, he pretended to read it, even though his mind was spinning in a vortex.

He risked another glance from behind the newspaper. That tenner, given to him a few weeks ago, had been a gift from heaven. When it came to food, he and his mate lived on whatever they could scrounge locally, including the stale bread and buns they salvaged from shop dustbins. Yet that bonus had afforded them a few bottles of cheap whisky, bringing comfort to the soul; it had soothed away the harshness of their lives for a while...

Somewhere in the mists of his deluded mind, Harry was convinced the girl was eloping with this young chap; the man pursuing them, a jilted lover. Unfortunately, that man had been one of the most frightening characters Harry had ever met. Waves of violence seemed to emanate from him; the chill of his voice and every unpredictable flash of movement. Harry had been terrified. With that in mind, could he afford not to pass on this information? Some nagging fear told him the man might discover his duplicity. He would have contacts. Word would get back, he had been sat here in this very café on a day the couple had finally broken cover. Harry felt a shudder rack his tired old bones. The consequences would be horrific... He glanced up again.

The young man turned away from the counter with two cups of coffee balanced on a tray. He brought them to one of the tables - oddly enough, the one closest to his own. Harry stole a peek at his profile; clocking the fine bone structure, straight forehead and shapely mouth. He was a handsome kid that was for sure. He couldn't blame the girl for running off with him.

From another side of the room, the girl was using the telephone. Old Harry tilted his head, his ears tuned in like radar.

"Can we see you today ... yes, I know it's short notice but we may not get another chance, see... We're about to leave the Capital..."

Harry froze. *They were leaving?*

The conversation hummed on for a few more minutes. Throughout her monologue, Harry overheard some reference to *Waterloo Station*. Unable to prevent the smirk that touched his lips, he continued to gaze at the paper. He turned the page. She was drifting back towards the table now where Harry couldn't resist lifting his head again.

Momentarily struck by her luminous golden eyes, he felt the breath catch in his throat. Yet she hardly seemed to notice him. She settled herself down opposite the boy, sipping coffee from a dainty white china cup. *Such a beauty,* he thought with regret. Could he really bring himself to turn them in? And what had that man said his name was? *Thakeham? Thurston?* Harry mentally rattled through the alphabet, searching... yet it came to him in a flash, as soon as the boy spoke.

"Do you think we have waited long enough to visit this place?" he muttered softly. "What if Theakston's men are hanging around?"

Theakston. That was it.

"But I've got an appointment now," Eleanor whispered back. "We can call into Holborn on the way to the station. 12.00 noon. It won't take up much time, I promise..."

Ending their conversation with an anxious nod, no more words were spoken.

Several minutes later, they had finished their coffee and rose from their seats. Harry noticed how attentive the young man was; the way he curled a protective arm around her shoulder, helping her gently to her feet. He picked up her holdall from the floor. He had a shoulder bag of his own, as well as a guitar in a leather case strapped to his back. Every little gesture demonstrated how fiercely he cared for this girl. Harry wrestled with his conscience; was it

127

right to destroy what they had? *They were just a couple of kids.*

The pain of guilt gnawed at his heart, although deep down, he *knew* what he had to do.

There was no choice really. It took one fleeting memory of the fearsome character who had hounded him that night, to send all doubts fleeing from his mind; if he was kicked to death for his failure to pass the information on, would anyone even care? Harry hauled himself to his feet and shuffled across the road. The bus stop lay ahead. He reluctantly joined the queue, to board the same bus; ready to locate the 'Dog and Duck' in Whitechapel.

As soon as Eleanor found a seat, she snuggled into Jake's embrace.

Closing her eyes, she feared what lay ahead. The bus started moving. Thus began their slow journey back towards the East End. At some point they would pass through the areas of Aldgate and Whitechapel; places, she knew their enemies would be lurking. Yet if they were to reach the centre of London, it was essential to travel on the London underground.

Their first stop however, would be Holborn.

Eleanor had been fortunate enough to secure an appointment with the firm known as *Simpson and Sharp Solicitors*; Sammie's lawyers. Surely enough time had lapsed by now to chance a visit? She was intrigued to learn a little more about the legacy Sammie Maxwell had left her.

One brief meeting would be enough to discover all she needed to know, before they concentrated their efforts on getting out of London. It meant more trains - more changes between underground stations - but essential if they were ever to make their escape from the city...

She opened her eyes as the bus hauled its way into the next road. The familiar dark brick architecture of the East End had already begun to manifest itself; the messy streets and crumbling brick work from partly demolished buildings. She bit her lip, glancing up at Jake. The sight brought back memories of the last time she had been here - memories she would rather forget as a creeping sensation of dread started to consume her.

II

Ironically, a short distance away, the very man who haunted her deepest fears was also thinking about her.

Resting in a leather chair in his new headquarters, sipping orange juice, Dominic Theakston could not have done more to try and find them. In over seven weeks, he had raked every square inch of East London looking for them, leaving no stone unturned... Yet he had sensed the *fruitlessness* of his mission a while ago. The trail had dried out. With no further sightings nor leads since the scene by the railway tunnel, *they seemed to have just vanished.*

He still had men on the lookout, brandishing photos at every opportunity, clinging to the hope that someone would stumble across a clue soon. Furthermore, he had upped his reward. Dominic wasn't used to failure, convinced he would track them down wherever they were hiding. The very notion they had outsmarted him brought out the more sadistic side of his nature, which had in turn led to the interrogation of Sammie's men. With ever increasing threats of violence, he was prepared to punish anyone who was helping them.

Every muscle in his face hardened. All he had gleaned from *that exercise* was the final taunt that *Ollie Chapman had returned* - albeit very briefly - but at a time when he had been too busy combing the streets looking for his daughter.

Closing his eyes, he pinched the bridge between his brows to massage out the tension. Time was running out and worse than anything, Inspector Hargreaves never stopped hassling him.

Dominic had been given an ultimatum: should he fail to complete his contract to find Jake and dispose of him within a six month period, *there would be consequences*; his elevated status on Sammie's patch torn away. There would be no more deals with the police and any historic crimes connected to his name would be addressed. Hargreaves had sworn, he could no longer cover up for him; that with the prospect of a criminal conviction looming, a prison sentence was not impossible.

Dominic turned cold. He genuinely liked living in Whitechapel.

It embraced just the sort of dark criminal underworld he thrived on, where his role as crime boss had been an overnight success. The East End was a thrilling place with its vibrant nightlife. There were plenty of opportunities to get your kicks. Clubs and parties were wild, people lost their inhibitions and there was no shortage of beautiful women to flirt with and date. In his new role, running Sammie's patch, there was no reason to live anywhere else. He had turned his back on North London, glad to be shot of the place; far enough away from the slums and the demons of the past to enjoy a new life.

Yet if his paymasters carried out their threat, he would be forced to go on the run.

Slamming down his empty glass, Dominic reached for a cigarette. He sensed the familiar signs of anxiety from the tremor in his hand. It wasn't fair! Hargreaves had effectively ordered him to kill that kid but what had he done to try and find him? Nothing!

Norman was prepared to lay money on it, both kids were still in London. They had to be! If they had left, there would be ripples by now. Something would have happened, something that threatened the very existence of the men who had ordered his death.

Dominic shuddered. He held no malice towards the kid, it was just business; nothing more than a cold blooded execution for which he would be well paid. His interest in Eleanor however, lay at a far more personal level...

The calculating nature of her escape had taught him he was dealing with no fool. She possessed a clear head not unlike that of his partner, Dan Levy, which in turn, made her a deadly adversary.

But there was another problem... an innocent sixteen year old, Eleanor Chapman had inflamed his lust like no other female. He could not deny, she was the subject of his most erotic fantasies and to possess her would be his ultimate victory.

Such thoughts regrettably, were a distraction...

He had to destroy her, as he intended to destroy her father. No one got the better of him! His entire reign was based on the understanding that those who crossed him paid a terrible price and to back down now would mark his downfall.

Dragging hard on his cigarette, he felt his desire darkening to hatred. This whole wretched situation was down to her and if ever a day came when he got his hands on her... Dominic smiled. He might not kill her but he was going to make her wish she had never crossed him

The ring of the telephone broke the silence, tearing him out his reverie. He ground down his half-smoked cigarette with a sigh and reached across his desk to answer it.

"Hello?" he barked into the receiver.

"Dominic," the man on the other end said silkily. "Got some news! Do you remember that old wino by the railway tunnel?"

At first he was silent, allowing the words to sink in. *Dan's timing could not have been better.*

"He's seen them," Dan continued. "The Jansen boy *and* Eleanor Chapman. Spotted 'em in some café over in Forest Haven..."

"Is that so?" Dominic whispered. "And are they still there?"

"Nah, they boarded a bus," Dan furnished him. "Looks like they're leaving..."

Dominic listened patiently as Dan gave him the full report.

Forest Haven. So they had been hiding there all along. Ironically, they were making their way across East London towards the centre. Interesting news. Question was, what to do about it? His initial instinct was to grab them and quickly - before they had a chance of slipping through the net again. Though on this occasion, he decided to exercise a little extra caution.

He dialled another number to talk to Inspector Hargreaves.

"You've done the right thing," Norman appeased him. "Good man!"

"So now what?" Dominic demanded.

"Get over to the pub and talk to that tramp!" he insisted. "Get as many

130

details as you can and I'll send someone over. This time, I prefer it if you stayed away… I hate to say it Dominic, but the moment they see your face, they're going to dive straight back underground again."

"Is that all the thanks I get?" Dominic sneered.

"We cannot afford to lose them," Norman whispered, "not after all this time. This is going to require some very careful planning if we are ever to succeed in capturing them..."

"Good luck to you then," Dominic finished coolly.

He rose, slipped on his jacket and left, his heart racing. Was it possible that this relentless search was finally about to draw to a close?

"Holborn!" Jake whispered in her ear. "C'mon my love, we are here!"

It seemed no time at all before they had travelled from Liverpool Street to Holborn. Eleanor felt sleepy on the underground. The atmosphere was airless and stuffy and even in the early stages of her pregnancy, she suffered from tiredness. Pulling herself drowsily to her feet, she grabbed the handrail, waiting for the train to slow. It lurched to a halt. Taking her hand, Jake pulled her gently from the train and dived into the nearest passage to find the escalator. A long ascent brought them to the top of the station where they gratefully made their exit.

An elegant part of London compared to the East End, the road seemed to stretch into infinity. No sooner had they swung around the next corner when a bank of clean white office blocks towered into view. Hundreds of windows reflected an expanse of blue sky and clouds; they already knew that *one of these blocks* housed the office of Simpson and Sharp Solicitors.

They continued walking, pausing at every block until they eventually reached the address printed on the card. Jake glanced around as if absorbing his surroundings then wandered towards the imposing black double door.

At the same time, a peculiar ripple of unease crept over them. *How many people had known about Sammie's will?* What if someone had leaked news of his legacy? That being the case, this would be an ideal location for Theakston to have a man stationed on the lookout and for all the while they were lingering they were visible...

Jake looked at her. "We have to go in," he urged, "before anyone sees us."

Eleanor pushed open the door. It felt solid and heavy but the moment they were inside, they found themselves drawn into a cool foyer with a reception desk. A man in livery smiled at her. At first it felt a little daunting; the world of business and finance was so unfamiliar. With no hesitation, she told him of her appointment with the law firm… a moment, the man turned and escorted them to an elevator.

The premises of Simpson and Sharp Solicitors were located on the fourth floor. Eleanor watched in a dream as the lift arrived. Hauling its way skywards, it paused with a wobble before the doors slid apart to reveal a higher level. Eleanor felt her stomach lurch.

A long corridor rolled out before them. She could see a succession of oak-panelled doors ahead, all furnished with brass plaques. Their escort led them a little further until they finally located the right one. He rapped on the door. Eleanor breathed deeply, relishing the breeze as it wafted from an open window, ferrying the fragrance of furniture polish.

"Ask them to ring reception when you're done," their escort finished pleasantly.

"Thank you," Jake nodded.

The solicitor she had agreed to meet was a man by the name of John Sharp.

Smartly clothed in an immaculate brown suit, he had thinning blonde hair and a long, lugubrious face; Eleanor was reminded of a foxhound. Once he had offered his condolences over Sammie's death, he gesticulated to Eleanor - just Eleanor - to take a seat in his office. It seemed only natural to ask if Jake could accompany her.

"Jake is my fiancé," she insisted. "We're planning to leave England today, so I would like him to hear whatever it is you have to say to me. Is that okay?"

"Of course," John said. "Please come through."

He lowered his gaze, shuffling through a file of papers. His long, smooth fingers stroked the pages, turning them one by one until he had found what he was looking for. He took a swallow, gazing at her with genuine concern.

"I understand this has been a difficult time for you. Mr Maxwell explained everything in a letter, or more specifically, the situation with regards your father... He was particularly worried you would be left out on a limb and with no one to take care of you."

Eleanor stared back at him as she perched in one of the leather chairs. His words had enkindled the threads of an idea; but for now she kept it to herself, urging him to continue.

"I'll spare you the legal jargon but this is basically what it says." He cleared his throat. "I Samuel Edward Maxwell make this request on behalf of my colleague, Oliver Chapman, that in the event of my death and should the situation prevail that he is still absent, unable to be found or contacted, I would like his daughter, Eleanor, to be left a sum of one thousand pounds..."

Eleanor let out a sharp gasp. Even she had not been expecting this.

"He made a further request that the money be paid into a bank account bearing your name; that on the day you made contact, to allow you full access to the account... There are no underlying conditions or restrictions. He just wanted you to be safe..." he stopped reading and gazed into her eyes.

"It has been quite a while since Sammie's funeral. I'm a little surprised it took you so long to get in touch with us."

"Yes, I know," Eleanor sighed, unsure how much to tell him. Her eyes flickered to Jake. "The truth is, Mr Sharp, we've been in hiding. I can't tell you everything. In fact, the only reason I came to you at all, was because Harvey sent me. You know Harvey from the club? I visited him at the Malibu a few weeks ago, just before he left the country..."

John nodded sagely. "Yes, I met most of Mr Maxwell's beneficiaries."

"Harvey told me about the legacy," Eleanor blurted. "He thought it would be better to wait a while. But a thousand pounds... that's a fortune."

"I imagine, it must seem a fortune to someone so young," John sighed. He gave a wry but sympathetic smile. "But this is 1972. The average house costs about £4,500 these days. You might consider using this as a down payment to buy a property of your own."

Eleanor nodded, her eyes filling up with tears. "I can't believe Sammie could be so kind."

"I know," John replied. "It is truly regrettable that a man of such calibre is deceased. We've been acting as his lawyers for years - at least, we always looked after the more legal aspects of his enterprise..."

A secretive smile lifted the corners of his mouth, his eyes betraying a twinkle. Eleanor felt herself relax. Of course he would know exactly the type of man Sammie was.

"So you know about Theakston do you?" she dared herself to say.

The outrage in John's expression spread like a thunder cloud.

"Oh yes," he said bitterly. "Terrible character! I am certain it was largely down to his activities that Sammie was driven to an early grave..."

"Yes," Eleanor admitted sadly, "and not just Sammie. Others have been hurt."

She looked at him directly; ready to divulge her earlier idea.

"Mr Sharp, may I ask you something? Has there been any news about my father?"

Going by his pained expression, he was still mulling over the demise of Sammie. His eyes softened. Yet he slowly shook his head. Eleanor felt her heart crumble...

"Is there a chance he will contact you?" Jake intervened. "He must know that Sammie has died. Does he know you are his lawyers?"

"Indeed," John sighed, "and I agree. Should Oliver ever contact us, we will let you know. Just keep in touch once in a while. I don't expect you to pass on your details but there is no reason why we couldn't use my firm as a communication channel."

"That would be very helpful," Jake nodded, catching Eleanor's eye.

"Anyway," John said, "returning to the matter in hand, I have your

133

documents. The money has been deposited in Barclays Bank in Charterhouse Street. So all you have to do next is to present the paperwork and a bank book will be issued in your name. Keep it somewhere safe, Eleanor. You will need it, any time you wish to withdraw funds."

"Pardon?" Eleanor frowned.

"Take money out," John said gently. "You've never had a bank account, have you, Eleanor?"

"No," she admitted, "only a post office savings account..."

"Well, you have no further money worries," John smiled. He rose to his feet where it was obvious the meeting was drawing to a close. "My only advice would be to use it wisely."

"Thank you, Mr Sharp," Eleanor finished, wiping a tear from her eye. "You don't know how much this means to me and I'll remember what you said about my father. I'll keep in touch."

"Just be careful, my dear," John smiled. "That's all Sammie ever wanted... for you to be safe. It was nice to meet you too, Jake," he added, shaking his hand.

They left the building in a daze. It was a humbling thought that in the midst of all their problems, someone still cared about them - even beyond the grave.

"God bless you, Sammie," Eleanor whispered, staring up at the sky. "If only you could hear me."

"If he can, he must know that the best thing we could do is escape," Jake pondered. "Can't you see, this changes everything. He has given us enough to start a whole new life..."

"I know, it's fantastic," Eleanor said and she gave a little shiver.

They wandered away, temporarily liberated from their worries.

Just a small path lay between the office block and the road. Captured in the joy of the moment, Jake clasped her hands, spun her around to face him and kissed her on the lips. Eleanor laughed lightly.

The sun illuminated the copper gleam of his hair. Despite the fact that Eleanor had insisted on cutting it, the colour was distinctive enough to draw attention. As the two of them embraced, they did not realise that new eyes were watching them from the other side of the path.

III

The man did not see them go into the office block but guessed they would be there; just a rumour, a rapid flurry of words he had picked up... He had to pass on a warning.

Fortunately, he found a street bench in the patch of green space near the office. He lingered in the shadow of trees until they appeared. Studying the young man, he noted every feature, from his slender build to the way he moved. He possessed an almost feline grace, the guitar in its case fixed to his back identifying him to be a musician.

This had to be Jake Jansen of course.

The female, he had spotted before but only very briefly. Her colouring gave her away; that shimmering dark hair braided and pinned to her head, revealing a delicate neck. Her flawless skin was just as he remembered, her eyes, two golden orbs.

As she turned, the flowing white fabric of her dress billowed out behind her. Jake took her arm, steering her down the path towards the very place where he waited...

He observed their cheerful, animated faces; the way they glanced at each other, touched each other. It was clear to see that they were lovers. Perhaps they would blend easily into a crowd, where few people would notice them. Yet somehow, he expected them to behave a little more warily. There was something quite brazen about the way they ambled around so freely without a care in the world. He stood up and stepped out of the shadows, blocking their path.

The two of them froze, so he spoke quickly.

"Excuse me, may I have a word? But not here out in the open. It isn't safe..."

"I'm sorry?" Eleanor gasped. She leapt back, without really knowing why.

"It's alright, I know who you are," The stranger said. Eleanor noted his soft, cultured voice. "I am aware of the danger you are in, which is the reason I had to warn you, that's all."

"Who are you?" Jake demanded.

The man looked at him; his face filled with compassion.

"I'm guessing you must be Jake." Since Jake gave no reply, he continued speaking. "Allow me to introduce myself. My name is Robin Whaley. Councillor Robin Whaley. I've been sent here to assist you, as I believe you could use an ally."

"Councillor Whaley?" Eleanor frowned. She found herself scrutinising him, trying to place his face. Oddly enough, he did look familiar.

"Do you know him?" Jake murmured.

"I'm not sure," she whispered back. She scratched around in her mind for a memory.

He seemed fairly young for a councillor, tall and dark haired. The tailored cut of his pin stripe suit gave him an air of professionalism. Handsome with regular features, he possessed a straight nose and a wide mouth with soft, shapely lips. His evenly spaced, pale blue eyes settled upon them beneath delicate eyebrow ridges.

The image came back to her in a flash, she remembered where she had seen him.

"Do you mean, you're an elected councillor?" she queried

"I am indeed," Robin replied, "but please... It isn't safe to stand here in full view. Can't we at least, get ourselves out of sight? This need only take a few minutes..."

Jake's eyes conveyed a look of worry as he glanced at Eleanor. She gave a light shrug.

Beckoning them to follow, he led them into a side street where a number of cafés lingered. He quickly selected one. It had an old-fashioned ice cream sign outside where one fleeting glance told them it was empty. He held the door open and ushered them inside.

"Take a seat," he muttered. "I'd better order us a drink, what would you like?"

"It's okay," Jake said. "We don't have much time. If you don't mind, will you please say whatever it is you have to say, so we can be on our way...?"

The subtle but musical lilt of his Dutch accent seemed strangely pronounced. The man perused him with sudden interest.

"I gather you are from Holland, Jake," he said softly. He followed it with a nervous smile. "Look, I understand your caution. You don't know me and you clearly don't trust me..."

Fishing into his breast pocket, he produced a card; it bore the distinct crest of Tower Hamlets Council along with the name, *Cllr. R. Whaley* and a telephone number.

"You can telephone them if you wish. They'll be more than happy to confirm my identity. I appreciate you shouldn't trust strangers."

"You know who *I* am though, don't you," Eleanor accused.

Trapped in her own memories, she was thrown back to a time when she had *just* released Jake from the basement of that house. She recalled their fear, their urgency to get out; that one transitory glance out of the window... *except there had been a man standing outside.* A wave of unease rolled over her. He had only been there for literally a second but it was enough...

Robin cleared his throat.

"Yes, I have seen you before," he relented. "You must be Eleanor. I don't mean to pry but it concerns me to hear of vulnerable young people in danger, especially when they happen to be living in my ward. I admit I saw you in the upstairs window of that house..."

"You know that place was a brothel then?" Eleanor retorted. "I was kept there as a prisoner. I supposed you thought I was a prostitute."

"It's immaterial," he said gently, "but in answer to your question, I was

136

well aware of the type of establishment it was. I received a number of complaints."

Jake was frowning. Glancing from Eleanor to Robin and back again, he was clearly confused.

"Jake," she said softly, "do you remember the time we escaped from Clark's brothel? We were about to climb out of the window but I made us wait... There was a man outside, which is the reason I hesitated. It was him."

"I see," Jake replied. He fiddled absent-mindedly with the business card, turning it over in his fingers. "So how has he managed to find us now?" He lifted his gaze, probing deep into the other man's eyes. "What were you doing outside that place, Mr Whaley?"

Robin let out a sigh before gesturing to the waitress; a small dark-skinned girl in a black dress and frilly apron. Without further delay, he asked her to bring a pot of tea and three cups.

No sooner had she disappeared, he looked back at Jake. He drew his head close.

"Jake, I want you to understand that local issues concern me. I decided to investigate that place after residents made complaints - late night noise, shouting, foul language, not to mention a number of girls parading themselves in skimpy outfits... It's a disgrace. There is a school not far from there. It's not appropriate to be running an establishment like that, not when there are children around. I agreed to launch a campaign to get the place closed down..."

Eleanor was stunned. His explanation actually sounded quite feasible.

"So how did you know about us?" she pressed.

"From the residents," he replied with an element of satisfaction. "News travels fast. I heard about some chase that occurred along that road - a young girl and a slim, auburn haired boy." His eyes slid towards Jake again where they lingered. "You were witnessed running for your lives, pursued by a car... I was also told the men in that car looked less than desirable."

Jake gave a snort. "It is no lie!"

"Those men were arrested for driving a motorbike through a public park," Robin continued with a cool smile. "Lucky you got away. As I said, it is my duty to keep abreast with problems in my ward, including any known criminal activity..."

"Did you talk to the police?" Jake queried.

"Oh yes," Robin sighed, "and this is something else that has come to my attention. I understand the police are very keen to find you, Jake."

Jake raised his eyebrows. "Really?"

Eleanor turned to him with a look of alarm.

"Yes," Robin replied, "you were reported missing. They also expressed concern for Eleanor's safety, which I gather had something to do with the men who were after you that day; a notoriously violent gang..."

Eleanor and Jake stared at each other, a wave of unease rising between them. Was there anything this man didn't know?

His version of events could hardly be dismissed; *the terrifying chase from all those weeks ago must have drawn attention, especially from members of the public.* Yet the involvement of the police had dredged up Eleanor's worse fears; especially their interest in Jake.

In the brief interlude of silence, the waitress returned with a tray of tea. She observed Councillor Whaley as he laid out three china cups; the way he proceeded to pour the tea - the slow, almost delicate movement of his hands which were so clean and soft, the nails perfectly manicured. She was struck with a sudden urge to hear what else he knew.

"Do you know why the police are looking for Jake?"

"Ssh, Eleanor," Jake cautioned, covering her hand with his own. "It doesn't matter." He inclined his head, his green eyes penetrating again. "Why have you brought us here, Mr Whaley? Could you please just explain the point of this meeting?"

"Yes," Robin murmured casually. "The reason I found you today was to pass on a warning. I've kept my ears and eyes open, you see... I know that those men are still out there, just waiting for you to surface."

"We have already guessed that," Jake said through gritted teeth.

"Then why are you walking around in broad daylight?" Robin demanded.

"We have a train to catch," Jake protested. "We do not want to be in London for any longer, does that answer your question? We are on our way to Waterloo Station..."

"You can't go there," Robin broke in quickly. "It's too dangerous."

"I don't understand," Eleanor frowned. She gratefully accepted the cup of tea Robin handed her and began to sip it gently, blowing the steam off the surface.

"This is exactly the type of location, your enemies will be waiting," Robin snapped. "You can't go anywhere near a mainline station. This is what they are hoping for..."

"Whose they?" Jake intercepted as if testing him.

Robin shot another circular glance as if to check they weren't being overheard. He seemed to choose his next words very carefully.

"I know who is behind this," he whispered. "A gangster by the name of Dominic Theakston."

Eleanor turned cold, the tremor in her hand almost causing her to drop her cup.

"Yes," Robin said, staring deep into her eyes, "I see I have your attention now. His men have been laying traps all over London and it sounds like you are about to step right into one."

Eleanor could not speak. The room seemed to spin. Just the sound of that name turned her giddy with fear. She knew Theakston had come close when he had visited Forest Haven... but this! *They had to leave London.* Staying here was no longer an option yet from what this man was saying, it was beginning to sound like an impossibility.

"I gather my news has alarmed you," Robin said.

His voice seemed strangely mocking, prompting Jake to glare at him.

"Well, what do you expect?" he hissed. "Of course we are scared. Have you any idea what this man will to do to us if he catches us?"

Robin's counter stare was equally challenging. "Go on."

"One question for you, Mr Whaley. Have you ever faced death before?" Jake taunted.

They witnessed the change in his expression. "Death?" Robin breathed.

"Yes, that is what I said," Jake repeated. He brushed his hand over his forehead, without meaning to, a look of despair clouding his features. "These men want to kill me, Mr Whaley and they might do the same to Eleanor. Neither of us really want to think about it too much."

Robin's expression did not change as he turned his attention back to Eleanor.

Jake could almost imagine how she must have appeared in his eyes; so young and fragile, so vulnerable. For the next few seconds, his eyes seemed to devour her. He took a sip from his tea cup and gently placed it down. As his hand fell to the table top, it brushed Jake's wrist as if to convey his sympathy.

"I'm sorry," he whispered sadly. "In that case, I'll get straight to the point. It's obvious you need help and there is a place I am going to suggest you go. Toynbee Hall. It's close to Aldgate East tube station, not hard to find. Look for a red brick building with bay windows. Go there and ask for a man by the name of Bernard James. As one of our carers in society, he helps all manner of people from drunks and vagrants to vulnerable young people such as yourselves. I'll phone him and let him know to expect you... I am certain he will offer a solution to your dilemma."

"Thank you," Jake replied. He saw the pity in Robin's eyes; a gaze so powerfully irresistible, it compelled him to unzip his holdall to find a pen. "Bernard James," he murmured dreamily. "Toynbee Hall..."

"Look for Commercial Street," Robin said, draining the last drop of tea from his cup. "It's just off Whitechapel Road. I know, it means you have to return to East London but this is possibly your only chance of saving yourselves. I must impress upon you to go there."

"And I have *your* details," Jake added, flashing the card.

"Indeed," Robin smiled at him.

Five minutes later, they slipped out of the door and with no delay, made their way back towards the tube station. Eleanor remained silent for the rest of the conversation. Jake guessed it had a lot to do with hearing their enemy's name spoken out loud.

It came as a devastating anti-climax. A few minutes ago, they had been revelling in their good fortune but this latest news had completely floored them.

They kept walking. They didn't even notice where Robin Whaley had gone but for now, they didn't care. Heads down, marching onwards, they waited until they were back inside the tube station before they spoke another word...

"Well," Jake breathed. "What did you make of that?"

"Did you trust him?" Eleanor said.

Jake heard the fear in her voice. "No," he answered bluntly. "Did you?"

Eleanor sighed. Her eyes flickered from left to right, as if checking for signs they were being watched. She seemed confident the throng of people passing back and forth were commuters.

"I wanted to," she said, "he seemed *so nice*. I really think he wanted to help us... but on the other hand, how did he know *so much* about us? I found that really disturbing."

"That is the problem," Jake agreed. "We don't know who he is. And what about this place he wants us to visit? It means going back to East London. Do you really want to risk it?"

Eleanor shook her head. "It's only going to delay us," she whispered, "and I don't want to go back to the East End. I'm certain there'll be more of Theakston's men crawling around in that part of London than anywhere. We're in danger wherever we go... but Whitechapel!"

"Then let us stick to our plan," Jake said firmly. Taking her hand, he offered her a gentle smile. "We've come this far, Eleanor so we need to keep going... We could jump on a train and be out of here within an hour!"

Eleanor squeezed his hand and nodded. The next time she looked at him, her golden eyes were full of fire. They had made their decision.

Chapter 8

I

They approached Waterloo station from the road where its grand facade loomed up impressively. Hearts racing, Jake and Eleanor skipped up the wide flight of steps and under a beautiful archway flanked by statues. Its famous four-faced clock hung above as they passed through the station. But there was no time to waste; they needed tickets and travel information.

Jake paused, eyes scanning the area. He felt an initial burst of excitement as he took in the scene, convinced they had made the right decision. A tiny part of him so much wanted to believe Robin Whaley. He had left the café, feeling somewhat comforted by the thought that someone wanted to help them. Unfortunately, that help had arrived too late... They were about to take their final leap towards freedom.

Crouching down, he unzipped his holdall and rifled around for the wallet he had bought from the market. Every so often he glanced up, aware of the tide of people. They flowed from all directions; a typical crowd consisting of suited businessmen and shoppers. Trendy young women swayed past in flares and mini-dresses, platforms clomping across the floor tiles...

He caught Eleanor's eye and flashed her a reassuring smile. How regrettable they hadn't seized a chance to visit the bank John Sharp had mentioned. It would have made sense to have done that before leaving but it would have to wait now. Robin's approach had thrown them off course.

Digging deeper into the holdall, he finally unearthed the wallet.

The moment he rose, Eleanor turned and subtly gestured towards the ticket office. A row of boards stretched out ahead of her, listing the timetables. Jake watched as she glided towards them, the enveloping white swathes of her dress fanning outwards as she moved. His eyes were fixed on the back of her head as he began to follow. Yet just as she reached the boards, a man unexpectedly emerged from behind them. He positioned himself right in front of her, hands on hips, a posture that seemed intimidating. Eleanor froze, stalled by his approach. Still as a statue, he gazed down at her; tall, reed thin and dressed in a cheap looking suit.

Jake felt himself drawn to the scene, before a chilling memory pierced his mind. He had seen this man before. All senses had been on red alert, that day; sounds of a rough and noisy neighbourhood, followed by the terror of being forced into a chair and handcuffed in some kitchen, engulfed by the stench of cooking fat. Only his vision had been obscured. He remembered the noose made from some sort of sacking; a splinter of time when the sack was pulled away to be replaced by a blindfold.

The image of the same man shimmered like a mirage. Jake experienced

the first prickle of goose bumps, only this time, he was seeing his face clearly
- the narrow light blue eyes boring into him like shards of ice.

"Shit!" Jake gasped unable to tear his gaze away.

The chilling eyes pinned him where he stood.

"What's wrong, Jake?" Eleanor cried, twisting her head around to look at
him but he had already grabbed her hand...

Overcome with a sudden terror, Jake tugged her away from the billboards,
away from this menacing stranger who refused to break eye contact.

He moved quickly, weaving his way in and out of the knots of people,
propelled back in the direction of the archway. Eleanor glanced around at the
man. He had also moved away from the billboards, a triumphant look
spreading across his face.

"Who is he?" she gasped as they staggered through the archway.

Jake did not answer. Fighting his way out of the station he was unable to
shake off his panic; he could no longer deny that this was one of the men
who'd plotted to kill him.

They reached the other side of the archway, pausing at the top of the
steps. Jake shuddered to a halt as if on a cliff edge. Was it his imagination or
had more people gathered outside the station? Maybe they had been there all
the time but in their haste they hadn't noticed them...

A spreading crowd of men took shape; *dangerous looking men*. One
lounged against the wall. Dark haired with a bushy black beard, he glowered
at them through a cloud of pipe smoke. Jake flinched as a movement caught
his eye from another direction. This time, it was the slow wind of a car
window opening. His glance shot towards a white Ford Cortina where two
more men materialised, both staring at him, their expressions hostile.

Everywhere he turned, someone seemed to be lingering.

Glancing down towards the foot of the steps, he saw yet another man
advancing, this time, on foot. Short and squat with an enormous belly
straining against his jacket buttons, his mean face bore the savagery of a
Rottweiler.

"Oh shit!" Jake spluttered again. "They are everywhere!"

He remembered something Eleanor had said, words that were gradually
transforming into reality... *the day we leave this place, Theakston's men are
going to close in on us like a pack of wolves.* She had been right all along.

Time stood still; the ever continuous lines of faceless people moving in
both directions, seemingly oblivious to it all. Jake snatched one final look at
the scene unfurling ahead of them and sensing the aggression that charged
the atmosphere, he spun towards the station again.

The man with the pale blue eyes loomed behind him, having finally
caught up. Jake gulped, overwhelmed by a wave of fear before he came to an
abrupt decision.

Turning to Eleanor, he pulled her around, lowering his head to kiss her. He trailed a forefinger over her profile then spoke very gently.

"Run, my love. Get yourself out of here while you still can, I am giving myself up..."

"Jake, no!" she whimpered, staring at him bolt eyed.

He shook her off then strode out into the open. Poised at the top of the steps and facing the crowd, he stretched his arms out wide as if offering himself as a sacrifice.

"Come on then!" he yelled down at the men. "What are you waiting for? Come and get me, you wankers!"

Not a single one of them moved.

Watching like a crowd of silent spectators, Jake wondered if something else was about to happen. He heard Eleanor sob. Spinning around again to peer over her shoulder, he was amazed to see the tall man still hovering; yet even he wasn't moving, the same cold smile stapled to his face. The tension in the air hung so thick now, people were beginning stare.

Then out of nowhere, rose the wail of a police siren. They saw the car carve its way through the crowd, a turquoise Morris Minor with the word POLICE emblazoned on its side panel.

In that precise second, Jake realised what was really going on as the car lurched its way right up to the steps.

"Fuck!" he gasped to himself.

Eleanor grasped his arm. Gifted with a hidden strength, she hauled him back under the archway and this time they *charged*. Jake glared once more at the tall man blocking their path before barging into him, catapulting him sideways.

"Stop those two!" a voice boomed though the tunnel arch.

The surrounding walls seemed to absorb the sound but Jake and Eleanor did not stop running; they staggered across the station floor, burdened with their belongings. Fortuitously, people moved aside to let them through where another exit beckoned. They flew towards it.

At first, the sunshine blinded them. Jake squinted. The exit had brought them out into a different road but it was lined with a rank of taxis. Without hesitation, Eleanor bounded towards the nearest one. Grasping the door handle to yank it open, she hurled herself inside, dragging Jake in beside her. She could hardly breathe, her heart was hammering so fast...

"We need a different tube station!" she panted. "Quickly!"

Their young, fair haired driver possessed a pleasant, rosy face. Turning to smile at her, he must have taken one glance at her panic stricken face before he obligingly started the engine. Eleanor stole a glance out of the back window horrified to see two policemen staggering out of the same exit. The glint of silver buttons on their helmets contrasted starkly with their dark uniforms.

"'Ere," muttered the cabbie, "you ain't in no trouble with the old bill, are you?"

"No!" Eleanor spluttered. "Not us! There are some *other* men in there we're running from! I think the police have turned up to arrest *them*. Oh please, get us out of here!"

"Alright, love, calm down," the driver grinned. "Cor! Can't wait to tell the missus about this! Love a good chase I do! So, where now? Embankment's the next underground station..."

"Will it get us to East London?" Eleanor said shakily.

"Should do," the cab driver said. "Follow the District line and it'll take you there direct."

"Eleanor," Jake whispered in her ear, "that was really good thinking..."

For now, they were hidden inside the cab as it sped along the streets, leaving their pursuers way behind. The couple took a moment to stare at each other.

"Oh, Jake," Eleanor breathed. "Maybe Mr Whaley was right..."

"I know," Jake replied, though she detected a darkness in his tone. "I guess, we have to find this place he told us about... Toynbee Hall. It is our only choice."

II

Just as Robin Whaley indicated, Toynbee Hall was not difficult to find. It lay a little further back from Whitechapel Road, a short distance from Aldgate East tube station.

There was no mistaking, it felt unnerving to be back in East London. Yet in the light of another electrifying chase, Eleanor was compelled to bury her fear just to get to this place.

An elegant building, Toynbee Hall was a welcome contrast to the dark and claustrophobic labyrinths of the East End; every mullioned window surrounded by stonework, creamy against the bricks. With walls smothered in ivy and a double pitched roof, it struck Eleanor as approachable. Relieved to have found it, she drifted towards the door, almost dizzy with exhaustion.

Once inside, she begged for a quiet few words with the man known as Bernard James.

They were asked to wait although it seemed only seconds before a man approached them. He looked to be in his late 50s; a tall man, casually dressed in a tweed sports jacket and faded cords. Gifted with a face, Eleanor would describe as kindly, his evenly spaced eyes shone a watery blue behind his steel-framed glasses. His complexion was threaded with soft lines. He did not smile and Eleanor noticed he was accompanied by another man. This one seemed considerably younger, his gaunt face partially concealed behind a beard.

"Good day," he began. "I gather you wanted to see me. I am Bernard James, one of the wardens here and this is my assistant, Reginald Magnus..."

Eleanor bit her lip. "I'm sorry to bother you but we were advised you might be able to help us? A man named Councillor Robin Whaley spoke to us..."

"Oh yes," Bernard murmured, "we did receive a call from him. Are you homeless?"

She risked a sideways glance where Jake stood in silence. Only now, she clocked the defeat in his expression. His complexion seemed drained of colour, his eyes harbouring a haunted look. This latest incident had affected him worse than she thought. He had barely spoken a word since their escape from Waterloo Station.

"I suppose we are really," Eleanor confessed miserably. "We're not without money... But we are in a lot of danger. I don't know how much to tell you."

"Perhaps we can offer you a refuge," the man began gently.

Eleanor froze. She wondered what he meant by *refuge*.

"You do realise that much of our work is to help the poor," he added.

Eleanor's lip started to tremble. She did not want to break down in front of these two strangers, her grip on Jake's hand tightening.

"I-is this why M-Mr Whaley sent us here?" she shivered. "I-it's not like we're a couple of tramps spending our days lying around in parks, high on meths all the time."

Bernard tilted his head, the benevolence of his smile bringing a little light to his eyes.

"I didn't think for a moment you were," he reassured her, "but I would still like to know a little more about you. You say you're in danger... does this mean someone intends to harm you?"

Eleanor nodded, reluctant to say too much.

"Have you spoken to the police?" the other man demanded.

Eleanor glanced at him, unnerved by his slightly condescending tone. Once again she bit her lip, fighting against the urge to cry.

"S-sorry," she began, "but the people we're hiding from are not the type of people you report to *the police*. They'd more likely slit your throat if you even got as far as the station door..."

Reginald Magnus gulped visibly. She saw the tell-tale wobble of his Adam's apple, satisfied her words seemed to have stifled him.

"It sounds to me like you need a place to hide," Bernard suggested.

"Yes," Eleanor nodded where at last his words brought hope. "I suppose we do..."

A frown shot across his face but it was momentary. He was peering over the edge of his glasses like an old schoolmaster. Turning his gaze to Jake as if to study him, the gentleness in his expression never wavered.

"Are you alright, sonny? You seem upset..."

"Sorry," Jake murmured. "I am not normally like this. I have always been the optimistic one until now." He gave Eleanor's hand an affectionate squeeze.

Bernard frowned again, jarred by the way he articulated his vowels; the hint of a foreign accent that swum in the melody of his voice. The reassuring light in his eyes did not fade as he took another step closer.

"You're not from England are you?" he whispered. "But don't give up hope… Perhaps there *is a way* we can help you."

He turned to his colleague with raised eyebrows. The other man gave a slight nod, as if some silent agreement had been made.

"It so happens," Bernard continued, "there are places to live where you would barely be seen. Believe me, we have helped many people who've said they're in trouble but they're often vagrants, not young people... It strikes me you need a safe house. So why don't we go up to my office and see what we can find for you?"

Without further question, they allowed themselves to be led upstairs. Eleanor could not fail to notice some of the other visitors; mostly old people but destitute. Their clothes looked worn, their expressions stricken and forlorn, as if somehow life had abandoned them. The only saving grace was, this was probably the last place Theakston would come looking for them…

They found themselves tucked in a tiny office and ushered into chairs. Bernard and his assistant Reginald positioned themselves on the other side of the desk. Eleanor watched in intrigue as Bernard dragged a heavy box file from the shelf. He fished out a map of London and spread it out over what little space there was. Reginald seized a clipboard and pen.

She caught Jake's eye, troubled by the enduring panic in his expression.

"It'll be okay, Jake," she whispered. "This won't be forever…"

"I so much wanted to get away from here," he answered through gritted teeth. "If only those men hadn't found us… We could be on a ferry by now."

Her eyes turned to Bernard; she saw a myriad of changing expressions on his face as he sifted through the file. In the moment Jake spoke, he seemed to freeze. He glanced up in a way that seemed anxious.

"I think I may have found something," he muttered, "but it may not be up to the standard you're used to. Is there anything else you want to tell me about your circumstances?"

"There is one thing," Jake said guardedly. "Eleanor is pregnant. All I want to do is to protect her." His hand folded over hers as it rested on the desk.

Bernard's expression changed again. "You're expecting a child?" he gasped. "How old are you, my dear?"

"It doesn't matter," Eleanor said, almost wishing Jake had kept quiet. "Please... just tell us what you've found."

"A-a bedsit," Bernard faltered. "Its former occupant was a vagrant who refused to move out when the plot was developed into high rise flats. He *was* eventually evicted and the building demolished but the original basement still stands. Do you know where Bethnal Green is?"

"I've heard of it," Eleanor said. "Is it far?"

"About a mile to the north of Whitechapel," Bernard replied. "Reggie, would you mind very much driving them over there? The accommodation is just beneath the ground floor and very much out of sight. No one will know you are there, not even the other tenants."

"It sounds perfect," Jake nodded.

"I warn you, it's no palace," Bernard added sadly. "You have only one room with the most basic cooking facilities and a bathroom."

"It doesn't matter," Jake said stiffly. "We will live anywhere, as long as we are safe from our enemies. Now how much do we owe you for rent?"

The words seemed to stall Bernard in his tracks. "That's very noble, Jake," he sighed, "but unnecessary. This is a charitable organisation destined to help those in need. Though we are more than happy to accept a donation... whatever you can afford."

The first hint of a smile lifted the corners of his mouth. "Thank you," Jake finished.

III

Their next journey took them through a maze of streets, the pavements crowded with people who in the main possessed a shabby look. There was no mistaking the austerity of the area, crammed with an odd mix of buildings. Rows of houses squatted together tightly in the shadow of the high rise blocks. They seemed stark and characterless in comparison. Modern development was infiltrating the area on a huge scale, the demolition of older terraces making way for compact suburban housing designed to accommodate the masses.

Rolling past the shops, Eleanor spotted a Saverstores, the same grocery chain run by Daliya's family in Forest Haven. The sight brought a painful tug of nostalgia. *Was it only this morning, they had crept away from that place?*

Reginald parked in a side street. Coaxing them out of the car, he hurried towards one of the ugliest buildings Eleanor had ever seen; a hideous, monolithic tower constructed in grey concrete, rising from the edge of a parched lawn. He unlocked the door and ushered them inside where a musty, dark lobby engulfed them. A flight of steps loomed ahead but just to the side of it, Reginald pointed towards a private door. Hidden in the shadows and barely visible, a few more steps drew them into the basement level.

"This is the door to the bedsit," Reginald explained in hushed tones. "It will enable you to lie low for a while. Keep in touch if you can and if you *do* manage to escape these enemies of yours, let us know…"

"Of course," Eleanor said, an echo of despair in her voice. "Thank you, Mr Magnus."

Jake unlocked the door to encounter a wall of darkness. Feeling for a light switch, he paused as the interior emerged. It was much as described; a bleak bedsit whose oppressive atmosphere contained a lingering smell of mould. Tucked below ground level, there were no windows. The only furniture inside was a double divan slumped on a threadbare carpet and a few flimsy cupboards. At the other end, lurked a door which they guessed was a bathroom.

"What a dump," Jake sighed. "I am so sorry, Eleanor."

"It doesn't matter," Eleanor said, desperately clinging onto the tiniest bit of hope she had left. "I guess it feels safe… and at least we have a roof over our heads."

As they began to settle into their new hiding place, Eleanor packed away the few things they had brought with them. Using one of the cupboards as a makeshift wardrobe, she tidily arranged their clothes. The poky bathroom was at least clean with a wash basin and toilet. At the other end of the room, rested an old electric cooker along with a medley of kitchen utensils.

Eleanor inched her way around the floor as if in a dream, trying hard not to concentrate on their conditions. Disturbed by the age of the floorboards, there was one in particular that emitted a groan every time she stepped on it. She pulled back the edge of the carpet to investigate. Sure enough, two of the boards appeared to be loose and as she slid her fingers into the groove, they lifted right up. A recess of about two feet opened up underneath. She could see the foundations on which the entire structure was built. Following her gaze, Jake gaped into the space in disbelief. Nothing but a configuration of breeze blocks stretched between the cold earth and the floor boards.

"It looks like the sort of place someone would hide a body," Eleanor said casually.

She intended it to be light humour but Jake did not smile. Absorbing the image of his frozen features, she felt a wave of despair roll right over her.

"Jake, who the hell were all those men at the station?"

"Can't you guess?" Jake shivered. "The tall man, I recognised. He was one of the men in the kitchen from the time they first captured me. I remember him."

"What? So he's definitely one of Theakston's men?" Eleanor gasped.

"Yes," Jake said darkly, "one of Theakston's top men. He gave a lot of orders. I remember his voice, i-it was musical with a strong London accent…"

His head drooped into his hands. Eleanor had never seen him like this; as if the very life essence had been siphoned out of him.

"Eleanor, we were completely outnumbered," he whimpered. "I cannot believe they were all there, just waiting for us. The police too…"

Only now did she recall the menace that had loomed inside that station, her mind's eye honing on one particular scene; the moment Jake had stepped over to that crowd of thugs, arms outstretched. She felt a shudder of horror.

"Jake, don't you ever do anything like that again," she said, her tone dropping to a snarl.

"I'm sorry?" Jake frowned.

"Offer yourself up like that!" she snapped, spinning round to face him. "How could you? After everything we've been through!"

"Eleanor, they set a trap!" Jake protested. "I really thought we had reached the end of the road. We have been in hiding for nearly two months. I thought we would be safe to move on but what happened today was a nightmare. They came so close and do you know what? I am sick of running!"

"We got away, didn't we?" Eleanor sobbed. "I thought we were in this together. If you go down, we both go down, understand? I can't go on without you…"

Jake shook his head, his eyes pleading. "No, Eleanor," he gasped. "What about our baby? Don't you think our child deserves a chance to live, even if we don't? If we are faced with that choice again and one of us can get away, then it *has to be* you."

She finally read the emotion in his mysterious eyes. He was braver than she realised.

Tears swum in her eyes, spilling down her cheeks. Jake exhaled a sigh. Stroking the tears from her cheeks, he ran his hands over the sides of her face, savouring every detail. He reached up, letting his fingertips sweep over the bridge of her nose, brushing the tops of her eyelashes. They came away wet with her tears. Last of all, he traced the outline of her lips. It felt as if he was trying to imprint every detail of her into his mind.

"I love you so very much," he whispered. "Whatever happens, the last weeks have been the happiest ever. I would not have wanted my life to be any different…"

Later in the evening they made love with fiercer passion than ever. During their long, lazy days in Forest Haven, everything happened in slow motion, as if they had all the time in the world. Yet something had changed in the last few hours. The clock seemed to be running faster.

Jake unbraided Eleanor's hair, relishing every tendril as he separated them out with his fingers. Gleaming like pitch, her hair was actually quite course. His lips brushed against her neck then in a single violent motion, he pushed her down onto the divan, pulling off her dress. The rest of her clothes followed. He gripped her arms with a strength she didn't know he possessed, leaving her struggling at first... Yet as he began to kiss her, she could feel her resistance melting, conscious of his lips pressing down harder than normal...

She kissed him back. In truth, she wanted him as badly as he desired her.

The moment she felt him relax a little, she knelt over and straddled him, locking him between her thighs. Wasting no time, she bore downwards, feeling the hardness of his manhood inside her. The ebb and flow of their bodies rose like a storm on the sea, the swelling waves rising higher. The bed springs squeaked but neither of them cared. Jake grasped her hair, pulling her head down to kiss her again and again, his hands on her breasts, kneading them with a lust that felt almost painful. But still she did not resist; it was as if they had reached another pivotal point in time...

Several times they changed position but their motion didn't waver. Swept in a continuous river of energy, Eleanor was aware of the familiar warm current spreading through her body, unable to stem her cries as she was driven to a climax which shook her in its intensity.

Jake rose with her. She felt him shudder, the enveloping warmth of his body pulsating against her own, the warmth of his breath like steam.

Yet the sound that echoed in the aftermath was more like a sob. He became very still, hands buried in her flowing, dark hair as he held his position, kneeling behind her.

As she turned to kiss him again, she discovered his face soaked with tears.

Chapter 9

I

For the next few weeks they managed to live in secret and as far as they could tell, remained invisible to the outside world. It was much as Bernard and his colleague had described. If they kept their heads down, no one need even know of their presence though there were times when it wasn't easy. People tended to loiter near the elevator and stairs. On occasions like these, they were forced to endure an existence of total silence.

It was a far cry from the life they had cherished.

Bethnal Green wasn't a million miles away from Whitechapel, which had formerly served as the nucleus of Sammie's empire. Neither of them could shake off the terror, those streets belonged to Dominic Theakston now... a forbidding area, grimy and noisy, with drunks lolling around right up until the early hours. They were frequently awoken by the sounds of fighting; of drunken abuse and screaming. Empty beer bottles accumulated in the gutters, where the periodic shatter of glass was combined with the rising echo of police sirens.

They craved the tranquillity of Forest Haven yet that neighbourhood seemed like a distant dream now. This was more about survival.

Occasionally they did venture out but only in disguise. Eleanor was fortunate enough to find some Muslim clothes at a nearby jumble sale and with so many women from Pakistan living in London, she did not look out of place. The floating gown and veil she had selected was sufficient to conceal her hair and her figure. Such a disguise enabled her to move around freely, affording her the confidence to take on the role of shopping.

She had also risked one or two calls from a public telephone box, although there were only two people she dared contact; one was Bernard James, the other Councillor Whaley.

Some while later, she revisited the jumble sale in the hope, she would find a suitable disguise for Jake. If ever they were to make an escape from this city, it was essential no one recognised him. The baggy old overcoat she had chosen was about three sizes too big for him but concealed his slender, light frame. With his distinctive auburn hair tucked under a woolly hat, along with some very dark, round glasses, people took him for a blind man; a deception that proved to be effective, especially on the days he went busking.

Clinging to the guitar like a lifeline, Jake had discovered the perfect spot on the edge of a modern shopping centre. Passing shoppers were enchanted by his music. In fact, the opportunity to practice his songs was one of the few positive pleasures that had arisen from this new and very challenging situation they found themselves in.

Jake saw this as a transitory phase; another chance to stay hidden, hoping the dust might eventually settle and people would forget about them.

At times, Eleanor had floated the suggestion that they should strive to escape from London. She seemed very set on the idea of a taxi; perhaps travel separately, in disguise, as they had done in Forest Haven.

Jake however was reluctant, unable to shake off the dread that overwhelmed him every time he recalled their ordeal at Waterloo Station. This was the second time they had escaped Theakston's men by a hair's breadth but it left him feeling anxious as to whether they would be so lucky a third time... and this was not the only scenario that was niggling him.

His overriding concern was for Eleanor, where his inner voice was crying out to him; he would rather spend the next seven months in hiding than risk the possibility of her ending up in Theakston's hands. Picturing the scene at Waterloo Station, another memory sprang to mind, a concept that terrified him more than anything: why had the police been there?

Shortly after they moved into the bedsit, Eleanor made a preliminary call to Robin Whaley. He seemed delighted they had taken his advice though curious to know where they were staying. Eleanor had declined to reveal this, a decision they had agreed beforehand. Never knowing who to trust (or who might be listening) it seemed far safer to protect their anonymity, so the fewer people who knew their whereabouts the better...

But given the troubled nature of Jake's thoughts, the next communication begged the killer question: *why had the police been after them?*

On this occasion, Robin had disclosed the most candid yet *disturbing* allegation.

Eleanor returned that day, numb with shock. It transpired, the police were seeking to arrest Jake on the suspicion *he was a drug dealer.*

His reaction seemed to surprise her. He laughed at the suggestion although it was a mirthless sound.

"That is fucking ridiculous! Is this the best they can come up with? Didn't I always say there was a police officer involved in this? I am certain, the only reason he wants to arrest me is so he can hand me straight back over to those thugs, so they finish what they started!"

"Don't say that!" Eleanor whimpered. "It's probably a rumour, one that's being banded about by Theakston's lot. Maybe this is their latest tactic."

Jake sighed, ripping the foil off a bottle of cheap German wine. Having unearthed a fold-up table for meals and two rickety wooden chairs, they could at least attempt some sort of civilised lifestyle. A saucepan of chilli was already simmering on the stove top.

"Don't you remember what I told you about the police inspector who interviewed me?" Jake persisted. "Hargreaves! He was quite hostile, Eleanor.

I can't help thinking, he is behind this..."

"But why would anyone say that?" Eleanor demanded. "They haven't got any proof."

"Maybe they think I am from Amsterdam," he mused. "I bet they don't even know I'm from Nijmegen. Amsterdam is one of the main drug routes to Britain. He saw me as some long haired hippy with a guitar, someone who goes around music festivals where drugs are easy to find and people like me go around selling them..."

"Oh Jake," Eleanor whispered, accepting the wine he had just poured. "This doesn't make our situation any easier does it? You've never even taken drugs... have you?"

He gave a furtive smile. "Don't all rock musicians? Look at the Rolling Stones..."

Eleanor's face froze. Lowering her glass to the table, she stared at him with displeasure.

"You haven't?" she whispered. "Please tell me you're joking. What sort of drugs?"

"Not hard drugs," he answered, amazed by her reaction. "I've smoked a little grass at times to relax after a performance. We tried LSD once too, just to see what it was like..."

When Eleanor still refused to speak, he tried to explain the effects.

"It changes stuff - makes life look a-a little weird. Sounds turn into colours... you are looking across a meadow and everything seems to dance - flowers turn into cakes. For a musician, it can be very inspiring. You are never going to tell me the Beatles didn't try it…"

Jake faltered. She wasn't even looking at him now.

"I am not trying to convert you, Eleanor. I have only taken drugs a few times, I promise... I am not an addict and I am definitely not a dealer!"

"I never thought that for a moment," Eleanor mumbled.

Glancing across the table, she must have spotted the hurt in his eyes.

She clasped his hand. "I'm sorry... I just cannot believe the police are saying these things. I'd hate it if they used anything like this against you."

"I don't see how they can," Jake whispered sadly. "This is all such bullshit."

"So why are they accusing you of this crime?" Eleanor shivered. "How do they imagine they'll get away with it, even if they *do* manage to arrest you?"

"I don't know," he murmured. "I think the police are looking for any excuse to reel us in now, even if it means spreading lies..."

II

Jake tried to appear casual when in truth his world was starting to crumble under the weight of the conspiracy he was caught up in.

Everything that had emerged, from the day of the car bomb, to this absurd rumour being circulated, seemed to add substance to the efforts people were prepared to go to, in order to silence him.

He turned the facts over in his mind one by one, analysing each part in sequence.

Who was the dark-haired man at Waterloo Station? His pale blue eyes had chilled him to the core. With the vision fixed in his mind, he tried to recall the scrap of conversation he had picked up; words spluttered in the kitchen when he had originally been taken prisoner...

You've been telling stories, son! Things people don't want no one to know.

They had warned him that someone out there wanted rid of him. So why had he just stood there, staring at them?

The more he thought about it, the more it occurred to him that not a single one of those men had moved, not even when he had offered himself up. *Bizarre.* So what was the purpose of them being there? If not to capture them, were they simply there to keep them trapped inside the station? They had behaved like a pack, every one of them lurking by the entrance to stop them leaving; perhaps holding them in situ until the police arrived...

There wasn't a shred of doubt, the police were immersed in this. They were as much their enemies as Theakston's men, although a tiny part of him had always known this.

He had been snatched by that gang, literally moments after the police inspector had released him. Such thoughts brought his mind back to his interrogation... Why had he detained him for so long? Was it possible, the only reason the inspector had summoned him was to discover how much he knew? Jake felt the grip of fear. He could remember his face clearly, those cold blue eyes boring into him, scouring his mind for every detail. He had picked up the disdain in his voice and buckled under his prejudice. Hadn't he even detected a degree of irritation when he had repeated his statement, a second time?

With that thought, another rolled into his mind. Was it possible, this man was trying to protect whoever was responsible for that car bomb? That single horrific event had claimed the life of a British MP, along with a few others...

Jake wandered along the grotty, litter strewn pavements, keeping his head down. The stream of memories just kept coming, capturing him in their flow. He wanted to stay focussed.

Gradually making his way towards the shopping centre, he found his footsteps turning slower. The clouds of confusion were beginning to break, a sinister truth sliding through the gaps as he clung to that last thought. *Albert Enfield.*

He had never understood why anyone wanted him dead in the first place. Recapturing his first impression from the party, Albert had come across as a pleasant, middle-aged man who simply wanted to deliver a better quality of life for his countrymen. Wasn't this the only viewpoint he had expressed? Jake tugged at his memories, where the threads of his speech came back to him.

I want to establish a society which is fairer... British culture is controlled by the greed of the ruling elite... The clue had been in those words.

Albert Enfield had vowed to change the nature of British politics, perhaps in a manner that threatened the very authority of those in power. *The ruling elite...* Was this what he had been assassinated for? One sector of society were determined to hold on to their power! Jake knew the IRA had been blamed for the car bomb but rapidly formed the opinion it was nothing but a smoke screen to protect those who were really responsible.

Yet he was the only witness; the only member of the public who had spotted the true culprits or more specifically, those men lingering in that lane. He could still picture them; the suited blonde man in the car. *A Daimler.* Inspector Hargreaves had been particularly scornful about that statement, a thought that drew a smile to his lips. To be driving a Daimler, that man must have been unquestionably wealthy. Perhaps he represented the very ruling elite Albert had threatened to unhinge. Or did the man harbour some secret, something Albert had threatened to expose perhaps? There was something particularly clandestine about the way he had been conversing with his colleagues, moments before the cake had been wheeled out...

So who were Albert's enemies? Someone in power obviously; someone who had sufficient clout to manipulate a corrupt police officer to do his bidding and hire a contract killer. Jake had known all along that he held the key to the mystery. In order to understand who had masterminded the car bomb atrocity and why, he needed to learn more about Albert Enfield.

In some ways, he was enjoying these flashes of intuition but as for his own fate: he had witnessed something no one was meant to see; unmissable details such as the car, a brief glimpse of the man inside... Such evidence unsuppressed harboured potentially damaging consequences for someone; some faceless individual who would stop at nothing to get rid of him.

Jake paused on the threshold of the shopping centre. All these things combined seemed so sinister... *and now they were accusing him of being a drug dealer*. He didn't want to think too hard about what his enemies had in store for him. Filled with a yearning to go home, he was beginning to wonder if he would ever be safe, even if they did escaped to the Netherlands. But what other steps could they take? Despite Eleanor's desperation to run, they had no choice but to stay underground for now; it was the only way they would survive...

155

He started walking again, curious to wonder if there was any other tactic they could try. He did not dare phone home or reach out to anyone, fearing his enemies would use the information to trace them. Whoever these people were, they were dangerous. They held more influence than either of them could have imagined and there was nothing he could do to change that.

As the shops came into view, Jake gazed blankly ahead, ready to settle down and lose himself in his music. This was the only thing he could do really; keep a low profile and for all the while the blood flowed in his veins, he would indulge in the one passion that gave a purpose in life. Inspired to perform a few songs, he unrolled his blanket and spread it out on the pavement. He removed the guitar from its case, plucking at the strings, twisting the keys to tune it.

He already knew a selection of songs people liked, popular numbers such as 'House of the Rising Sun' which he had practised to perfection, as well as songs by the Beatles. 'Yellow Submarine' and 'Lady Madonna' in particular, brought smiles to the faces of strangers.

He had also started writing more of his own songs. Lyrics came to him in the darkness of night, when his troubled mind refused to switch off. They imprinted themselves in his thoughts, ready to be scrawled down in daylight. And as he wrote them down, new melodies entwined themselves around them, transforming them into songs. He had written two but was working on a third. One of these new songs meandered its way into head right now as he gripped the guitar. He gazed down at his hands, seeing the long, pale fingers that were connected to his soul, the tips hardened to calluses as they brushed the strings.

People froze where they stood, stirred by the beautiful arpeggios which sprang from the instrument. Added to a series of slow and haunting chords, he had developed a long 'intro' until eventually, he started singing - the words projected in his soft and distinctive tone.

The sound began to permeate through the precinct in every direction. Through his round, dark lenses he was moved by people's expressions. They looked at each other and smiled. Jake felt his heart swell, grateful for the opportunity to evoke such joy.

From the far end of the street however, one particular man was halted mid-step.

He craned his head, searching for the source until his eyes fell on the solitary figure hunched on the pavement. He spun around before Jake had a chance of recognising him.

His music played on. It echoed in ripples, bringing colour to the stark surround of grey walls and littered pavements but in those final moments before he reached the end of his song, that man found it impossible to tear himself away...

One glance at a nearby clock told him an hour had passed.

Jake knew when to call it a day. Packing away his guitar, he rose to his feet, ready to sneak his way back to the bedsit. He scooped up the handful of coins which lay scattered on the blanket, dropping them into one of his massive coat pockets. Finally, he rolled up the blanket and started walking. Once again, he kept his head down, desperate to remain inconspicuous as he inched his way through the grimy maze. He had just turned the corner of the next block, when someone bumped into him.

Jake glared up in outrage. He had practically been knocked off his feet. To his further annoyance, the clumsy oaf clung to his shoulders, using him like a wall to retain his balance; a gangly youth of about six foot tall with messy, slightly long hair. He bore the inane grin of someone who had drunk too much. Furthermore, he was staggering all over the place.

"Get your hands off me, you idiot!" Jake hissed.

The boy kept on grinning. "Hey, keep yer cool, man!" he laughed back.

It suddenly dawned on him, there was someone behind him too; some alien hand clawing at his coat pocket. He suspected, the two of them must have seen him scoop up all that cash, obviously intent on robbing him.

Jake spun around and with a single violent shove, sent the second youth sprawling to the ground.

"Get off me, you bastard!" he bellowed. "Piss off! Both of you!"

Shaking with rage, Jake was not the sort of person who lost his temper easily but in the light of all his other problems, he really didn't need this. He watched, as the first youth helped the second to his feet and the two of them went reeling out of sight. Jake released a sigh, brushing his hands over his coat to ward off the touch of their filthy hands. He felt violated and to think, he had practically been mugged on top!

Only a little later, did he finally get around to checking his pockets.

It was mid-day. Stirring some soup in a saucepan, Eleanor just happened to mention they were getting short of bread and butter. Jake began to empty out his pockets to count up all the loose change he had collected. The coins lay heavily in his pocket but as his hand closed around them, he could feel something else buried among them.

With a deepening frown, he extracted the contents and deposited them onto the table. There, in the middle of the spreading pile of change lay a package wrapped in cling film. Jake sat very still. He experienced the same feeling of violation as before, coupled with an escalating sense of unease.

"What's that?" Eleanor queried, wandering up to the table.

Jake remained where he sat, megalith still. His mind was already flickering back to those two youths who had bumped into him. There was never any doubt they had done it on purpose; one at the front, hanging onto his shoulders to distract him while the other sifted through his pockets. Jake felt his blood turn to ice as he stared at the package. Picking it up, he let it roll into his palm. The tightly wrapped contents seemed compact; some powdery substance, pale in colour.

"I have never seen it before," he replied dazedly.

Eleanor stared at him as he held it out for her to look at. Already he could see the panic glowing in her eyes before another thought occurred to him…

"Oh, no," he murmured, "it cannot be… Oh Jesus!"

"What?" Eleanor gasped.

"I thought it was nothing," he continued. "Some kid walked right into me. I thought he was drunk but there was another one behind me. I thought they were trying to steal the cash from my pockets…" his voice trailed off.

"Oh, Jake," Eleanor whispered, "and you didn't think to check your pockets?"

"I was angry," Jake sighed. He dropped the suspicious package onto the table top. "I'm sorry Eleanor but I have a very bad feeling about this."

"Drugs?" she suggested fearfully.

"Possibly," Jake sighed. He banged his fist down on the table, making her jump. "What the hell are we going to do now? Can't you see… this must have something to do with the *drug dealing* rumour! Do you remember what you said about the police having no proof? Well now they do! Somebody has planted it on me!"

Eleanor plucked the package from the table top and sniffed it. Turning it over in her hand as if to examine it, she must have noticed how solid it felt but so light. It emitted no smell yet the texture of the powder was reminiscent of brown sugar.

"Take it to the police," she challenged him. "Let's challenge them… a-ask them if they want it b-back." Her voice started to wobble. "Oh Jake, this is horrible!"

He felt his stomach tighten. The net was closing in on him, he could sense it. Watching Eleanor, moved by her storm of emotions, he knew what they needed to do.

"I have a better idea," he said stiffly. "Let us show this package to Bernard James. See what he has to say…"

"Why him?" Eleanor questioned. "Shouldn't we mention it to Councillor Whaley? After all, he was the one who told me about this rumour. Wouldn't this be an ideal opportunity to prove to him that you're innocent?"

"No," Jake said firmly. "Not him. There was something about Councillor Whaley that left me cold. I can't explain it but he gave me the creeps… Bernard, I trusted. I am sure he is the most sensible person to talk to."

"Okay," Eleanor sniffled. "I guess you're right."

She was trying hard not to cry, her bottom lip trembling. Their eyes met. He shot to his feet, gathering her in his arms before she finally gave way to tears. But as he cuddled her tightly, feeling the warmth of her young body pressed up against him, he was disturbingly aware of the baby growing inside her, *his child*. How much more misery she could take? And at the back of his mind, he was also left wondering, how the hell those two youths had known who *he* was.

III

The journey to Toynbee Hall took around twenty minutes, drawing them down familiar paths. Taking it one stage at a time, they moved more cautiously than ever, driven by a new and deeper fear. At the forefront of their minds lay an awareness that the police had good grounds to arrest them now. Coupled with the chilling notion that Theakston's men were still hunting them, they felt like mice trapped in an alleyway.

Eleanor moved first. Racing across the road towards the railway bridge, she ducked inside. Jake followed, seconds later. They proceeded in the same fashion, flitting from one street corner to the next, fading in and out of view like shadows. No sooner had they crept into the tube station and found their platform, they tucked themselves behind a concrete pillar. Well concealed until the train arrived, they could only pray that no one had followed them.

Eleanor was first to arrive at Toynbee Hall. As the familiar brick architecture loomed in sight, she darted across the courtyard and through the entrance. A couple of minutes later, Jake emerged from behind a bush. Enshrouded in his enormous tweed overcoat, anyone who spotted him would have mistaken him for a vagrant.

The instant they were hidden inside the building, Eleanor pulled the veil away from her face, her eyes scanning the area. She was looking for Bernard, desperate to speak to none other than him, not even his assistant, Mr Magnus, who she found a little disdainful. Her heart beat faster as she took in the scene. A number of wardens circulated around the hall, pausing to converse with some of the elderly people. Yet Bernard was not among them. Eleanor drew in a long, deep breath. Fixing her gaze on one of the staff members, she eventually found the courage to approach her. The woman must have recognised the panic in her eyes as she guided her gently aside.

"Mr James is extremely busy," she said in a tone which sounded almost apologetic. "He has an important meeting with the council tonight and engaged with other staff, right now. I'm sure he'll agree to see you. That is, if you don't mind waiting..."

"Of course not," Eleanor murmured.

Eyes lowered, she felt somewhat deflated though her fear gradually began to disperse. *It didn't matter really.* It wasn't as if they had anywhere else to go. In fact, the longer they remained in this establishment, the better. They were out of sight and in a place where no one would come looking for them. Backing out of the main reception area, they found a canteen.

Jake and Eleanor chose a table. Tucked in the farthest corner, the light from the windows didn't quite reach them. They sat in silence, sipping tea from dull china cups; but what was there left to say? Their situation had become grave. Jake had already voiced his concerns about the youths, wondering why they had targeted him. He had never ventured out without a disguise. It implied someone had identified him and in that case, did they also know who Eleanor was?

He was seized by a sudden shiver, lowering his teacup as he turned to her. Shuffling his chair a little closer, he curled his arm around her shoulder almost by instinct.

"Perhaps you were right," he sighed. "Maybe I should have agreed when you wanted to try to escape from London again. But after what happened the last time..."

Eleanor rested her head on his shoulder. "We still could, you know," she murmured. "It's not too late. It would help if I could open my bank account, so why don't we think about it."

They remained in the canteen for another hour, silently observing the people as they moved in circles around them.

Another ten minutes passed before Bernard finally appeared in the doorway. Eleanor braced herself. Filled with a sudden hope, neither of them could ignore how harassed he looked.

"I am so dreadfully sorry to have kept you waiting all this time," he flapped as they hurried up the staircase. "These meetings take up so much of our time. I couldn't get away."

He held the door open, ushering them inside his office before anyone else could distract them, waving towards the same wooden chairs as before.

"Don't apologise," Eleanor said as he closed the door. "We knew you were busy but thanks for agreeing to see us."

"Is everything alright with the bedsit?" Bernard enquired. "It's been a few weeks now... So how are things?"

"Not good," Jake said darkly, "which is the reason we came to see you."

Bernard seemed to study him. They saw him frown, wondering if he could sense their torment - Jake's expression must have reflected it.

"Whatever is wrong," he whispered anxiously.

Jake did not hold back. "Do you remember what we told you about having to hide from dangerous men? We think they may have found us.

Something very strange happened today. Two kids knocked into me. I thought they were drunk but they planted *this* inside my pocket."

Jake placed the suspicious package onto the desk. At first, Bernard looked at it as if reluctant to touch it. He gingerly picked it up.

"It's a package of drugs, isn't it?" Jake disclosed.

"Yes," Bernard replied without hesitation.

"Do you know what exactly?" Jake pressed him.

Bernard's frown deepened. Jake did not like the secrecy that was buried in his expression; as if he knew something they had been excluded from. Nevertheless, he waited patiently for an answer.

"It looks like heroin," Bernard nodded knowingly. "Nasty stuff and very addictive. Have you any idea of the mess people end up in? I've seen some terrible cases..."

"But someone planted it on him," Eleanor insisted. "Why would they do that?"

"I have no idea," Bernard sighed. "Is it possible, they were trying to get rid of it? I have to admit, this does seem a little strange..."

"There is something we haven't told you," Jake confessed, leaning closer. The distrust was still there, clearly mapped across Bernard's face but for now, he chose to ignore it. "First, can you promise to keep this secret? You are the only person we feel we can trust."

"Of course," Bernard murmured. A humble smile finally broke the lingering suspicion on his face. "I told you that from the start - anything you say will be kept in confidence."

"Okay," Jake continued. "In that case, I will tell you something else that is worrying us. We hear the police are after us. We found this out from Councillor Whaley. There are rumours going around that I am a drug dealer..."

He found himself scrutinising Bernard's face even closer. His features turned rigid. Jake swallowed deeply before he continued.

"It is a lie, Bernard. The gang who are hunting us are on our trail but this has nothing to do with *drug dealing*. We think the same men may have started this rumour, which makes our lives very difficult. It means we cannot go to the police for help even if we wanted to..."

"And you're certain about this?" Bernard questioned in horror.

"Yes," Jake said firmly. "The police tried to grab me at Waterloo Station! We had no idea why. We were hoping to get away. Worse, the station was full of men from this gang. They tried to trap us and I recognised one of them! These are the same men who tried to kill me, back in July!"

"Kill you?" Bernard gasped. The shock in his voice drained all the volume out of it.

"This is the reason we were desperate to find *you*," Eleanor insisted.

"Councillor Whaley warned us not to go to a mainline station but we ignored his advice. We had no idea something like this would happen. Jake is right, the police did turn up. Neither of us knew why they sprung on us like they did so we just ran! Maybe we shouldn't have done that but we were scared..."

"This is an outrage," Bernard whispered. Removing his glasses to polish them, there was no denying the distress in his eyes. "Why on earth would someone want to kill you, Jake?"

Jake sucked in another deep breath, unsure how much to tell him. Studying the older man's face, it struck him, he had nothing to lose. Whatever Bernard thought, *he was a good man.*

"It is a contract killing," he said shakily. "These men are from a criminal gang. I know this must sound strange but hiding from them is not enough any more - not now the police are involved. They say I'm a drug dealer yet someone planted this on me today."

"Do you believe us, Mr James?" Eleanor added, her tone filled with sorrow.

"Of course," Bernard said, his voice heavy with conviction. "I can tell you're not a drug dealer, Jake. I've met dealers! Some of our work regrettably brings us into contact with them but they are not like you! Shifty, arrogant and cocky for the most part, not at all nice people. You need no longer worry. I know you are telling the truth!"

Jake felt himself relax slightly. Twisting his hands together, he wondered what to say next. With time running out, they had almost reached the end of the line. Fear thudded its way through him though it appeared, Bernard had recognised their dilemma...

"Where is it you are trying to get to?" he asked him gently.

"Away from London," Jake said, "to Dover where we can catch a boat. I am from the Netherlands, Mr James and I just want to go home, where we can be safe; for Eleanor to meet my family. One day, maybe we will seek out the truth - find out why our lives have been threatened. But for now, it would be nice to get married - to look forward to the birth of our baby."

Bernard's eyes emitted a glint. Looking at Jake intently, he seemed to be hovering on the brink of a decision...

"I'll tell you what I am going to do then," he said. "I am going to drive you out of London and take you to the docks myself!"

Eleanor stared at him in amazement. "Would you really do that for us?" she gasped.

"Yes," Bernard nodded. "It horrifies me to hear your story. I can't understand why the police aren't doing more to protect you and as for these crime gangs... They are a blight on our city!"

"This is the best thing you could do for us, Mr James," Jake added softly. "Are you sure about this?"

"I'm true to my word," Bernard said. "First thing tomorrow, I will collect you from the bedsit. I'd do it tonight if I could but I've got this wretched meeting..."

"We understand," Jake said. He felt the beginnings of a smile but the moment was short-lived as another thought plagued him. "Just one more thing... Now these drugs have been planted, what happens if the police come round tonight? What if I am arrested?"

"If they arrest you, Jake, I will vouch for you," Bernard reassured him. "You were right to come to me. My word should carry some weight where the law is concerned and for that reason, I will keep this package as proof... in case I am required to give evidence. In the meantime, get yourself back to your flat and pack your things."

"Thank you, Mr James," Eleanor whispered.

In a world filled with dangerous enemies, his altruistic offer could not have been more timely. She wanted to hug him.

"You've been so very kind to us."

"I'll see you in the morning," Bernard smiled back. "Be ready by eight."

IV

They picked their way cautiously back along the same well-trodden path. The autumn days drew in faster now and it was already getting dark. Jake let himself into the bedsit first. After a tense interlude, a second figure slipped through the shadows. Eleanor crept into the tower block, grateful to see the lobby empty before she turned to the hidden corner by the staircase.

They gradually started to gather their belongings together. A chilly night, the thin concrete walls did nothing to ward off the cold. Eleanor put on her jeans, together with the cardigan she had brought with her. Unrolling the blanket Jake used for busking, she wrapped it around her shoulders.

Jake had settled into one of the thin wooden chairs, plucking at the strings of the guitar. He was still working on his third song. They had often wondered if the little rifts of music might be overheard from the communal lobby. If so, no one had shown any curiosity. They had met none of the other residents. This was the one place they had truly been on their own; a mysterious, subterranean existence, they were finally about to abandon. Jake gave a shiver of excitement.

"That's a pretty tune," Eleanor smiled. "Another new song?"

"Uh-Hmm," Jake murmured, working the chords into an introduction. "I finished writing it this morning before I went out. This is a song I wrote for *us*."

"Really?" Eleanor whispered, drawing herself close. "I can't wait to hear it. Have you played any of your new songs while you've been out?"

163

"Yes, I have," Jake grinned. A faint hint of colour warmed his cheeks. "I played the one with the long 'intro.' People actually seemed to *like it.*"

Eleanor pulled the blanket tighter around her shoulders and gazed at him. The light in the room was very dim. Cast by a single lamp, the glare of the bulb was obscured by a truncated shade. Yet it was a cold, insipid light, lacking in any warmth, unlike the candles they had grown to love in their previous home. It illuminated the planes of Jake's face. Shadows rested in the contours and his pale complexion gleamed. Eleanor studied him, taking in every little detail. His hair was beginning to grow long again; the silky auburn strands creeping to his collar. He was strumming a few experimental chords, his eyes lowered beneath their slender brows. The shadow of his eyelashes fell in soft, fine spikes.

"So, are you going to let me hear your new song?" she pressed.

Jake stopped playing, leaving the hum of the last note suspended.

"If you like. Just as long as it doesn't make you feel sad. I was inspired by everything we have been through. So this is how it goes..."

His long fingers worked the strings, filling the room with music.

"Memories like butterflies paint colours in my mind
From memories, come melodies, the words are hard to find
Our lives have been a mystery, where do we go from here?
The net around us closing tight, like birds we disappear...

We step into the dawn again, another brand new day
Who knows where we might find ourselves, the melody can't say
As birds we might fly free again should fortune have its way
To make the choice, to run, to hide, be predator or prey..."

Eleanor sat very still. At the end of each verse, Jake threaded in a light instrumental phrase; an enchanting melody in its own right. He launched into the final verse and as Eleanor listened, a rush of emotion sent shivers over her.

"Memories come floating in, the words are in this song
There is nothing I would want to change and nothing we did wrong
Our love has been a constant race, too strong to fade away,
Should love survive through life or death, our melodies will stay..."

The last chord trailed away into the silence and he stopped singing. For several seconds, neither of them moved. Eleanor appeared to be in some sort of trance as the fading notes of his song lingered. She looked up at him. Her eyes were like jewels as tears shone across the surface. He flashed her a gentle smile.

"Jake, that was beautiful," she whispered, her voice breaking huskily.

"You liked it?" he beamed, placing the guitar down on the bed. "Great!"

"Do you think you'll get back together with your band again?" she said, "once we're settled."

"Of course," he replied cheerfully. "It's been over three months since I saw them last so I hope we will keep going... If not, I will start a new band."

"Free Spirit," she pondered. "Is there a Dutch translation?"

"There is only one translation," Jake replied. "Vrije Geest but it doesn't have the correct meaning. Geest means ghost, which is not quite the same. Most bands have English names these days, anyway."

The interior of the room hung in silence again. Eleanor looked at her watch. It was almost midnight. Glancing around the room, it appeared just as bare and shabby as the day they had moved in. Like Jake, she seemed thrilled to finally be escaping from this place.

Peeling the blanket from her shoulders, she rose to her feet and wandered right up to him. He was still resting in the chair. She stroked the back of his hair and he closed his eyes, comforted by the tenderness of her touch...

For the short interim, they relished the ambience they had created.

Seconds later, a sound materialised outside the bedsit, causing Eleanor to flinch.

Jake's eyes flew open as he too braced himself. *Footsteps. Slow, creeping footsteps drawing themselves right up to the concealed entrance.* Jake felt the first prickle of cold. Rising to his feet, he found himself staring at the door, craning his head towards it. There was no longer any doubt that someone was outside. They gaped at each other in confusion.

Next, came the dull thud of a fist; a resolute, almost urgent sound which could not be ignored. Eleanor let out a gasp.

"Police?" Jake said in the faintest whisper. "Do you know I had a really bad feeling they might come here tonight. Eleanor, you have to hide..."

Without a moment's hesitation, Jake hauled back the carpet to expose the floorboards. He pulled them up one at a time, revealing the recess below. Eleanor shook her head, her face stark with panic as she stared into the gap. Jake took her arm gently.

"Come on, quick," he breathed into her ear. "We cannot ignore them forever. What if they break the door down? Bernard said if they arrested me, he would vouch for me."

The hammering resounded again. Eleanor gaped back at him, her eyes wide with terror.

Jake lowered his head and kissed her hard on the lips. "Please, Eleanor we agreed," he begged her.

He threw another glance at the gap in the floor.

The pounding on the door was resumed with a sudden violence. Whoever was outside, they were getting impatient. Crouching by the gap in the floor, Eleanor clutched Jake's hands.

"Jake, I'm so scared for you," she whimpered.

"Don't be," he replied, his voice barely audible.

He helped her into the space. Lowering herself onto the bare earth, she lay on her back, never once breaking eye contact...

"Why can't we *both* hide?" she hissed.

"Because they know I am here," Jake answered rapidly. "They will arrest us both, so just lie still and don't make a sound. Come and find me in the morning but for now, just remember how much I love you. We will be together again very soon..."

Once again, came the intrusive pounding on the other side of the door. Knowing he couldn't ignore it for very much longer, Jake replaced the first of the floor boards. He was beginning to fear, the police would kick their way in and if that happened, both of them would be detained and with no one on the outside to help them...

"Jake, please," Eleanor gasped as the boards started to close over her.

"Ssh, my love," Jake whispered. He gave a gentle smile. "Just keep yourself safe and keep our child safe. Everything will be fine..."

He had been about to replace the last floor board yet in the fragment of time left, he leaned down into the gap. Drawing his face close, his lips brushed over her own.

"I love you so much," she mumbled.

"And I love you," he finished tenderly. He hauled himself away from the recess.

With the boards slotted back in place, Eleanor was securely hidden beneath the floor.

The darkness enclosed her totally and as she lay there, eyes closed, she could feel the embers of his last kiss melting on her lips.

Jake rolled the carpet back over the floorboards and retreated from the space.

Creeping slowly towards the door, the thumping returned, only this time it was accompanied by a voice...

"Open up!" someone growled. "We know you're in there."

"Okay," Jake called back, "I'm coming! Can't a man even put some clothes on?"

He took a deep breath, ready to face whoever was out there. His hand trembled as he lowered it, gingerly reaching for the key; he was just on the

166

verge of turning it...

"You bastards," he muttered under his breath, unable to stop himself.

The key turned with a click.

Yet the door banged open without warning, causing Jake to leap back in shock.

One of them must have kicked it.

Recoiling into the room, he drank in the sight of the men filling the doorway but it was not the police. Jake felt the breath leave his body as he met the chilling, pale blue eyes of Dan Levy; the man he had recognised at Waterloo Station...

V

He backed into the shadows, unable to fend off the dread assailing his senses. Legs trembling, he watched as three men strolled into the room. The third locked the door, trapping them inside. Jake could hardly drag his eyes away from the blue-eyed one, yet couldn't resist seizing a glance at the other two... One was short and stockily built, his gnarled face similar to a bulldog. *Hired muscle,* Jake suspected. The third man was as tall as the first but with a muscular frame and a face which could only be described as craggy. His drooping dark moustache gave him the appearance of a Mexican bandit.

Hostile eyes raked over him as they made their advance, though Jake's thoughts were focussed on *one* person: *Eleanor. Thank God, he had hidden her.*

Breathing deeply, he felt a sudden charge of adrenalin; gripped by a fear so powerful, his limbs felt like jelly. Whatever happened next - one careless move, one glance in the wrong direction and her presence would be betrayed...

"Hallo, Jake," said the man with the blue eyes. "Long time, no see."

The pleasant cockney ring sounded almost friendly. Eyes picking over the bedsit, he seemed to scrutinise every detail.

Jake said nothing, any preliminary words eluding him. He dragged his fingers through his hair, his heart pumping wildly. Dan smiled.

"Best chain 'im up, Eddie," he ordered.

The short, ugly little man, known as *Eddie the Pit Bull* strode over and seized Jake's arms, hauling him back into the centre of the room. Jake struggled but it was pointless; the man was powerfully built and strong as an ox. Seconds later, he had wrestled Jake into the chair, his arms yanked behind his back. He felt the metallic snap of handcuffs around his wrists.

He felt his whole body freeze, reliving the nightmare from before...

"H-how did you f-find us?" he finally blurted. "Who told you we were here?"

"Doesn't matter," Dan snapped. "Thing is, we caught up with you in the end but first things first... Where's the girl, Jake?"

"She left," Jake replied, staring defiantly back at him.

"Bollocks!" Dan spat, drawing himself close. His eyes cut into him like scalpels. "See, we've been keeping an eye on this place, watching your every move. We know exactly 'ow you've been disguising yourselves... You in your big overcoat and woolly 'at! We've seen 'er an all, dressed as one of them Pakis. So where is she, Jake? I'm all ears!"

"I c-cannot help you," Jake spluttered, twisting his face away. "We separated. I told her to leave. I am the one everyone is after and I-I didn't want to put her in any more danger..."

Dan Levy narrowed his eyes.

"Right!" he muttered icily. "Have it yer own way. Let's tear this place apart, boys!"

Jake could barely take in the horror of it as the three men proceeded to turn the place upside down. They began by hauling the bed away from the wall. They tipped it on its side sending the covers sliding to the floor then tore away the mattress.

Next, they started on the cupboards; each one wrenched open and emptied as if they somehow expected to find Eleanor squashed inside. A mass of cooking pots rolled out of the first, followed by a volley of smashing crockery. Cups and glasses shattered as they landed on the floor. Jake closed his eyes, unable to bear the savagery of their actions.

Moving from one end of the flat to the other, their frenzied hunt continued.

One of them then stepped over the loose floor board. Jake tensed as the tell-tale creak sighed into the room but fortunately no one seemed to notice. Convinced they were sufficiently engrossed, Jake shuffled his chair over a fraction, repositioning the leg so that it rested on top of the board to pin it down. By this time they had reached the bathroom, which was so small, it would be impossible to conceal anyone. All the same, Levy and his men prodded at the panels lining the ceiling, as if hoping they would find some sort of loft space up there.

Face like thunder, he marched back into the living area. Yet Jake didn't move. Cuffed in his chair, he sat as still as a statue.

"Where is she?" Dan demanded.

"I have no idea," Jake replied. "Looking for her father maybe... Why are you so desperate to find her? I thought I was the one you wanted dead."

"Yeah, well the boss wants 'er found," Dan hissed back. "Far as we're concerned, you two are in this together... She complicated things, see, by letting you out of that cellar!"

"Does this mean you are going to kill her too?" Jake whispered in dread.

"Nah!" Dan smiled evilly. "Not kill! Though, I wouldn't want to be in that girl's shoes. She shouldn't 'ave interfered in our business... She knew who was she was taking on and she has to learn the rules. Little girls shouldn't fuck with the big boys! Not to forget that she's Chapman's daughter..."

"Yes," Jake said sadly, "I know. She told me about Theakston's vendetta. So why isn't he here tonight?"

"Oh, Dominic's on 'is way as we speak," Dan gloated. "Just as long as the coast is clear. 'E wouldn't wanna miss this for the world. In fact, he'll be pleased to see you, Jake."

A chill ran over him on hearing those words; it stemmed the very breath in his lungs. Jake lowered his eyes again. Deep down, he couldn't drive away the fear that Eleanor was still here, literally inches from where he sat... *and Theakston was coming.* He had to brace every muscle in his body to stop himself from trembling.

"Thank G-God she left," he shivered under his breath. "Y-you see, I would do anything to protect her from that monster..."

His words were cut off as Dan lashed out, delivering a hard slap across the side of his head. The force of it sent the stars spinning.

"Shut your mouth, boy!" he snarled. "No one insults the boss!"

"I am sure he's been called worse things," Jake taunted back and raising his eyes, a sudden anger consumed him. "What sort of man is he to rape a man's sixteen year old daughter? And to threaten to film it! I have never heard anything so monstrous!"

"So Dominic wanted a bit of fun with 'er!" Dan sneered. "So what? This was a gang war and there ain't no happy endings. But this ain't just about some *frightened little girl* no more, this is about you, Jake and you were ours! She 'ad no right to interfere..."

Next came a gentle tap on the door.

Dan inclined his head, glancing at the hard-faced man with a nod. "Speak of the devil!" his voice rang out tunefully. He cast his eyes back to Jake and smiled. "Or shall we call 'im *the monster?* Let 'im in, Monty."

Jake froze as he heard the click of the key being turned.

A fourth man entered the room.

Jake did not even have to look around. His very presence seeped into the bedsit from those slow, sauntering footsteps to the towering shadow thrown across the carpet. Jake's heart had already started pounding again. Theakston strolled casually around to the front of the chair he was confined in and stared into his eyes.

This was the first time Jake had ever really seen the man properly; younger than expected, *maybe only a few years older than himself.* The cold light in the room captured the planes of his face, the hardness of his complexion gleaming and unlined. His face wore no expression yet his slanted eyes burned black as they penetrated his own.

"Jake Jansen," Dominic muttered tonelessly. "Finally, we meet again. Been a long search, but we found you in the end, just as you knew we would."

Jake was momentarily stunned, unable to shake off the notion, this man was here to kill him.

"Where's the girl?" he added, an evilness creeping into his voice.

"She is gone," Jake whispered. His voice left a melancholy echo. He could feel his breath trembling on his lips as he said it, wishing more than anything else that this could be a dream.

"Afraid it's true, Dominic," Dan confirmed. "As you see, we've turned this place on its 'ead but with no luck..."

Dominic started to pace around the bedsit, observing the chaos; the damage left by his men who had clearly ripped it apart. His expression remained blank though Jake sensed a shift in the atmosphere; the flicker of tension in the man's jaw, the way every contour in his face tightened. Jake could imagine his desolation.

With a deep sigh, Dominic reached into his top pocket and pulled out his cigarettes. He plucked one from the tin and lit it.

"Shame," he muttered coldly. "But never fear, we will track her down. As you've probably guessed, I am not a man to back down."

In the next second, he spun on his heel, glaring at Jake with growing malevolence. He stepped closer to the chair. Jake struggled instinctively against the biting cuffs, unable to control the sudden fear that arose in him.

"Please," he gasped. "You don't have to do this! Eleanor and I are no threat to you people, why can't you just let this go?"

"Aw c'mon, Jake," Dominic drawled, "you know we can't do that. If we don't see this through tonight they're only gonna hire someone else to do it. Besides, I stand to lose a lot, if this all goes tits up again. But that's life for you... and life's full of shit."

Jake shook his head in despair, his torment finally rising to the surface.

"Face facts," Dominic continued icily. "You were never gonna get away from this, kid, you're a *marked man*. There ain't a single place you could go where they wouldn't have followed you. Not even Holland. Fact is, someone quite high up wants you dead, son. We'd have dealt with you three months ago if your girlfriend hadn't got in the way."

"Stop it," Jake shivered. "None of this had anything to do with Eleanor. She has never meant you any harm..."

"But that's where you're wrong," Dominic hissed. "Have you any idea of the shit I've had to put up with, since she let you out of that basement?"

"She knew I was about to be killed!" Jake protested.

"So?" Dominic spat back. "What were you to her? Nothing! She didn't even know you. We had you right where we wanted and she couldn't resist fucking it up!"

Jake closed his eyes in dread. The man was obsessed.

"She said she couldn't leave me," he whispered, desperate to make the man see reason. "That is the sort of person she is. She cared for my life, even if I *was* just some stranger."

"Oh, spare me the sentimental crap," Dominic sneered. He turned to the others in the room. "You sure she's not here? You absolutely positive?"

The stifling silence confirmed everything Jake wanted them to believe. His heart slowed to a slow and heavy thump and he felt the weight of the other man's stare. Their eyes locked.

"Best get this over with then," Dominic whispered.

The tension in the room had reached breaking point where nobody spoke or moved. Jake waited, empty of the desire to fight any more. *It was almost over.*

Dominic took one last drag of his cigarette before stamping it out on the floor. Reaching inside his leather coat, he drew out a gun.

Jake watched in a dream, assailed by a sudden bleakness. "So, this is the end is it?"

"Yeah," Dominic sighed, "afraid so. Though I must say, it gives me no pleasure, son."

Pausing for a moment, he said something that surprised everyone in the room.

"If you really wanna know, I think it's a tragic waste. You've got talent, kid. You see, I heard you busking by the shops today... and you were good!"

Jake battled against the sting of tears, determined to stay strong.

Raising his head he stared directly into Dominic's eyes. The other man stared back at him, his expression as cold and deadpan as ever. He pointed the weapon at his forehead. Jake noticed, he was left-handed; it seemed such a trivial detail... Yet strangely enough, he felt no more fear, the atmosphere inside the bedsit growing ever more dreamlike.

Dan Levy snatched a cushion from the floor. Jake watched numbly and for that moment, he could see his whole life flashing before his eyes... Yet his focus clung to the last three months spent with Eleanor. Theakston was right in one respect; *he should have died the first time his men planned to kill him.* No one would have known a thing about it. He would have silently vanished.

Eleanor had bought him some extra time; time to fall in love and end his life on a high note. He knew he couldn't cheat death a second time. He clung to the hope that she and their child would be safe; that *someone* lived on to tell his tale and that somehow, his life would never completely be over... Just as he cherished that thought, Dan stepped forward and pressed the cushion against his head. Jake closed his eyes.

"Anything else you wanna say?" Dominic's voice registered subliminally.

"I hope I won't be forgotten," Jake finished softly, "and as for Eleanor... I do love her, you know. I will always be watching over her..."

He sensed the proximity of the gun looming, the weapon cocked, the trigger about to be pulled... And within the blink of an eye, his life was extinguished in a single shot.

PART 4. THE AFTERMATH

Chapter 10

I

She was starting to come round. The next time Eleanor opened her eyes, she found herself in a hospital bed, surrounded by white walls and an all-consuming silence... Her head felt heavy from the sedatives they had given her but they did nothing to block out the memories.

They were slipping back into place right now.

Hidden beneath the floorboards, she had been entombed in the darkness. The bare earth felt chilly and as the cold seeped into her bones she started to shiver.

The crash of the door had jolted her. Next came the distinctive voice of the man Jake had described; *musical with a strong London accent.*

Theakston's men were in the flat, sending her mind into chaos.

She had heard every word of their chilling conversation; the destruction they had wreaked while searching for her. She could never understand how she had managed to lie so still... Yet she had recognised the drag of Jake's chair across the floorboard, stifling its creak; he was so desperate to protect her. *So where was he now?*

Eleanor gripped the bedcovers, her mind spinning in terror. There was no mistaking Dominic Theakston's entrance, a notion that compelled her to freeze. As the sound of his voice echoed directly above, her hands had wound themselves around her belly by instinct. Starkly aware of the baby growing inside her, she was driven by her pledge to protect it.

Words drifted in and out of focus as the hideous scene played out. She was recalling every warning... *It's not money Theakston rules by, it's terror... He's a sadistic piece of scum!* They were Sammie's words. Next, Harvey's warnings came flooding back to her... *we all know he's a man with no mercy, 'specially when he starts swinging that little sack of stones of his...* Her breath starting coming faster. What if he was planning to use that weapon on her? The chances were she would lose the baby. Eleanor closed her eyes.

The icy chill was beginning to overwhelm her. Numb with cold, she started shivering, the tremors gradually increasing in intensity. They came in spasms, each more violent than the last and as the iciness penetrated her body, she could no longer feel her fingers or toes. Even her legs were beginning to lose feeling. The blackness had been closing in on her, moments before Theakston's final words cut through the floorboards... *Anything else you wanna say?*

She had assimilated Jake's response, the words almost amplified. The detail had been so sharp, he could have been whispering in her ear; the subtle break in his voice blended with the slur of his beautiful Dutch accent... Yet she heard the muted 'pop' that followed; the last thing that registered before her mind plunged into a state of obscurity.

Delirious with shock, coupled with the bitter cold, Eleanor drifted in and in and out of consciousness, unsure whether she was alive or dead. She could no longer discern what was imagination or real... only that some while later, there had been another disturbance.

Obviously, the police had arrived. People were lingering... There was a rumpus of activity. Only then did Eleanor start sobbing. Her fists thumped against the floor boards, until finally one of them shifted and someone was aware of her presence.

"Dear God, she's been buried alive..."

She was barely conscious as her trembling body was lifted out of the recess. Shapes moved all around her; faceless shadows, wrapping her in blankets, cautiously guiding her outside. An even sharper chill snapped at her senses. There were blue lights everywhere. They flashed and rotated, alternately turning the world from darkness to brightness. She felt as if she was hallucinating, staring blankly ahead, searching for him. *But where was he? Where was Jake?*

Somewhere in the fog of her consciousness, a car caught her eye but it was not a police car.

Dark and gleaming, it lurked in the shadows, not quite out of range of the blue light shimmering across its bonnet. The face of a man had been illuminated. *Councillor Whaley?* He saw her too, a moment his eyes turned shifty. Like a rabbit caught in a glare of headlights, he had fired up the ignition and without delay, sped away into the night.

Eleanor could no longer make sense of it. She thought he was their ally. Couldn't he have at least stepped out of his car to ask what had happened? Even in her confused state, her mind grappled at the truth. Theakston's men had known exactly where to find them; it implied that someone else had revealed their hiding place! Could that person have been Councillor Whaley? For what other reason would he be hidden there, observing the scene?

Eleanor started shaking again but next, came the onset of hysteria. From the moment they wrestled her into an ambulance, she could not stop screaming...

The aftermath was a blur but here she was, lost in some hospital and still the memories kept barging into her mind; the nurses, the needles, the consensus that she was suffering from *hypothermia* and *shock*. Yet from some secret corner of her mind, the worst truth of all was beginning to emerge. *Jake couldn't be dead, he just couldn't be.*

174

Eleanor felt the misery swelling inside her as the horror of it sank in. She started to cry. To think, they had been on the verge of leaving for the docks, away from London, away from their enemies and now it was all too late! Her sobs were coming harder just as another nurse slipped into the room.

"You poor child," she muttered. "Come on, don't get yourself into a state again."

She seemed kind, fussing over her in an attempt to calm her. She tried adjusting the pillows to make her more comfortable, stroking her hair from her forehead. Except nothing could ease the shudders that wracked her body, nor prevent her cries of torment.

Minutes later, Eleanor found herself staring at a tall elderly man. Dressed in a white coat, his face wore a grave expression.

"Take a deep breath, now," he ordered her gently.

He took her hand. But no sooner had he done this when the nurse reappeared at his side, a syringe positioned between her deft fingers.

Eleanor gaped at them in horror, her gasps of breath accelerating. There was no denying what they were about to do yet she seemed powerless to prevent it.

"Please," she managed to whimper.

"This is for your own good," the doctor reassured her. "You've had a terrible shock... you'll feel better in a moment."

She watched in a dream as the nurse slid the needle into the crook of her elbow. Gradually her surroundings became hazy, her head heavy as a cannon ball and as she slumped against the pillows, she could feel herself sinking back into a world of oblivion.

They kept her heavily sedated but what else could they do? Doctor Matherson was of the *old school*. Fully knowledgeable in curing physical ailments, dealing with a patient's emotional condition was all a bit of a mystery to him... He was baffled to know what to do in Eleanor's case; a girl discovered buried beneath a high rise block of flats. As if to make matters worse, there was talk of her boyfriend being murdered in the same room.

He shuddered to imagine the ordeal she had suffered yet there were other patients to attend to. Every time the sedatives wore off, Eleanor became hysterical. Her screams echoed around the corridors, sending staff and patients into panic.

So they kept administering the sedatives. It wasn't an ideal solution but filled him with the hope, her demons might eventually settle...

Regrettably there had been visitors.

First on the scene was the social worker; a man by the name of Bernard James. He seemed exceptionally distressed over her circumstances, wishing for nothing more than to reassure her... Doctor Matherson was reluctant.

Right now, Eleanor was no fit state to talk to anyone. Just before he left however, he had divulged the news that she was also pregnant.

The second, more persistent visitor was the police officer: *Inspector Norman Hargreaves*. Driven by a dogged sense of duty, he was yearning to question her over what had happened that night. Matherson shook his head. The poor girl was too traumatised to be interrogated over such a sensitive matter, though he had some problem explaining this...

Hargreaves on the other hand, refused to give in and after two days of pressure, the doctor had finally consented to a visit.

"Try not to upset her," he pleaded. "Her condition is extremely fragile."

Norman Hargreaves knew he was being unreasonable but what else could he do?

Almost everything had gone to plan. After a painstakingly long wait, they had achieved their goal; six insufferably long weeks, biding their time, waiting for the couple to settle, thinking they were safe... until Theakston had dealt with Jake with the same cold-blooded efficiency Hargreaves expected of him.

The killing was over. With his body wrapped in a blanket they had driven off into the night unseen. Just before departing, a few more wraps of heroin were hidden inside the bedsit, adding substance to Jake's death sentence. Few people would question the nature of this crime; it would go down as another drug-related murder between gangs.

With Norman insistent on leading the murder enquiry, he recruited his two most incompetent detectives to handle the finer details. This included a forensic examination of the bedsit as well as the victim; a body, which had been discarded in an empty warehouse only to be discovered 24 hours later. He guessed the detectives hadn't been that thorough in the way they logged the evidence - nor did they find any other suspicious circumstances. He hoped they were in the clear; that whatever secrets Jake had discovered had died with him and no one had anything to fear...

But nothing was ever straight forward. Just as the horrors of that night began to settle like a deep, dark pool, ripples disturbed the surface and now their plans lay in jeopardy.

Despite all their careful planning, Eleanor Chapman had resurfaced. She had never gone her separate way as Jake had implied. To think, for all that time she had been hidden under the floorboards.

Residents in the block had become curious, alerted to a disturbance. Someone called the police. Convinced they had heard a banging sound, they discovered the door to the secret bedsit. For some reason it had been left unlocked. This was the moment they had discovered her, still alive but hanging onto her sanity by a thread.

Norman felt a creeping chill. Eleanor Chapman stood on the verge of ruining everything and this was what had brought him to the London Royal Hospital.

Hovering outside her room, he allowed the doctor's words to sink in. He couldn't help wondering how serious her condition really was. Yet at the same time, he was hankering to meet her; this enigmatic girl who had rescued Jake from captivity, the half-caste daughter of the notorious Ollie Chapman, who Theakston was obsessed in finding...

Norman took a deep breath then wandered into her room.

There was something ethereal about her appearance. Slumped against the pillows, her long hair fanned out from the sides of her face, her slender arm hooked to a drip.

Studying her features, Norman had expected her to be different; darker perhaps, more discernibly Afro-Caribbean. Yet her complexion was drained of colour, pale as plaster of Paris against the shining tendrils of dark hair. Dressed in a plain white nightdress, her face free of makeup, she looked vulnerable like a child.

He lowered himself into a chair, his mind so crammed with questions he could not resist tapping her shoulder to arouse her. Shifting slightly, she gradually opened her eyes. At first she emitted a gasp before shrinking deeper into the pillows. Norman was not deterred. Despite his ruthless attitude, he knew how to handle people who were victims...

"Eleanor Chapman?" he began lightly. "It's okay. There is no need to be frightened."

She turned very still and for a second, the two of them surveyed one another. Norman was initially stunned by the beauty of her eyes, yet troubled by the look of pain in them. He didn't think he had ever witnessed such torment on the face of another human being.

"I am so sorry to disturb you," he continued. "I gather you went through a dreadful ordeal but I do need to ask some questions about what happened that night..."

Eleanor struggled into a sitting position.

"Jake's dead, isn't he," she croaked.

"I'm afraid so," Norman sighed.

The sound that escaped her lips made him flinch; an unrelenting wail of anguish which reminded him of a tortured puppy. The next thing he knew, she was crying.

He lowered a caressing hand on her arm, discovering skin that was meltingly soft. Once again, it struck him, how child-like she seemed.

"Come now, don't cry," he responded firmly. "He is at peace now. Whatever happened, the end was very quick. I doubt if he would have felt a thing..."

"But Jake was *murdered*," she managed to splutter through her sobs.

"So I gather," Norman nodded, "which is the reason I am here. Now is it possible, you could explain what you were doing beneath those floor boards?"

"Hiding," Eleanor shivered. "It was the only place... somewhere they'd never find me."

"Hiding?" Norman repeated, leaning his face close. "You mean you already *suspected* you were in danger?"

Her startled eyes danced in terror. "Jake and I have been in hiding for weeks! We've known all along that someone was trying to kill him..."

Norman raised his eyebrows, prompting her to continue, even though her tears hadn't yet abated; they spilled over her cheeks like raindrops down a window pane.

"I believe you, Eleanor," he kept pressing her. "I am leading the murder enquiry, so it is essential you tell me everything you know. Now, for how long were you were under the floorboards and did you hear anything?"

Gradually, she became less agitated. He saw her frown, wishing he could read the thoughts turning themselves over in her mind. There was something hidden in her expression that stirred him and despite his cold heart, this blatant exposure of grief was beginning to niggle a little...

"Tell me," he begged her.

She pressed her eyes shut in agony then finally started speaking.

Every scene was articulated painfully; from the moment a number of men had barged their way into the flat, to the savagery of their search...

"They smashed the place apart, looking for me," she kept sobbing, "b-but Jake never gave in. He told them I'd left, I could hear them interrogating him..."

Pausing for a second, she seemed to be panting as if she had run out of breath.

"Go on," Norman encouraged.

"They told him, Theakston was coming. He's the one who's been searching for us, the man we were hiding from... He was there!"

Hargreaves squirmed in his chair, wary of her sudden mood shift. Her tears may have subsided but what he was witnessing now was a fear so powerful, it unnerved him.

"And you're certain, it was the same man?" he frowned.

"Yes," she whispered. "I went into shock. He does that to people... That scary voice of his, the sound of his footsteps pacing around like he does. I knew straight away, it was him."

"I see," Norman responded numbly. *She depicted him so well.* "So what else can you tell me?"

Fresh tears rolled over her wet cheeks. Norman passed her a tissue.

"I felt s-so cold. I could hardly move. Part of me wanted to fade away and die. I loved him, you see. I loved Jake so much..."

Hargreaves felt his jaw tense up. He was finding this more difficult than he had imagined. He could no longer deny, he wanted Jake Jansen dead more than anyone but to see this girl, poleaxed with grief...

"I'm sorry," he said gently. "I wish I knew what to say. You on the other hand, *survived*. You could have died too, that night, it is lucky you were found."

Eleanor's hands slid down to her abdomen. Norman frowned. For the first time, he noticed the subtle curve in her shape. It seemed incongruous, given how thin she was.

"Yes, I suppose I am lucky in one way," she murmured through her tears. "At least we've saved our child..."

"You're pregnant?" Norman breathed.

"Yes," Eleanor said.

Once again, the two of them looked at one another. Eleanor's face seemed calmer now, almost at peace. Norman however, was experiencing a swell of guilt; something he had never expected. Shoving it to one side, he forced himself to concentrate on his true motives.

"I'm sorry," he repeated. "This must be terrible for you. Is there anything else you remember?"

"I-I thought I heard a gun shot," she finished shakily.

"But did you manage to catch any further conversation?" Norman frowned.

He saw the fear spread across her face again, a sudden desolation in her eyes. "Only that he's coming after me now," she whimpered.

"Coming after you," Norman echoed. "But that is not going to happen, Eleanor." His cool, professional tone sounded unconvincing even to him.

"Theakston will never stop searching for me," she whispered. "He'll hurt me, I know he will! I could lose my baby. He's just killed the man I loved..."

She broke off again, the sobs rising violently. With growing dread, Hargreaves sensed she was on the verge of hysteria.

"Th-this is an-another thing..." she shuddered. "There was a p-policeman involved! Someone on the inside, s-someone who helped them! H-how will I ever be safe?"

Norman rose to his feet, his heart crashing inside his ribs as the implications of her words sliced through him.

"Please help me," she just about managed to squeak. "You h-have got to arrest him..."

"Eleanor, calm down," Norman ordered, desperate to resume some authority. "The police will do whatever it takes to protect you. You have no reason to be afraid, this is nonsense..."

He felt the lie trip off the edge of his tongue, wary of the dilemma he now faced. Could he really bring himself to hand her over to Theakston, knowing she was pregnant? Only *he* knew the atrocities about to be committed and the notion pained him; more so, now he had met her. Unable to bear it a second longer, he needed time to think. *He had to close the interview.*

Rising to his feet, he peered through the glass partition. His eyes scoured the corridor, desperate to capture someone's attention. People shuffled backwards and forwards in staggered lines until he caught the eye of a nurse. Norman gave Eleanor one last sympathetic glance before he inched his way towards the door.

"I think I had better leave," he said. "I'm sorry if my questions have upset you..."

Turning, just as the nurse swooped to her side, he could not handle any more torment. He had barely managed to escape however, when he came face to face with doctor Matherson.

The other man's eyes grew cold.

"I thought I asked you not to upset her," he snapped.

"I didn't mean to," Norman retorted. "It was just an interview. I *had to* know the truth..."

"A truth that is very painful," the doctor persisted. "I suspect we'll have to sedate her again."

"Seems the best solution," Norman finished, offering his most reassuring a smile.

By the time he vacated the hospital, he definitely wasn't smiling.

Eleanor's words clanged inside his head like a warning bell; a situation that left him floundering. With a silent shiver, he knew who he had to contact next...

By the time he returned to his desk, he felt drained. The sight of Eleanor in her bereaved state had derailed him - but there was more... A sharper fragment of his brain had long wrestled with the notion of what she knew. *She had mentioned a policeman*; did this imply, she had some inkling of the real reason Jake had been killed?

Palms clammy with sweat, Norman slumped into his chair.

He glanced at the notes scribbled on his telephone pad, which included three missed telephone messages from Theakston, the last marked URGENT. Norman felt the atmosphere around him turn black. In truth, he had been ignoring his calls on the grounds, he was too busy.

Plagued with the same fear he had experienced since leaving the hospital, time was of the essence. He was going to have to talk to him at some point and now seemed an opportune time to suggest a meeting; somewhere private.

"Finally!" Dominic snarled into the receiver. "You took your time, didn't you? What the fuck is going on?"

"I'd listen to what I have to say before you take that tone," Norman snapped icily. "First, I suggest you get yourself a rock solid alibi. *She knows everything.*"

His words were met with a gulf of silence.

"Yes," he added with a hint of satisfaction. "I've just spoken to the girl."

"Where is she?" Dominic whispered dangerously.

"Never mind that," Norman said. "The fact is, she identified you, which means I'll have to issue a warrant for your arrest. I can't discuss this now but I will be calling round to your apartment after dark. So make sure you're there and as for an alibi... make sure it's one that will stick."

He slammed down the receiver, without even bothering to catch a reply.

II

In the daytime, Whitechapel was filled with a heady jumble of activity. Lively shop owners and market traders ran their day to day lives, whilst colourful characters such as musicians and clowns entertained the crowds; people spilled out of pub doorways, there was much shouting and occasionally fights broke out. But by nightfall, the mood changed with the darkness of the sky; a place where the high brick walls trapped the residents like rats in a maze. Danger lurked in every hidden corner. There were drunks sleeping in doorways and in the boots of abandoned cars, a litter of broken bottles, cigarette butts and beer cans scattered in the gutter.

Most menacing of all, those streets were regularly patrolled by Theakston's men. Cruel-faced, shady thugs for the main part, they injected a terror into the community that excelled Sammie Maxwell's reign. A growing volume of business owners paid for 'protection' without quibbling and few defaulted. Those who did were dealt with brutally, more so than Norman Hargreaves would have liked. He could detect an atmosphere of violence in the chilly air as he stepped out of his car. Theakston's home lingered a few yards away in a shabby apartment block.

Norman hauled the communal door open, wrinkling his nose with distaste. The hallway stunk of floor cleaner which did not quite disguise the underlying smell of piss... a niggling legacy left by the younger residents. Out all night partying, they would stagger home drunk, creating extra noise and havoc. He couldn't understand how Dominic could stand it, despite growing up in an even *worse* slum. Closing his mind to the squalor of his environment, Norman marched down the hallway to the far end and rapped on the apartment door.

The door was opened. Shuffling inside, Norman closed it quietly where Dominic stood facing him. Neither man spoke at first. He made a small gesture with his head as if to coax him into the lounge. A sparsely furnished room, it contained a brown leather settee and matching armchair. The only other item of furniture was a flimsy-looking unit sagging under the weight of a record player and TV set. The telephone lay on the floor, unplugged. In fact, there was nothing cosy about this room. Minimalist and functional, it lacked any ambience. The only light source appeared to be a desk lamp. It threw a dim white flare across the floor which reminded Norman of an interrogation cell.

"Take a seat," Dominic said softly. "Want anything to drink?"

"Got any beer?" Norman replied. He massaged his throat, which was as dry as sandpaper.

Without a word, Dominic spun around and vanished into a tiny kitchen. Norman lowered himself into the armchair just as he reappeared with a can of beer but no glass. With a sigh, he yanked back the ring pull and took a swallow. The other man crashed down in the settee opposite, fixing him with his cold, blank stare. He reached for his cigarettes and lit one.

"So," Dominic began, "Eleanor Chapman was hidden there all along."

"I'm afraid so," Norman replied. He saw Dominic's eyes narrow, quick to raise a palm to silence him. "No... Don't say anything, just let me finish. She knows you were there, Dominic! She heard your men talking about you and she heard your voice... Naturally, I'm as dismayed about this as anyone. I'd be the first to congratulate you on your success in handling this job, but this does rather put you in the frame..."

"She won't say anything," Dominic interrupted him. "I'll see to that! This bitch just needs a good scare..."

"That won't be necessary," Norman scoffed, taking another swig of beer. "You never saw the state she was in earlier. She is terrified of you!"

"Good," Dominic said icily. "Then let's make sure it stays that way, then maybe she'll keep her mouth shut. Now you can start by telling me where she is."

"She's in hospital," Norman answered, "suffering from severe shock. Staff are keeping a very close eye on her but apart from that, she's being sedated."

A heavy pause ensued as Dominic took this in. Silent and still, he sat there smoking, pondering over what Norman had divulged. Gradually the tension in his face began to drop. But as Norman guessed, he felt no pity; more irritation, they hadn't found her and pulled her out from under the floorboards themselves. The moment was short-lived. The fact was Eleanor was confined inside the walls of a hospital, scared out of her wits and powerless to do a thing.

A feeling of sudden triumph pounded in his veins. He let his head roll back and blew out a smoke ring. *She was as good as theirs.*

"What are you worried about?" he drawled. "Finally got rid of the Jansen boy and we've pretty much got Eleanor in our hands... Couple of months back, you were giving me shit because they escaped. So why all the doom and gloom?"

He released a smile, unable to hold back his euphoria.

"You seem very confident about all this," Norman sneered. "You do realise, I have to arrest you now. So did you do as I suggested and find an alibi?"

"Of course," Dominic said, his smile lingering. "At least a dozen people will swear I was at the Dog and Duck, right up until closing time - had a couple of whiskies then hung about outside until well after midnight, chatting up a couple of birds! That good enough for you?"

"Who's willing to vouch for you?" Norman pressed.

"Landlord and a few of the regulars," Dominic said, "including old Harry."

"Old Harry," Hargreaves spluttered. "Like anyone is going to listen to that old piss head."

"Still an alibi," Dominic argued. "So what happens now?"

"We'll be back tomorrow," Norman told him. "I'll bring a couple of regular officers to make the arrest, so just go along with it for the sake of appearances. Don't worry. We won't be bringing charges, especially if your alibi sticks and as for young Eleanor... Let's just say that if she even gets as far as making a statement, which I doubt, it won't be reliable. Given her state of mind, anything she says is going to sound delusional and paranoid..."

"The sooner you hand her over to me, the quicker we can make sure she never says anything," Dominic added in a chilling tone.

Norman drained his beer, belched softly and crushed the can in his fist. He exhaled a troubled sigh as the more harrowing memories of Eleanor's interview came back to him. Dominic, who seemed to be him watching him carefully, tilted his head to one side.

"Well?" he pressed.

"I can't do that," Norman disclosed. "You see, there's a further complication..."

"You what?" Dominic hissed, springing to his feet. "We had an agreement, Hargreaves! I swore we'd deal with the Jansen boy if you offered me Eleanor in return!"

With his earlier self-satisfied smile truly wiped off his face, he glowered down in fury. Before Norman could draw breath, he had already started pacing from one side the room to the other.

"I made no assurances, Dominic," Norman insisted. "Situations change. The first problem is her emotional state! She is aware you're after her and the very concept sent her into hysterics. She knows you intend to hurt her."

"So what?" Dominic threw back at him. "I spent over three months hunting for that bitch and it's time she paid the price for all the trouble she's caused. What, you're telling me you want to let her off the hook now? What the hell's turned you so soft?"

"She's pregnant," Norman told him bluntly.

Dominic paused mid step and spun around. "So?" he sneered.

"Isn't it obvious," Norman spat, eyes narrowing in contempt. "She's scared she'll lose the baby! Got some notion you're going to beat the shit out of her and she's right isn't she?"

Dominic released a hiss. The news seemed to have floored him but as he slumped back down on the settee and grabbed another cigarette, his fury had clearly not abated; it blazed in his eyes and manifested itself in every flash of movement.

"Okay, so we won't go overboard," he said a little too quickly, "not if she's pregnant. Shit, Norman, even I've got some principles! I take it, this is Jansen's kid?"

"Yes," Norman snapped. "The trouble is, it is not just your future at stake but mine and I'm not sure I can trust you. You said you wanted to *teach her a lesson*. That, coupled with the fact, she is Ollie Chapman's daughter suggests you're hell-bent on revenge."

Dominic gave a shrug. "Chapman returned before didn't he? Before we even laid a finger on her..."

"But you're a violent man, Dominic," Hargreaves argued, "and everyone knows that. Men like you don't back down and I'm sorry if I'm concerned about the girl's safety but all things considered, it's not a matter of whether you can promise not to hurt her... more a case of how will you be able to stop yourself?"

Dominic's eyes flashed.

"There is of course, another reason I can't hand her over to you," Norman finished, fixing him with his own cold stare. "We don't know how much she knows, which is why I prefer to keep her under my supervision for now. So try and get a grip will you. We got rid of the Jansen boy, which means you've redeemed yourself. You get to keep your status as crime boss and will receive a substantial pay packet on top."

"I'm giving half to Dan," Dominic intervened, drawing deeply on his cigarette. "No one could have helped me more with this business than he did."

"That's up to you," Norman finished. "Just as long as you stay away from

184

the Chapman girl. We are in the middle of a very delicate situation here and until I get to interrogate her properly, we could be sitting on a powder keg... So leave her be. Because you might as well know, she saw Robin that night too and he is shitting himself!"

With those words, Dominic let out a loud laugh.

"Brilliant," he smirked. "That'll teach the stuck up bastard, not everything in this world runs like clockwork. So what's *he* planning to do about it?"

Norman's icy stare didn't waver. "Stirring up as much shit in the press about young Jansen as possible, which those drugs your men planted should substantiate very nicely! You see, whatever Eleanor knows about this killing, I intend to quash it. She has no one left to turn to, nor anyone who will back up *her* version of events. We should be safe, just as long as we're careful."

"Fair enough," Dominic relented. "Just one last thing. I want you to keep me informed! Watch her every move, where she goes and when she has her kid... Do that for me and I promise I'll stay well away from her."

"That's okay then," Hargreaves said and rising to his feet, he forced a smile.

"At least for now," Dominic finished, offering him a chilling smile in return.

III

As the days wore on, Eleanor's world sank deeper into the darkness, a silent tunnel of oblivion where the pain couldn't reach her. The further she retreated, the more she could escape from the heart-breaking reality of everything that had happened to her. This was the only way she could suppress the memories; forget that terrible night in the bedsit and languish in a surreal world where she felt anaesthetised and safe.

Yet every time the drugs wore off, that world crumbled away, leaving her broken.

At times, she made a feeble attempt to crawl forward; to accept the pain and face up to her loss but it was unbearable. Her mind filled up with memories; delightful chapters of the life they had shared in Forest Haven. Despite being in hiding, her mind and body had been awakened; the books, the conversations, the bedrooms where they had blissfully made love...

She could see Jake now. The clarity of detail teased her senses, from the depths of his green eyes to his wonderful wide smile - his curtain of auburn hair gleaming as he moved. These brief recollections revived all the pain, a torment so excruciating it brought the tears flowing... and in no time at all, she found herself shuddering in the grip of hysteria again.

At times like this, she was thankful of the sedatives they kept administering, her only respite from the agony of losing him.

On one of those nights however and just as she found herself slipping towards consciousness, she chose to lie very still. Dimly aware of a nurse watching over her, the doctor seemed to be hovering. She could hear a murmur of conversation but on this occasion, she did not stir. Cocooned under the bed covers, she let the words drift over her head, listening but not quite connected to the real world. They must have assumed she was sleeping, their words fading in and out like intermittent radio waves...

"Is there nothing more we can do? How long has she been here now?"

"Five days," resounded the voice of Doctor Matherson, "and you're right. Maybe she is beyond our help. I feel sure she should have turned a corner by now yet she doesn't seem to be making much progress."

"We can't keep her sedated indefinitely..." the nurse whispered back.

The doctor exhaled a sigh. "No, we can't but her mind is too fragile to accept the magnitude of what has happened..."

Eleanor sensed the woman turning away. A slight breeze as she moved, she heard her shoe scrape across the floor.

"Some people can cope with the burden of grief," the doctor kept saying, "but others are not so strong. She is also very young..."

"What are you suggesting?" the nurse's voice echoed, further away now.

"A psychiatrist would be the next step. Maybe she'd be better off in an institution. She's obviously suffered some sort of breakdown, which means I cannot help her any more..."

Eleanor turned numb. Every muscle in her body froze and she didn't dare make a move, nor betray the truth that she was hanging onto every thread of their discussion.

"Seems a little extreme," the nurse's voice rose up sharply. "What about her baby?"

"This is out of our hands," replied the doctor. *Eleanor could almost hear the shrug in his voice.* "Let the authorities take over. They'll know what is best for her..."

Eleanor opened her eyes. The room had lapsed into shadow and as she stared at the wall, those final devastating words sank in. She flung back the bedcovers with a gasp.

She allowed her hand to slide into her lap, stroking her abdomen. A single tear trickled down her cheek as she remembered her promise to keep their child safe. The truth came charging at her with a devastating force. Ever since that fateful night, she had done nothing but lie here and let herself be sedated and now they were talking about sending her to some sort of institution... *in other words a mental hospital.*

Their words had jolted her but in some respect, forced her to accept the gravity of her grief. It could not be repressed forever. She had to face it, no matter how harrowing.

Still a little drowsy, she could sense the drugs wearing off, the clouds in her mind gradually clearing. The next stage was to keep her emotions under control; give them no further reason to sedate her. How could she forget that horrific moment in Clark's brothel; another time when she had been repressed by drugs?

At last her breathing slowed itself, her panic subsiding. Pushing herself down into the bed again, she drew the covers right up to her chin. She could sense the dark tunnel beckoning but now she had crossed to the other side... She allowed her thoughts to drift, tip-toeing back into 'painful territory.' The sweetness of past memories caught up with her but this time she clung to them. She relived the first time she had seen Jake; that startled face peering out of the darkness in an underground cell... and every episode that had followed. She let them run through her mind like a film; from the moment they had wandered into the park, to their final night in the bedsit. In her mist of her mind, she could hear his enchanting song, feel the brush of his lips, moments the floorboards had closed over her head...

But with the memories came sorrow; wave after wave of torment twisting and writhing around her mind, compelling her to squeeze her body into a ball beneath the bedclothes.

The sobs started, softer this time as she fought control them. She hauled the pillows over her head, so no one would hear them.

Over the next few hours, Eleanor wept for him. There was no point living in denial, Jake's life was over. She was never going to see him again where at times, the pain seemed so great, she felt as if she was drowning... Yet she rode with it. Somehow, she managed to get through the night.

Before the first grey light of dawn crept in through the window, she even managed to doze off as she recalled the last words Jake had spoken. They were a distant echo in her dreams. *Just keep yourself safe and keep our child safe. Everything will be fine...* She had almost forgotten that his very last words were to say how much he *loved her.*

The weather felt chilly, typical of November with leaden-grey clouds bulging in the sky. Bernard shivered as he climbed out of his car, the large hospital building looming ahead of him.

He couldn't stay away for any longer. It had been nearly a week since the tragic death of Jake and he was desperate to find out how Eleanor was... Today he was not going to be refused, his lips fixed in a grim line as he marched through the corridor in search of her.

He came face to face with one of the nurses and froze, wondering what he might say to her.

To his surprise, she gave a warm smile. "Mr James, I'm pleased you came. Miss Chapman seems a little better and this is the first day we haven't had to sedate her."

She guided him into a small room. Eleanor was propped up against the pillows, sipping a cup of tea. The first thing he noticed was her eyes, red from crying, her eyelids puffy. Yet her lips squeezed into a smile in the instant she saw him.

"Bernard," she gasped.

She finished her tea and placed the cup down as he lowered himself into a chair.

"How are you feeling, my dear?" he whispered gently.

Tears glittered in her eyes, her lip betraying a sudden quiver.

"Heartbroken," she croaked. "I haven't coped very well. They've been giving me sedatives to calm me down..."

"I know," Bernard nodded gravely. "I visited you before but no one would let me near you. This must be such a harrowing time for you and I so much wanted to be there... They insisted you were in no fit state to talk."

"I expect they were right," she sighed, "but everything changed last night..." Drawing her head closer, her voice lowered to a whisper. "They thought I was losing my mind. They were even talking about putting me into some sort of institution. I just had to pull myself together."

The pain in her eyes reflected a burden of grief too great for someone so young. He squeezed her hand, his mind full of questions.

"I'm sorry," he murmured sadly, "but can you bear to tell me what happened?"

Eleanor closed her eyes. "Jake was shot. Someone came to the bedsit around midnight and practically forced their way in... h-he only just managed to hide me in time. It was horrible, Bernard. We thought it was the police b-but we were wrong. I-it was Jake's killers..."

An expression of anguish tore her features and then came the tears; a swelling rise of pain, which could no longer be contained. Bernard could barely imagine her torment. Reaching out, he gathered her into his big, warm arms, holding her as she wept.

She was not the only one affected. As one of the last people who had seen Jake alive, he had already visited the police station to give evidence. He had even been asked to identify the body; a memory that would haunt him forever.

"Oh, Eleanor," he whimpered, "this never should have happened."

The moment passed, her sobs subsiding. It didn't seem long before she became still again, her body no longer shuddering. Easing herself out his embrace, she sank back into the pillows and tucked them around herself.

"Of course it shouldn't have happened," she sniffed. "It's only *now* I realise how I really feel. Not just unhappy, Bernard, outraged!" Grabbing for a tissue, she blew her nose loudly. "A policeman came to see me, did you know that? I didn't trust him. He seemed a bit shifty... and I'm sure there were others involved. I mean, how did they know where to find us? And this is another thing... Whaley was there that night, Councillor Whaley! I've got a horrible feeling he had something to do with this..."

She broke off, staring at him in dread. It left Bernard wondering if he had exposed something in himself. *Guilt maybe?* An emotion he could no longer disguise...

"What's wrong?" Eleanor shivered.

"You *were* betrayed," he muttered in a voice of doom, "and this is the most terrible thing of all. I sensed something was wrong but I never acted on it. When you and Jake came to see me and showed me those drugs, I realised what I should have done all along." Tears welled in his eyes as he took in the sight of her frozen features.

"What are you talking about?"

"Someone did reveal where you were living," his voice broke softly, "but Eleanor, that person was *me*."

Submerged in his own personal torment, Bernard found himself floundering. It started, one beautiful autumnal morning in September when he had received a very strange phone call. The man had introduced himself as *Councillor Whaley* no less. He had no reason to be suspicious, particularly when he voiced his concern over a situation in his ward; one which involved two young people, an organised crime gang and the uglier issue of drug dealing.

Eleanor's face turned rigid.

He described the man alleged to be at the heart of the story; irresistibly handsome, auburn haired and with an easy going charm, someone like Bernard might be taken in by. Dutch by birth, he went by the name of *Jake Jansen*. Bernard couldn't deny his intrigue; rumours that *he was using frequent trips between Holland and London as a channel to traffic heroin*. The police had been trying to track him down for weeks yet he had always slipped through the net.

But how the tide had turned when he had attracted the attention of one of London's more powerful crime gangs. Accused of defaulting on some deal, this mysterious young man had been forced to lie low for a while, along with his teenage girlfriend.

Councillor Whaley had disclosed all this in that very first conversation.

News like this meant a lot to Bernard and everything their organisation stood for. Robin went on to say that he had *met the couple* and *directed them to Toynbee Hall*. Ever willing to offer assistance, Bernard was stirred by his motives. If this man was as sophisticated a drug dealer as he implied, he might be skilfully introducing more drugs into the Capital... and this was an opportune time to entrap him.

Thus on that same morning, they had made a pact. If these two people turned up at Toynbee Hall looking for a sanctuary, then Bernard was to offer it. The plan was to allow Jake to settle; give the police a little more time to gather the evidence they needed to convict him.

Added to Jake's illicit activities, Robin had suggested they would have their own story. Ostensibly on the run from a dangerous gang leader, their plight was a cover to trick him.

Eleanor's image blurred on the edge of his vision. Eyes lowered, he could barely look at her.

"Unfortunately everything added up," he added miserably. "Councillor Whaley's predictions turned out to be spot on and by the time you arrived, your story was as he predicted."

Eleanor stared back at him wide-eyed. Unpicking the memories turned him cold. He could clearly remember how he felt when he had met them.

Scrutinising Jake carefully, he appeared exactly as described. Yet something in his demeanour didn't quite add up. Bernard would have expected someone more confident, maybe a little cocky; Jake looked visibly shaken, a fear that had left him hollow. *Was it possible, they really were being hunted?* And if so, was it so wrong to offer them a shelter? The underground bedsit in Bethnal Green seemed the perfect place.

A day later however, Councillor Whaley had demanded to know of their location. Using the same argument, that this was for the greater good of society, he swore he only intended to pass the details onto the police. Naturally, Bernard felt obliged to comply, but it was a deceit left him uncomfortable.

Stranger still, nothing happened. In the weeks that followed, Bernard kept in tune with current affairs, especially around London. An avid reader of newspapers, he would have expected to hear something affirmative by now, some clue, the police were closing in on them.

Adamant the police were being cautious, Whaley's assurances did nothing to shake off his unease. Something felt wrong and regrettably Bernard had done nothing about it; at least, not until the day Eleanor and Jake turned up at Toynbee Hall again.

There had been something in their faces beyond fear that had him panicking; *not everything was how it seemed*. The very notion that Jake was showing him drugs that were planted on him was all the proof Bernard needed to realise he had been lied to. He suspected all along that Jake didn't fit the mould of a true drug dealer. The boy possessed a deep inner calm that seemed completely incongruous with a true criminal mind.

Not until that day did Bernard finally hear their version of events; the revelation left him not just angry but with an agonising sense of guilt. Jake's last words had touched him deeply; his uncomplicated sincerity that he was an ordinary man who loved his girlfriend - someone who yearned to go home and look forward to becoming a parent... but it was too late now. The consequences had been devastating.

Bernard removed his glasses to dab his eyes. He would never forgive himself for revealing their whereabouts to Robin Whaley. There were so many questions he should have asked.

"I feel dreadful," he whispered to Eleanor. "If only I had thought to get you out of there sooner..."

Eleanor's hands gripped the pillows, pulling them tight against her body. *So Bernard and his assistant had been expecting them.* Worse, they had moved into that squalid bedsit, convinced they were helping them. Looking at Bernard now, she saw a mantle of suffering that matched her own. But despite the emotions raging inside her, she couldn't imagine that any of this was his fault. He had been manipulated by someone far more calculating and evil...

Yes, Councillor Whaley had come across as so sincere. Recalling the day they bumped into him, it had been impossible not to be swayed; everything seemed convincing, from his professional attire to the pity in his eyes... Yet every word he had uttered was a lie, a reality that pressed down painfully.

Eleanor blinked back tears. "I thought it was strange how he turned up in Holborn," she murmured. "We went there to visit a solicitor; it was one of the places we always feared someone might come looking for us..."

Bernard frowned deeply.

"Jake was right not to trust him," she added wistfully, "and we didn't follow his advice straight away. We'd come so far, all we wanted to do was to jump on a train... then that awful business at Waterloo Station happened."

Her eyes widened. Was it possible, even that had been engineered; a clever means to dupe them into trusting him? Whaley, the police, the circle of men from Theakston's gang... Was it feasible, that entire set up had been co-ordinated between them all?

At last everything locked into place.

"It was a ploy wasn't it, to drive us back into hiding..." She stared directly into Bernard's eyes. "Don't blame yourself. You only did what you thought was right. It's Whaley, I despise. From what you've told me, I'm guessing that he was the one who shopped us..."

"Oh, Eleanor," Bernard groaned. "I wish I'd kept quiet about the bedsit..."

"But you promised to help us in the end..." she placated him. "You offered to drive us to Dover!"

"I should have done it sooner," Bernard said curtly. "Then Jake might still be alive... But I am not going to abandon you *now*, Eleanor."

With a face set like stone and his hands twisted in sorrow, his very stance reflected the frustration battling inside him. He let out a shuddering sigh.

"It seems we have much to talk about but somewhere more private. Is there any chance, you're in a fit enough condition to leave hospital? We need to mull over the facts..."

"Yes," she threw back at him. "I've been here too long already b-but where will I go?"

"That needn't be a problem," he muttered. "I'd like to invite you to come and stay with me. My wife has already agreed to it and we're more than happy to take care of you. Please, Eleanor... It's the very least we can do."

"Thank you," she whispered numbly.

"And another thing," Bernard finished. "Your belongings have already been collected from the bedsit. I've been keeping them safe for you. I know I can never truly make up for what happened but I'll do whatever I can to help you through this..."

Chapter 11

I

Eleanor was finally discharged from hospital, escorted by Bernard.

Much to the relief of the hospital staff, it seemed fairly obvious she was in good hands. Happy to see her leave with him, they were not without sympathy...

Only a little later however, the doctor took a urgent call from Inspector Hargreaves, issuing a further demand to speak to her. A little aggrieved by his anger, he had no wish to detain her. Eleanor had struggled through the worst of her trauma and was healthy enough to be discharged.

Best of all, someone had offered to take care of her: a social worker no less.

Norman was forced to accept his authority though he did so through gritted teeth. Ending the call abruptly, he just about managed to retain a professional front.

Yet this prevailing situation worried him. It would be down to him to explain this unexpected turn of events to the other parties. *Trust a soft-hearted fool of a social worker like Bernard James to interfere.*

All he could pray was that Eleanor would cause no trouble; that whatever she knew about their conspiracy was shrouded with ambiguity. He lived in hope, there would never come a time when they would be forced to do something about her.

Bernard's home was squeezed into a row of typical Victorian terraced houses. Tall and narrow with decorative stonework around the windows, they stood slightly back from the road.

Inside it was cluttered but cosy. Bernard took her coat and hung it on a rack, then guided her into a lounge crammed with furniture. A large unit stood against the wall, books almost spilling from the shelves. In another corner, perched a dainty wooden bureau, groaning under a weight of paperwork. Two comfortable matching armchairs upholstered in green and orange dominated what little space there was left, as well as an old settee. With the chairs positioned on both sides of the hearth, a flickering gas fire radiated warmth into the room.

At first Eleanor stood there awkwardly.

"Make yourself at home, my dear," Bernard coaxed her gently. "Take a seat by the fire and get yourself warm. My wife, Edna, will be down in a moment..."

Eleanor did as advised but not before snatching a second glance at her surroundings. After the confines of the hospital, the outside world seemed huge, bringing back a sense of vulnerability. Neither did she miss the position of the window. It looked directly out onto the street. For that reason, she chose the armchair facing away from it.

Mercifully concealed from view, her eyes settled upon the fireplace. The luminous glow of orange bars had an almost hypnotic effect, allowing her thoughts to settle.

"This is very kind of you," she murmured, struggling to find the right words. "I don't know what I would have done otherwise..."

"Please," Bernard sighed, taking the chair opposite. "It is no trouble. We have two grown-up daughters and both of them have flown the nest. Our oldest, Celia, is getting married next year so there are two empty rooms. You can take your pick."

Next came a creak from the stairs followed by the slow shuffle of slippers. Eleanor peeped up just as a sweet middle-aged lady plodded into the room. She was about the same height as Eleanor but plumper. Wearing an apron over her dress and fluffy slippers on her stockinged feet, her greying blonde hair was piled up in curls.

The moment their eyes met, her face broke into a motherly smile,

"Hello, love, I'm Edna. Bernard told me all about you. Welcome to our home."

"How nice to meet you," Eleanor replied, rising from her chair, "and thank you for inviting me to stay with you."

Edna glanced at her feet as if humbled. "Oh, it's nothing," she mumbled. "Sit down, love and I'll make us a nice cup of tea. How do you take yours?"

"Just a little milk p-please," Eleanor stammered.

Her voice had already started to crack a little. Maybe it was the homely ambience, such a contrast to the last place she had lived; or the heart-felt warmth emanating from these kind people. Suddenly it overwhelmed her, bringing her emotions frothing to the surface.

With little hesitation, Edna gathered her up in her arms. Eleanor's whole body shuddered as the sobs consumed her again. *When was it ever going to end?* She must have cried enough tears to fill up a lake but sadly, what she hadn't yet realised, was the real process of grieving had just begun.

The next few days were hard, both for Eleanor and the couple who had chosen to take care of her. After almost a week in hospital doped with sedatives, she felt physically weak, her emotions in shreds. Her preliminary heartache, stirred into the mix of fear and betrayal had been suppressed for too long. Yet those feelings let loose shook her with their intensity.

Like a volcano erupting, Eleanor endured a storm of emotions...

At times she wanted to die. She missed Jake terribly; it seemed impossible for life to go on without him being a part of it. These were the times when she would sit silently brooding, the tears running down her face like waterfalls.

Only when these feelings subsided, did she ponder over the shocking revelations Bernard had imparted. To think of the lies that had been spread; the cutting rumour that Jake had been a drug dealer... How powerless they had been to fight such a calculating conspiracy to end his life. The truth released waves of fury so strong she could barely contain them at times.

Bernard bought all the newspapers. Details of Jake's killing had been published but he chose to keep them away from her. The way the story had been depicted would only add to her misery. Somehow, this was typical of the British tabloid press. They were over sensationalising the tragedy in a way that seemed particularly insensitive. So for now, he offered her novels to read and found boxes of glossy fashion magazines stashed in the bedrooms of his daughters.

The hum of a wireless in the background retained a sort of harmony in the household. One sunny day, Edna had even sent her outside to dig over the vegetable patch, removing all straggly remains of this season's carrots, marrows and runner beans. She seemed convinced a little physical work might help her to shake off all that inner turmoil and rage.

Bernard hadn't failed to notice how much weight Eleanor had lost; it carved a hollowness into her face which sharpened her cheekbones. Her arms were as thin as sticks and from the top of her cardigan, her collar bones stuck out like iron bars. Edna took on the task of feeding her up with plenty of home-cooked meals, from hearty stews and dumplings to piping hot pies filled with chicken and ham, served with fresh vegetables. As Eleanor tucked in, it put the first bloom of colour back into her cheeks and gradually her strength began to return. Naturally, Edna never stopped nagging her that she was *feeding for two now* - a harsh reminder of the unborn baby growing inside her, which she had pledged to protect at all costs.

The one factor that won her over was their incredible patience. At times Eleanor feared the effects her behaviour would have on them, from floods of tears one minute to episodes of uncontrollable rage the next. How fortunate, they both worked in caring professions. Edna too, had much experience working with the less fortunate, including her current mission as a volunteer with the Salvation Army. Both spent their lives alleviating the terrible burden of sadness which prevailed in society, especially among the poor.

"Just give her time," Bernard said to Edna, one night. "What that girl has been through is truly terrible... She won't heal overnight."

Ultimately, it took more than the kindness of these two extraordinary people to shake her out of her gloom. The couple shared their home with two pets; notably a yellow Labrador called Buttons. Intrigued by the sad, silent girl in the way animals are often drawn to those in need of comfort, he couldn't resist plodding up to her chair. Her hand trailed over the side. Pressing his wet nose into her palm to stir her, she would stroke his silky head. If that failed, he would shuffle right up close, lifting a big yellow paw to rest upon her knee. His gentle attempts to engage her made her smile; those soft brown eyes, coupled with an expression of bewilderment.

Their other pet was a long haired cat. Aptly named Treacle, her dark fur took on a rich brown shine in the sunlight. She had never actually been much of a lap cat. Yet there was something about Eleanor's stillness that tempted her to investigate. One day, she had leapt into her chair. After a systematic kneading of paws and rotating circles, the cat had finally curled herself into a ball and settled, purring with the force of an engine. Instantly comforted by her warm weight, Eleanor sank her fingers into fur that felt luxuriously soft and thick, the effect unquestionably therapeutic.

Love and affection surrounded her from every corner and she started to accept it. It felt like an embrace which grew stronger with each passing day, pushing the pain from her heart and within that first week, she was finally beginning to heal.

II

Bernard sensed the change in her and as they drifted into the second week, she started to engage in a little more conversation. On one of those chilly winter evenings, he settled himself in the armchair on the opposite side of the fireplace. Their eyes met.

Only now, did he dare bring up the mystery surrounding Jake's murder. Eleanor nodded. She seemed calm and sedate as the warmth of the fire caressed them. With the curtains drawn, an ambience of secrecy united them and suddenly she wanted to tell him everything.

It began on the day she had stumbled across Jake; incarcerated in an underground dungeon, they were all too aware, he was about to be the victim of a contract killing.

Next, she disclosed everything there was to know about the gang leader hired to kill him. Had he ever come across a man named Dominic Theakston? Bernard blinked. *Yes, he knew the name but only as a result of the media stories...*

She spoke in hushed tones as if fearing they might be overheard. With an element of fear, she described the car bomb explosion Jake had witnessed; the call to Scotland Yard to give evidence and the men he had seen just hours before the atrocity. One moment, Jake had been a cog in the wheel of a massive police investigation before his world was flipped upside down. Theakston's men had ambushed him, his life dangling on a thread...

Bernard listened in silence. An unexpected wave of dread swept over him at the mere mention of that car bomb. A stalwart supporter of Albert Enfield, it seemed unbelievable that Jake could have witnessed something so contentious.

Resisting the urge to interrupt, he allowed her to finish her story, right up to the day they had left Forest Haven. He already knew the rest. He had played his own part in it.

"A police officer came to see you didn't he?" he whispered.

Hands folded in her lap, she stared at the fire, mesmerised. There was no other sound in the house other than the clock ticking. Edna had joined her friends at the local Bingo hall.

"I was hanging about in the hospital as he was leaving," Bernard continued. "I recognised him. He took a statement from me earlier that week."

"I see," Eleanor mumbled. She dreamily twisted a strand of hair around her finger. "What did you tell him?"

"Everything, Eleanor, from the day you visited Toynbee Hall. I said as much as I could to vouch for Jake's character... the drugs that were planted on him, the last day I saw him alive."

"And did they believe you?" Eleanor piped up.

He lowered his eyes, feeling a shadow descend. "He seemed convinced the package was a ploy to get me on your side. Furthermore, the police confiscated it. We can no longer use it as evidence. I am sorry, Eleanor, but the police officer in charge is very powerful. He's the same officer who visited you..." He unfolded a newspaper. "It was this man, wasn't it?"

Eleanor's heart began to quicken. She could not fail to recognise those granite hard features and silver hair. His blue eyes chilled her with their intensity. Nodding as she studied the photograph, her eyes then drifted to the caption.

"Hargreaves!" she gasped. "Bernard, this is the man Jake mentioned, the one who took his statement..." Her eyes widened. "It was shortly after that interview he was snatched by those thugs... and he's leading the murder enquiry?"

"So it would appear," Bernard said.

Eleanor frowned as she poked around in her head for answers. From her own recollections, the inspector had come across as solicitous and kind. Yet this single revelation changed everything. *Was it possible, the only reason he had spoken to her was to ascertain how much she knew about Jake's killing?* He had been particularly curious to know what she had overheard whilst hidden beneath those floorboards... A whisper of cold ran over her. Jake lived in fear that someone in the police had been involved and he had specifically named this man.

"What else have you got there?" she dared to ask. She had already spotted the newspapers piled untidily by the side of Bernard's chair.

"The rest of the media coverage," Bernard sighed. "There's even mention of this *Dominic Theakston...*" He bit his lip. "There is one thing I should warn you though. The news surrounding Jake's death wasn't particularly tactful. In fact, it is probably going to upset you..."

"Just show me," Eleanor snapped.

"They did arrest this man," Bernard added warily, "but the charges were dropped..."

With a growing sense of dread, Eleanor stared at the paper. The very exposure of his face felt like a stab in the heart; a picture taken of Theakston just as he was leaving the police station.

It so much reminded her of the press cutting Sammie had revealed all those months ago, same slanted eyes, same cocky smile. Described as a 28 year old gang leader rumoured to be a new face in organised crime, the article went on to report that he had been released without charge; how several people had accounted for his whereabouts at the time of the murder.

"Liars!" Eleanor hissed in fury. "I bet they were paid off!"

Bernard winced. "I told you, you wouldn't like it."

"But he's a killer! I was there! I heard his voice and it's not a voice you forget easily!"

With a sob, she flung the paper to one side.

She had never wanted to be reminded of that hateful man and to think, he was still out there, no doubt terrorising the streets in the wake of Sammie's demise.

"Doesn't my evidence count for anything?" she added numbly. "This Hargreaves promised me, he'd be arrested and now they've just let him go! I wonder if they're in this together!"

"You could well be right," Bernard snapped. "In fact, I'm unhappy about the way this entire investigation has been handled! Inspector Hargreaves was not at all thorough in his analysis and I am sorry, my dear, but you only have to read the headlines to see what they really wanted the public to believe."

She clocked his rising fury. Whatever lurked in those papers had outraged him. Eleanor braced herself, reluctant to see what was written but on the other hand, she had to know. Bernard gave a sigh. Scooping up an armful of newspapers and passing them to her, he collapsed in his chair as if resigned to the effects they were about to have on her...

Another Gangland Murder shakes the East End of London. She glanced quickly over the article, then lifted the paper to reveal the next headline...

Suspected Drug Dealer shot dead by London Crime Gang.

"No!" Eleanor whimpered. "This can't be true!"

She kept sifting through the papers, flipping them aside more quickly... In one particularly damning article, it was claimed that Jake had *buried her under the floorboards to get rid of her.* Eleanor wilted to tears, dropping the papers on the floor.

"How could they report such lies?" she sobbed. "He did it to save me. There's no proof he dealt in drugs! For God's sake, we were in hiding for three months..."

She broke off suddenly, her eyes spilling over with tears.

"Councillor Whaley!" she spluttered. "I bet he had something to do with this..."

"Possibly," Bernard sighed, "especially given the manner of the investigation... They discovered more drugs when they searched your bedsit, Eleanor."

"So that's it, is it," she shivered, drawing her arms around herself. "Jake has been framed! I suppose the whole world is going to think he really was some drug dealer..."

"Regrettably so," Bernard lamented. "I think Hargreaves knew exactly what the forensic officers were going to find. It was virtually a foregone conclusion."

"But we can't let them get away with this!" Eleanor breathed. "We have got to protest Jake's innocence. Because if we don't, he'll be forgotten. It'll be as if he never existed."

"Maybe we should concentrate on the real reason Jake was killed," Bernard finished sagely. He scooped up the newspapers. "Let's just take this one step at a time..."

They decided to continue their analysis next day, after Edna had cooked a hearty breakfast of bacon and eggs. Being a weekend, Bernard had plenty of free time to engage in further discussion. Once again, they chose the sitting room. A weak winter sunshine gleamed outside, casting thin beams through the net curtains.

Earlier that morning, Eleanor had finally bucked up the courage to sort through Jake's things.

Up until now, they had been hidden in a cupboard to spare her more torment. Yet the sight of the guitar in its leather case unleashed a spasm of anguish. Eleanor fought back tears as she persevered. Unzipping the holdall where his clothes lay neatly folded, she sank her hands into the depths. His sweet male fragrance was dispensed into the air as she sifted through it. Further down, she found the sheets of paper where he had scrawled his song lyrics - wishing she could have recorded the beautiful ballad he had sung on their final night.

Bernard had also given her a plastic bag collected from the police station. It contained his wallet along with the little green pendant he had been wearing from the very first day she had met him. Eleanor clung to it for a moment, then looped it around her own neck. The coolness of stone felt soothing against her heart, evoking an immediate sense of connection.

"It was such a part of him," she murmured to herself as she rolled it between her fingers. "His songs too..." and these were the only keepsakes she yearned for. As for his clothes... she would offer them to a refuge so that others could make use of them. Jake would have liked that.

The task, no matter how small, seemed a huge step in the right direction. It drew her towards acceptance; Jake had departed from this world. Sadness hung heavily in her heart as she hedged towards the next question begging to be asked. *Why?*

"Did they ever f-find his b-body?" she shivered.

"Yes, Eleanor," Bernard confessed. "I was the one who identified him."

He fought to keep his voice steady. Even though Jake appeared to be at peace, there had been something deeply shocking about the stillness of death in his face. He was relieved Eleanor chose not to question him any further about this.

"What about his funeral arrangements?" she added.

"My understanding is that Jake was returned to his homeland," Bernard said.

Eleanor sank slowly into the armchair, her face ashen. "So I can't even say goodbye to him?"

Sensing her desolation, Bernard moved a little closer. He lowered a gentle hand to her shoulder though to his surprise, she didn't break down in tears. The news had left her frozen.

"You could always establish your own memorial in London, Eleanor. Perhaps there is a special place where you can picture him... pay a tribute."

Eleanor nodded. She spoke again yet there was little strength in her voice.

"I'd like to know where he's buried, so I can visit his grave some time. I wonder if we could trace his family."

"Talk to the authorities in Holland," Bernard responded, lowering himself into the other chair. "I have already made enquiries. It would help if I knew where Jake came from."

"Nijmegen," Eleanor murmured dazedly. She seemed to be in a trance as if his last words hadn't quite sunk in. "Have you heard of it?"

"Yes!" he blustered. "The Germans invaded the city in the war. There was a famous battle which involved the blowing up of a bridge... and you're certain about this?"

"Of course I'm sure," she said, snapping out of her dream world. "Jake told me loads about his homeland. This is where his band was based, in fact the other musicians could still be living there. Maybe we could trace them too… as well as Jake's family!"

"There seems to be a little confusion," Bernard added anxiously. "Holland was mentioned, the most obvious assumption being Amsterdam. I supposed it stems from the notion it's a notorious drug capital. Yet there never any mention of Nijmegen…"

"But why would the truth about Jake's home be kept quiet?" Eleanor pressed.

"I confess, I am as shocked as you are," Bernard said. "I wonder if the British press wanted him to appear faceless and anonymous so the stories wouldn't raise suspicion amongst his townsfolk - in other words, those who knew him…"

Staring at each other in incredulity, they digested the facts; their minds joined by a similar thread.

"That's it!" Eleanor squeaked. "The other band members will confirm that Jake was on tour with them… They definitely know he wasn't a drug dealer."

A flicker of light loomed in Bernard's mind like a candle.

"The answers lie in Jake's homeland," she continued. "If we only we could talk to his friends… Jake was far too into his music to be involved in drugs and as for these 'trips' between Holland and London to traffic heroin… How would he have had the time?"

"It would be impossible!" Bernard snapped, his irritation spiralling. "This is only what Councillor Whaley wanted us to believe."

Eleanor's eyes smouldered with hate. "So we will prove him wrong! Jake and his band, *Free Spirit*, were far too busy touring the music festivals and in July, they were hired to play at that birthday party. The politician, Albert Enfield…"

"Oh yes, I wondered when we would get to him," Bernard said. Wrenching his mind from the brutality of the press coverage, he raised his eyebrows. "We both know this drug dealing business was a cover up. Jake was murdered for another reason, wasn't he?"

With those last words left dangling, it seemed obvious where the conversation was leading; the subject of Albert Enfield.

"What do you know about him?" Eleanor probed. "What's more, who would have wanted him dead? Do you think it was the IRA?"

"It's not impossible," Bernard frowned. "The threat of terrorism arose earlier in the year; the troubles in Northern Ireland. There was a car bomb at an Army barracks in Aldershot."

"Albert Enfield was killed by a car bomb," Eleanor reflected.

"Yes," Bernard muttered, "though the IRA never actually claimed responsibility."

"So if it wasn't the IRA who else could it be?" Eleanor pressed. *How strange, her thoughts were following the same pattern as Jake's had. They had talked about this...*

"Those in authority considered Enfield to be a socialist," Bernard began, "yet he wasn't always that way inclined. His politics used to be a little more liberal, that was, until his son was killed in a tragic accident at school. Something in him changed. He turned notably anti-establishment."

Eleanor shook her head sadly. In truth, she was finding it a little hard to take in. Bernard gave a sigh, leaning forward to catch her eye.

"What I mean is, he turned against the system! He didn't approve of our ruling elite, their wealth, their public schools or their power. Does that make sense?"

"I guess so," Eleanor said as he clung to her gaze. "He didn't like the rich."

Bernard cast her a warm smile, as if touched by the simplicity of that concept.

"I suppose not. He accused such people of being hoarders; greedy, unwilling to give more to the people. He campaigned for higher wages which unfortunately our current prime minister, Ted Heath, has failed to do. I mean look at this country!" he waved a hand in the air. "The economy's a mess, people are discontented, there are strikes and power cuts... People are fed up with politicians! They were looking for a saviour and I have to say, Albert Enfield appealed to them! But the more he grew in popularity, the more other parliamentary members maligned him."

"But why?" Eleanor said, her frown deepening.

"They feared his reforms would encourage revolution," Bernard shrugged. "Strip the ruling elite of their power and turn this country into some sort of Soviet state... It was all such rubbish! I personally didn't believe a word of it! The trade unions have already risen to enormous power but at a price. People are sick of all the strikes, they don't want these militants!"

"Yet someone believed it," Eleanor intervened, "and they chose to kill him... What a horrible way to do it, a car bomb. Jake often wondered if the Secret Service was involved..."

Shifting where he sat, Bernard frowned and fiddled with his glasses.

"No," he argued. "My first guess would be someone in power, given what you told me about the car Jake saw and the man inside..."

"So how do you imagine someone like Whaley became involved?" Eleanor said, drawn to an earlier mind walk. "Wasn't he the one who spread the lie about the drug dealing? He's in politics, well spoken... would he have friends in high places?"

Bernard took a deep breath, replaced his glasses and sat back again.

"Where was it you said he found you? Holborn... What was the significance of that location?"

"Sammie Maxwell left me a legacy," Eleanor said. *She had already explained snippets of her past.* "We went there to visit his solicitor... We were always a bit nervous about it, never sure how much Theakston knew. He said he raided Sammie's office and went through his files."

"Do you think, he may have passed the information on?" Bernard pondered. "Which is how Councillor Whaley might have traced you?"

"Yes," Eleanor responded. "He bumped into us - pretended to be our ally to set his trap..." She looked at him with growing dread. *Could it have been just seconds after they parted, he had made his damning call and coerced Bernard into helping him?*

"That man has a lot to answer for," Bernard shuddered.

"Have you spoken to him since this happened?" Eleanor snapped.

"How can I?" Bernard whispered, "and I urge you not contact him either! I know I was manipulated by that man and I'm as upset about this as you are! My job is to help people, not to aid and abet killers!"

"So what now?" Eleanor demanded. "We know he's in on this, Bernard, and he always has been. But how do we prove it?"

"By treading very carefully," Bernard finished. "Hard though it seems, you cannot go charging in with all guns blazing. So let's just go through the facts again, shall we?"

Eleanor hardly slept that night, her mind battling to make sense of it all. Lying on her back, she stretched out her spine, anything to make herself more comfortable. Twisting from side to side, the echo of her heart pounded in her ears... it was no use. She found it impossible to relax.

Rising from her bed she slipped into a borrowed dressing gown and crept downstairs.

Every newspaper clipping had been tucked inside a folder by now, including the press coverage surrounding the car bomb atrocity. Eleanor stared at it; hit with a sudden hankering to compile her own report. She settled herself down on the settee.

Treacle immediately sprang onto the cushions, about to trample all over the newspapers. Eleanor felt the touch of a smile as she ran her palm down her back, relishing the softness of fur beneath her fingers. *Such a beautiful cat.* For a few seconds, she savoured the moment, then pushed her away so she landed neatly back onto the carpet.

She found a notebook and pen, then reached for the folder. At first, she clung to it, almost fearful to look at it again. She closed her eyes. A vision of Jake's lovely face immediately flickered in her mind, sending a twist of sadness through her. No sooner had the moment passed when she felt the soaring anger that replaced it.

She didn't yet know who was responsible for the bomb explosion in July.

But she knew with absolute certainty the identities of three men who had conspired to kill Jake; Inspector Hargreaves, Councillor Whaley and ultimately, Dominic Theakston.

She was beginning to picture Whaley as the co-ordinator; a shadowy figure who always been hovering in the background. He had been stalking around outside Clark's brothel, maybe curious to see the building where their doomed victim was held captive. He had appeared again on the night of the murder; Eleanor would never forget the sight of his car tucked in the shadows, before a wheel of blue light had illuminated his face. Taking the pen in her hand, she began to record her thoughts...

How Inspector Hargreaves fitted into this equation seemed obvious; a man so corrupt, he had abused his power, from his initial interrogation of Jake, to the carefully co-ordinated ambush organised by Theakston's men. In all the hours Jake had been detained, she could almost imagine the sinister instruction behind the scenes; a calculating ploy to *get rid of him*.

Theakston's role was even more clear cut; the man contracted to terminate Jake's life.

Tears burned in her eyes as she recalled the horrific night of the murder. He sounded so calm. Did he even know the reason he had been hired to take an innocent life? He had said something very strange that night too ... *you're a marked man. There ain't a single place you could go where they wouldn't have followed you. Not even Holland.* He left the chilling implication that Jake's fate was sealed wherever they went.

Eleanor kept scribbling, listing the most crucial elements until she felt sure she must have covered everything. She re-wrote the entire script in a neater hand; wondering if there was any significance to this - something yet to be realised.

III

Sunday passed in a blur. Due to her restless night, Eleanor slept late, so Bernard and Edna decided to leave her in bed while they attended Church.

A little later, she helped Edna prepare a lavish Sunday dinner, which they enjoyed at the kitchen table. As they settled down in the lounge afterwards, Bernard dozed off in his chair and Edna watched a film on their small black and white television.

Eleanor read through her notes again: *her own secret dossier*. Inspired by this notion, she decided to embellish them with a selection of Bernard's press clippings.

"I want to take a trip to central London," she announced next day, over a coffee.

Bernard's face pinched into a frown. "Are you sure that's wise, my dear?"

"It's only to sort out a few personal matters," she assured him. "That's all."

She could guess what he was thinking. What was there to say, she wouldn't go storming into the police headquarters, demanding answers? Yet she had fought hard to keep her sentiments under control, despite the unforgivable way Jake's murder had been trivialised.

"So why don't I drive you?" he conceded. "It'll be safer, Eleanor. From what you've been saying, your old enemy, Dominic Theakston, could still be after you. You can't take any risks."

Their first stop was Charterhouse Street to find Barclays Bank.

More than two months had passed since she'd learned of Sammie's legacy. Yet she had never had a chance to issue the documents John Sharp had given her. It so happened, the bank lay close to Holborn, only a short distance from his office.

With a bank account finally authorised in her name, along with a cheque book and guarantee card, she was overcome with a sudden thrill; especially when she made a cash withdrawal. Her first impulse was to offer Edna £10 as a contribution towards food and housekeeping.

Her eyes remained downcast as she left the bank. She couldn't help but feel haunted, unable to cast aside the memory of the last time she had been here. Today the streets were teaming with business people; men in dark suits and bowler hats pacing alongside smartly groomed women in short dresses worn with tight-fitting jackets and boots. This was clearly a commercial area. Tidy ranks of shops ducked beneath the towering office blocks. She found Bernard resting in his car, drinking in the scene as she dropped herself into the passenger seat.

"Everything alright?" he smiled as he started the engine.

"Fine," Eleanor said softly. "I've finally got a bank account. There's just one more thing I'd like to do now and that's visit Sammie's solicitor again..."

Bernard shot her a shrewd, sideways glance. She had showed him the notes she had drafted and as soon as the road was clear, he swerved away from the curb.

Heading down the busy main road, his Triumph Herald seemed tiny amongst the tide of black taxis and giant red buses. As soon as they reached the traffic lights, they were drawn towards a bank of high rise offices. Eleanor pointed out a distinctive white building.

"Looks very posh," Bernard commented, pulling into the curb. "Must be a top drawer firm."

"Oh, it is," Eleanor said gently. "I won't be long, I promise."

She was glad of another opportunity to speak to John Sharp, even though the circumstances were less than joyful. Devastated by the news of Jake's death, John was resolute in offering whatever professional assistance she required.

During their brief meeting, she settled three matters of crucial importance.

First, she needed to make a will; nothing complicated. All she desired was that everything she owned, including Sammie's legacy, would be left to her child; the one exception being a £20 donation to aid the charitable work of Toynbee Hall.

Second on the list, she could not resist asking if there was any news of her father. Regrettably there had been no word... Sammie's estate had been dissolved, the Malibu sold to a private developer who had no plans to run it as an entertainment venue. Organised crime continued to flourish but under the power of a deadly new crime boss. All Eleanor hoped was that one day, John would find an opportunity to pass a message on. But until that day came he assured her, this channel of communication would remain forever open to her.

This left the third and final matter to be addressed.

Bernard had sprung the idea to lodge her file here. This included all the notes she had recorded, in addition to his press clippings. No one could dismiss the grim possibility, she was under the radar and if her enemies chose to deal with her in the way they had done with Jake...

Among the press articles lurked a single breaking headline of the car bomb attack in July. Attached to it with a paperclip was an account of everything Jake had witnessed.

Next came the clippings, which portrayed his murder; details of a gangland shooting right up to the arrest of Theakston, the accused. Each article was illuminated with Eleanor's account of what had really happened; names including Inspector Hargreaves and Councillor Whaley, who she unashamedly named as the main perpetrator of the conspiracy.

Bernard seemed adamant, this secret dossier of documents would blow the lid off the establishment if revealed. In the event that Eleanor might 'disappear,' her file would be released into the hands of the media and the courts.

Eleanor felt somewhat cleansed by her actions; a subtle tribute. She had at least tried to do something to chronicle the mystery behind Jake's death.

Yet somehow, it still didn't seem enough...

She wandered wearily back to the car, her face pale in the liquid sunshine. Bernard could not help but notice how haunted she looked.

"Did you sort everything out?" he asked her.

"I suppose so," Eleanor replied, her voice lacking in any substance.

"Look," he said, turning the key in the ignition. "Why don't we go and grab a bite to eat. I don't really need to go back to work until this afternoon and it's lunchtime..."

By the time he had driven from Holborn, he was fortunate to find another empty parking place. Walking briskly along the pavement, Eleanor kept her head down. Within a few yards, they arrived at the 'Golden Egg,' a popular chain of diners. With a busy, colourful atmosphere they found a table inside an alcove with soft leather seats. A waitress brought them each a menu and took their drinks order. The instant she left however, Bernard met Eleanor's eye.

"My dear, whatever is wrong?" he muttered, his hand light on her wrist.

Eleanor gave a shudder. "Nothing," she sighed. "It's just that Dad used to take me to one of these restaurants. There's still no word of him. I don't understand it, Bernard, where the hell could he have gone? I can't help thinking he might be dead!"

"I'm sure there's a perfectly reasonable explanation," Bernard assured her.

A sudden bitterness edged her tone. "Too right there is! Dominic Theakston! He rules the area of East London now, the place where Dad and Sammie used to operate..."

"Eleanor," Bernard whispered, "for God's sake keep your voice down." His fingers squeezed her wrist a little harder than he intended, causing her to flinch. "I'm sorry but you never know who's listening..." he added guardedly.

"But what if I'm right?" Eleanor said, her voice dropping to a whisper. "Sammie warned us about Theakston. He was obsessed with revenge and as for Jake... as if I haven't got enough reason to hate that man."

"Shush," Bernard soothed. "You've got to try and control your emotions, Eleanor."

The waitress shimmied up to their table with a tray of drinks balanced in her hand. Glancing over the menu, Eleanor ordered a cheese and mushroom omelette. Bernard chose ham and eggs. Both came with chips. Looking at her again, he felt unnerved by her despondency.

"Eleanor," he whispered. "What happened to Jake was utterly deplorable but Theakston was only hired as the executioner. What about those who sanctioned that killing? The men at the top, people who abused their power, especially Hargreaves. As for Councillor Whaley... wasn't it his deception that ultimately sealed Jake's fate? He is evil, Eleanor. You should be far more worried about him?"

"So what happens now?" Eleanor shivered. "So my solicitor has agreed to keep my file secure yet it all seems so - so - pointless against such powerful men!"

"It may seem a small step to you," Bernard replied, "but think of the contents of that file. They could be quite devastating." He gazed into her eyes. "All we can do is to add to that file. Find Jake's friends in Holland... prove that he was not the shady character they depicted him as."

"Do you think it will work?" Eleanor gasped.

He felt a smile tug the corners of his mouth. "If we gather enough proof, I swear to you that Hargreaves and Whaley are the ones who will be panicking! It will completely unhinge their story. People will demand the truth, which is where your secret file comes into play..."

The waitress returned with their meals.

In that fleeting moment of silence, he was thankful to catch Eleanor's smile.

IV

Bernard's fears were not without foundation. In another part of London, Robin Whaley stared at the clean white walls of his apartment, smoking a cigarette. It rested limply in his hand, a thread of smoke trickling towards an open window. Ever since Eleanor had spotted him on the night of the murder, his world had been thrown into turmoil.

She was out there, right now; a loose cannon primed to destroy everything they had worked for. Robin clenched his teeth, lost in a chokehold of anxiety. Bernard James had been so easy to manipulate. There was a time, Robin genuinely believed he was on their side; except they had underestimated him. According to Hargreaves, he was outraged by Jake's murder, convinced the entire drug dealing scenario was a set up.

The question in his mind now was how much did Eleanor know? And was Bernard party to the same information?

Drawing hard on his cigarette, he satisfied his craving. He had never intended to start smoking so much but if only Hargreaves had made better use of his power. Given the drugs found in the bedsit, he could have arrested Eleanor but he hadn't! He had been clinging to the notion she was suffering from some sort of breakdown; on the verge of being institutionalised where she would be of no threat to anyone...

But of course, it hadn't happened. Bernard James had seen to that, landing him in the perilous situation he was in now. He no longer knew where he stood any more.

Getting rid of Jake should have been so straight forward. Those thugs had planted enough drugs to convince a battalion of journalists a typical gangland murder had occurred... and the resulting press coverage had been quite satisfying.

The fact was, Robin had developed a skill for surreptitiously planting evidence to incriminate people and it had begun from a very early age.

What people didn't know about Robin was that he had grown up on a rough council estate. The youngest of four children, his parents came from a working class background. Life was harsh, kids played in the streets and got themselves dirty but Robin had never really been that sort of boy.

Small, pale and skinny for his age, the other kids picked on him. His older brothers too gave him a hard time; both big, strapping lads, good at sport, especially on the football pitch. His father, an avid West Ham supporter, was proud of them. Yet he had never really stuck up for Robin who he regarded as a maggot.

But where Robin lacked any physical prowess, he possessed a brilliant mind. Elevated to the top of his class, he attracted the school's worst bullies. Yet despite the swelling tide of antagonism on all sides, he persevered with his academic studies, one of the few children in his school expected to pass the 'Eleven Plus.'

Throughout his growing years however, those deepening layers of misery and frustration ignited a hatred in him. Robin decided to put his devious mind to better uses. He had been 10 years old when he had stolen a bar of chocolate from the headmaster's office, smuggling it into the desk of one of the classroom bullies.

Everyone feared the headmaster. A brute of a man, he was devoutly religious with a passion for the Ten Commandments, especially stealing. So when every child was forced to turn out their desk that day, Robin waited in anticipation for his enemy to be chastised. The vicious caning in front of the entire class had been his moment of pure triumph.

Robin no longer cared what others in his class thought of him but he endeared himself to the teachers. Given, a lot of the kids were noisy, disruptive and not at all interested in learning, to teachers like these, Robin was a breath of fresh air so naturally they encouraged him.

By the time he left school at sixteen, he had eight O levels to his name and was even considering university. *Any other parent would be proud.* Unfortunately Robin's parents were no such people and it pained him to this day. Scornful of intellectuals, they had treated him with utter ridicule. All his father really cared about was that he couldn't kick a football around a field and he finally saw him for what he was; an unshaven, beer swilling lout and his brothers were turning into replicas of him! His mother was too weak to stick up for him; a typical working class crone with hair in curlers and a fag drooping from her mouth.

Sadly, the only family member who had ever shown him any affection was his sister. Yet even she had slipped up, got herself pregnant and left home at the age of 17.

He was determined never to become like them. Driven by a relentless sense of ambition, Robin did apply for university and as he had developed an interest in politics, he dedicated the next three years to studying a PPE in London.

Installed in university halls of residence, he had at last detached himself from his family. Yet the emotional pain of his upbringing had darkened his personality. A ruthless, damaged man, he came to despise the working classes; forever whining about a lack of money yet too lazy and lacking in ambition to do anything about it.

Working on his accent, he became more cultured. He modelled himself on the sophisticated young men at university, many of whom hailed from the public school. Slowly but surely, he elevated himself to their status. But as he grew older, he became obsessed with power.

Anyone who met Robin couldn't resist being swayed; charming, solicitous and above all, convincing, his looks too, were an asset. His alluring features and blue eyes conveyed a sympathetic nature and this in turn, made him popular in politics. Robin's success soared at the age of 25 when he was elected councillor for a ward in Poplar. Not particularly an area of his choosing, it nonetheless afforded him that first 'step up the ladder' in the political world.

But university had opened other doors for him. It had introduced him to influential men who were not only wealthy, but well connected with the establishment. Robin lived in hope that one day, there would be an opportunity to prove his true worth...

The opportunity arose in 1972, three years after he had been elected a ward councillor. It happened in an era when a new political face in the form of Albert Enfield had arisen. He seemed destined to threaten the very people Robin wanted to ally himself with. So how ironic that someone in power had already spotted his potential for corruptibility; an unknown but sinister politician.

The man must have guessed that Robin loathed Enfield and everything he stood for. He never bothered to hide his contempt of socialism. So when a smear campaign to ruin Albert's political career failed, Robin was not the slightest bit surprised when a conspiracy was devised to destroy him. Anyone brave enough to inaugurate a car bomb attack, would surely be doing the establishment a favour. It was the very callousness of his attitude that attracted the other man's interest; his clawing ambition to succeed in politics, his hunger for power...

In the aftermath of the explosion however, a very secret meeting cropped up; Robin had been drawn into a conspiracy so dark, he knew it would change his life forever. Enfield may have perished but not everything had gone to plan. A witness had surfaced and they were desperate to silence him.

Robin would never forget the euphoria that hit him as soon as he realised that he was the one being propositioned. Added to the allure of an attractive four-figure pay out, his ally agreed to use whatever influence he possessed to launch him higher up in politics. Robin felt no shame in agreeing to his pact. In fact, he was thrilled by it. To be a part of something so secret, a darker side of him relished the thought of getting rid of someone. Wasn't this the ultimate testament of power? Conversing with Norman Hargreaves, the inspector had already agreed to interview the witness as well as delay him from leaving the building.

In the crucial moment Jake was captured, Robin had been hiding in the shadows. He had observed the boy as he left the police headquarters - his slenderness, the sheen of flowing hair, those pale handsome features which made him look so vulnerable. The moment those thugs grabbed him, Robin experienced a frisson of excitement as they hurled him into their van. So turned on was he by the concept of what he was getting himself into, he had made a decision there and then; on the night Jake was killed, he yearned to be there to witness it.

But of course, that never happened. Jake had escaped.

No one could have been more devastated. He had taken an instant dislike to Dominic Theakston, as it was; irritated by his cockiness, his towering height and muscle-bound physique which reminded him all too harshly of the boys who had tormented him at school. It had been Robin's idea to impose the six month deadline; that if Theakston failed to find Jake, Hargreaves would have sufficient jurisdiction to lock him up!

The next two months had been insufferable. If Robin did not see this through, there would never be another chance to appeal to his mentor. His career in politics might even be over. So when Jake had finally resurfaced, together with that troublesome female, he formulated a plan so devious, they would have no chance of escaping a second time.

He was delighted to have found them in Holborn, all thanks to a tip from some old vagrant. And what a wonderful encounter it was too! Using his charm and his manipulative skills to maximum effect, he had captured their interest from the start. He chose words he knew would frighten them, especially the female. Girls as beautiful as Eleanor were a threat to him. He had enjoyed playing on her fear and if they did chance a visit to Waterloo, the stage was set... a scenario that would send them running to Toynbee Hall at the first hint of trouble.

Their plan had been perfect and finally Jake had been dealt with. Unfortunately, he had never counted on the fact that Eleanor would resurface.

All too aware Theakston wanted her for his own personal vendetta, Robin was convinced she would be captured. Yet she had evaded them. Somehow, they had discovered a hiding place where their enemies would never find her… and now she was walking free, a threat to them all. Robin closed his eyes, conscious of the charge of his heart. It was no use. They *had* to do something about her before it was too late.

The police inspector's home lay in a moderately inconspicuous location.

Some distance from both Poplar and Whitechapel, his modern semi-detached house was tucked in a small suburban side street, away from the bright city lights. Robin concealed his car well out of sight. Glancing round the area, he was grateful of the cloak of darkness.

Norman led him into a tidy, comfortably furnished lounge but Robin had no desire to waste time on pleasantries. He got straight to the point.

"Why did you let her go, Norman?"

"I didn't," Norman snapped. "She was discharged from hospital and you know it."

"Not good enough," Robin whispered, drawing a step closer.

Norman did not move, refusing to be intimidated.

"We had her right in our hands! All the while she was in that hospital, we were safe. Couldn't you have at least told the doctor, she was *wanted by the police* for questioning?"

"Except she wasn't," Norman said coldly. "The doctor knew she was the girlfriend of a murder victim. Furthermore, she was close to a mental breakdown. So just be reasonable, will you? They had no choice but to let her leave…"

"Except you weren't counting on someone like *Bernard James* to go poking his nose in, were you?" Robin interrupted.

"At least the girl's being looked after," Norman shrugged, "and I personally don't have a problem with that."

Robin's eyes took on a flicker of contempt. Sinking his hands in the pockets of his overcoat, he slowly shook his head. He released a sigh of frustration.

Norman braced himself, appalled to witness such malice; without warning, the veil had been drawn back, exposing Councillor Whaley's true persona.

"What's the matter with you, Norman?" he sneered. "You know damn well this presents a problem. I met Bernard James and you didn't have to look hard to see that he's a typical socialist; just the type of person who would support Enfield. Does it not worry you, what Eleanor may have told him?"

"Oh, for Christ's sake, will you calm down!" Norman spat. "Whatever

Eleanor may or may not have said, she has no proof! At the end of the day, we got what *we* wanted. The Jansen boy is dead."

"But she is still walking free," Robin said icily, "a danger to us all and you can't even see it!" He gave a chilling smile. "I thought you were going to hand her over to Dominic..."

"Well I changed my mind!" Norman snarled. "Eleanor is sixteen and furthermore she is pregnant, which makes her an extremely vulnerable young girl..."

"Oh yes, I did hear the Jansen boy knocked her up!" Whaley snorted callously.

"As a senior police officer, I can't take the risk," Norman continued, ignoring that last remark. "It's a miracle we bluffed our way through Jansen's murder but as for Eleanor... You have no idea how vicious Dominic can be especially when he holds a vendetta..."

"Are you sure you're not turning soft, Norman?" Robin taunted. "She is after all a very pretty girl, isn't she?"

"That's enough, Councillor Whaley," Norman said softly. "Think about our positions. Would you want to risk throwing away everything, on the very slim chance that Eleanor might say something? I think you're being paranoid, so let me put your mind at rest." He took two lead crystal glasses from the sideboard and filled them with a fine, single malt whisky. Handing one to Robin, he waved him towards to a swivel armchair. "Sit down."

For once, Robin didn't argue. With look of disdain, he accepted the drink and lowered himself into the chair. Norman sensed he was fuming but at the same time, he was damned if he was going to be manipulated. Taking the chair opposite, he stared deep into the other man's eyes, a technique that had always worked for him.

"So you're worried the Chapman girl poses a threat are you?" he muttered. "Well let me remind you, I've already stuck my neck out for you, Robin."

"For which you've been richly rewarded," Robin shot back nastily.

"Yes, and I am about to be promoted," he ploughed on, "which puts me under a certain obligation to protect people. Now while I agree, it is possible that Eleanor may know something, the truth is, she is a sixteen year old kid with no proof. Anything she says will sound like a fairy tale! Even the hospital staff have confirmed her state of mind was fragile."

He allowed himself a pause, waiting for the words to sink in. Robin remained silent, staring dazedly into space. Hand tightening around his glass, his knuckles had turned white.

"We, on the other hand obtained enough evidence to prove that Jake Jansen was involved in drug dealing. He was wanted by the police and it is common belief within the force, he was murdered by a criminal gang; one which remains anonymous since Dominic had an alibi. There is nothing she can say or do to incriminate any of us."

"But she saw me," Robin said in a tone of pure venom. He raised his glass and hurled the whisky down his throat, slamming the glass down on the table. "That little bitch has been a problem from the start! She saw me outside the brothel before she set the boy free! As if that wasn't enough! It took us weeks to find him! Then, just when everything was back on course, she appeared in the road and saw me. And you accuse me of being paranoid?"

"What if she did see you?" Norman replied. "It doesn't prove anything. I expect there were lots of people hanging around, as is usually the case when there's some sort of incident and the police are involved."

"What about Bernard James?" Robin continued, eyes narrowing. "He must have his suspicions... I am the only person he passed their address to!"

Norman froze, fearing there was nothing he could say to put his mind at rest. Yet he was still not prepared to give up. He had visited Eleanor just the once; a frightened young girl who had begged him to protect her.

"Look," he said through gritted teeth, "we seem to be going round in circles! So Bernard James is suspicious. I took his statement for God's sake but what are either of those two going to do about it? Like you say, old James is some woolly minded 'lefty' who would say anything to have a go at the authorities, especially the police..."

"So that's your solution is it?" Robin hissed. "To do nothing!"

Norman shrugged again, unable to prevent the smile that teased his lips. "It's the only option as far as I'm concerned. If we start marching around, interrogating people like Bernard James, we are only going to draw attention to ourselves. There's already enough talk of police 'cover ups' and as for detaining Eleanor... Forget it and that is my final decision! You and Dominic can go fuck yourselves!"

Robin's eyes flashed. A valley of silence hung between them as he pulled out his cigarettes. He fumbled around with the pack for a moment before lighting one.

"I suppose I'll have to talk to Dominic then," he drawled.

"Dominic hates your guts," Norman responded harshly.

"Not many people like *him* either," Robin taunted.

"Difference is, Dominic doesn't give a shit!" Norman smirked.

"Well, I'm not really that concerned," Robin sighed, pinning him with his cold eyes again. "Just one last question. Is anyone having her watched?"

"We know where she's living," Norman retorted. "I said I'd keep an eye on her but that's all and there is nothing to report. If there was, you'd be the first to know."

"I see," Robin finished, rising to his feet. "Well, you may not feel she is a threat, Norman, but I do. At the very least, she needs a warning - something to remind her that it's in her best interests to keep quiet. I hope you understand..."

V

Eleanor did not venture out much. Yet there came a time when she loathed being cooped up all day. It was not for lack of things to do; she had plenty of magazines, she could watch TV if she wanted to or listen to a play on the wireless. Nevertheless, she felt frustrated. The ache in her heart from losing Jake had never fully subsided; not a day went past where she could ignore the terrible emptiness in her life. She missed him so much.

Today the clouds had receded, giving way to sunshine; one of those bracing winter days when Eleanor would have liked nothing better than to go for a brisk walk. The bite of cold would be refreshing, allowing her troubled thoughts to clear... In fact, she had never felt more restless.

She had spent the morning pottering. Engrossing herself in chores, she had washed up, swept the stairs and mopped the kitchen floor. With nothing more to do, she had reached that point in the day where she would sit comatose in the same armchair, watching the world go by...

Buttons lay curled up on the rug by the fireplace. Gazing silently into space, Eleanor's hand swept over the subtle curve of her belly. At least she had the birth of her child to look forward to, her last legacy to Jake. Yet that wouldn't be until May. It seemed an eternity.

Expelling a sigh, she dragged herself out of her armchair. In the same instant, Buttons sprang to his feet, gazing up with his wistful brown eyes. With his tail swishing from side to side in anticipation, he was clearly longing for a walk.

Perhaps this was her opportunity to go outdoors and grab some fresh air. Eleanor bit her lip, her eyes drifting to the door, where his lead hung on a hook. Unable to resist that look for second more, she clipped it to his collar. Pushing her feet into her boots, she slipped on a warm overcoat Edna had given her and stepped cautiously out onto the pavement.

At first it felt strange. She glanced from one end of the street to the other, where the rows of Victorian terraces stretched in both directions. Breathing deeply, she felt the cool air fill her lungs. There was a faint whiff of rubbish in the air, but sweetened with the more pleasing aroma of wood smoke drifting from surrounding chimneys. She began to stroll up the road with Buttons trotting along beside her. *Only now did she feel exposed.* There were a few people meandering around on the pavements; but they were mostly middle-aged housewives in overcoats and headscarves, pulling shopping trolleys behind them. Eleanor let go of her tension a little. It was a pleasure to be outside where the chill of the winter air felt refreshing, bringing a tingling sensation to her cheeks.

By the time she reached the end of the road, several shops began to materialise. She proceeded to poke around the area, clocking the different stores; a café, a traditional London pub and a betting shop. What she didn't notice was the blue transit van pulling into the side of the road. The dark shape lurked on the edge of her vision but didn't quite register.

Immersed in her reverie, she found herself drawn to a florist. A tall woman with a blonde beehive hairdo was fussing around outside, arranging buckets of pretty blooms. Eleanor smiled to herself. The sight of the flowers reminded her of something else she had been meaning to do. Hadn't she been yearning to pay some kind of tribute to Jake?

Pausing by the front of the shop, she couldn't resist lingering to gaze at the blooms; colourful chrysanthemums blazed brightly against the more delicate pastel shades of carnations and roses. The woman turned to her and smiled.

"Anyfink take yer fancy, love?" she chirped in a rich cockney accent.

"I was thinking about setting up a memorial for someone," Eleanor replied dreamily. "A place I could visit from time to time... relive our memories together..."

As her words petered away, she could feel the tears welling. The woman placed a gentle, rubber-gloved hand on her shoulder. Despite the tired worn look she carried on her lined face, she surveyed her with a look of genuine sympathy.

"Ow's about the Garden of Remembrance?" she muttered. "There's a special little area in the park. It's fenced off with railings. Some folk lay a little plaque or an urn full o' plants. You should ask the council, they take care o' them things..."

"Thank you," Eleanor whispered, forcing a smile. "It sounds perfect."

Already she could picture the place she was talking about. She had only ever seen one park in this area; the same place she and Jake had sprinted across, pursued by Theakston's gang. It made perfect sense. That pivotal scene had occurred just moments after they had met and marked the beginning of a whole new chapter. If only their lives had turned out differently and the ending could be re-written... Feeling a tug on the lead, she remembered Buttons. Inspired to buy a bunch of pale pink carnations, she decided to head back home.

As soon as she moved, the van fired up its engine, ready to follow.

Yet over the next few moments, Eleanor felt strangely at peace. She glided along the pavement where the watery sunshine added a little colour to the streets, transforming the grimy brickwork into a mosaic of terracotta reds and browns. She had almost returned to Bernard's house when the van swerved around the corner. It crawled right up to the pavement. Then at last she saw it.

Peering over her shoulder, she froze. Buttons gave a little whimper as if sensing her panic and for the next second, she could hardly breath...

It must have been there all along yet only now did she become more wary of it. The hovering presence seemed threatening. She thought she even recognised it; a van that was uncannily similar to the one Jake had spotted in the driveway of Clark's brothel. Could this be the same vehicle they had used to capture him?

Eleanor spun towards the house, her face rigid as she rummaged in her coat pocket for the key. She had been a fool to think her enemies wouldn't watching her. Even with Jake dead, her situation had never changed. Didn't they say all along, they intended to track her down?

Of course they had discovered where she was living. She was jarred by a metallic rumble as the van door slid open. Someone jumped out, a set of boots landing heavily on the pavement from behind. She could not bear to look around to see who it was; a tiny part of her already knew. With trembling hands, she rammed the key into the door to open it and leapt indoors, slamming it firmly closed behind her.

"Bernard, I have to leave," she announced.

He had returned from work and only just sat down with a mug of tea. Edna could be heard shuffling about in the kitchen, putting away groceries.

His mouth dropped open. Lowering his mug to the table, he rose to his feet.

"You can't!" he spluttered. "What about your baby?"

"The reason I have to leave is for the protection of my baby," Eleanor whimpered. "They know I'm living here! I saw a van and it was the same one used by Theakston's thugs. They came here, Bernard! They pulled up right outside your house!" She started to cry.

"Oh, surely not," Bernard breathed, gathering her into an embrace.

Edna, who had clearly heard every word, waddled into the room. Her face was stricken with misery, mouth open, as she gaped at Eleanor.

"Oh Eleanor! When did this happen?"

Pulling herself out of Bernard's embrace, she clasped the woman's hands.

"This afternoon," she said tearfully. "I took Buttons for a walk. They probably knew I was living here all along..." She released Edna's hands and spun back to Bernard. "I can't face them, Bernard, not yet. They killed Jake and it almost destroyed me. If they get their hands on me now, I won't survive, especially if something happens to my baby and this is why I've got

217

to get away from here. I just want my baby to be safe..."

"We can protect you," Bernard insisted. "If we see them again, we'll call the police."

"No!" Eleanor protested. "As you know, the police are powerless against Theakston and I couldn't bear it if they hurt you. You've been so kind to me..."

"But where will you go?" Bernard argued.

"I've already been thinking about this," Eleanor sniffed. "A neighbourhood called Forest Haven. Jake and I hid there for a couple of months. This is the place we shared our happiest memories and we always swore we'd return the guitar..."

Bernard shook his head, his expression taut with anxiety. *Of course, she had told him.* The truth was they had squatted in someone's house over the summer. How could she be sure what type of reception she'd get? The residents might be furious!

"The worse they can do is tell me to clear off," she shrugged, "but I owe them an explanation. I think it's only fair to give the guitar back to its rightful owner don't you? Once that's settled, who knows? I'll find some lodgings..." She surveyed him timidly. "There was a nice Asian family who ran a shop and they always had postcards in their window advertising rooms. Don't worry, I'll find somewhere. I just have to get away from this area."

"But what if these people call the police?" Edna whimpered. "What if they decide to prosecute you for squatting in their house?"

Eleanor swallowed. "If that's the way they react, I'll deal with it." A sad smile lifted the corners of her mouth as she pictured a photo of the Merriman family. "Though somehow, I can't imagine they're that sort of people..."

PART 5. THE MERRIMANS

Chapter 12

I

Eleanor couldn't be swayed, convinced she had made the right decision. The sight of the blue van had unleashed a savage fear and she was never going to feel safe again, knowing that Theakston's men had started tailing her...

Hastily gathering her belongings, she packed a few extra clothes Edna had given her and the guitar in its leather case. No sooner had she piled them into Bernard's car, they set off just as the sun started to disappear beneath the roof tops.

"I hope my stay hasn't put you in any danger," she murmured from the back seat. "What if they come back and start hassling you?"

"How can they, Eleanor?" Bernard sighed. "We've been looking after you, that is all. As for the other matters we discussed... I suppose they will have to be kept secret for now, though I still think you should try to trace Jake's friends."

"One day," Eleanor nodded.

Glancing from left to right, she couldn't help scouring the streets for enemies, never quite sure if they were being followed.

They approached Forest Haven from the west. The area seemed more built up from this side; a stark contrast to the murky neighbourhood she had stalked with Jake. That night seemed like a dream now yet she could still recall the industrial wastelands and railway embankment...

They found themselves drawn into a narrow road, observing the little houses tucked behind their hedges. By the time they reached the crossroads, Eleanor braced herself. The sight of the shops brought a twist of sadness, the tiny café where they had enjoyed a last coffee.

"This is it," she gasped. "Turn left and we should be able to find the road where the house is. Jake and I always used a little footpath which led into the back garden..."

She didn't need to explain further. Fortunately, it wasn't difficult to find. The main road led into a warren of side streets and there at the back, soared an imposing row of detached houses, the slope of the embankment not yet visible. Eleanor asked Bernard to pull over. Hit with an unexpected bolt of anxiety, she knew there was no turning back now...

"Promise to stay in touch, love," Edna whispered tearfully, pushing a tin of shortbread biscuits into her hands.

"Oh, thank you!" she gasped. "I love shortbread! And of course I'll keep in touch. I don't know what I'd have done without you two..."

"Such a pity you had to leave," Bernard added gently. His lined, hang-dog face was etched with sadness. "But you know where we are, if it doesn't work out. Just take care, Eleanor..."

Her heart sank as she backed away from them, waving as the gulf stretched wider.

Braced outside the house, this was the first time she had viewed it from the front side; the sash windows looked startlingly familiar as did the grey stucco walls. Eleanor glanced at the VW camper van in the driveway with a gulp, then finally tapped on the door.

A tall, middle-aged woman materialised. Gazing down through widely spaced green eyes, she bore the deep leather tan of one who spent many hours in the sun. Her features were strong and almost masculine. Eleanor couldn't help but feel a little intimidated by her; the heavy jaw, high forehead and full lips. Casually dressed in a long, crinkle cotton skirt, her mane of long, silver hair cascaded almost to her waist.

A strange encounter where neither of them spoke, Eleanor took a deep breath. Her hand trembled as she held out the guitar. Her mouth had turned dry. The woman offered her a twisted smile, leaning into the door frame, surveying her.

"Well, hello," she said coolly. She almost seemed to be expecting her.

"I thought I should b-bring this back," Eleanor faltered. "I-I believe it belongs to your son?"

The woman pursed her lips and with a resigned sigh, snatched the guitar.

"You'd better come in," she sighed.

Eleanor's eyebrows shot upwards yet the woman's face simmered with questions. Flicking her head towards the lounge, she turned from the door, compelling Eleanor to follow.

Nothing could have prepared her for the rush of emotion she experienced, the moment she was back in that lounge; the shimmers of light emanating from the crystals, the books, the clutter of candles and ornaments. A pungent scent of roses filled the air, tinged with a familiar trace of incense. Eleanor could no longer hang onto her composure. She broke down in tears.

"I think you had better sit down," the woman muttered. Her voice held no anger, only a hint of suspicion. "Come on in, don't be shy. I'm guessing, you're one of the people who lived in my house over the summer... and yet you brought my son's guitar back."

"Are - are y-you Mrs. Merriman?" Eleanor faltered.

"I am indeed," the woman said, "but you may call me Rosemary." Coaxing Eleanor towards the little leather tub chair, she lowered herself into the settee. "So what about you? Are you going to tell me *your* name? I'm curious to know why you came back…"

"My name is Eleanor," she began. "I wanted to put things right and return your son's guitar… I also wanted to meet *you*."

"An unusual decision," Rosemary pondered. "I could still inform the police."

Eleanor raised her head, heart thumping. "I-I know that… b-but we weren't really squatters. We just needed a place to hide."

Rosemary raised her eyebrows but if there was ever a glint of accusation, it faded in that instant, leaving a touch of curiosity. In many ways, she was exactly as Eleanor imagined; intelligent, calm… a deep inner goodness seemed to radiate from her soul.

"Okay, so now you've met me, what now? You see, I sense your grief… So come on, you might as well tell me the rest. What were your reasons for staying in my house?"

Eleanor drew her arms slowly around herself. "As I said, we were desperate for somewhere to hide. We thought the house had been abandoned…"

"So how did you get in?" Rosemary kept pressing.

"J-Jake found the key in the jam jar," Eleanor mumbled. "We only meant to stay for one night and yet we felt so safe here…"

"You decided to stay a little longer," Rosemary finished.

Eleanor nodded. *Yes, this was the only place they had ever felt truly safe.* Even now, she could feel its protective mantle embracing her. It forced the memories to come bubbling to the surface; the night of their escape being the sharpest. Strange though her explanation may sound, she felt a hankering to share her story…

It began with the chase across East London. Although Eleanor was desperate to get her story out, Rosemary couldn't seem to resist interrupting - picking over every detail.

"It was a long night," Eleanor shivered, "we walked and ran for miles. It was getting cold a-and we were terrified…"

"So who were these people?" Rosemary pressed, the horror in her expression growing.

"A dangerous gang," Eleanor shivered, "ruled by a contract killer. I'm sorry if it sounds far-fetched but London can be a very scary place at times."

"Some people say the whole of the East End is run by villains," Rosemary nodded knowingly, "but why were they after you?"

"It's complicated," Eleanor sniffed. Another tear escaped her eye but she wiped it away savagely. "They were after Jake, more than me…"

"So where is Jake now?" Rosemary whispered.

221

The light in her eyes dwindled as she said it. There was no holding back, she had to tell her.

"Jake's dead," Eleanor's voice withered. "They got him in the end..."

"No!" Rosemary gasped. "Oh, I am so sorry!"

A moment of uncomfortable silence ensued as she absorbed this. Yet Eleanor knew they had only scratched the surface. She had so much more to tell her; the notion of a contract killing, the men who had sanctioned it, men in power... the more she talked, the more Rosemary's expression flared with outrage, to a point where she had to break her flow.

"It's alright, I know you're telling the truth," Rosemary shuddered. "I am fully aware of the corruption in Scotland Yard. The police and organised crime practically go hand in hand in this city. But it doesn't really help *you* much does it? Your story is horrendous!"

"I had a feeling you'd understand," Eleanor whispered, swallowing back her tears. Without realising it, her hand had fallen to her abdomen, stroking the spot where she could imagine her baby's heart beating. Jake's presence had filled this whole house once. She could almost sense a part of him lingering here right now.

"You loved him very much didn't you?" Rosemary concluded.

"Yes,' Eleanor replied, her breathing slowing itself at last.

"You poor child!" she added softly. "I know what it means to lose someone and you're with child too, aren't you?"

Eleanor could hardly speak. She gave the slightest nod.

"Okay," Rosemary nodded, "so now I know a little more about you, I'm somewhat *reassured* that you found my house and made it your sanctuary. So why don't we continue this conversation over a glass of home-made wine? I can tell you sampled some of it..."

She rose and swept from the room, skirt swishing over the floorboards. Eleanor watched mesmerised. Pleased to have finally met her, she felt as if she had turned another corner.

The familiarity of her surroundings brought a painful sense of nostalgia as daytime slipped into evening. The light drained from the sky. Eleanor gazed out of the kitchen window as Rosemary poured the wine; absorbing the sight of the long garden before the shadows crept in. By the time they had settled down to renew their conversation, Rosemary had drawn the curtains. She switched on one of the cane lamps, engulfing the room in a ball of warm light.

How could she forget the cosy evenings spent with Jake? Yet she was fascinated by Rosemary, a woman who appeared to be deeply spiritual. In very little time, she seemed to have absorbed all her troubles; from the prolonged absence of her father, to the threat of her enemies who were still stalking her. She had told her about Bernard and Edna. Their warmth and hospitality had helped her overcome the worst of her grief, until the unexpected manifestation of that van today.

"And this is what brought you back here," Rosemary deduced. "It completes the circle. You said you always wanted to return..."

Eleanor lowered her eyes where Edna's tin of shortbread nestled in her lap. Absentmindedly picking the Sellotape off the lid, she found herself pondering over what she had said.

Next she heard the sound of footsteps erupting outside. A jumble of voices accompanied it before a key was thrust into the door. Someone else had arrived home. Eleanor sat up sharply, tense with anxiety.

"Oh, that'll be the kids!" Rosemary said with a casual wave of her hand.

A small group of young people piled into the lounge where they stopped dead. Eleanor turned and gazed at each of them in turn.

Wary she had reached another hurdle, their questioning faces demanded an explanation... Her eyes were drawn to the taller of the two boys, instantly struck by the resemblance to his mother. He possessed the same pale green eyes, powerful jaw and generous mouth. But remodelled on the face of a male, those features were incredibly handsome. With smooth, dark hair and smart attire, this was obviously the older, more conservative of the two brothers.

As her gaze shifted to the second boy, there was little doubt, this was the guitarist. With longer, golden brown hair flopping around an animated face, he was mouthing silent words as if singing to himself. His jeans had several rips in them, below the hem of his afghan coat.

The girl however, stared back through eyes which were undeniably hostile. She possessed a lovely face with long silver eyes, similar to those of the younger boy; her silky blonde hair tumbling to her waist.

"Who's she?" she demanded in a high, girlish voice.

"This is Eleanor," Rosemary smiled. "She wanted to meet us. She also brought your guitar back, Joshua..."

"Cool!" the one with the long hair piped up.

"Just a sec!" The girl hissed. "Does this mean she's one of the squatters who lived here?"

"Alison, calm down," Rosemary sighed. "She's here to make amends..."

"Maybe I should leave," Eleanor said softly, sensing the waves of animosity.

"No, stay!" Rosemary begged her.

Alison had started to retreat towards the stairs. "Why did you even let her in?" she shouted, "after they slept in our beds, helped themselves to food... They even took our things!"

"That's why she came back!" Rosemary pressed, "to return your brother's guitar. She's just explained her reasons for living in our house..."

"Yeah, our house!" Alison echoed mid-rant. "Not some hostel for anyone to doss down in!"

"Oh, for goodness sake, stop it," Rosemary argued. "So she stayed in our house whilst it was stood empty. She was desperate... Don't you understand the importance of sharing?"

The last thing Eleanor saw was the fury writhe in her face before she stormed out of the room. The bedroom door was slammed above, followed by an intolerable thump of rock music.

Rosemary rolled her eyes and sat back down. "Ignore her!" she sighed, gazing sadly back at Eleanor. "She's just angry."

The music pounding through the floorboards however refused to be ignored.

Several minutes passed before Rosemary ground her teeth. She too, flounced up the stairs to have a word with her daughter; by the time she returned, she had at least persuaded her to turn her music down a little.

It was pitch black outside by now and the candles had been lit. The older boy poured himself a glass of wine before he joined the discussion. A sensitive boy, he seemed intrigued by Eleanor's story. The other boy sat cross legged on one of the floor cushions. He had already started fumbling with the guitar, adjusting the pegs, running his fingers over the strings, where a series of soft notes hummed through the murmur of adult conversation.

Eleanor was telling them about the day they had left Forest Haven.

Rosemary seemed surprised, given the perilousness of their circumstances. Yet how could they stay, knowing the owners were due home? There was no question they would have been offended. Eleanor had tried to relay this, though looking at Rosemary now, maybe they should have taken a gamble... It could have changed everything. Jake might still be alive.

The conversation moved on. She mentioned Sammie's solicitor in Holborn, a point at which the older boy's interest peaked. His name was Luke.

"Sammie Maxwell," he mused. "I can't believe you were remembered in the will of the late Sammie Maxwell. Wow, that is just so cool!"

"You've heard of him?" Eleanor frowned.

"You bet!" Luke grinned. "My boss used to go to his club, the Malibu, said it was the hottest place in London for a good night out... Some say, he was a shady character but I would have loved to have gone there. I hear it's closed down."

"What happened next?" Rosemary intervened, determined to keep Eleanor on track.

She started twisting a strand of hair between her fingers. She had never wanted to mention Councillor Whaley, but how could she avoid it?

"We were betrayed," she finished numbly.

In the moment of silence, even Joshua paused in his musical reverie. All three of them clung to her words, desperate to know where the story was heading; an emotional journey that catapulted her from Waterloo Station to Toynbee Hall...

"A place for people to turn when they're desperate," Rosemary smiled knowingly. "They can live there for next to nothing, so long as they volunteer to help the community."

Luke nodded sagely, sufficiently enlightened. Unable to sit still, Joshua began gently plucking the guitar strings again, repeating the same bars, over and over.

"They tried to help by moving us into a bedsit," Eleanor added bitterly, "but it was awful."

Tears blurred her vision, as she found herself funnelled towards the worst memories of all. Luke chanced a timid smile. Rosemary was helping herself to a piece of shortbread while the other boy seemed engrossed in his guitar; though Eleanor suspected he was listening with half an ear. Rosemary touched her hand, as if picking up her tension...

"It's okay, there is no need to continue," she whispered uneasily. "You've already explained what happened to Jake..."

"He was killed?" Luke whispered. There was something very cautious about the way he said it; no morbid curiosity just a deep-hearted concern.

Fighting hard to keep her emotions under control, Eleanor nodded, her lip quivering.

"I think that's enough," Rosemary finished tactfully. "Let's not talk about it any more, not tonight. It's time I cooked us a meal."

Already, Eleanor loved their company. They were just the type of family she imagined them to be, people she yearned to get to know better. Their patience soothed her, enabling her to share her tale without disintegrating. It was a shame about the daughter but she clung to the hope that maybe she could reach out to her some day and discover what lay at the root of her anger.

Slowly she rose, glancing across the room to seek out her coat. "Thanks for being so nice about this..." She picked up her hold-all.

"Hang on," Luke gasped. "Where are you going?"

"To find somewhere to stay, of course," Eleanor said with genuine sincerity. "I'm sure there's a boarding house somewhere."

"You can't go!" Luke gasped. "Not now. Tell her, Mum!"

"Eleanor, I'd like you to stay with us," Rosemary announced with an air of authority.

"Oh, no," Eleanor said uncomfortably. "That's not fair... what about

Alison?"

"You leave me to deal with Alison," Rosemary said firmly. Arms folded, her eyes turned granite hard as they pinned her where she stood. "You're sixteen. I won't let you to go wandering off in the dark, not now, given the danger you're in... especially as you're pregnant?"

Tears sprang to Eleanor's eyes again, the holdall slipping from her hand. "I-I don't know how t-to thank you," she mumbled. "I could always sleep on the sofa..."

"There's no need," Rosemary finished boldly. "You can sleep on the camp bed in my room. The camp bed, which one of you two boys can get ready. Okay, boys?"

"I'll do it!" Luke volunteered, jumping to his feet.

II

Her return to the house evoked a riot of emotions; from an initial sense of safety to unexpected waves of sadness. The gratitude she felt towards the Merrimans was indescribable. They had not only welcomed her into their home but showed incredible tolerance. In some way, she felt embarrassed if not a little guilty. She and Jake had taken incredible liberties living in their home. Yet they were surprisingly forgiving and genuinely wanted to help her; such undisguised compassion moved her deeply.

Rosemary with her powerful sense of perception had a good idea of what she was going through. Well-read, intelligent and motherly, she was unlike anyone Eleanor had ever met before. The boys too, were great and displayed a similar warmth towards her.

Luke, unmistakably the more chatty of the two, couldn't deny the strange feeling that stirred him when they had returned home from Ibiza. Evidently the house had been lived in; things seemed to have been moved, some of his clothes were missing. Yet as soon as the initial shock wore off, he and Joshua couldn't help wondering if it was someone they knew... They had travelled around France, Spain and the Balearics, where strangers often put them up for a day or two; likeminded, bohemian folk with whom they had swapped addresses.

Joshua felt the same way; a quieter boy who tended to talk in monosyllables. He eventually confessed he preferred the older guitar to his new one, delighted Eleanor had returned it. Quick to reassure him, the guitar had been put to good use, she told him about Jake; his band, 'Free Spirit' and his songs. She even showed him Jake's song lyrics.

"Cool words!" was his straightforward comment.

If only she could recall the melody of his final song, though she tried to explain its meaning. "It was a song about us," she said gently. "That bit about *predator and prey*, I think what he meant is, people live their lives as they are meant to. But when they die, their memories live on; in Jake's case, his songs..."

"Nice," Joshua said - and looking at her through his clear, grey eyes added: "Sad that he died. What a waste..."

Settling into familiar surroundings, Eleanor realised that the process of grieving had to undergo a number of stages.

In the immediate aftermath of Jake's killing, she was left in a void of such shock she never imagined she would survive it. Yet Bernard had thrown her a lifeline. Throughout her short stay, she had overcome the worst of her heartache.

Her return to Forest Haven had initiated the final stage; a pain that would never subside yet she could cling to the memories of Jake without feeling traumatised. It inspired her to ask Rosemary what had become of *her* husband. She had never forgotten that first cryptic clue; *I know what it means to lose someone*.

Rosemary had met her husband, Jonathan in the 1950s. As the daughter of a wealthy, private doctor, she had attended an exclusive boarding school for girls. She merged into society a polished, sophisticated young lady but even private school failed to suppress the wilder side of her nature. A fleeting tour with friends across France and Italy had ultimately brought her into contact with him. Worlds apart from the stuffy, middle class life she was used to, Jonathan introduced her to a more nomadic lifestyle; one that involved a fair amount of travelling and a chance to make new friends. From the very first night she had met him, relaxing around a camp fire, strumming his guitar, she knew she had found a kindred spirit...

Her family did not approve at first and hoped the relationship would be a passing phase. But one year later - a day they had nervously announced their plans to marry - they had no choice but to accept, their daughter was in love and finally consented to the union.

Delighted by the birth of their baby son in 1953, the couple decided to settle in London.

Two years later, Joshua was born and within a few more months, Rosemary fell pregnant again with Alison. Delirious with happiness, they knew would need a bigger house.

Determined to find a place they could live happily for the rest of their lives, they were blessed to discover Forest Haven; a small community confined within an ever expanding sprawl of modern housing and industrial estates. Yet as the walls of urbanisation squeezed tighter, the neighbourhood managed to retain its charm.

Their lives could not have been happier. They were living in a house of their dreams and as soon as the children were old enough, they introduced them to the joys of travelling. A lumberjack by trade, Jonathan worked hard to support his family. Yet as the kids entered their teens, so they outgrew the camper van. This was the reason they had purchased the caravan, sadly abandoned in the back garden. Tragedy had struck the previous year, when Jonathan suffered a terrible fall from a ladder. He had eventually died from head injuries. Rosemary never imagined how she would survive such heartache but as the only remaining parent, she needed to summon the strength to cope with her own grief, as well as comfort their children.

Their long sabbatical in Ibiza had been a tribute to Jonathan. The idea of spending a whole summer in this notorious 'hippie paradise' would have appealed to him. The caravan however was never used again. Rosemary considered it a bad omen and wanted to sell it.

The story touched a nerve in Eleanor. Rosemary had endured the same emotional turmoil as she was going through and it bonded them even closer.

And as for Rosemary... Eleanor's plight had jarred her too.

Fearing the effects on someone so young (and with her child not even born yet), this was the one factor that had brought out her fierce protective instincts. From the depth of her heart, she felt that Eleanor belonged here. The love she had nurtured, coupled with the magical conception of a child had forged a connection here; the reason she was unable to let her go on that first night...

The only one who continued to disrupt the harmony was Alison. It didn't matter how much Eleanor helped around the house; from washing cars and cleaning the sooty grime off the windows, to helping their mother prepare meals.

Resentful of her presence, she never bothered to hide her contempt. Refusing to speak to her or even look at her, she stuck her nose in the air whenever Eleanor loomed close. Her behaviour created a mood of tension which at times, lingered like a storm, provoking frequent rows with her mother. Eleanor wondered if life would be easier if she just left and found some lodgings.

Rosemary refused to even consider it but Eleanor couldn't let the situation prevail. Time was slipping by and they were approaching Christmas. Unable to bear the thought of such a special time of year being tarnished by Alison's bitterness, she knew she had to confront her, if not just to find out what was really gnawing inside her.

There were times when she made a tentative approach; like the morning she awoken early and slipping silently from her camp bed, crept into the kitchen to make tea. She had been gazing silently out of the window. The sky was indigo, the garden illuminated by an iridescent moon where the spiky silhouettes of trees stretched into the cold light of dawn

Alison had wandered through the door.

"What are you doing up?" she spat.

"Can't we just talk?" Eleanor pleaded. "At least tell me why you feel like this?"

It was useless. Alison clenched her jaw in a way which sent her chin jutting outwards and over the next few minutes, uttered some very unpleasant words. *"Maybe I'm the only one who thinks it's wrong to help yourself... You're not on the run! I reckon you made that up to get sympathy... somewhere cushy to sit out the final months of your pregnancy."*

Eleanor wished she could pinpoint the real reason for her hatred. The death of her father had clearly left a hole in her life and maybe she saw her presence as an intrusion. But there was something else. Alison was possessive, driven by a powerful urge to cling to all she had left. Her bedroom was her private domain and she felt violated. Like the three bears in the Goldilocks fairy tale, the concept that someone had been in there and borrowed her things, infuriated her beyond all reason.

"How can you be like this?" Eleanor croaked. "Everyone else in your family's so kind!"

Wary of the tears prickling, she couldn't bear the sight of Alison's cruel face, a feeling that had sent her fleeing back upstairs again.

The argument left her drained. Alison worked on Saturdays. Her part time job in a Covent Garden boutique dragged her out of bed early to catch the bus, leaving Rosemary to gather the rest of her family in the kitchen for a weekly cooked breakfast. The moment Eleanor wandered into the kitchen however she felt a grip of nausea.

"Are you not feeling well today?" Rosemary queried as the boys tucked in ravenously.

A combination of pregnancy and her churning emotions caused her to retch, sending her rushing up to the bathroom. For the rest of that day, she had been subdued.

Yet Eleanor couldn't bring herself to give up.

Every so often, she tentatively held out an olive branch. Yet however hard she tried to engage with Alison, she always had some nasty retort... until a day came when she finally lost her temper. She had been in the garden when Alison unexpectedly slipped through the hedge.

"I've had enough of this! Don't you think I've had my heart broken enough? I fell in love with Jake in this house and he was murdered..."

"Really?" Alison said evilly, drawing her face close. "I'm not even sure I believe that! You sure he didn't just dump you...?"

Eleanor jumped back as if scolded. She could have hit her but in the same moment she spotted the Supersavers carrier bag in Alison's hand, bulging with groceries.

"I see you've been to the corner shop," she said through gritted teeth. "Do you know the girl who works there? Daliya? Ask her if she remembers Jake. Theakston's gang visited their shop once, when he came looking for us! Go on, ask her, I dare you!"

Everything changed that night. Eleanor couldn't deny she felt nervous as she began to chop up vegetables for dinner. The anger which festered inside had transformed into panic. *How could she face Alison after that horrible exchange?*

Breathing deeply, she tried concentrating on the carrots and potatoes to be washed and peeled. Rosemary was a great believer in home cooking and loathed all the processed and packet foods packed with chemicals which were starting to creep into British supermarkets.

Eleanor felt her stomach heave as she glanced at the kitchen clock. Seconds later, a movement caught her eye, a shadow flickering across the lawn, drawing right up to the back door.

The expression on Alison's face was priceless.

"Oh my God, Eleanor..." She was white to the lips.

To everyone's even greater amazement she clasped Eleanor's shoulders.

"I'm so sorry..." was all she could say, at first.

So Daliya had borne out everything she had told her. She had even kept a copy of the newspaper, chronicling Theakston's arrest, having instantly recognised him as the gang leader who had interrogated them that summer.

III

With their inner wounds healed and differences patched up, Eleanor felt they could move forward at last. Later in the evening, they had settled in the lounge for a proper girlie chat. The room was warm, the shadows soft in the flutter of candlelight and as Alison sat cross-legged on the floor cushion, she confessed how close she had been to her father.

Jonathan had always referred to her as his 'special little princess' with a tendency to overindulge her. But while Rosemary possessed a heart that could easily wield the love of two parents, Eleanor sensed something irreplaceable had been torn from Alison's life.

It struck another painful chord; the mystery of her own dad. Their shared grief for an absent father was the one thing that ultimately bonded them...

But as the harmony inside the Merriman household shifted into balance, time began to pass more quickly. It didn't seem long before the family were caught up in the festivities of Christmas. The house almost lent itself to the season; enhanced with a log fire, baskets filled with fir cones and a real fir tree. There was no safer place on earth where Eleanor could be, thankful for the chance to forget about her enemies for a while and protect her unborn baby.

She sent a card to Bernard and Edna, reassuring them that everything had worked out favourably. The only other card she had written was to John Sharp, Sammie's solicitor; clutching at the ever prevailing possibility, there might be news of her father...

On the evening the tree went up, she collapsed into the depths of the baggy sofa and closed her eyes. She thought of Jake; how much he would have loved all this. In some way, she could almost imagine his spirit hovering, watching beyond the grave and it magnified her love for the Merriman family. She was already wondering what she could buy them for Christmas.

As Christmas was the one season which brought London to life, Rosemary agreed to drive both her and Alison into the heart of the West End, where they arranged to meet the boys.

It so happened, they both worked at the Grosvenor Hotel; a large and magnificent establishment, situated near Victoria Station. Luke held the privileged position of a wine waiter, dapper in his uniform waistcoat, formal trousers and bow tie. He confessed wines were his passion; his ultimate dream to open an exclusive wine shop, perhaps in Forest Haven one day.

Joshua worked as an apprentice painter and decorator, since the luxurious interior was currently undergoing refurbishment. Apart from his job, he enjoyed socialising. His favourite pastime was browsing the record shops, especially in pursuit of rare and unusual bands.

He had already put out a few feelers, regarding the Dutch band, 'Free Spirit.' One of the more alternative hippy shops, hidden in a side street, was a place he had finally stumbled across mention of them. In a summer 1971 back issue of 'New Musical Express,' the band appeared very briefly as part of a line up for the Weeley Festival of Progressive Music.

It seemed almost uncanny; so much so, the store owner (who specialised in foreign imports and bootleg tapes) was captivated by the idea of discovering more about this unknown band and promised he would track down their music.

It seemed however, that Joshua was not the only one thinking about 'Free Spirit' nor for that matter, Eleanor...

In the busy streets of the West End, hung a lovely atmosphere - the warming fragrance of hot chestnuts and toffee apples sold by street vendors - shop windows decorated with fake snow and pretty lights. Somewhere in the distance, echoed the haunting sound of a Salvation Army brass band playing Christmas carols. And as the evocative melody of 'God Rest Ye Merry

Gentlemen' rose into the air, Robin Whaley felt the hairs on the back of his neck prickle before he spotted them.

Watching the two girls wandering along the pavement arm in arm he saw them disappear inside Selfridges. His eyes were fixed on just one of them, never able to forget the graceful, gliding step of Eleanor Chapman. She might be wearing a fluffy white hat over her distinctive hair yet this was a girl he would have picked out anywhere.

Concealed in the shadowy doorway of a nearby cafe, his eyes narrowed as they momentarily slipped out of sight. The other girl, he barely noticed - his heart was thumping.

He knew he had to be careful. He had recognised Eleanor instantly but there was every chance that she would recognise him, if he crept up too close to her. How many weeks had it been since she had disappeared from the area where Bernard James lived? Hargreaves had promised they would keep tabs on her. Right now, Robin wondered if he dared set the wheels into motion and have her followed. He bit his lip, eyes scouring the area for a public phone box.

Fortunately, he spotted one a little further down the road. With his head lowered and his hands buried deep in the pockets of his winter coat, he inched cautiously towards it.

"Oxford Street," he whispered into the receiver. "Christmas shopping with a friend, they're in Selfridges. How soon can you get here and start tailing them?"

Five minutes later, a typical London taxi drew to a pause outside the department store. Robin watched with pleasure, delighted to have located her again...

Eleanor felt the burn of tears but blinked them back, refusing to let her melancholy surface in the midst of such joviality. In truth, she felt uneasy wandering from shop to shop and as an extra precaution, chose to buy all her presents in this single department store.

With Alison accompanying her to help her choose, she started picking out gifts; an ornamental glass decanter filled with bubble bath for Rosemary. In the menswear department, she spotted a fashionably striped grey shirt for Luke.

By the time they left the store, it had turned dark but the busy pavements were illuminated by the gleam of lanterns emanating from the shop windows. In the fraction of time they had left before meeting the others, Eleanor dashed into a record shop to buy the latest Rolling Stones album for Joshua: 'Exile on Main St,' which he had been wanting for ages. Fighting their way through the crowds they headed towards a corner of Oxford Street, where the boys awaited them. Wrapped in scarves and woolly hats, they breathed great clouds into the crisp winter air. It had been a hugely enjoyable venture and safe to be reunited with them, Eleanor couldn't wait to return home and start present wrapping.

Chapter 13

I
January 1973

Christmas came and went. The world flipped over like an hourglass and as the year drew to a close, so emerged the dawn of a brand new year.

Eleanor tried to imagine the life she had led a year ago. Distant memories loomed of Christmas spent in her old home; a muddle of suited men, cigars and card games not to forget the mysterious telephone calls which drew Oliver away from the house at night...

A whole new future lay ahead of her now with the imminent birth of her own child.

It seemed a good time to install the memorial she had been planning for Jake; something personal in a place that connected them and relive a part of their journey. Later in the year, she planned to visit Holland, in respect of everything she and Bernard had talked about. It would be therapeutic to trace Jake's friends and visit his final resting place. But for now, the park in Poplar still appealed to her.

Escorted by Rosemary, they found themselves wandering along in the chilly January air, where a sparkle of frost cloaked the ground. As the woman in the flower shop had mentioned, a circle of railings enclosed the area designated the *Garden of Remembrance*. Unfastening the latch on the heavy wrought iron gate, they crept inside.

The garden was designed in a series of concentric circles. As Eleanor moved forwards, she was drawn to the central flower bed filled with rose bushes. The branches were bare but she could picture them in summer, smothered in fragrant blooms. An array of wooden memorial plaques surrounded them. Eleanor spun around to gaze at the shrubbery. More rose bushes reared up before her; but they were blended in amongst other species of shrub. As Eleanor peered more closely, she began to notice the other memorials peering out of the shadows; they included more crosses, rocks and even a stone urn nestling on the ground.

She closed her eyes. Could she really lay him to rest here? Thrown back in time to the day they raced through this park together, the essence of him flowed through her mind; the sunshine hazy, the paths that had granted them an escape route... She would never forget the power of his spirit.

Yes, it was a perfect place.

Rosemary appeared to be watching her. Intuitive as ever, perhaps she felt him too; that fleeting presence of Jake, which lingered like a footprint...

Eleanor gave a nod. Nothing more needed to be said; all that had to be done was to consult the council for permission. Sensing threat, Eleanor took a gulp of the icy air. Tower Hamlets Council; a place connected with Robin Whaley and this park lay in the boundaries of his ward.

Rosemary handled the paperwork, liaising with the department who managed parks and gardens. By the middle of February and with the application complete, Eleanor commissioned a local mason to create a memorial stone; a subtle, green-grained marble with the inscription of just a few words:

My beloved Jake
Never to be Forgotten

Beneath the stone, she buried a tiny wooden casket as a token of their love. Inside hid a lock of her own hair and a folded note onto which she had re-written the lyrics of his last song. He would never know how much those words had touched her, his most beautiful song of all... Furthermore, his little stone pendant kept him close to her heart at all times and she continued to wear the engagement ring he had bought her.

In the final seconds before she tore herself away, she paused at the gate, her face wet with tears. Pressed against the cold iron bars, she could see the stone gazing out from the undergrowth and as it caught her eye, she gave a tiny wave.

II

In the following weeks, Rosemary witnessed a change in her. There was a lightness in her mood as if a burden had been lifted. An unexpected bloom of health manifested itself in her appearance; a peachy glow to her complexion and a renewed shine in her honey coloured eyes. Her dark hair had grown thicker, the swelling of her pregnancy quite visible by now, like a ripe water melon.

In March however, the media was rocked by news that the provisional IRA had exploded more bombs, this time in Central London. It was the start of a campaign of terrorism that shook fear into the nation but for Eleanor, it couldn't have happened at a worse time. The IRA had never admitted responsibility for the bomb which had killed the politician, Albert Enfield. Yet such devastating news seemed destined to confirm what people believed; while the true perpetrators, those people Jake had spotted, were even more likely to get away with their atrocities...

It set her thoughts spinning into motion, wishing there was a way of infiltrating the media. If only they could expose the truth. How could a rock musician from Holland witness something so significant and end up murdered? Worse, how could he be so falsely portrayed as a drug dealer to mask a sinister contract killing?

But whatever flames had been fanned by this latest terrorist threat, the wheels of every day life kept rolling.

On April 6th Eleanor turned 17. The Merriman family had been enthusing for days as to how they could make this a memorable celebration. With her baby due in just a few weeks' time, this could be her last chance to enjoy life as an irresponsible teenager.

Her birthday fell on a Friday which meant everyone was working. Alison however, had a half day at drama school and was planning to be home by mid-day. She suggested they could have lunch in the local pub the 'White Swan.'

By mid-afternoon, sunshine poured through the windows, drawing her into the garden where she settled into a deckchair. The encircling borders had begun to burst into to life - clumps of daffodils in full bloom, their bright yellow heads nodding in the breeze. Fat buds glistened on the bushes and the surrounding trees were cloaked in a haze of green as new leaves began to emerge. It all seemed symbolic. What a joy to be reaching the final stage of her pregnancy in the spring; to be a part of a continuing cycle of creation that radiated in the world all around her. She felt ripe and fertile, her body a temple, harbouring a new life and as her hand moved over her mound, she couldn't resist a smile, enjoying the sense of connection.

The main celebration took place in the evening. Eleanor had plenty of time to rest in the lounge, having changed and put on a little makeup before the others started piling through the door. They brought an effervescent mood into the house. Rosemary made pizzas which they arranged on the table and ate with their fingers, leaving strings of cheese trailing over the plates. The sky outside had darkened to an inky blue, the candles lit. Luke then surprised them all by producing a bottle of champagne to celebrate the occasion.

Proud to show off his skills as a wine waiter, he gracefully popped out the cork. Eleanor watched, mesmerised. A wisp of vapour curled like smoke from the bottle neck before he poured out five glasses, waiting for the foam to settle before topping them up.

"To Eleanor!" he announced. "Happy seventeenth birthday!"

"Thanks Luke," she sighed. "This is so sweet of you..."

Their eyes met. Luke held her stare, his wide green eyes shining with affection as Eleanor sipped her champagne. It tingled on her tongue, refreshing and dry, infused with a hint of creaminess as the bubbles exploded inside her mouth.

Joshua burped loudly, clamped his hand over his mouth in embarrassment then jumped to his feet. Ever since he had arrived home, he seemed agitated;

hopping his way across the lounge, whispering away in song. Yet there was an extra bounce in his step.

"We found a special present for you," Rosemary said, gazing deeply into her eyes.

The room fell silent. Everyone seemed tense yet at the same time, thrilled.

By the time Joshua returned to the table, he was holding out a small, gift-wrapped parcel, his face illuminated with a cheeky grin.

Eleanor took it, recognising the shape of an audio cassette before she unwrapped it. Her heart gave a little leap as she drank in the cover; the logo of a pink elephant beneath a set of chunky letters: FREE SPIRIT - DEMO 1972. She gave a cry of pleasure.

"Jake's band! I don't know what to say..."

"Happy birthday, sweetheart," Rosemary said, leaning back in her chair.

"Told you I'd find something!" Joshua smiled proudly.

"It's a bootleg tape," Luke added. "Some weird guy Josh knows always manages to find stuff. He told him Jake's band were from Holland... got a copy from their recording studio."

Eleanor glanced at each one of them in turn. Turning the cassette over in her hands, she could have cried. This was Jake's music. To think, a part of him had been resurrected, leaving her with a peculiar feeling inside.

It took a little prompting for her to agree to listen to it. Fighting tears, she passed the tape to Joshua.

He bounded across the floor and slipped it into the stereo. After an initial hiss of lead tape, a fast and heady drumbeat pounded into the room. A bass guitar joined in and with an explosion of power, the first song was launched.

Eleanor sat very still, waiting for the voices to kick in; a chorus of them to begin with. Yet they receded into the background, leaving a single soloist. She pressed her eyes shut. There was no mistaking that gentle mid-range voice - breaking huskily as he hit the high notes - deepening to a whisper as it dipped to the lower ones. An army of shivers ran over her body, the hairs on the back of her neck tingling. Without warning, she could feel the tears coming...

"Oh Jake," she sobbed, pressing her hand to her mouth.

The music played on, a lively, intoxicating tune which would have had the crowds stamping their feet in any concert hall. Joshua tapped his foot in time to the drum beat. Alison's face was lit with an expression of pure joy. Only Luke remained still. He must have spotted the trail of tears on her face in the candlelight and as the first track ended, so a second began. This one was more of a folk tune, the beautiful guitar rifts accompanied by a saxophone.

"Wow!" Alison whispered. "They're bloody good!"

"Ssh!" Rosemary whispered.

Jake had started singing again. Everyone fell silent as the sound of his exquisite voice flooded the room. A single candle flame suddenly shot upwards like a flare.

Eleanor gasped, bracing herself. Jake's face materialised in her mind and for a second, it was as if he was stood right next to her. She could almost sense him; the subtle fragrance of his skin, the purity of love which shone in his mysterious green eyes. Every characteristic was embossed in her mind... and as the beautiful song played on, the flame abruptly flickered back down again.

"I-I don't think I can listen to any more, right now," she shivered.

"Did you see the candle?" Alison whispered. "That was spooky!"

Joshua beamed at her, reluctantly hitting the stop button.

"Love it!" he piped up. "Can I have a copy?"

"Of course," Eleanor murmured, "let's make lots of copies. Can you believe, this is the first time I've heard Jake's band? They're brilliant! I want as many people to hear them as possible..."

"Yes," Rosemary said as she hovered in the background.

Detaching herself from the group, she stood by the sink, glancing out of the window. The garden lay in darkness. She too, had seen the eerie way the candle had shot upwards; an ethereal presence which *had to be* connected to Jake.

But it also set her mind working. How on earth could it be right for such a talented young man to have his life cut short so brutally? It served as a sharp reminder of the injustice they needed to expose... but only when Eleanor was ready.

Eleanor left the debris of the party for a while to enjoy a walk with Luke and grab some fresh air. The sound of Free Spirit had exposed her heartache; although she was deeply moved by the Merriman family's gesture, not to mention everything else they had done to make the evening special. Right now, she had a yearning to step back into the past; to explain to Luke how they had arrived here on the night she and Jake had escaped...

Sliding through the gap in the hedge, she beckoned Luke to follow. The path eventually led up to the embankment. There were railings protecting it from the overhanging brambles now.

"Be careful," Luke whispered, "don't fall."

He curled his hand around her waist to steady her as they pushed their way to the top.

An extensive view across London was unveiled. A clear night, the stars made sharp pinpoints of light in the sky above them.

"We came to this embankment from somewhere over there," Eleanor said, pointing.

Luke followed her gaze, seeing the silhouettes of factory buildings, towering cranes and a pair of gas containers in the distance. The area was as cold and industrial as Eleanor remembered; they could just about make out the rows of houses crammed together further away.

Eleanor exhaled a sigh. "Jake would have been killed if I hadn't found him. Yet they got him in the end... What was it all for, Luke? None of it made any difference."

"That's not quite true," Luke reassured her. "You're expecting *his baby*. It's the sort of thing my Mum would say *was meant to be*, a chance to pass on his family line. If you hadn't escaped together, there would be no one left to tell his story."

"True," Eleanor admitted. She could not help but feel a wave of sadness. It shouldn't have ended this way; their escape, the start of a brand new life together.

The thought brought an involuntary shiver.

"Are you cold?"

"I'm scared. There's something that still worries me, see. Like what will happen, once my baby's born. What if Theakston and his gang catch up with me again?"

"I can protect you," Luke said softly. She observed his profile, silhouetted against the sky; the straight forehead and strong line of his jaw. He turned and looked at her. "I'd look after you, Eleanor and the baby. You must know I have feelings for you..."

Eleanor bit her lip, lowering her eyes. She suddenly couldn't look at him. "Luke, that's sweet," she mumbled, "but we both know things aren't that simple."

To think, Luke could have easily captured her heart. He was handsome, kind, engaging... but right now, she felt nothing for him; her love for Jake eclipsed everything. In time, she would heal but for now, Jake held a very special place in her heart and she was not yet ready to let that feeling go. Drifting into a relationship was not impossible, just not yet. The timing was all wrong.

"I don't think you understand how dangerous Dominic Theakston is," she relented, desperate to spare his feelings. "I'm Ollie Chapman's daughter, which means he could still use me to get back at him! He's a powerful gangster, Luke, and that could bring danger for you..."

"Okay," he said, "but I meant what I said. I'd do anything to keep you safe. We could even get a flat together..."

They wandered back along the railway tracks and just before they reached the house, his hand slipped into hers. Eleanor smiled secretly; it was comforting to know that someone cared for her. Maybe one day, she would love again... but it was going to take a very long time.

Robin Whaley glanced at the inner walls of the exquisite mansion in awe.

The light was soft; a subdued gleam cast by the pendants of a chandelier seemed to mirror the secrecy of this meeting. Still, at least Theakston's intelligence had paid off...

"It appears she is living in Forest Haven," he smiled.

The other man leant back in his deep leather chair, his face veiled in shadow. It was impossible to gauge the expression on his face as he lit a cigar.

"Forest Haven..." his deep voice pulsed into the room. "The same place they were hiding in the first instance? Is it possible, she might know someone there?" He appeared to be thinking out loud, the drawl of his English public school accent pronounced in the electrical pause.

He took a short puff from his cigar.

"What has she told them about the Jansen boy, I wonder?"

"We don't know," Robin responded warily.

"So we need to up our offensive," his companion whispered. "See if we can catch her on her own at some point."

Robin braced himself, sensing the potential threat that lurked in the wake of their discovery; a matter that was never going to go away until they dealt with her...

III

On the dawn of May 3rd, Eleanor and Jake's child was finally delivered into the world.

Her labour started in the night as the house lay in stillness. The only sound in the room was the tick of the clock on the dressing table; it merged with Rosemary's breathing. The sky gleamed a luminous blue from a dazzling full moon but as she squirmed in her camp bed, she could no longer ignore the spasms of pain tugging inside her body.

"Rosemary!" she whimpered, gripping her belly with both hands.

Instantly aroused from sleep, Rosemary swooped to her bedside to comfort her.

The contractions continued. They ebbed and swelled like the waves of a sea, growing in strength, the pain steadily worsening...

"Can you take me to hospital?" she moaned through gritted teeth.

"Of course," Rosemary said gently, "you'd better pack a bag..."

Looking at Rosemary's face, she absorbed the compassion in her eyes; she reminded her of some sort of earth mother.

She picked out her flowing white dress of cheesecloth. *Jake had loved her in this dress.* Catching a glance at her reflection, she couldn't help but smile. Her belly was huge, big as a space hopper, her honey coloured eyes glittering. Her hair hung almost to her waist, the rippling tresses luxuriously thick as they shimmered in the light. In fact she had never looked more beautiful. Powerfully connected to the child inside her, she was reassured, they had survived this far...

Venturing into the night, the full moon beamed a pool of white light over the road as if to guide them. Rosemary began their journey towards East London, the familiar streets marking dangerous territory. Yet there was so little traffic at this time of night. Within 15 minutes they had reached the London Royal Hospital in Whitechapel.

Time passed in a blur. Examined by a doctor and then a midwife, she had to face a barrage of questions; from the name of her doctor to the date of her last check up.

"You've been pregnant all this time and you've never seen a doctor?" the midwife scolded her.

Eleanor closed her eyes as the nurse tut-tutted. How could she begin to explain? *Hiding from dangerous enemies; there was a time they had virtually sprung up outside Bernard's door.* Eleanor shivered. She didn't want to consider her fearsome past, not when the only thing she cared about was the birth of her child.

As time wore on, she wondered if she would ever survive this. She was exhausted, giddy and soaked in sweat; rolling around in a sea of pain as she pushed and pushed. Her memories of Jake were the driving force that kept her going until after what seemed like an eternity, their son finally made it into the world, healthy and whole.

The next time she awoke, the room was flooded with sunshine. A light breeze fanned the curtains and as she absorbed her surroundings, she was dimly aware of a melody tinkling inside her head. It sounded eerily familiar; something she had been trying to recall for days. Drifting into her mind shortly after her baby was born, the mysterious tune stayed with her. At the same time, she was struck by a sense of emptiness. They had left her in a room on her own.

Eleanor sat up abruptly. One glance at her watch told her, it was almost noon so why were they keeping her isolated? Surprised she had not been transferred to a ward by now, she was uncannily reminded of the last time she had been here. A tiny part of her expected to see Inspector Hargreaves looming in the doorway. Already, she could feel the tears fighting their way out, her emotions raw. Without warning, she was struck with a feeling of vulnerability; memories of the tiny scrap of life they had lain on her chest earlier, *her baby.* For all the time the child had been gestating in her womb, he had been safe. Yet how on earth was she going to protect him now?

Eleanor felt a sudden weight of responsibility. The outside world seemed huge, filled with the same hostile enemies as before. She had sworn to Jake she would protect their baby. Yet right at this moment, she was unsure if she would be able to keep that promise, a feeling which left her in pieces.

Jolted by the swing of the door opening, she was relieved to see the nurse. Even better, she was accompanied by Rosemary and Alison. She forced a smile.

"Whatever's the matter, sweetheart," Rosemary sighed, flopping into a chair next to her bed.

"Thank God you're here," Eleanor whispered.

Alison found another chair, dragging it around to the other side. Leaning forward, she kissed Eleanor's cheek.

"What are you upset about?" she muttered. "I thought the worst bit was over. I hear you did great! So where's the baby?"

"Midwife says she's going to bring him in a minute," the nurse answered. Beaming down at Eleanor, she possessed a face that appeared plump and matronly. "We thought we'd leave you to rest a while, you looked exhausted. How do you feel now?"

She hadn't really thought much about her physical condition but now they mentioned it... Yes, her body did feel battered and sore, her breasts tender as they swelled against the satin of her nightie. She touched one of them and winced.

"Sore boobies?" the nurse added sweetly. "That's your milk coming, dear. Baby needs feeding."

Eleanor turned to Rosemary with a look of alarm.

"Stop worrying," Rosemary fussed. She caressed her shoulder. "Let nature take its course, you've got nothing to feel frightened about."

"So why do I feel so scared?" Eleanor bleated. "Why do I feel as if my enemies are stood out there in ranks, waiting to grab me? Especially, now I'm not pregnant any more..."

"There's no one out there, Eleanor," Rosemary muttered. She rubbed her hand tenderly over Eleanor's back, easing the tension from her shoulders. "It's perfectly normal to feel anxious after a birth. Every woman does, it's the hormones. Face it dear, you've battled your way through the worst part so just relax. You've given birth to a beautiful baby boy."

"Here he is now!" Alison gasped, rising from her chair.

She wore a half smile, her silver eyes lit with pleasure as the door swung open again. Craning her neck, she seemed desperate for a peak, as the midwife lowered the infant into Eleanor's waiting arms. He was wrapped in a clean white blanket. At first Eleanor said nothing. Cradling him in her arms, she just stared at him. But as the image of the child materialised, her senses were flooded with a feeling she could not describe.

Her baby's face was no longer crinkled like crepe paper but had evened out to a smooth, pearlescent pink. Stroking the top of his head, she encountered a fuzz of soft baby hair. Unusually fine, it was almost without substance like the filament of a feather; a soft brown in colour and as Eleanor studied him, she saw a subtle underlying hue of auburn. At last, the baby opened his eyes. She felt her heart squeeze with emotion. The child's eyes danced, unfocused, a clear blue in colour and for a brief second they met her own.

"Oh my goodness," Eleanor gasped, "he's beautiful."

She had never felt a force of love so powerful as she was experiencing now.

"Wow, he is too," Alison blurted. "Lucky you! Most new-borns are really ugly."

"Alison!" her mother scolded, though her eyes twinkled with amusement.

Her gaze settled on Eleanor as she carefully manoeuvred the baby towards her breast. One plump little hand pushed against her flesh, tiny fingers stretching outwards. She managed to rest him down comfortably, before his sweet pink lips found her nipple. Eleanor felt a lump rise in her throat, letting go of her troubled thoughts as she bonded with her baby.

This was Jake's child. A precious life form she had vowed to safeguard for all the while she carried him, he was a real person now. She knew without any further doubt, she would love and protect this child, whatever future lay ahead of them.

IV

Eleanor remained in hospital for two days. Only after Rosemary's visit was she finally moved into a ward. She not only felt safer but enjoyed mingling with the other mums. Touched by the level of care offered by the staff here, they checked her constantly to see how she was faring.

A little later, the boys popped by. Joshua charmed the nurses with his alluring smile while Luke, armed with flowers, fussed over her like a big brother.

The following afternoon, Eleanor was enchanted to see Bernard and Edna poke their heads around the door.

"We thought it was about time we paid you a visit," Bernard announced.

Edna, stirred by the sight of the tiny baby, turned a little tearful.

"Oh, what a bonny little chap," she crooned, rocking him in her motherly arms. Eleanor studied her face, wreathed in soft lines. She had never been more comforted by their presence.

"We're so very happy for you, my dear," Bernard smiled.

Eleanor gazed back at him with affection. "Thank you! It's lovely to see you both and I've missed you. But just to put your minds at rest, the Merrimans have been absolute treasures."

They stayed for a good half-hour, chatting and fussing over the baby. Before they left, they hugged her warmly, kissing her on the cheeks like long lost parents.

Relishing such tenderness, Eleanor could feel a sense of joy spreading over her like a smile. A number of cards perched on the table alongside three bunches of flowers. The nurses had arranged them in vases: frilly white carnations from Luke, an array of coloured tulips from the rest of the family and a huge bouquet from the James's.

Before she left however, a different nurse appeared at her bedside.

"These are for you too..." she said.

Eleanor glanced at the flowers and frowned. Just a few red roses poked out of a paper cone, their petals misted with a faint dew. Spotting the small card taped inside the paper, she started picking it loose with her finger nails.

Congratulations, hope to catch up with you soon.

Such a stark, cryptic message left her confused. Studying the handwriting, every spiky letter had been scrawled untidily across the card. This was not the script of anyone she recognised. But for some reason, she turned completely cold.

An hour later, she was safely back inside the fold of the Merriman family

Oddly enough, that melody had latched itself to her mind again. But whatever memories were associated with it, they raced away before she had a chance to recapture them...

Huddled inside the lounge, everyone was fighting for a turn to hold her baby. Only Joshua seemed a little awkward, as if afraid he might drop him. Alison snatched him back. Eleanor couldn't help but savour the look on her face; glowing with such euphoria, it seemed as though her child was the most wonderful thing to slip into their home for years.

"Do you know what you want to call him?" she asked, stroking his cheek.

"I have actually," Eleanor smiled back. She had thought of it last night whilst feeding him, resisting the urge to name him Jake. "I was looking for something meaningful. Something that included both our names, Jake and Eleanor. I was wondering about *Elijah...*"

"That's lovely," Alison agreed.

"Unusual too," Rosemary added. "Where did you get the idea?"

"When Jake and I visited Toynbee Hall to see Bernard," Eleanor said dreamily. "The original designer of the building was a man named Elijah Hoole. The name sort of stuck..."

Rosemary gave an intuitive smile.

"Can I cuddle him?" Luke intervened, rising. "Come on, Alison, stop hogging him."

She reluctantly allowed him to peel the baby away from her arms. Cradling him gently, it must have seemed a tad strange. Luke had never had much to do with babies but like Alison, he displayed a genuine fondness towards this delicate creature.

The baby started to squirm a little. Luke shifted him to his other side but within a few more seconds, the infant started wriggling again before he screwed up his face and bawled.

"Sorry," Luke mumbled, "I can't seem to get him comfy..."

"It's okay," Eleanor laughed, "maybe he's got wind or something. Here, let me take him."

Turning to pass him back, their eyes met. They shared a heartfelt smile. Eleanor snuggled the baby close to comfort him but as she did so, she automatically started humming *that tune* to herself; that distant, forgotten melody, which continued to haunt her...

"Who are the roses from?" Luke suddenly questioned her.

"Oh, those..." Eleanor mumbled. She turned rigid, unsure what it was about those roses that unnerved her. Wary of her baby still fighting and wrestling, she struggled to find the right words. Perhaps she should have just left them at the hospital.

"I don't know who they're from," she blurted. "The note didn't say."

She turned and stared at Rosemary. If anyone could throw a light on the mystery, she could; Rosemary with her incredible sense of perception. Already, she detected a hint of trepidation.

"An anonymous bunch of red roses," Luke murmured.

"Do you still have the note?" Rosemary asked her. "Can I see it?"

"Of course," Eleanor replied. She was too preoccupied to think about it right now, her arms locked around her child, rocking him as gently as possible as she paced the room.

"I'll have to look in my bag," she added, "but let me see to Elijah. He might need changing..."

Only a little later, Rosemary pulled Eleanor to one side, desperate to talk to her alone. Sloping off upstairs to the master bedroom, she closed the door. Elijah was settled in the same room, sleeping peacefully.

"It's about those roses isn't it?" Eleanor whispered with a creeping sense of dread.

"Yes," Rosemary nodded. "You'd better sit down, Eleanor, because before I say anything else, I am certain, those roses were sent by an enemy..."

Eleanor lowered herself onto the bed, taut with anxiety.

"The clue is in the flowers. Think about it, red roses are usually the flowers one sends to a lover. But try looking at it another way. Imagine a mirror where you can see the same thing in reverse. The opposite of love is hate. Red is the colour of love but also the colour of violence."

"But who could have sent them?" Eleanor shuddered.

Lowering herself down at the dressing table, Rosemary fished out the card. She turned it over in her hands where the same jagged letters leapt out at her.

"I'll get straight to the point. I cannot believe this came from the police inspector nor for that matter, the councillor. Neither of them would have handwriting like this! Both are professional men. I am certain their writing would be neater, which only leaves one other person..."

"Theakston?" Eleanor gasped, her eyes widening.

"The writing is scruffy," Rosemary continued, holding the card up. "Scrawled without a lot of thought... I've studied graphology and there is something very aggressive in this style. I think whoever wrote it might also be left handed."

"But why would he send me flowers?" Eleanor breathed. "It doesn't make sense!"

Sagging onto the bed, she felt as if all the substance had been knocked out of her.

"There's a message hidden in the words," Rosemary added sadly. "*Congratulations*... He knows you've had your baby but the words that follow, *hope to catch up with you soon*... I'm guessing he plans to find you again; that your quarrel is not quite over. I'm sorry Eleanor, but I've got a funny feeling, these words could be a veiled threat..."

Eleanor shivered again. Already she could hear the sense in her words.

"So what the hell am I going to do?" she whispered. "What about my baby? I would die if anything happened to him."

"Don't dwell," Rosemary soothed her. "He may be doing this just to intimidate you."

"But what if the threat is real?" Eleanor pressed. "You don't know this man. You don't know what he's capable of! People have told me some of the things he does to his victims..."

Glancing at the card again, the words seemed to mock her *'hope to catch up with you soon.'* She turned very still, hit with a rapid fear and at the same time, her fingers crept towards Jake's stone pendant.

"Rosemary, will you promise me something? If anything ever did happen to me, would you take care of Elijah? I am not suggesting you keep him. Just see that he goes to a good home, somewhere where he'll be safe..."

Rosemary sighed. "Eleanor, you know I will but nothing is going to happen to you. Are you trying to suggest this man might actually kill you? Because if this is the case, you should talk to the police. You cannot live your life in fear."

"There's nothing the police can do," Eleanor sighed. "Inspector Hargreaves has already covered up for Theakston once. How do you think he got away with Jake's murder? And that's what's so terrible! This is how organised crime works. Theakston has a huge number of villains working for him; take the two lads who planted drugs on Jake for example. I could meet someone in the street and be snatched without even knowing who they were..."

"Then it's time you did something," Rosemary insisted. "You cannot let this man control your life. Where the law has failed to bring justice to Jake's killers, there has to be another way... a young man died! Shouldn't that raise questions?"

"Not if he was some drug dealer bumped off by a criminal gang, it seems," Eleanor said miserably, "and this is how they covered it up - using fake evidence - the same story they printed in the papers. If only I could prove what really happened and I bet this is why Theakston's trying to scare me. I know too much."

"You mentioned the papers..." Rosemary murmured. Her voice spooled into the room like a loose thread. Eleanor fell silent before she added something very strange. "There has to be another story hidden in this, can't you see? When it comes to the papers, it's not what's staring you in the face that matters. It's what's missing..."

V

Eleanor laid the baby onto a cushion and settled down on the floor next to him. She couldn't bear to be parted from him for long, driven by a powerful maternal instinct to keep an eye on him. It had been three weeks since his birth and already he was changing. His tiny limbs were becoming plumper. A cap of baby hair spread over his whole head, fine and silky, a warm chestnut brown. Right now he was making sweet gurgling noises, his eyes wide open. Eleanor stroked his face, marvelling at the pearly smoothness of his skin.

She was curious to know why his eyes were blue, an enigma Rosemary had explained; *all babies were born with blue eyes.* Their true colour would develop in time, which left her wondering if his eyes would be green like Jake's...

Rosemary lingered in the doorway with Luke, as she crooned over her infant.

Waves of music emanated from the stereo; the distinctive sound of 'Free Spirit.' A huge hit among the family, they loved the harmonious blend of ballad and rock, an energetic beat reminiscent of 'T-Rex' married with softer undertones akin to 'Lindisfarne.' It spoke volumes that both groups had been headline acts in the festival line up Joshua had spotted in NME and this was the one issue where 'Free Spirit' had received a mention. It suggested their music more than fitted the genre of the era.

For Eleanor, the sound of Jake's band was a gift. Nothing delighted her more than fussing over their child, whilst immersed in the power of his songs... Clocking the presence of the others, she turned from her baby and smiled at them.

"I was just gonna make some tea," Luke beamed, "fancy a cup?"

It was Saturday midday. Alison had hung onto her job at the trendy fashion boutique in central London and had plans to go out after she had finished. Bubbling with excitement over some new boy she had met, she wasn't expected home until later.

Joshua on the other hand had been to a party the previous night. Staggering home drunk, well beyond midnight, he was heard galumphing around the house, bumping into furniture and making enough noise to wake up the entire household. Rosemary had decided to leave him in bed to sleep off his hangover. Though it was evident he was up now, from the flush of the lavatory upstairs.

"I swear I'm going to kill that little sod," she hissed.

"Oh, don't be too hard on him," Eleanor pleaded, "not after he found this tape! He's made so many copies of it too... I bet all his friends know about Jake's band by now."

"About the only good thing he has done!" Rosemary snorted.

Eleanor fought back a smile. The whole family suffered the occasional bout of conflict; though on the whole, she thought they got on pretty well. She had feared the presence of a newborn would turn their lives upside down. Yet they had been incredibly tolerant, even when he cried at night. Resuming her cosseting, she was kissing his bare foot when Joshua burst into the room, almost knocking Luke over.

"Watch it, you bloody idiot!" Luke shouted, shoving him back.

"Sorry, bro'," Joshua mumbled with a grin. Swaying slightly, he clamped an affectionate arm around his shoulder to hug him.

"Piss off," Luke growled, shaking him off.

"Boys!" Rosemary exclaimed. "And you Joshua have got some explaining to do! How dare you come in so late and make all that noise, crashing around like a bull in a china shop!"

"Sorry, Mum," the boy spluttered, "didn't do it on purpose, honest..."

He loped across the lounge in ripped jeans and a stripy black and red T-shirt like 'Dennis the Menace,' long hair flopping in his eyes as he rubbed them.

"You woke Elijah," Eleanor said accusingly. "It took me ages to get him to sleep again. He wouldn't stop howling and that disturbed Alison. So she's furious with you too!"

"You know she had to get up early for work," Rosemary scolded.

"Aw, c'mon, I am really sorry," Joshua repeated. Raking his fingers through his hair to sweep it away from his eyes again, he did at least look a little sheepish. "But hey! Listen to what I gotta tell you! S'important!"

Luke narrowed his eyes, all plans of making tea, forgotten.

Refusing to be ignored, Joshua sagged into the sofa next to him. Eleanor clocked the animation in his face; a look of glee that couldn't be suppressed.

"Eleanor!" he grinned at her. "You'll never guess what?"

"I can't possibly imagine," Luke drawled, hurling him a withering look.

"Shut up, bro! Seriously, this is news, good news!" Speaking a lot faster, he was clearly building up to something. Joshua was a boy of few words but whenever he did have something to say, it was like a dam bursting… "Met Adam Morrison! Writes for NME and guess what? There's been some news about 'Free Spirit…' Some Dutch guy wrote an article!"

"What?" Eleanor gasped. Stirred by his words, she found herself rising to a kneeling position. "Did he tell you what the article said?"

"Yeah," Joshua muttered, the smile falling from his face. He lowered his eyes.

Yet to reveal everything this editor had told him, he felt a little nervous at first. He had memorised the story so well now, it was engraved on his mind like an epitaph.

Piece by piece, he attempted to explain it, though struggling to find the right words...

It had been reported that 'Free Spirit' had split up.

They could no longer continue without knowing what had happened to their lead singer, Jake, who had disappeared without a trace, back in July 1972.

Later that same year, the tragedy of his murder hit them with devastating impact. News that his body had turned up in the darkest avenues of East London began to filter through; reports that he had been shot, that drugs had been found on him and police suspected the involvement of a criminal gang.

Such reports spread waves of horror across Nijmegen. Fans of the band were left reeling, the other three musicians perplexed as to where such stories had arisen from. They thought they knew their front man better than anyone.

"I offered him my last copy of their tape," Joshua finished proudly, pointing at the speakers. "Said he'd listen to it and get back to me. Told him, I might know stuff about what really happened if they were interested…"

Eleanor stared into his clear grey eyes as the essence of the story began to permeate. Of course! Why hadn't they thought of it before? The mainstream press had maligned Jake in the most terrible way but the *music press...* They would look at the story from a completely different angle.

This was everything Rosemary had hinted at. In fact, the more Eleanor recalled their covert discussion about the media, the more she realised that this was the key: *it's not what's staring you in the face that matters. It's what's missing...*

There was never any mention that Jake had been a musician; nor that he was a member of a rock band, or more specifically, a band teetering on the brink of success.

"Joshua, this is fantastic!" she gasped. "Is there any way you could get hold of the article?"

"Yeah," he responded, his cheeks flushing pink.

"Clever boy," Luke relented. "Just one question. Did you tell him anything?"

Joshua shifted anxiously in his seat. "Wasn't sure how much to say, what with these people hanging around in London like - you know - Eleanor's enemies..."

"Oh, well done, Joshua!" Rosemary praised, ruffling his hair. "And you were wise not to say too much. It will keep him intrigued. In fact, maybe we should suggest a press conference. This could be the very solution we've been looking for..."

"Yes," Eleanor murmured.

She was gazing dreamily down at Elijah when without warning, that mysterious tune crept into her head again. A second later, she felt a shiver of cold sweep over her entire body, remembering where she had heard it...

"Jake's last song!" she gasped, yanking her body upright.

The other three people in the room gaped at her. Yet the memory slotted into place from nowhere. Right now, she was picturing Jake's face in the cold light of the bedsit; his smooth white hands as they brushed the guitar strings. The sound of that beautiful song flowing into the room completed the scene... She thought she had forgotten it when it had been hiding there all along, driven to the deepest recesses of her mind as a result of the horrific event in the aftermath. Eleanor pressed her eyes shut, the torment of that night almost suffocating her.

"What did you say?" Rosemary pressed, leaning her head close.

"Jake's song, the l-last he ever wrote..." Eleanor trembled. "I've been hearing a tune in my head for weeks now and I couldn't remember what it was... It came to me, just then." She turned her eyes to Joshua. "The lyrics! Do you know where they are?"

"Sure," Joshua muttered, springing from the settee. "Just gimme a sec.'"

He disappeared upstairs for a few minutes. In his absence, Eleanor reached down and gingerly picked up Elijah. She hugged him to her chest.

"This is amazing," she whispered dazedly. "When I think of all the months I could not remember how it went."

"When did you start hearing it?" Luke frowned.

"Moments after Elijah was born," Eleanor replied, suppressing another shiver.

Rosemary was looking at her in a peculiar way, her green eyes penetrating. Eleanor knew she held some chilling notion that a thread of communication existed between the real world and the spirit world. Though what she said next seemed more logical.

"The mind can play strange tricks - repress memories that are painful - but allow them to resurface later. Eleanor, I think you were so worried about the safety of your unborn child, you were forced to forget everything associated with the night of Jake's murder..."

"Here you go!" Joshua piped up, bounding into the room before she had a chance to reply.

He passed her a sheet of paper. Staring at it with trepidation, Eleanor took it, her eyes scanning the page. This was the original; a page that had been written in Jake's own distinctive script, the letters rounded and small.

"This means more to me than anything," she whispered, pushing it towards Rosemary. "Read the words..." Her fingers trailed towards the stone pendant dangling from her neck.

Rosemary's eyes wandered over the lines of verse. "Do you know what? Reading between the lines, I've got a feeling that when he wrote this,he already feared he was about to die: *Should love survive through life or death, our melodies will stay.*"

Eleanor swallowed back a sob. "We have to do something," she added shakily.

"Yes," Rosemary consented. "We need to offer this editor as much help as we can, Joshua, and we can start with Eleanor's news clippings. Those should more than substantiate the disgraceful way Jake's murder was treated... Can you retrieve them, Eleanor?"

"Of course," she nodded. "They're lodged in a file with my solicitor."

"Good," Rosemary muttered. "Next, why don't we suggest to your journalist friend, he speaks to Inspector Hargreaves. He led the murder enquiry. Any information we expose, I'm certain the music press will pick up on..."

"Bloody right," Luke intervened. "I wonder how fans in Holland will react when they see how their idol was slandered in the press. This could be sensational!"

"So what next?" Eleanor pressed. "I mean how do we get all these people together to discuss it? I'm certain the editor from NME will be interested but

Hargreaves?"

"Let's invite them to the Grosvenor," Luke said. "Joshua and I, seeing as we both work there! Get them all in the same room together and thrash it out. Who knows what'll happen."

The two boys glanced at each other with a conspiratorial nod.

"I wish I could be there," Eleanor added. "Maybe not in person but hidden away somewhere. I wouldn't want to miss this for the world..."

Having reached a momentous decision they knew that if all went to plan, Adam Morrison would almost certainly be in touch with the Dutchman at the heart of the NME article.

Not only were they going to expose the tactless way Jake's murder had been portrayed in the press but stir ripples in the music world. It might even result in the entire drug dealing farce being shattered. This had to be a first step towards unlocking the real mystery. With that thought, Eleanor was seized by a second shiver, but this time, in excitement.

Bouncing Elijah in her lap in time to the music, her energy was revived. Finally they had found a way to fight Jake's corner. Now all they had to do was to lay the battleground.

For the first time in a long time, Norman Hargreaves was in a foul mood. He had spent the last six months revelling in the glory of his promotion to Chief Inspector.

Inflated with a new sense of power, he had soared to the challenge; and with his secret connections in the criminal underworld, he also succeeded in keeping Theakston and his men under control. With recent reports the police were doing a better job the future was looking rosy. Yet just at a time when he hoped, that unaccountable, drug-related murder in an East End bedsit had been forgotten, a disturbing article had risen out of the ashes...

Norman had it right in front of him. *Mystery Surrounds the Death of Lead Singer*

Finally, he'd received communications from a Dutchman known as *Jordaan Van Rosendal*. He had summoned him to a press conference, curious to know more about the mysterious death of Jake Jansen. Norman clenched his teeth. The boy couldn't just be some nobody could he? Oh no, he had to be a bloody rock musician! Van Rosendal happened to be their manager, owner of the record label who had signed up Jake's band in May 1972.

This left Norman in turmoil; not one of them, not even Whaley, had considered the possibility of something like this kicking up a stink!

His mind drifted back to July, the aftermath of that car bomb barging into his thoughts. The assassination was nothing unusual. Such sinister campaigns took place in all corners of the world. Occasionally situations arose when government officials were forced to take matters into their own hands;

especially if a political storm was about to gain momentum. Norman had to admit even *he* had been shocked by the magnitude of that bomb attack; the promise of power and a substantial pay out being the two factors that had lured him into the conspiracy...

So, he had abused his powers to protect those responsible. How regrettable, Jake Jansen had seen that car in the lane. But they could afford no risks; Norman had to get to him first. The boy's memories - the car in particular - set the alarm bells ringing. If this story came to light, what was there to say that others might remember seeing that same car or worse, identify the owner? He would never forget his instructions: *Jake Jansen was a liability and they had to get rid of him.*

Norman shivered, the events of that day sharp in his mind; how he had kept Jake in a room by himself, away from the anti-terrorist squad and interviewed him personally - a statement he had promptly destroyed. Last of all, came the instruction from his fellow conspirator, to source a contract killer. Norman could think of no better hit man than Theakston, not to forget, the man owed him! He had virtually given him the green light to destroy Sammie Maxwell and with a dossier of serious crimes to wave in his face, Dominic really had no choice.

With a van summoned and waiting, he didn't want to dwell on it any more... They had done their job, ended Jake's life and covered their tracks. Nothing remained to connect Jake Jansen to that car bomb atrocity and he truly believed that nothing ever would.

Right now Norman felt trapped, squeezed into a tight spot and with no choice but to agree to the press conference. Attention had been drawn to Jake's murder and it was never going to go away. All they had to do was to stick to their own version of events.

He ran his mind through it all again, secretly wondering if there was any element they could have handled better; the detectives who had unearthed the evidence - the drugs found in the bedsit, as well as in Jake's possession. There had been an inquest confirming the cause of death; a single bullet to the brain. The entire investigation had ultimately met a dead end with no more clues as to who they could pin the murder on - not even Dominic. Now all he had to do was authenticate those lies, persuade this Dutchman that Jake must have ditched his band in favour of making better riches in London, smuggling drugs...

Sucking in his breath, he stared out of the window of his office, across the skyline of London, pondering over the enormity of the task which now faced him.

Yet it wasn't just down to him was it? There were others involved. Desperate for backup, maybe it was time to reel in a few allies. His hand hovered over the telephone, his decision made. He dialled the private telephone number of Robin Whaley.

"So, it appears we have a problem," Robin responded smoothly.

Hargreaves was a little taken aback, given the obsessive paranoia he had revealed a few months back. "Problem?" he spluttered. "This is a bloody nightmare! You do realise, this could unhinge everything?"

"You got rid of Jansen's statement, didn't you?" the other man drawled. "Any suggestion that the boy may have witnessed something at that party?"

"Of course," Norman sighed. "That was quashed months ago. But I'm not talking about that. These people want to know the finer details of his murder!"

"We have nothing to worry about," Robin said coldly. "No one knows why Jansen was really killed, apart from the Chapman girl and she's still hiding in Forest Haven. So let's just hammer home the drugs issue and present the same evidence as before."

Norman cleared his throat. "Is there anything you can say to substantiate these points? For example, could you use the same story you used to convince Bernard James?"

"Of course," Robin answered in the same superior tone. "You know I have a way with words. It's what makes me a good politician..."

Chapter 14

On the night of the press conference, the Merriman kids were fizzing with excitement.

Each had their role to play. Luke was scheduled to work his usual shift but with the added responsibility of looking after Eleanor (who he had sworn to conceal from sight.) She had agreed to be on the lookout. If she spotted any significant faces, Luke would schmooze up to them and ply them with the fine wines the Grosvenor Hotel was renowned for. He had also dragged his brother along. Joshua was looking forward to seeing Adam Morrison again as well as intrigued to meet Jordaan Van Rosendal, manager of a Dutch recording studio.

Rosemary had made good use of the photocopier at the publishing house in Wapping where she worked. Having secretly run off copies of the press cuttings and Jake's song lyrics, Luke was hoping for Joshua to assist him tonight. They needed someone to slip copies into the hands of any journalists who might turn up.

Alison meanwhile, had nagged her brothers relentlessly for a part in this showdown, by pretending to be a journalist. Currently studying to be an actress, not only did she belong to an amateur dramatics society but confident she could create the right persona. She could even raise a few contentious questions, should there be any attempts to sideline the issue.

Rosemary was not entirely happy about this idea, wary of the danger. It would be a disaster if the opposition discovered her true identity.

Seized by the drama of the event, Alison couldn't be swayed. In the end, she had no choice but to accept her daughter's decision and agreed to stay at home with Elijah. Yet she couldn't help worrying about her children. Plagued by the notion they were about to face Jake's killers, she insisted they were to phone her at the slightest hint of trouble…

At around 5:30 that evening, the four of them leapt onto an underground train bound for Victoria. It was still daylight, so they proceeded with caution. Smartly turned out, they blended easily amongst the river of people sweeping their way along the pavements.

Passing the front of the hotel, the boys were the first to make their way through the revolving doors. The girls settled in a café where they would linger for the next half hour.

The conference was scheduled to start at 6:30. From the moment they were inside however, Luke ushered his brother towards the cloakroom, instead coming face to face with his boss. The man's eyes raked over them, glinting with suspicion. Renowned to be something of a shady character Martin Williams was not unknown for mixing social activities with a little wheeler-dealing. At 35 years of age, he was reed thin with slicked back hair and sharp, rat-like features.

"Luke!" he remarked, with a clap of the hands. "Good of you to get here early, it's going to be busy tonight!"

"Good evening, Mr Williams," Luke answered politely. "You don't happen to know where this press conference is taking place do you?"

"Bessborough Suite," Martin said curtly, "right out the way. Expect some of 'em will be quaffing drinks in the lounge bar to begin with, why?"

"Is it okay if I serve them?" Luke offered. "I hear there might be some important people here tonight and you can rely on me to recommend our best wines..."

Martin gave him a long, appraising stare, his gaze flickering to Joshua.

"What's he doing here?"

"Um - well, he's my brother," Luke said softly, "and he works here too."

"Yeah as a decorator," Martin sneered.

"Look, Mr Williams," Luke confided, sidling up close. "It's largely down to Josh, this event's happening at all. He knows Adam Morrison, one of the journalists from NME. I was wondering if he could be on hand - you know, help me out a bit perhaps?"

"With hair like that?" Martin said, throwing an icy glare at Joshua. "No way, now fuck off!"

"Aw, don't be like that, Sir," Joshua whined, looking crestfallen. "I'll tie it back, right?"

He gazed up at him with soft, puppy dog eyes. Martin exhaled a sigh.

"Please, Mr Williams," Luke begged. "You said it was going to be busy tonight. Couldn't he just collect empty glasses and wipe tables or something?"

"I'll do it unpaid," Joshua piped up.

"Okay, you're on!" Martin snapped. "But smarten yourself up and wear a uniform. This is the Grosvenor and we don't employ no scruffy oiks."

"Yes, Sir," Joshua mumbled, betraying the tiniest hint of a grin.

Hidden in the cloakroom, Luke felt a sigh of relief leave his body. He collected his uniform, before requesting another one for Joshua in a smaller size. Luke helped him fasten the cuffs of his dress shirt and tied his bow tie. Brushing his hair away from his forehead, he fastened it with a rubber band, then stood back and observed him.

"Mum'd be proud of you," he smiled. "You look the biz! Now remember what Mr Williams said and don't cock this up, okay?"

With a timid smile, Joshua nodded. The last thing he did was to dip into the envelope they had brought along with them, extracting the folded copies of Eleanor's news clippings. He slid them inside his trouser pockets. The first set featured the news breaking headline of the car bomb attack; the second, the stories about Jake's murder including Theakston's arrest.

He gave a shiver of excitement, conscious of what he had to do.

By 6:00 Eleanor wove her way through the same revolving glass doors and glided into the foyer. Lingering by the side of the reception desk, she pretended to study a brochure.

Luke, who had straight away spotted her, rushed to her side. After a quick flurry of words, he escorted her into the corridor. They wandered past glossy marble pillars reflecting the gleam of chandeliers. Soft piano music trickled into their surroundings. Satisfied no one was watching, Luke steered her towards an alcove in the wall; it was guarded by a line of colossal rubber plants.

"I'll bring you something to drink," he whispered. "Just don't move until the press conference is about to start and I'll come and collect you. It's taking place in a private meeting room."

"Thanks, Luke," she said softly.

Another advantage of this table was, it afforded her a good view of the foyer from behind the rubber plants.

The revolving doors kept turning, dispensing more people into the hotel. They included two men, both reasonably young looking. Sweeping through the entrance they paused in the luxurious foyer, glancing around in awe. In the next instant, Joshua spotted them. One of them looked up in surprise, gave a broad smile and patted him on the back. *These had to be the journalists,* Eleanor deduced. Next, they were joined by two more people, a man and a woman, their necks slung with cameras. Alison innocently wandered in behind them.

She had dressed up tonight and looked stunning; a knee length dress tailored in plum red velvet teamed up with a black jacket. Her carefully made up face added a certain maturity; layers of mascara that made her grey eyes look huge under her pencil thin eyebrows.

The hotel was just beginning to shrug itself to life, so Luke snatched an opportunity to join them.

"Adam Morrison," one of the men smiled, extending a hand. Luke shook it gratefully. "I already know your brother, of course..."

"Great to meet you," Luke said quickly. "I haven't got much time, so here's the plan. Joshua is going to give you some news clippings to look at. If any other journalists turn up, do you think you could circulate them?"

One of the men was already glancing at the clippings, eyebrows raised.

"Oh, and this is my sister, Alison. Is it okay for her to join you? She's already agreed to heckle these people if they try to fool you."

"It will be my pleasure," Adam purred. He gave her a cool, lop-sided smile. "You can pretend to be my PA..."

There was no denying he was attractive; tall and slim, with a complexion like satin and widely spaced, dark eyes. Dressed in an immaculate sports jacket with fashionable flares, his mop of lustrous brown curls hung almost to his collar. Alison smiled back.

"Take care," Luke managed to whisper as the journalists moved towards the lounge.

"Wow, he is gorgeous," Alison breathed.

"Flirt with him by all means," Luke grinned, "as long as you don't let him seduce you. It's rumoured he has a way with the ladies!"

"I can look after myself," Alison sniffed. "I've got Steve now!"

From her concealed position behind the foliage, Eleanor waited in silence. Her eyes danced, taking in her surroundings. She felt tense but at the same time, focussed, thinking about Jake.

Her eyes stopped dead as two men wandered into view, zooming in on a face she would never forget. Robin Whaley. Poised where he stood, head inclined, his cold eyes flickered around the foyer. He looked immaculate in his beautifully tailored dinner suit. His dark hair gleamed beneath the warm light of the chandelier, enhancing his flawless features.

Eleanor sat very still, feeling the first thread of cold snake its way through her veins.

He was accompanied by a second man, also donning a dress suit. Yet this was no one Eleanor recognised. Slightly shorter than Whaley, he commanded a huge presence; it was depicted in the way he moved, forceful and arrogant with an air of authority. Of slightly stocky build, his thick blonde hair framed a face that was florid and square, his grey eyes pale in comparison.

She watched as the two men swept into the corridor. Momentarily masked by the foliage, she huddled in dread before they turned into the lounge and slipped out of sight.

Eleanor dared not move; hidden, but now trapped.

A moment later, Luke glided across with a tray of drinks. Darting covertly into the alcove to join her, he lowered a glass of coca-cola into her hand. With a quick, furtive glance, he bobbed down by her side to share a few words.

"The journalists are here," he muttered beneath his breath.

"I know," she whispered, "but listen. The next time you're in the lounge, take a good look at the two men in dinner suits who have just arrived, especially the dark haired one..."

Luke frowned at her.

"It's Councillor Whaley," she added fearfully. "Is it possible you could talk to him? And if so, try and find out who the other one is."

"Okay," Luke responded warily and within a second, he had disappeared again.

The next time Luke sailed into the lounge, he carried a leather bound folder containing their exclusive wine list. Spotting the two men just as Eleanor had described, he sidled up to their table and with practised formality, opened the folder to present the list.

"Good evening, gentlemen," he began politely. "May I offer you something to drink? Perhaps an opportunity to sample one of our very fine wines?"

"Sounds good to me," the blonde man drawled, without looking at him.

Robin, on the other hand, stared directly back, his blue eyes devouring him. Luke offered his most charming smile.

"Is there anything you could recommend?" he said lightly. Luke noted his cultured accent.

"That would depend on whether you prefer red or white," he replied.

"Perry?" Robin murmured, glancing at the other man.

"Red, of course," the other man said. Luke paid attention to his voice; the oozing public school accent, which seemed a little exaggerated. "Nothing common. A Burgundy perhaps, something with a good vintage."

Luke fought against the urge to smirk. "May I recommend our Chateau Moreau 1970 St Emilion?" he suggested. "1970 was a very good vintage. This is a ruby red wine with a spicy aroma, slightly plum in flavour..."

"Hmm," the man pondered, gazing down the price column. "Anything more impressive?"

In other words more expensive, Luke thought, amused by such self-aggrandisement. He pointed a little further down the list where the wines soared in price.

"In that case," he said pleasantly, "and seeing as you have a preference for wines of the *Burgundy* region, we have an excellent Bordeaux from 1961. The good weather produced an outstanding vintage. Our Chateau La Garde is a medium bodied red, firm and concentrated with a cherry flavour at its core."

"That sounds better!" the man agreed pompously.

"You seem very knowledgeable," Robin added. He was studying Luke with far more interest than he would have liked. "Have you been in this job for long?"

"I've been working as a wine waiter for almost a year," Luke replied. "Wines are such an interesting subject. There is so much to the grape and how it relates to its climate."

"Interesting," Robin smiled.

"And what line of work are *you two* gentlemen engaged in?" Luke enquired, his eyes moving to the other man. "You clearly have an appreciation for fine wines. Are you a connoisseur?"

The man chuckled. "For my sins, dear boy, I am a humble politician, a member of the Conservative Party, though I have yet to secure my place in Parliament."

"Good luck," Luke said with feigned enthusiasm, "and how about you, Sir?"

"Me?" Robin added coolly. "I'm a local councillor in London."

"Impressive," Luke replied in a monotone. "Can't say I understand much about politics."

"Who does?" Robin murmured.

He lay a caressing hand on Luke's forearm, capturing his eye again.

Luke fought to suppress a shiver. "I'll bring you your wine," he said, desperate to end the conversation and with no further word, he turned and gracefully left their table.

"Jesus! What a creep!" Luke spluttered, as soon as he was behind the scenes again. Joshua was busily polishing wine glasses beneath the fierce scrutiny of Luke's boss, Martin. "Tell you what, Josh, you would not want to get into his car if he offered you sweeties..."

"Don't cheek our customers," Martin warned. He glanced at Luke's order pad. "Fucking hell! Not short of a bob or two then?"

"Yeah, I reckon his friend only ordered that to rub our noses in it," Luke sneered.

"Who you talking about?" Joshua whispered, as Martin disappeared to fetch the wine.

"This Councillor Whaley, Eleanor keeps on about," Luke muttered though right now, he was experiencing a creeping unease about the whole business.

"He's here?" Joshua beamed. "Interesting!"

"Yeah and the other one's a politician," Luke added. "I need to tell Eleanor..."

No sooner had Martin surfaced when Luke briefly vanished again.

He caught Alison's eye and flashed a smile, carefully inching his way towards Whaley's table. Proudly bearing the wine on a silver tray, he sloshed a drop into each glass.

"I hope this is to your liking," he remarked pleasantly.

"I'm sure it will be splendid," Robin's friend smirked, swilling the wine in the glass before sipping it. "Yes, very good. Thank you, young Sir!"

Luke gave a slight bow and left them.

The next place he headed was the table where the journalists sat at the opposite end of the lounge. Immersed in a hushed conversation, they were pouring over the news clippings. Luke swooped in to take their drinks order, unable to resist touching base with them.

The next person to saunter into the corridor was a silver haired man in a police uniform. He was accompanied by an officer of lower rank and a man in a grey suit; possibly a detective.

"Hey!" Adam announced. "Looks like the cops are here. Nearly time to get the ball rolling."

Looking at his watch, it was 6:20.

"Can I fetch some drinks for you first?" Luke volunteered. "Or are you going straight up to the Bessborough Suite?"

"Best wait," Adam answered. "Give them a chance to get their bearings. I'd like a tonic water, please and whatever your sister's having. Has anyone had a chance to read the press cuttings?"

Luke studied his face, which appeared somewhat grim.

"They are outrageous," a second man murmured in a soft, throaty accent.

As Luke scrawled down the drinks order, he took an opportunity to observe him. He had already picked up the musical lilt in his deep voice. This had to be the Dutchman, the man Adam had traced in response to Joshua's lead. If his theory was correct, he was the instigator of the press conference; Jordaan Van Rosendal, manager of the record label, Pink Elephant, who had signed up Jake's band. Jordaan was very tall with long fair hair tied into a ponytail. Casually dressed in a pale blue shirt and faded cords, he kept his fashionable suede jacket draped over his arm.

Luke caught his eye and smiled.

"Beer please," he muttered.

"It was good of you to come tonight, Sir," Luke added bravely. "Free Spirit have written some brilliant songs and there is no way, Jake was ever a drug dealer..."

With a lengthy sigh, Jordaan lowered his eyes. He did not smile back.

Luke left the table, wishing he could be present at the press conference; yet there was no way Martin would allow him to abandon the bar as more and more people trickled in. It was really down to Joshua to hover in the background and keep an eye on things.

Everyone was here now; Eleanor hidden in the corridor behind the rubber plants, the journalists huddled at their own table... Councillor Whaley and his snobbish companion lurked in the heart of the lounge, enjoying their expensive wine.

Luke needed one more opportunity to touch base with her. This would be his last chance before the press conference began and confident no one was paying any attention to him, he sneaked into the corridor for a secret word.

"Everyone's here," he whispered. "The conference is about to start at any moment."

"I saw Inspector Hargreaves," Eleanor mumbled, keeping her head down. "I'm so scared, Luke..."

She peered up at him and for a moment, he felt a rush of emotion. Despite her startled look, she looked so lovely tonight. Alison had helped get her ready, picking out a long black evening gown and pearl beads to wear around her graceful neck. She had even suggested arranging her luxurious hair into a French pleat. But Eleanor, filled with a hankering to embrace her Afro-Caribbean heritage, chose to wear it loose and curly with just the sides pinned back with combs. Her only makeup was a little mascara, which made her eyes look even bigger; her full lips enhanced with a slick of neutral coloured lipstick.

"You've got nothing to worry about," Luke soothed her. "Nearly everyone's on your side. All you have to do is stay out of sight."

"I know," Eleanor sighed, wringing her hands together. "It's bad enough that Hargreaves is here, but Whaley... I feel sick. These are the people who conspired to kill Jake."

"Which is the probably reason they're here. Maybe Adam and his colleagues will expose the truth when they start grilling them."

A ghost of a smile tweaked Eleanor's lips. "We'll see."

"It's time we made a move," Luke muttered. "Bessborough Suite is open, so let's get you up there and quickly, before anyone sees us."

"Thanks, Luke," she muttered, rising to her feet.

He carefully manoeuvred himself behind her, hoping it would be enough to conceal her from Whaley as well as Hargreaves' gathering. Creeping along the corridor, Luke stole a furtive backward glance towards the lounge and confident to see that none of them were making an exit just yet, they quickened their pace.

Moments later, they were inside the Bessborough Suite.

With richly panelled walls and a large board room table sprawling under another sparkling chandelier, this was the location the press conference was about to take place. A row of arched windows lined the left wall. They were dressed in heavy drapes and crowned with decorative pelmets. Luke pointed towards the central one.

"Sit yourself down on the window sill behind those curtains," he said. "Keep perfectly still and no one will know you're here... but you should still be able to hear them."

Eleanor threw him a last panic-stricken look and with a nervous smile, she leapt up onto the window sill where the drapes fell softly closed behind her.

The first people to be shown into the Bessborough Suite were Chief Inspector Hargreaves and his colleagues. Martin had agreed to spare Joshua to act as a doorman and supply refreshments. He was carefully positioning a jug of iced water onto the boardroom table, when a volley of footsteps rolled in from behind. Turning, he gave a quick smile and without speaking, waved a hand towards the chairs at the far side of the table.

Norman gave him a curt nod, his stony features composed.

Next to appear was Robin Whaley. Barely taking in his surroundings as he adjusted his bow tie, he failed to notice Joshua hovering in the background.

"Good evening, Norman," he muttered, moving towards the table. "So - are we ready to give these people their little media circus?"

Norman emitted a harsh cough as if clearing his throat, compelling Robin to look up. He was instantly alerted to Joshua's presence. Their eyes locked.

The moment passed without comment as another group of people congregated outside.

Two of the journalists stepped over the threshold, cameras poised. They looked tense yet visibly thrilled before they honed in on the group of visitors. The girl raised her camera and a flashbulb exploded. Norman shifted uncomfortably in his seat.

Adam strolled in their wake, sidling right up to the table. A curious smile spread across his face as he took a moment to observe them all.

"Gentlemen!" he greeted them. "First, I'd like to thank you for agreeing to this meeting. I'm Adam Morrison, feature editor for NME."

Lowering a copy of the tabloid publication right in front of them, he took the chair opposite Norman. The police inspector gave a polite nod though his eyes remained frosty.

He was not the only one who appeared diffident. From the moment Jordaan approached, a noticeable chill swept around the table. Joining Adam in the neighbouring chair, he positioned himself right opposite Robin Whaley and his companion.

Joshua tactfully pulled out a chair on Adam's left for Alison, while the two remaining journalists settled themselves down next to her.

Adam wasted no time, his eyes latching onto the police officer.

"As you probably know, Sir," he began gravely, "there has been some confusion in the media over a musician by the name of Jake Jansen. My associate here, Jordaan Van Rosendal, signed up his band last year. They had just completed a tour before Jake disappeared. It later transpired, he was murdered. Mr Hargreaves, I gather that you led the investigation..."

Norman gazed back, any last traces of hostility fading as an expression of regret touched his features.

"First, I offer my condolences?" he sighed. His gaze momentarily drifted towards Jordaan. "I understand this has been distressing for you as well as for the band. To answer your first question, the murder took place at around midnight in October last year. We were alerted by the residents of a tower block in Bethnal Green."

"I see," Adam nodded. He paused for a moment, ruminating over the facts. "So you went into the flat and then what? What did you find there?"

"The flat appeared empty," Norman replied. "There was no visible blood, nor any signs that a murder had taken place. The room however, had been completely ransacked; cupboards emptied, a bed turned on its side. Whoever was there was obviously looking for something..."

Adam raised an eyebrow, urging him to continue. The only other sound in the room was the frenzied scratch of pencils as his fellow journalists filled their notepads.

"From what we deduced, they were searching for drugs," Norman concluded. Tilting his body forward slightly, he pressed him with a stare that was strangely penetrating. "The detectives discovered the drugs later. They were hidden in various locations around the flat; under the cooker, for example and in the bathroom cabinet..."

"Your detectives found drugs that Jake's killers did not?" Adam remarked acidly.

"My colleagues were extremely thorough in their search," Norman bounced back. "We already had our suspicions that Mr Jansen was involved in a drug dealing cartel. In fact, we were planning an arrest, as soon as we had sufficient evidence..."

Adam frowned, tilting his head to one side. "What sort of drugs?"

"Hard drugs," Norman answered. "Heroin. This may come as something as a shock but it is alleged that Mr Jansen was operating in another neighbourhood. Furthermore, he was on the run. A social worker we spoke to claims that Mr Jansen was being hunted by a notoriously violent criminal gang. The man offered him the flat as a refuge. He later identified his body..."

Adam could not help but shake his head, though Jordaan remained unmoving. Pinning the police chief with an unwavering stare, his eyes never lost their chill.

"I'm sorry, but do you dispute what I'm saying?" Norman sniffed.

"I'm not exactly disputing it," Adam said crisply, "but I do find it a bit odd. What led you to believe that Jake was involved in a drugs cartel? You mentioned another neighbourhood..."

"Ah, yes," Norman muttered. "I thought we might get to that, which is the reason I invited an elected councillor from Tower Hamlets. He has very kindly agreed to explain some of the circumstances that led to our investigation..."

All journalists turned to Robin as if joined by a single thread. He sat very still, smooth hands resting neatly on the polished wood surface.

"A few months earlier," Robin began, "I was aware of a situation in my own community."

"Sorry," Adam interrupted, "but could you tell us your name please?"

"Councillor Robin Whaley," he announced. "My ward is in Poplar; an area of East London near the Docks. Rumours came to my attention of a suspected drug dealer operating in the neighbourhood; a young man in his 20s with long, dark reddish hair."

"When was this?" Adam demanded.

"Oh, let me see," Robin pondered, "it must have been around late August, early September."

From her concealed spot, Eleanor listened to the drawl of his voice and shivered.

"Naturally, I passed the information to the police. I felt it was my duty. I alerted the social worker too and he consented to do whatever he could. It so happens, Mr Jansen visited his premises, demanding his help. There was indeed mention of a gang... The young man was scared out of his wits and this is why he offered him a sanctuary. Somewhere to lie low for a while..."

Adam narrowed his eyes. "Do you have any proof of this?"

"I beg your pardon?" Robin challenged him.

"You talk of rumours, Mr Whaley," Adam pressed. "Not hard facts. Did anyone in your ward actually *witness* any drug transactions?"

Robin paused as if carefully rehearsing his words. "I could summon at least *two* addicts in the area who would confirm my story. There was no shortage of heroin at that time and it was easy to obtain... It comes as no coincidence that a substantial quantity was found in his flat."

"How do you know those drugs belonged to Jake?" Adam fired back at him.

"The exact same type was found on the victim in person," Norman intervened, before turning to the suited man sat next to him. "Isn't that right?"

"Regrettably so," the man nodded, his expression pained. "Mr Jansen's body turned up in a disused warehouse. He'd been shot in the head. On further investigation, we found traces of drugs on his clothes, along with a few more packages of the same substance. This boy had even hollowed out a cavity in the heel of his shoe; the perfect place to conceal yet another package..."

Eleanor froze in disbelief - the hole in Jake's shoe! Was there anything these people wouldn't exploit to nail down their lies?

"But did anyone ever witness Jake selling drugs?" Adam repeated. "You see, this is what we are finding hard to believe, Sir. Jake was not that type of person!"

"With due respects," Norman said silkily, "there is no specific personality type when it comes to drug smuggling. It takes all sorts."

"Right," Adam snapped, "well, in that case, it is time for my friend Jordaan to say a few words. He was the one who called this meeting... not just to learn what happened to Jake, but to enlighten you a little about his background. Over to you, Jordaan."

All eyes turned to the enigmatic, fair haired man looming next to Adam. He had barely moved since the conference began; a strong, silent figure who given his cue, now braced himself. Several news clippings lay in front of him. He spread them out with his large hands.

"My name is Jordaan Van Rosendal," he began. "I am manager of the record company who signed up 'Free Spirit' in May last year."

"Free Spirit was Jake's band, in case you didn't know," Adam added quickly.

"The band were doing so well," Jordaan sighed, pinning Norman with his cool stare. "Audiences across the Netherlands loved them, as did your English people when they performed at the music festivals. Every band member was a talented musician. Matthias a drummer, Youf a brilliant saxophone player. Andries played bass guitar, friends with Jake since they were at school. Even as boys they played guitar together. And Jake could sing, he had a beautiful voice... He was probably the most talented of them all... He wrote their songs. This is why it has been so difficult for the band to continue w-without him..."

A subtle catch resounded in his throat as the words withered. There was no doubt in anyone's mind that this gentle giant of a man had been badly affected by the horror of Jake's death.

Eleanor felt a sting of tears, absorbing the echo of his deep voice; each word enriched with an accent more pronounced than Jake's had ever been.

"I have spoken with Andries and he is outraged by this story, as I am. He is certain that Jake was never involved in drugs."

"I understand, Sir," Norman said gently. "I realise this must be hurtful for you and you have my sympathy. But this is in the past. People change."

Jordaan glared at him. "No," he contested icily, "Andries knew Jake was a good person. He did not care about making money, all he wanted was to play music. Entertain people. He cannot believe his friend would change overnight - not when they were so close to success!"

"You have a very good point there, Jordaan," Adam said indulgently.

"He cannot understand why Jake disappeared at all!" Jordaan reinforced, his voice gaining fury. "The last time he saw him, the group were in London! And there is something else you should know. Their last performance was at a birthday party... the 40th birthday party of your ill-fated politician, Mr Enfield!"

An icy silence spread across the table like a membrane; so taut and fragile, it would have taken just one more damning word to shatter their entire conspiracy.

Eleanor braced herself, waiting for the silence to crack.

Without warning, Robin Whaley intervened. "No one could ever forget that day," he remarked portentously. "Nor the dramatic way it ended. An entire nation was shocked by the atrocity of that car bomb..."

"Andries told me Jake saw something," Jordaan added, a dangerous tone creeping into his voice. "The police wanted to interview him and this is the last time they saw him - a little strange, don't you think?"

"What exactly are you implying?" Norman said guardedly. "As far as I am concerned, there were no witnesses. Did this friend divulge any details to you?"

"Jake saw a man by the roadside," Jordaan persisted, staring fixedly back at him.

"You sure he wasn't hallucinating?" Robin muttered with sarcasm.

Jordaan shot him a look of pure loathing.

"Gentlemen," Norman interjected. "The consensus is, the IRA were responsible for that car bomb. I assure you, no one else was implicated. Whatever Mr Jansen claims he saw, we have no record of interviewing him... nor was any statement made."

"This is crazy!" Jordaan thundered. "Andries would not make this up. Jake left all his belongings at the hotel, even his passport. He disappeared without a trace and no one knew what happened to him…. until this story was printed!"

Shaking with rage, he scooped one of the news clippings and dangled it between his forefinger and thumb.

"And this is how your English reporters treat him," he whispered, unable to disguise his contempt, "like he was some vermin! Some drug dealing hippy. No one thought to report the truth, that this '*victim of another gangland murder*' was a talented musician..." Dropping the clipping to the table, he stabbed at the headline with his finger.

"The papers only published what they knew," Robin placated him.

"Except they didn't know who he was, did they?" Adam retorted with equal disgust. "Furthermore, they didn't bother to find out. They chose to demonise him. Jordaan is right to be outraged! There was never any mention of Jake's musical talent, nor a word about Free Spirit!"

"Well, I can only apologise on behalf of the tabloids," Norman replied. "I appreciate how tactless this seems but it appears no connection was made between the murder victim and the missing member of your band. Has anyone here actually heard of - um - *Free Spirit?*"

"Well obviously Albert Enfield must have heard of them," Alison intervened, her smile calculating.

Robin writhed in his chair, glancing shiftily in her direction. The tension stretched tightly between them.

"I wonder if this was kept quiet for another reason," Adam drawled, leaning back in his chair.

Once again, the room lapsed into a mantle of disquiet as everyone took this in.

Joshua hovered in the wings, still as a statue. His heart was pounding... In truth, he could not believe the lies that were being pushed around this table.

Councillor Whaley had turned noticeably paler. The man next to him sat motionless, his face flushed by comparison as he emptied the last few drops from their wine bottle into his glass. He had not uttered a single word, Joshua acknowledged.

Chief Inspector Hargreaves on the other hand, retained his composure; only the granite hardness of his eyes betrayed displeasure as they bore into Adam.

"Are you suggesting some sort of conspiracy?" he drawled.

Adam shrugged his shoulders. "Those are your words, not mine. You say no connection was made between the murder victim and a young musician who went missing several months earlier. What I am more concerned about is, there seems to be very little evidence which connects Jake with these drug dealing allegations..."

"I thought we had already covered that," Norman insisted.

"Did you?" Adam snapped. "Well, I'm not convinced. In fact, in the light of everything I've heard tonight, I remain even less convinced. A young man mysteriously disappears in London; a member of a rock band on the brink of success - described as gentle and *easy-going with no record of drug dealing.* Three months later, it transpires he ditched all that to deal drugs in some crappy neighbourhood in East London? Do you know what, Mr Hargreaves? I think this is a crock of shit!"

"Now you listen to me, young man..." Norman growled, rearing up in his chair.

"No! You listen to me!" Adam retorted. "Fact is, you don't have a shred of proof, do you?"

"Excuse me, but did we not sufficiently explain the evidence our forensic team uncovered?" Norman continued. "Drugs were found in his flat and found on him! I have the forensic report here in front of me. Would you like to see it?"

Alison swallowed deeply before she raised her hand.

"Yes?" Norman barked.

"Supposing the drugs were planted," she dropped into the discussion. "What if someone was deliberately trying to frame Jake?"

Robin Whaley laughed. "How very cloak and dagger!"

Alison gritted her teeth, her hatred of this man becoming more and more evident.

"It's not impossible," she hissed, glancing at him from beneath her feathery dark eyelashes. "I don't believe he was a drug dealer. I think this is all a great big cover up!"

She had captured Robin's attention.

His cold eyes nailed her for a second, sizing her up; a blonde female whose beauty unleashed a wave of hatred and she was about the same age as Eleanor.

"And who..." he whispered, "might you be, young lady?"

Joshua was observing the scene with horror. He nibbled his lip, just as Robin caught his eye again.

The moment was short lived. Adam hastily sprang to her defence. "Don't speak to my assistant like that!" he berated him. "She does have a point, you know!"

"So, tell me her name," Robin pressed in his quiet, interrogatory tone. "Who is she working for?"

"I thought I just I told you," Adam retorted. "My PA works for NME magazine. You have no right to be so unpleasant. All we are trying to establish is how someone like Jake could have ended up in such a terrible place and some report about a few bags of heroin stashed in a flat, doesn't really cut it as far as I'm concerned!"

"What else can we tell you?" Norman sighed.

He was beginning to look uneasy as he fiddled with his shirt cuffs. Joshua was still lingering by the doorway. Norman glanced across and pointing to the empty water jug, he signalled for a top up. Joshua gave a nod and reluctantly left the room.

"Right," Adam continued. "Well, assuming this all happened as you claim, my next question is this. What did you do to resolve this crime? Drug dealer or not, Mr Hargreaves, a young man was shot. How far did you go to try and catch his killer?"

"Regrettably, we've been unable to convict anyone as yet," Norman confessed. "We interviewed a number of the residents but no one actually saw anything."

"Yet there was one arrest, wasn't there?" Adam said. Sifting through the news clippings, he gave a twisted smile. "I understand you arrested a man named Dominic Theakston; described here as a *'28 year old gang leader rumoured to be a new face in organised crime...'* Now in my mind, that would seem to fit in with everything you have told us. You mentioned the involvement of a criminal gang... and once again, those were your words, Mr Hargreaves."

"Name me a crime in the East End that hasn't been blamed on Dominic Theakston lately?" Norman shrugged. He gave a sniff of amusement.

"Why did you let him go?" Adam probed, refusing to be patronised.

"He was drinking in his local pub," Norman insisted. "Several people confirmed this, including one of the young ladies he was flirting with, which was well after midnight. The murder took place at around midnight. Theakston could not have travelled from Whitechapel to Bethnal Green in the time. I have a crime report that rules him out as the killer."

"But no one else was arrested?" Adam pressed. "So you have closed the case."

"That's not true," Norman argued. "All I'm saying is, there have been no further suspects yet. If any new evidence comes to light, we will act on it but for the time being, Mr Jansen's murder will be confined to the cold case unit. I'm very sorry..."

Adam froze, dismayed by their lack of commitment. In fact in anything, he seemed to be drawing the meeting to a close. There was a shuffle of movement around the table, followed by the snap of a briefcase; the suited detective was already stashing away his paperwork...

Jordaan on the other hand, did not move. Anchored to his seat as if carved from stone, he continued to study the news clippings.

Joshua slipped back into the room with a jug of fresh water.

The silence hung heavily as he approached the table. Robin was scrutinising his face again but no sooner had he lowered the jug when Norman raised his hand.

"There's no need," he announced, levering himself to his feet. "I don't really think there is anything left to discuss..."

"Oh, but there is," Jordaan interrupted. The displeasure in his eyes was replaced by the first glint of a smirk. "I have something very important to ask you. So, please... If I could have just a few more minutes of your time."

Norman glowered at him, his patience finally dissolving.

"What now?" he demanded. "Wasn't this supposed to be a press conference? Funny, because it actually feels more like a trial!"

"That was not our intention," Adam placated him. "But you have to understand, Dutch fans are mourning the loss of a much-loved musician. All we want is an explanation! What were you going to say, Jordaan?"

He brandished another news clipping but not one of Eleanor's. This extract appeared to be one of the more malicious accounts, she had chosen to discard; a news item, he had stumbled across himself.

"It says here that *a girl* was hidden under the floorboards..." His voice dropped so low, it was almost a whisper. "Eleanor Chapman. I understand she was Jake's girlfriend. Why have you not even mentioned her?"

"I spoke at length with Miss Chapman!" Norman snapped. "She was in hospital at the time and deeply traumatised. She would never have been able to handle the intrusion of the media."

"Yet you interviewed her all the same?" Adam piped up with renewed enthusiasm. "What did she tell you about the murder?"

"She was hiding!" Norman said icily. "She saw nothing! What is more, she was suffering from a breakdown and had to be sedated. There was nothing she could tell us that could be relied upon..."

Alison started to shake her head, her mouth dropping open. "But that is ridiculous!"

"If she was hiding beneath the floorboards," Adam added cynically, "she must have heard everything that happened in that room. Wasn't she the most vital witness of all?"

"Her mind was undeniably fragile," Norman argued, "as confirmed by her doctor. I would have spoken to her again if she hadn't discharged herself. No one has seen her since!"

"But I would still like to know a little more about her," Jordaan pressed. His eyes turned more penetrating as he stared deep into the police officer's eyes.

"Well, perhaps I can enlighten you," Robin's voice cut through the lull of silence. Returning Jordaan's smile, his eyes disguised a coldness. "From my understanding, Eleanor Chapman grew up in a background of organised crime. Her father was employed by the late Sammie Maxwell, a notorious gangster involved in prostitution, protection rackets and drugs. Who knows what this girl may have experienced in her lifetime? More significantly, her father is said to be on the run, as a result of a gangland shooting incident..."

He let the words float in the frozen silence.

From her concealed position behind the curtain, Eleanor started to tremble.

"In fact, given the evidence that Mr Jansen was involved in drug dealing," he finished coolly, "wouldn't she have made the perfect accomplice in a saga like this?"

"I don't believe you," Adam said flatly.

"Councillor Whaley speaks the truth," Norman corroborated. "Eleanor's father, Oliver was indeed involved in organised crime. I thank you for raising this, Mr Van Rosendal."

"I guess that concludes our discussion," Robin smiled, catching Alison's eye. "I'm sorry if it wasn't what you wanted to hear but if you feel the need to raise any complaints with regards the press coverage..."

"*You bastard!*" a voice shuddered across the room.

Several heads turned. No one had spotted a ripple in the folds of the window drapes until Eleanor pushed them apart. But they could see her now, perched on the window sill.

A look of shock registered on several faces, as she slowly lowered her feet to the ground. Her face gleamed in the shimmering light of the chandelier, her eyes illuminated like flames as she glided towards their table.

Norman appeared to stumble slightly, his stony features turning ashen.

"What are you doing here?" he spluttered. "What on earth is going on?"

"This whole event was a set up, wasn't it?" Robin said. He gave a mirthless smile. "So aren't you going to introduce yourself, *Eleanor*?"

Jordaan and Adam reared up in their chairs. The girl with the camera meanwhile was quick to seize a photo opportunity sending another blinding flash into the room; the young reporter seated next to her was scribbling away on his notepad again...

"Put that fucking camera away!" the man next to Robin then hissed.

The camera girl paused. This was the first time anyone had heard him speak. Joshua's mouth dropped open in shock before a second flash was detonated.

"Calm down, Perry," Robin whispered. He gazed up at Joshua in a way that was chilling before switching his eyes back to Eleanor. "Let us hear what she has to say..."

"No," the other man groaned. "We should end this madness now."

Robin seemed unperturbed, surveying her with curiosity as she continued to drift towards the table. There was something alarmingly confident about the way he lounged in his chair, one pale hand draped over the arm rest. He offered her a mocking smile.

"Eleanor," he said gently. "How are you, my dear?"

She shook her head in disbelief. "How can you say that?" she gasped. "Jake was never a drug dealer! I cannot believe the lies you've told tonight... We spent the last few months of our time in hiding together!"

"Eleanor, please don't make a scene!" Norman said. He spoke through gritted teeth. "We all know how distressed you've been and I realise this is hard for you to accept but..."

"Accept what, Mr Hargreaves?" Eleanor challenged, turning to stare at him. "And stop saying, my mind is *fragile*. That evidence was fabricated, all of it. We found one of those packages when Jake was alive! Bernard James knew he was innocent..."

"Bernard James was a soft-hearted fool," Robin added softly. "He would have believed anything. I suppose you only made this up to get him on your side."

"Bernard James was the only person who tried to help us!" Eleanor protested with a sob.

Jordaan took in the scene with a sigh.

"You are really Eleanor Chapman?" he probed.

"Yes!" she replied, turning to look at him. Finally a smile squeezed itself through the anguish on her face. "And you must be Jordaan! I'm so glad you came!"

Fumbling in her handbag, she absorbed the sight of this tall man with awe. Honoured to meet him at last, he was effectively the band's *manager*. But time was short; she knew it would be unwise to remain in this room for very much longer...

"I have some of Jake's lyrics for you," she blurted.

Wandering into the space between Robin Whaley and Norman Hargreaves, she leant across the table and passed him a photocopied sheet containing Jake's song lyrics. She could feel the sea of anger that swelled between the two powerful men with no other choice than to keep talking.

"This is Jake's last song! He sung it to me on the night he was killed. Pass it to Andries and if there's ever an opportunity to record it, I can remember the tune... It would be a lovely tribute."

"Thank you," Jordaan smiled, taking the sheet. "You were brave to come here tonight."

Norman's eyes flashed.

"Eleanor," Adam intervened, "do you have anything you can tell us? It could really make a difference..."

"You've already g-guessed the truth," Eleanor said shakily, "but for now, all I want is for the media to show some respect... to recognise what a talented musician Jake was!"

"If he wasn't killed because of drugs, then what *was* he killed for?" Adam pressed her.

She stared into his intense dark eyes - pleading eyes. "I-I can't tell you!" she faltered. "All I know is that his friend *Andries* spoke the truth when he told you that Jake *witnessed something*. Just follow the clues!"

Something in the air turned black.

From the other corner of the table, Robin's friend squirmed in his chair, the rage in him swelling again. He clutched his tie as if choking, his face turning purple.

"Get her out of here," he snarled to Whaley in a voice that shook with outrage. "Don't let her say another word…"

Without warning, he had drawn attention to himself. Despite the rising levels of danger that were closing in on all sides, Eleanor found herself staring at him.

"Eleanor, I think you should leave *now*," Norman said quickly. "I don't know how you came to be here tonight, but I am not happy about this intrusion…"

"No, well you wouldn't be would you?" she snapped. "And I thought you were a good man, Mr Hargreaves. The day you interviewed me in hospital, you were kind to me. I can at least give you that credit…"

Her eyes turned to Robin.

"You, on the other hand, Councillor Whaley, are pure evil."

Alison smiled.

"But who are you?" she added, her voice dreamlike as she stared at his companion. "Why are *you* here tonight? Do you know the truth? I have a feeling you do…"

"You know absolutely nothing!" the man spluttered, fighting to regain some composure.

"Yes, I do," Eleanor murmured, inching away from the table. "Someone had Jake killed to protect a secret and you might as well know, I wrote it down. I've got an account of everything Jake told me - from the day he left the police station - to the moment he was captured by the hit man hired to kill him - and it was Dominic Theakston…"

"Be careful, Eleanor," Norman muttered in a soft and dangerous tone. "You don't know what you're saying…"

"It's the truth, Mr Hargreaves," she pressed. She was close to the door now, ready to make an escape yet the words kept leaking out like a torrent and there was nothing she could do to stem them. "So I might as well warn you, my notes are filed and if I end up dead like Jake, that file is going to be published!"

"You have a very overactive imagination, my girl," Perry sneered, also rising, "and if you do not leave, right now, I am going to haul you through the court for slander, you lying harpy!"

"Well, this is never going to go away," Eleanor's voice broke tearfully. "I won't let Jake's death be forgotten. One day, I'll prove what really went on, even if it takes me a lifetime!"

Shuddering with fear, she stumbled back a few steps and with no further delay, turned and fled from the doorway, leaving the assembly gaping after her.

"Outrageous!" Norman bellowed. "This event has been a bloody farce!

Who organised it? We've deliberately been made to look like fools!"

"I'm sorry, Sir," Adam said softly. "I was the one who suggested that Jordaan should call the conference though I swear to you none of us had any idea this girl was going to show up..."

"Yes, well I am warning you, young man," Norman spat, "you are not to publish a word of what she said..." His blue eyes were blazing; impaling Adam with such fury, the man did not move. "Tomorrow morning I will be talking to officials at Scotland Yard with regards to issuing a D-notice. Do you know what that is?"

"Of course," Adam sighed, "I appreciate your concern. We meant no harm, especially if such allegations are unsubstantiated. We asked you here tonight to explain the story behind Jake's murder. As for our own article; all we ever wanted to do was put right the damage that was done to Jake's character, to honour his band and his musical talent out of respect to those in Holland..."

The room fell silent as the journalist packed away their camera and notes.

There was an air of tension as they prepared to leave. Joshua flitted around the table, collecting glasses. The police, as well as the suited men however, did not move.

"There were others involved," Robin remarked icily as Joshua loomed close.

Observing him for a few seconds and just at the point, he reached down to scoop up his wine glass, his hand clamped across his forearm like a manacle. Joshua gasped, desperate to tear himself away yet Robin's grip was like iron.

"You!" he snarled. "You're in on this, aren't you?"

"No!" Joshua squeaked.

"Let him go!" Alison shrieked, staggering back towards the table.

Robin captured her eye with a smirk. "Who are you really, young lady?" he whispered.

"They're brother and sister," Perry commented nastily. "You can see the resemblance. Don't you think it's obvious who they are?"

Joshua's face was a picture of anguish. Having finally wrenched his arm from Robin's grasp, he turned and sped from the room. The two men pushed their way out of their seats to follow but it was Jordaan who swayed in front of them, his towering frame denying them access.

"Enough, gentlemen," he ordered frostily. "I think there has been enough conflict for one night. Now let us all go home!"

III

Eleanor did not look back. She fled from the hotel and a few minutes later, was hurtling down the steps of Victoria tube station, to head for home.

Her heart was racing. Though in some ways, it could not have gone better. The journalists had definitely grasped the idea, there was something more sinister attached to Jake's death. She had no idea how her enemies would react, praying that her secret file might protect her.

Robin meanwhile, had also left the hotel, quick to install Perry into a taxi...

There was no denying, he was appalled by his reaction to Eleanor's unforeseen arrival, wishing he had never brought him. Anyone who had witnessed his outrage would be suspicious; everything they had worked so hard to hide wobbling on the edge of a tight rope.

Dragging deeply on his cigarette, he shivered, despite the warmth of the evening.

"Well, didn't I always warn you, she was dangerous," he snapped at Norman.

By 8:00, they had moved to a discreet restaurant in the Mayfair area. Just a taxi ride from the Grosvenor Hotel, they chose to continue their discussion in private.

"Yes, well even I never expected that," Norman whispered. "Though I cannot believe she pulled a stunt like that on her own. Do you suppose, she knew that journalist from NME?"

"I'll lay money on it, one of her friends did," Robin said coldly. "Probably the long haired boy; the one pretending to be a waiter, which I knew he wasn't, no more than his sister was Adam Morrison's PA!"

Yes, he had been dubious of Joshua from the start. Young waiters usually made themselves more scarce, their eyes averted... Yet this boy had stared openly back at him and he had read the fear in his eyes. Stubbing out his cigarette, he glanced back at Norman.

"Like I said all along, you really should have let Dominic deal with her, then maybe none of this would have happened. Eleanor has clearly made new friends... and she's stirring things."

"So what now?" Norman pondered. He shifted uncomfortably in his chair. "I am still not happy about involving Dominic. We don't want to run the risk of him killing her..."

"What's the problem?" Robin said evilly. "It's not as if she's pregnant now. We kept a close eye on her and she's had her brat! Dominic sent flowers, remember? We've known for some time where she's living, which is probably where those kids came from."

Norman felt his stomach tighten.

"It is too dangerous," he whispered under his breath, "especially if this file she spoke of exists and I doubt if she was lying... Whatever it contains could destroy us."

With those words, he longed to be anywhere else but here. Squeezing his eyes shut, he could hardly bear to look at Whaley's face; Jake's murder was going to haunt him forever, he knew it.

"I wasn't going to suggest killing her," Robin softly retorted.

Norman blinked, shaken out of his reverie.

"Even I agree, that would be risky..."

"Then what are you suggesting?" Norman probed. "Bearing in mind that any form of assault will have repercussions. She is a seventeen year old single mother."

Robin's smile chilled him. "We drive home a threat that will completely unhinge her," he drawled. "Dominic is a master when it comes to injecting fear into people. It's what he does best..."

"It'd have to be something seriously bad to throw her off the scent!" Norman snorted.

"Oh, it will," Robin's voice continued to drip nastily, "and you're right. She did step very close to the truth tonight, a little too close. This time, we are going to give her such a scare, she will never dare challenge us again."

Staring back at him, Norman was woefully seeing the man for who he was; the arctic chill of his eyes was enough to make his skin crawl.

"Don't tell me you and Dominic are friends now," he breathed. "I thought you couldn't stand each other! You'll never get a man like him to dance to your tune."

"I will, if it benefits us both," Robin snapped. "He stands to lose as much as I do."

"Yes, well I hear he's living the life of Riley, these days," Norman taunted. "He runs the criminal underworld like a business and he's got himself a very nice house; even nicer than mine, Robin, which is a big step up from the last shit hole he was living in! He's lodging with Dan Levy's family until the sale goes through. I also hear he's got a steady girlfriend. I have to admit, even I'm surprised at that, given his track record. He must be mellowing..."

"Well, I wouldn't get your hopes up, Norman," Robin finished. "As far as I know, he still rules by fear and he has one more little job to do for me..."

PART 6. DEPARTURE

Chapter 15

I

The Merriman children were still reeling in the aftermath of the press conference.

Even a week later, it was the most talked about subject in their household. Pushing aside the preliminary fear of being singled out by Whaley, Alison was adamant that this had been one of the most thrilling events in her life.

By the time they vacated the Bessborough Suite, Joshua had vanished behind the scenes to spend the next couple of hours immersed in the task of washing up glasses. Relieved to have escaped, he didn't dare show his face again... The consensus was, he would finish work at the same time as Luke and the two of them would travel home by taxi.

Alison on the other hand, had been delighted to accept a lift from the journalists.

It gave her an opportunity to quiz Adam; curious to wonder if he was going to print any of the suspicious allegations that had arisen.

"We will have to be careful," he told her gravely. "If that blonde guy turns out to be some political big wig, there could be some very damaging repercussions..."

With regret, he also warned of the potential legal action they might face, particularly if the police felt they had been slandered in any way.

Cautiously explaining what a *D-notice* was, he knew it would be unwise to print anything contentious until further proof had been uncovered. Yet he seemed confident that Eleanor should not give up. At the very least, a spotlight had been cast; the uncertainty surrounding Jake's killing had been exposed and there were bound to be further clues...

Back in the secure embrace of the Merriman household, Rosemary enjoyed listening to their banter. At the same time, she could not eliminate the churning worry she felt for her children, especially Joshua. Unlike the other two, he was visibly shaken by the event. His decision to infiltrate the press conference in the guise of a waiter had been a clever one; although Rosemary guessed he was a little too young to pull it off successfully.

No one had been fooled, especially the Councillor.

Their description of the man left her cold. Having long suspected he was corrupt, she was beginning to sense a more predatory nature. Her vulnerable son was even considering handing in his notice but Rosemary refused to allow him to give in to such intimidation; not with his mother around to protect him...

"If anything, that Councillor Whaley should be scared of *me*," she enlivened him. "He clearly has a fetish for teenage boys. Something like that could ruin a man's political career."

Luke smiled at that.

Out of the five of them, he felt the most optimistic. He didn't really want to speculate about the danger they might have landed themselves in. They were fighting against an appalling injustice and it felt good! Right now it was simply a matter of waiting to see what emerged from the press conference; the next edition of NME due out in just a few days' time.

His main concern was for Eleanor and her child.

While it was a delight to see her safely back in Forest Haven with Elijah, he couldn't ignore the potential threat unravelling its way into her world. Eleanor seemed so blissfully oblivious to it. It was almost as if she had forgotten about Theakston; the anonymous bunch of flowers, the chilling undertone of violence...

She had voiced a desire to go out, specifically to visit the park where Jake's 'memorial' was located. Jubilant they had set the wheels in motion to expose the truth behind his murder, she cherished the idea of slipping a lock of Elijah's hair beneath his stone.

"A keepsake from our baby boy," she chuckled as she played with him.

Luke felt a lump in his throat as her words tumbled into the lounge and for a few seconds he could not take his eyes off them. He was moved by the way Eleanor demonstrated her love for this child and to everyone's delight, he was in such excellent health too. Staff at the Forest Haven Clinic never stopped complimenting her on how well he was developing; the perfect weight for his age and with no signs of ill health, not even nappy rash.

She smiled with pleasure as he pushed his hand into the air, spreading out his tiny fingers. Unable to resist stroking the flesh of his palm, those same little fingers closed around her own, making a dumpling of a fist. Eleanor lowered her lips and kissed it, his marbled white skin evocative of apple blossom.

The only other difference was his eyes which were finally beginning to change colour. Flecks of green and gold had materialised.

Though right now, his eyelids were fluttering and as Eleanor continued to watch over him, he stretched his arms above his head and exhaled a toothless yawn.

"Looks like somebody's tired," Eleanor murmured. "Time to take you upstairs for your nap. I'll be back in a moment, Luke..."

Luke watched her go, struck with a pang of disappointment. He guessed, she would probably want to stay by her infant's side for now but he was wrong. On this occasion, he could hear her feet padding softly back downstairs before she rejoined him in the lounge.

"Sleeping like a log," she said, collapsing into the wing-backed armchair. "It's nice that he settles down so quickly. He's growing fast, Luke, he's going to need some new things."

"Mum can get you anything you want," Luke replied. "Or Alison..."

"I know," Eleanor sighed, tucking her feet underneath her knees, "but there are times when I think how nice it would be to browse around some of the bigger shops. Supersavers is fine for stuff like talc and baby oil. But I want to buy some cute clothes for him and some toys."

"Why don't we order a few catalogues then?" Luke suggested. No sooner had the idea slipped into his mind when he sat up straight. "It would be a lot safer than wandering around in London, surely."

"Oh, Luke!" Eleanor sighed, gazing fondly back at him. "I know you mean well, but I'm the one who needs to go out! I've been cooped up for so long. The last time I ventured out shopping was at Christmas and I could do with some new clothes myself. I can't keep wearing Alison's cast-offs forever."

Luke sighed. True to her word, she was dressed in one of Alison's old cat suits, olive green with flared trousers, a fashion trend from the previous year. With her lustrous, long locks swept back with a hairband, she conveyed the appearance of a TV character from 'The Avengers.'

"Mum's not happy about you going out on your own," he mumbled.

Eleanor bit her lip. "I know... but I'm going to have to step out into the big wide world again, one day. I love your Mum and I know she means well."

"We've all been a bit jumpy since the press conference," he added darkly. A shiver of goose bumps crawled over him as he said it; confused as to how she could remain so unfazed. "Can't you imagine the fury those men must be feeling? We all know Joshua experienced it first hand, especially from Whaley, but they've had a bit of time to reflect now..."

"I'm sorry about Joshua," Eleanor whispered. Eyes lowered, she seemed to mull it over. "I always knew Whaley was evil. I've never known anyone lie like he does or twist things! He's a horrible, manipulative man and the thought of him getting into politics makes me feel sick!"

"So what about the other one?" Luke probed. "We haven't actually discussed him much, have we? He was a politician too, you know..."

"You're talking about his friend aren't you?" Eleanor sighed. "The blonde man. He called me a *lying harpy*! I thought he was going to have a seizure!"

"Why do you think he reacted like that?" Luke pondered. "Is it possible, he might be even more dangerous? He seemed to have a lot more authority than Whaley."

"You spoke to him," she nodded. "Who was he, can you remember?"

Luke raked through his memory. "He said he was a member of the Conservative Party but yet to make his way into Parliament. I'm guessing he was 'public school' from his accent... and filthy rich! He made a real big deal of ordering one of our most expensive wines!"

"Really?" Eleanor gasped.

"Yes," Luke pressed. "His name was Perry! I remember Whaley calling him by that name. Perry, I guess it must be short for Peregrine."

"How very upper class," Eleanor mused. The light in her eyes faded. "Do you know what I think? I actually wonder if we met the man who was behind this whole thing."

"You mean Jake's murder?" Luke frowned.

"Yes, but not just Jake," she whispered fearfully. "What about Albert Enfield? What if he's *the man Jake saw by the roadside?* Fancy car, cigar... He was clearly somebody wealthy!"

"Not to forget the way he flipped as soon as you appeared," Luke reminded her. He gave a sigh. "Eleanor, we really need to find out who this man is."

Eleanor nodded. She had turned strangely silent as if chewing over the facts.

There had been a certain degree of satisfaction seeing those men squirming in that conference. Yet Luke was right about this man. He had kept his emotions well under guard; that was, until the very first hint Jake had witnessed something... and it had driven him wild.

II

The day the latest edition of New Musical Express hit the shops, Joshua squandered 70p of his hard-earned pocket money to bag ten copies. The black and white tabloid lay invitingly on the kitchen table, immediately distinguishable by its red logo. The whole family swarmed around the table, almost reluctant to open it.

"Oh come on, what are we waiting for?" Alison snapped.

Diving into the pages, she skipped all the other articles and reviews, until a headline leapt out at them.

MURDER OF LEAD VOCALIST REMAINS UNSOLVED
by Feature Editor Adam Morrison

Did fans from Nijmegen, Holland, ever expect justice, when newly emerging folk/rock band FREE SPIRIT lost their lead singer in July last year? This could be the first serious attempt by

the UK music press to acknowledge the link between an unresolved killing and the disappearance of a talented young musician on the verge of success...

Last month we brought you the sad news that lead vocalist, Jake Jansen, from the Netherlands-based rock group 'Free Spirit' was discovered dead in a violent East London neighbourhood. This story not only shocked fans in Holland, but drew our attention to a number of flaws concerning the media coverage of this tragedy at the time.

It seems the British Press were only too keen to suppress the true identity of the murder victim, when details of this crime hit the headlines last year. The story was instead sensationalised by the sleazier issue of drugs and perhaps typical of a media caught up in the tide of organised crime which has gripped London throughout the 70s. It is now certain that these reports put greater emphasis on the slim chance that this was a drug related killing carried out by a criminal gang, as opposed to recognising the victim as lead singer/guitarist, band members of Free Spirit had reported missing three months earlier.

Details of the murder, as well as the handling of the case, were discussed last week during a heated interview between Jordaan Van Rosendal, manager of *Pink Elephant,* (the recording company who signed up the band) and Chief Inspector Norman Hargreaves from the Metropolitan Police. It has since been acknowledged that the young man discovered shot turned out to be unsung legend Jake Jansen. Though the reason he was murdered sadly remains unsolved which must come as something of a huge disappointment to fans both in the UK and Holland.

Free Spirit made their debut appearance in Britain when they played as a supporting act at the Wheeley Festival of Progressive Music in Clacton On Sea, Essex, back in August 1971. Audiences were captivated by their awe-inspiring music, which likened them to popular British bands such as chart champions T-Rex, yet softened by haunting guitar solos and the subdued, sensitive vocals of folk groups like Lindisfarne. Free Spirit were renowned for their singalong melodies and maintained their musical consistency, as demonstrated by a recent recording and further commemorated by (as yet) unseen lyrics written by Jake during the closing chapters of his life. The band completed their triumphant year in the UK with a recent tour in the spring and summer of 1972 and were specifically chosen to play at the private party of the late Albert Enfield, who tragically died in a terrorist car bomb attack, thought to be instigated by the IRA.

Jordaan Van Rosendal accused the British police force of doing little to catch Jake's killers and contested any suggestion that Jake was involved in drug dealing, based on evidence that drugs were found in his flat. In his closing statement, Chief Inspector Norman Hargreaves apologised on behalf of the British press concerning the tactless way the story was handled and is reported to have said:

"If any new evidence comes to light, we will act on it but for the time being, Mr Jansen's murder will be confined to the cold case unit."

Pink Elephant plan to release a compilation album featuring some of their better known songs later in the year. They also hope to produce a new recording of one of Jake's final songs to pay tribute to the musical talent and song-writing ability he was best known for.

"It's not a bad result," Luke sighed. "At least it puts Jake's *music* in the spotlight. I think this is as much as you could hope for, Eleanor."

"Thank God for this article," she whispered, pointing to a small photo insert of the band on stage. She would have recognised Jake's pale, striking features if he had been submerged in a crowd. "At least I have a picture of him now..."

III

The days rolled towards another Saturday. They had moved into July now, where the shifting weather patterns delivered a spate of warm, dry days. Yet the air was beginning to turn muggy, bringing a forecast of rain and possibly storms.

Eleanor was determined to do some shopping beforehand with a yearning to choose some new baby clothes. But there was more to it than that. Aspiring to her role of motherhood, she was beginning to crave other things; a pram for example. There were times when she spotted other young mums wheeling their babies around in the fresh air and felt a prick of envy.

Determined to take another trip into Central London, she was convinced the danger would be minimal. With busy high streets packed with shoppers, it was way too crowded for her enemies to risk an ambush, especially in broad daylight.

Rosemary suggested the West End and Kensington; insistent she was to travel by public transport at all times and to absolutely promise to be home by mid-day.

Unable to suppress her glee, Eleanor journeyed to Kensington.

Located a fair distance from the East End, the buildings were tall and gracefully elegant with arched windows and pillared doorways. The area was characterised by its huge open spaces, the beautiful parks enclosed within black railings. The shops too, shared the same grandeur; sprawling and wide fronted with signs stretching high above their glass windows. Eleanor peered inside, enthralled by the colourful displays of furniture and lamps, the jewellery, clothes and shoes...

Drifting along the busy street, she was drawn to a halt whenever anything captured her attention.

At the same time, she found her mind slipping into the past; a time when she relished exploring London. These were the days she had lived in blissful ignorance with her father. Everything seemed so routine and uncomplicated. With a pressing sadness, Eleanor realised an entire year had passed since the terrible day she had said goodbye to him. She felt a sudden shiver. Ollie Chapman was a grandfather now... Yet she was pained to wonder if she would ever see him again.

Before long, the heat was beginning to stifle her. The weather *was* changing, the air closing in; oppressive and heavy with the increasing threat of a thunderstorm. She wore the dark blue dress she had originally borrowed from Alison. Spun from cool cotton, it allowed her to move freely, to ward off the worst of the heat as a gentle breeze wafted around the hem.

Perhaps the next time she felt brave enough to venture out, she would indulge in a long overdue shopping spree with Alison. Her new friend was gifted with good fashion sense and knew the best haunts for hunting out bargains.

Her motive today however, was for Elijah. Choosing her gifts carefully, she picked out several romper suits and a cashmere cardigan so soft, it felt almost weightless. She discovered padded booties made for tiny feet, a sight that drew a smile. Her gaze was also drawn to a candlewick blanket and ultimately a little teddy bear with creamy white fur and golden eyes.

Ecstatic with her purchases, she poured over the prams and pushchairs but turned away. Perhaps she should invite Rosemary to accompany her on the day she purchased one of these; she was bound to offer the most practical advice... and with this in mind, she tucked her merchandise into a roomy shoulder bag, all set to begin her homeward journey.

She had one more stop; to pay a visit to the Garden of Remembrance hiding in its own quiet corner of the park.

Despite the heat, it was easy to relax on a shaded bench and allow her mind to wander. The memories of Jake had already surfaced. She could picture him now, a fleeting backward glance as they raced across the park. Eleanor held her breath, her vision blurred by tears. She found herself drawn towards his memorial plaque, an enduring symbol of her love for him.

True to her word, she had snipped away a wisp of her baby son's hair. It resembled a feather, as fine and silky as Jake's, a burnished brown enriched with a subtle hint of auburn. Locating the small wooden box embedded in the earth beneath the stone, she plucked it from its crater and opened it. The box already concealed a lock of her own hair looped around Jake's song lyrics. Poking in the few silken strands of Elijah's hair, she felt an immediate breeze of connection...

"We have a son, Jake," she whispered, trailing her hand over the polished stone, "a beautiful boy. I named him Elijah, for both of us..."

Reassured that no one was lurking or watching her, she eventually tore herself away to find the bus stop. Her heart felt heavy, dragged down with sadness, yet it was the overwhelming love for her child that kept her going. Eleanor wandered past the railings which led to Commercial Road. Several buses were already queued along the pavement, including one destined for Forest Haven. She did not look back. Wasting no more time she jumped aboard.

The bus began to heave its way through the streets.

It veered to the right far sooner than she expected. Eleanor frowned. She was experiencing a moment of panic now, desperate to attract the attention of the bus conductor.

"This bus does go to Forest Haven doesn't it?"

Surveying her with irritation, he reassured her that *this was indeed the bus to Forest Haven* and just happened to travel the slightly longer route!

Eleanor lowered her eyes, wary of the dingy streets closing in on her. She instantly recognised the tightly packed terraces; these were the same streets she and Jake had crept along, on the night of their escape. In one way it felt nostalgic; like retracing old footsteps and reliving a memory... It took a good ten minutes for the bus to chug its way through the neighbourhood and after numerous stops, finally inched its way around the industrial estates.

The railway embankment loomed on the skyline like a landmark. On the other hand, she didn't want to be late home. Charged with a sudden hankering to disembark, she knew Forest Haven lingered just to the other side of that tunnel. It would do no good to have Rosemary worrying. With some reluctance, she stepped off the bus.

Adjusting her bag so that it rested comfortably over her shoulder, she numbly wandered towards the tunnel. She was sucked into its yawning interior, the curving brick walls enveloping her in a cape of shadow. At least it was cooler in here; silent and tranquil, where nothing but the tap of her own footsteps echoed through the void.

Yet the next sound wrenched her out of her dream world. No longer was it just her own footsteps, there were others... Powerful and menacing, they had gradually manifested themselves in her wake and already gaining ground.

Eleanor braced herself, resisting the urge to look around. Eyes fixed rigidly ahead of her, she kept walking. Except there was a chilling familiarity about this scenario. It reminded her of the time she had been walking Bernard's dog; the dark blue transit van hovering on the edge of her vision, that sinking sense of being followed. She quickened her pace.

Her pursuers were drawing closer. Eleanor flung a glance over her shoulder, unable to contain her curiosity for another second. She had to check who was there. The shadows of three men reared in her vision, silhouetted against the light of the tunnel mouth; but it was the towering, broad-shouldered shape of just one of them that finally unleashed her fear.

Propelled towards the exit, she charged into a run... The tunnel exit beckoned, a semi-circle of light. She was only yards away when a fourth man loomed into view; a man whose appearance seemed to mock her as the emerging daylight fell across his hawk like features. This was none other than the man from Waterloo Station. Positioning himself directly in front of her, his pale blue eyes skewered into her. He offered her a cold smile.

With a gasp, Eleanor skidded to a halt, staggering backwards without a second thought. Disorientated by panic, she receded back into the tunnel, having momentarily forgotten about the other men in there...

Nothing could prepare her for the shock she was about to experience as she collided with Theakston; encountering a wall of rock hard muscle, she backed right into him. She felt the heat of his palm as it clamped across her mouth, the power of his arm locked around her waist, strong as a python before he dragged her deep inside the tunnel.

He gripped the front of her dress and thrust her against the cold brick wall. Eleanor stared up at him in dread, her heart pounding.

Trying to fight them was pointless, *they had finally caught up with her.* She blinked back her terror, forcing herself to stay calm. His appearance had not changed. Only a short-sleeved shirt replaced the black leather coat she remembered him for but it was the only difference. His familiar, slanted dark eyes smouldered as he drank in her image, his face rigid and cold.

"Eleanor Chapman," his voice echoed into the silence.

"Dominic," she whispered huskily.

Slowly releasing his hold on her, he took a step back.

"Well, what can I say?" he drawled. "I'll give you this, love, you're either very brave or downright stupid to take on a man like me... unless you've got some sort of death wish!"

"Maybe I have," she said and this was the only thing she could throw back at him; a fruitless display of courage. There was no denying, she was terrified, all the months of pent up fear charging through her mind like a train.

The words seemed to stifle him. He took a deep breath.

"Thing is, you crossed the line again didn't you?"

"I did?" Eleanor responded dazedly.

Once again he stepped up to her, drawing his head close. "You know damn well you did!" his voice lowered to a hiss. "No one ever mentions my name and murder in the same sentence... or calls me a *hit man*. Especially in a room full of fucking journalists! You've well overstepped the mark this time, bitch! Time I taught you a lesson..."

Eleanor flinched, feeling the force of his wrath like fire as he towered over her. She could already sense her courage wavering.

"I-I'm sorry," she croaked tearfully, "but they knew your name from the papers..."

"Yeah and it was you who got me arrested in the first place," Dominic sneered, "which makes you a grass. Do you know what I do to people who grass me up?"

Eleanor swallowed, at the same time tilting her head slightly. Her eyes never left his face.

"Please!" she protested. "This was never about you, i-it was about Jake! All I wanted was for people to know the truth. The p-papers were full of lies, I wanted to put the record straight."

"Really?" Dominic said. "Not the story I heard!"

"Why should you people get away with what you did?" she blurted, unable to stem the sob in her throat. "You *did* kill him! I know it was you, I heard you!"

"Doesn't matter," he snapped, "fact is, it's time you learned some rules, girl! You've pissed me off more than anyone would ever dare in these last few months and now you pay the price."

In a flash of movement, he reached into his belt and withdrew his knife, brandishing it right in front of her eyes. Its polished surface shone in the glimmer of light from the tunnel exit.

Eleanor felt her throat turn dry.

"Such a lovely face," he whispered evilly, "what a waste..."

He pressed the flat of the blade against her cheek, allowing her to feel its cold metal surface. Eleanor pressed her eyes shut. The seconds passed slowly, her lip beginning to tremble; with some reluctance, she opened her eyes a crack but still he did not move. He wanted to prolong the torture.

"NO," she whimpered, inching her face away. "Please!"

She had never wanted to plead with him but how could she not? The proximity of the blade was unbearable as he continued to taunt her with it, not to mention sharp. His eyes filled with sadistic pleasure as he flicked back his wrist, ready to strike. With the knife suspended just inches from her face he casually slashed downwards.

Eleanor let out a yelp of terror.

But there was no pain, no sensation of bleeding, nothing... She slowly opened her eyes.

The sight of her enemy soared in front of her, the knife gripped in one hand, a severed hank of her own dark curls draped in the other. He met her terror-filled eyes and laughed.

Eleanor released a sob, filled with a sense of shock so pronounced, it was like waking up from a nightmare. The other men were laughing too, the sound echoing nastily in the surround of the tunnel. She felt her world crumble, painfully reminded of the night of Jake's murder; that same crushing defeat.

Unable to help herself, she started to cry. *They had no absolutely right to do this to her.*

"Don't cry, Eleanor," Dominic said almost tenderly. "Think yourself lucky! Up until now, you got off lightly..."

"Lightly?" she shuddered through her sobs. "You're going to kill me anyway! A-and do you know what? I don't care any more!"

Their laughter faded, leaving a chilling echo. Dominic looked at her with a sudden curiosity, his face illuminated by his cocky smile as he sauntered right up to her again.

"You already did the worst thing you could ever do to me!" Eleanor whimpered. "You killed the man I loved..."

He gave a casual shrug.

"Why?" Eleanor sobbed. "Why did you do it? Why did you have to kill him?"

"Dunno," Dominic said curtly. "Do you think I care?"

She shook her head in disbelief as his expression turned more sinister.

"Just a job, darling!"

"You took a man's life!" Eleanor yelled back at him. "Someone who meant you no harm!"

Sliding the knife slowly back inside its hidden sheath, he was yet to reveal the true callousness of his nature.

"So what? I only did what I was ordered. He was a *condemned man*, Eleanor and he was never gonna escape from those who wanted him dead..."

From the other side of the tunnel, Eleanor glimpsed the man with the pale blue eyes, watching them intensely. He turned away in the second she met his eye.

"Besides," Dominic continued, "none of this would have happened, if you hadn't interfered and let him out of that cell. Not my fault you fell in love with him. Sorry love, but he was nothing to me, so I really couldn't give a shit!"

Eleanor felt the brutality of his words. They pierced her heart, delivering more agony than the blade of his knife could ever do. It took one more glance at his taunting dark eyes before she felt the last of her self-control slip away.

"You bastard!" she gasped.

Fresh tears spilled from her eyes and with a scream of fury, she launched herself at him. To everyone's surprise, she started pounding him with her fists.

"You bastard, you bastard, you bastard!' she kept screaming.

Dominic laughed again, unfazed. Her tiny fists bounced off his muscular chest like raindrops.

Sobbing uncontrollably, she was tempted to kick him in the balls but somehow, he anticipated her move, twisting his lower body away just in time. As far as Eleanor was concerned, she had nothing more to lose; her fury had escalated beyond reason.

In a final gesture of defiance, she drew back her head and spat in his face.

Unfortunately, this got a reaction.

She saw the growing rage darken his eyes as he wiped the spit from his cheek. A second later, he drew back his fist and punched her. It was like a rock smashing into her face. Eleanor was floored by the sheer impact of it.

For a moment, she could not move; weeping with all the torment of a child. Her fingers touched the top of her lip where she tasted blood. There was not a man in the land who would not have been moved by the sight of such fragility. But these were no such men. She could feel their eyes feasting on her, savouring her ordeal.

"Silly little girl," Dominic snarled. "I could stamp on you like an ant! Now get up!"

Reaching down, he grasped a handful of her hair to haul her upwards. Within a flash, he had her pinned against the tunnel wall again; one hand around her throat, the other stretched high above her head, palm flat against the brickwork.

The image of his hate-filled face swam before her.

"So this is where I'm going to die, right?" she forced herself to splutter.

"No... I'm not going to kill you," Dominic whispered. "That would be far too simple. Fact is, we've been issued with strict instructions *not to kill you*, thanks to your little charade at that press conference. But I *am* going to give you one final warning..."

A heavy silence descended as he let the words sink in - yet to deliver a most deadly ultimatum.

"If you cause any more trouble... and if you ever mention my name again, in front of the press, the police, or in any public place, I'm gonna make you suffer another way, Eleanor Chapman."

"You said you can't touch me," she blurted, a little too soon.

"True," Dominic smiled evilly, "but you've got a kid now, ain't you?"

Nothing could have delivered more horror than those words.

"Shame if something happened to him," he added softly.

"How can you say that?" she whimpered.

"What, didn't Sammie warn you?" Dominic taunted, his grip around her throat tightening. "This is what I do..."

"B-but he - he's just a baby," Eleanor shivered.

He held her paralysed, his eyes boring into her. The power of his words hung in the silence yet at the same time, she noticed his arm suspended above her head. Her gaze was drawn to a pattern of scars. Small and circular, they wove a distinctive trail along the inside of his forearm. In truth, it looked as if someone had played a game of *join the dots*, using a burning cigarette.

"Yeah," Dominic sighed, following the path of her stare. "You understand, don't you? Cause me any more grief and I could snatch hold of that son of yours... I could make him suffer in ways you couldn't even imagine and make you watch!"

"You can't mean that!" Eleanor sobbed.

"Just try me!" he finished icily and with a final stab of his eyes, he released her. "One last thing," he added. "I don't want you around here no more, you're to leave London."

"What?" Eleanor gasped.

He was refusing to meet her eye now...

In those few seconds of electrifying silence, Eleanor crouched down to retrieve her shoulder bag. It had flown to the ground in the moment he punched her. She was shaking all over, her face wet with tears, a droplet of blood swelling in her lip; and as she hugged her bag, remembering all the lovely things that she had bought for Elijah, she knew without a doubt, Theakston had won. She would never cross him again.

"You heard what I said," he whispered after an agonisingly long pause.

Eleanor nodded her head.

"I'll give you 24 hours," he finished brutally, "and in case you didn't know, we've sussed out where you're living. Seen all those *hippy weirdos* you're lodging with and as for those boys, who I know work at the Grosvenor... tell 'em they'd better watch their backs. In fact, if you're still here this time tomorrow, we're gonna torch that place with them inside! Do you understand?"

"Yes," Eleanor replied in a tiny voice. "I-I'll leave, I promise..."

He shot her a final warning look; except her eyes were drawn to the tunnel exit. Dan Levy lingered, hands shoved deep inside his jacket pockets. He was staring at her strangely. Eleanor couldn't quite fathom the expression in his eyes; a glimmer of some unspoken emotion which might even have been regret...

"C'mon, Dan," Dominic snapped, tailed by his other two men.

They headed towards a familiar dark blue van, conveniently parked on the other side of the tunnel.

Eleanor did not move. The last part of that conversation had left her frozen.

She heard the sound of the van doors closing, followed by the rumble of an engine. It finally drove away. Yet still she crouched inside the tunnel; immersed in such a dark place, she almost wished Theakston had ended her life there and then, as he had done Jake's...

The air outside felt dense, choked with imminent thunder. Then the rain began to fall, lightly at first, before a scattering of fat droplets hit the pavements.

By the time she hauled herself out of the tunnel, she was caught in a heavy deluge. She hardly noticed... The rain soaked her clothes and hair as she drifted along the path towards the house. Her eyes stared blankly, empty of emotion until she had finally reached the back garden.

She stood there for a moment, staring at the house, *her home*, filled with the people she loved; and she was about to give it all up. Only then did her face crumple in anguish.

Chapter 16

I

Rosemary had been fretting for some time. Eleanor was late. She had promised she would be home by early afternoon and it was 4:00. Unable to suppress her anxiety, she stared out at the streets again. What troubled her equally was this savage downturn in the weather. The blackness of the clouds seemed particularly threatening. She couldn't help wondering if Eleanor had lost track of time; maybe she had dived into the cafe for shelter...

Any last hopes were shattered as a shout from Joshua resounded from above. He came pounding down the stairs. Luke, who was sprawled across the sofa, reading a newspaper, leapt to his feet.

"What's up?" he gasped.

"She's out the back!" Joshua spluttered. "Something's wrong!"

The three of them surged into the kitchen. Rosemary yanked the back door open just as Eleanor staggered up to it. Yet one glance at her terror stricken face told them everything.

"C'mon, let's get you indoors," Rosemary soothed, gathering her up in her arms.

Her soaking wet hair hung limply; the fabric of her dress drenched as it clung to her slender frame, leaking rainwater onto the floor. At the same time, Rosemary could feel the tremors emanating across her whole body.

"Can one of you fetch some towels?" she muttered to the boys.

Joshua responded immediately, bounding back up the stairs.

Luke on the other hand stood frozen. There was no denying her deathly pallor; the startled shock in her eyes. A purple flush of bruising had spread from her cheek to her mouth, a split in her upper lip filled with blood.

He shook his head, rendered speechless.

Rosemary lowered her gently into one of the kitchen chairs. "What happened?" she demanded, stroking her wet hair away from her forehead.

"Th-they got me..." The words were forced out painfully.

"Who?" Rosemary pressed her gently. "Not Theakston..."

Eleanor nodded, the shivers growing more violent before she completely broke down in tears. Rosemary wrapped her in her arms as she sobbed.

Finally torn from his trance, Luke crouched down next to her. He gently squeezed her hand.

"Bastard," he breathed through clenched teeth. "Fucking bastard!"

For once, his mother didn't complain about his choice of language. Eyes hard with anger, her first concern was to comfort Eleanor.

Joshua squeezed his way back into the kitchen, arms overflowing with fluffy towels. Luke grabbed one and wrapped it around Eleanor's shaking shoulders. Rosemary pulled another from the stack and started dabbing it against her hair.

"Make us a cup of tea, sweetheart," she muttered to Joshua.

Plonking the remaining towels onto the table, he turned to fill up the kettle. He could not resist the occasional backward glance. Like Luke, he sensed that something violent had taken place.

"That's it!" Luke snarled, rising to his feet. "This has gone too far, I'm calling the police!"

"You stay right there, Luke," Rosemary ordered curtly.

"But look at her!" Luke yelled. "How dare he do this to her!"

"Luke, p-please don't call th-the police," Eleanor stammered weakly through her sobs.

For several minutes, she could not stop crying.

The damage that had been done was more than physical; a prolonged psychological torment that had left her in tatters. The tears she wept were not just for today. This was a tidal wave of misery, arising from everything she had suffered. In less than a year, Dominic Theakston had destroyed her. His very existence threatened the safety of everyone she loved, including this gentle family... including her baby son.

"Elijah!" she whimpered. "Where is he?"

"He's upstairs, sleeping," Rosemary frowned.

"I want to see him!" Eleanor gasped, hauling herself out of her chair.

Rosemary eased her gently back into it, hands gentle as they pressed on her shoulders.

"Please, Rosemary!"

"Shall I go and fetch him?" Luke offered.

Eleanor nodded.

"Why don't you just tell us what happened," Rosemary sighed.

Joshua placed two mugs of tea down on the table.

"I will," Eleanor shuddered, "I just want to see my son first..."

Luke returned to the kitchen with her baby. Securely tucked in the folds of a blanket, he appeared to be sleeping blissfully. Eleanor peered at his face, her senses stirred by the sight of his delicate little features. Already, she could feel a bubble of fresh tears brewing.

"Oh Eli," she whispered, touching the baby's cheek. Gazing up at the adults poised fearfully in front of her, she dreaded what she was about to say next. "I have to leave! I have to get out of London forever..."

"What?" Luke whispered in disbelief, "but..."

"No, hear me out," Eleanor interrupted. "Theakston knows I live here. He's probably known all along. They've been watching me..."

Drawing Elijah from his arms, she swallowed back her tears.

293

"It was only a matter of time before he *caught up with me*. They had me trapped, Rosemary. They followed me inside the railway tunnel..."

"Good God, Eleanor," Rosemary fretted, "why did you choose to go through there?"

"It doesn't matter," Eleanor said. "If it hadn't happened there, it would have happened somewhere else... The fact is, everyone in this house is in danger including Elijah. He threatened him, Rosemary. He threatened to harm my baby..."

Her words trailed off, leaving a void of stunned silence.

It was Luke who eventually spoke. "Scum bag," he whispered, unable to conceal his fury. "What did he do to you, Eleanor, did he hurt you?"

She touched her lip, wincing at the tenderness. "He punched me, though I've only got myself to blame for that. I spat in his face! I couldn't help it, I hate him so much for killing Jake..."

"That's no excuse!" Rosemary snapped.

"B-but the things he hinted to do to Elijah..." she shivered, "and you may as well know something else. He threatened all of you and this is the reason, I have to leave! 24 hours he said, otherwise they'll be coming here..."

"Let them try!" Luke hissed, fists clenched by his sides.

Joshua on the other hand, had turned white.

"Luke, you can't fight a man like him!" Eleanor yelled. "If I'm not out of here by tomorrow, Theakston and his men are going to come to this house and set fire to it! We could be burned alive..."

"Oh, are they now?" Rosemary raged. "Well in that case, I bloody well am going to call the police! I will not tolerate these threats! If he's planning to come here tomorrow, I'll make sure the police are notified and ready for them."

Eleanor was shaking her head again. "It's no use," she squeaked. "It might not even happen tomorrow, it could be any time! I won't put your lives in danger!"

A sense of panic consumed her. Baby Elijah meanwhile started to stir, his sleep disrupted by the raised voices. He must have picked up on the fear bouncing around the kitchen. Wrestling in her arms, he emitted a series of thin cries.

The only problem facing them now was where to go? How easy would it be to find somewhere; some place right away from London where her enemies would never find her?

II

"This is all my fault," Eleanor whispered, a little later that evening.

By this time Alison too, had returned. She had stepped into the house, knowing that something had happened. A veil of malaise hung in the atmosphere like stale cigarette smoke. It lurked in the eyes of her two brothers. No sooner had she dashed upstairs when she was faced by the sight of her mother dabbing Eleanor's face with witch hazel.

With little choice but to enjoy a last meal together, the pitiful subject was resumed after dinner. A persistent bank of heavy cloud continued to press out the light. They settled down in the lounge, where the glimmer of candles felt comforting. Alison's eyes were glued to Elijah rolling around on the floor in one of his new romper suits, clutching his teddy bear. *She was going to miss him so much.*

"You were right, Luke," Eleanor continued sadly. "This was the result of the press conference."

"But darling, you only wanted people to know the truth," Rosemary argued.

"I know," Eleanor said sadly. "I loved Jake. He was my whole world. We even agreed to get married..."

She twisted the intricate silver ring on her third finger; *her engagement ring.*

"The memory of his last song," she mumbled. "It brought it back it all back; that horrible night, he was murdered... that mention in NME."

"Eleanor, we all supported you," Luke protested. "The press conference was a great idea! No one believed any of that drug dealing crap. They paid a tribute to the person Jake really was, which was the whole point of it..."

"Yes, but if only I'd kept quiet!" she whimpered. "They would never have known I was there! Do you know what angered Theakston the most? I convinced everyone, he was the *murderer*. You just don't do that in his world!"

"Oh, Eleanor," Alison said miserably.

A breath of fear was discharged into the room. Elijah started to cry. Eleanor knelt down and gathered him up from the floor, clucking in his ear to comfort him.

From another corner of the room, Luke sat forward, hands clasped in front of him. His whole face harboured a look of despair.

"Eleanor, you did nothing wrong. All you did was put up a fight."

"Men like Theakston rule by terror," Eleanor murmured, rocking the infant in her arms. "This was one of the first things Sammie warned me. You can't fight someone like him, I already knew he was dangerous." Hit by a wave after wave of fear, she remembered his last sinister words. *He knew where the boys worked.* "Promise me you'll look out for yourselves. He could still target you and this is what I worry about more than anything..."

"That monster should be put behind bars," Rosemary spat in outrage. "Why should we live our lives in terror? Something has to be done."

"Until the police stand up to organised crime, there is nothing we can do," Eleanor protested. "and I'm betting, he's still got Hargreaves protecting his back! They've won. I've got no choice other than to move away, so at least my son can be safe."

A sense of purpose crept into her mind as she said it. *She had to protect Jake's son.* This was her last legacy to him and they would never be safe in London, all the while Theakston dominated the criminal underworld! A tiny part of her had always known he would track her down one day and he was not a man to back down.

"Eleanor, do you remember what I said?" Luke proposed. "We could still get a flat together, you know. Perhaps we could ask about police protection..."

Eleanor clocked the surprise on the faces of the other family members. Luke had clearly never mentioned this. Gazing down at Elijah whose wails had subsided, her emotions felt torn... Everything about him was so fragile; his ears like tiny pink shells, his lips puckered up like a rosebud. She felt a burn of tears as she recalled Theakston's horrifying threat. Could she really bring herself to tempt fate?

"It wouldn't be fair on you," she intercepted. "I don't want to put you in any more danger. You've already done enough for me and I've only got 24 hours, remember?"

"But I can't bear to think of you being on your own!" Luke protested.

A tear leapt from her eye as she kissed her baby's forehead. Planting a dummy between his lips, she formulated her next words cautiously.

"Luke... I never wanted to tell you this but Theakston knows that you and Josh work at the Grosvenor! He said, you should *watch your backs...*"

She picked up the tension coiling its way into the atmosphere.

"All the while we stay in contact you'll be putting yourselves at risk. Can't you understand that? Danger will follow me wherever I go... whoever I am friends with..." She glanced at Rosemary, who had turned very still. "Tell him, Rosemary, he's your son!" Finally, she understood the powerful protective instincts that came with motherhood.

Rosemary's green eyes conveyed an unanticipated panic. "I'm sorry, but I have to go along with Eleanor on this... You're my children! I was worried enough about the press conference, especially when you were all so desperate to get involved. I knew it was risky! I suppose Hargreaves along with that odious councillor gave Theakston a report... I cannot allow you to put yourselves in the firing line any more."

Joshua had not said much all day. But as the conversation floated across the room, he was absorbing every word. He chewed his nails and looked up.

"There must be something we can do to help," he mumbled. "Where you gonna go?"

With a smile of surprise, Eleanor turned to him.

"Maybe there is," she murmured. "I thought about this earlier but are you still thinking about selling your caravan?"

Rosemary sat up sharply and their eyes locked. "Of course," she whispered. "That is the solution. I don't want the caravan any more... It doesn't really suit our purpose now but it could be perfect for you."

"How much do you want for it?" Eleanor pressed.

"Nothing," Rosemary beamed at her. "Just take it! You'd be doing us a favour..."

Luke's expression on the other hand, turned to outrage. "She can't live in a caravan! How can that be safe?"

"Luke, can't you see, this is perfect," Eleanor said tenderly. "I need a new home and fast..."

"I realise, it's not ideal," Rosemary consoled him, "but we do need to get Eleanor out of town. London is where the danger lies yet there is no reason why she couldn't be safe."

"The only problem is where to move it," Eleanor added. "What about some place in the country? Is there any way we could find a site?"

The silence fell again as they pondered on those words. A decision had been reached and in those closing seconds, Eleanor allowed her eyes to circle the room, capturing every person: Alison, with her serene beauty - Joshua with his enchanting, puppy dog eyes - and finally Luke.

For a second, she felt the magnetic pull of attraction, clocking his impish smile, his mesmerising, pale green eyes. *If only.* Out of the three of them, Eleanor knew she would miss him the most. The concept of a relationship flitted momentarily but faded, the instant Jake crept into her thoughts. No, there had not been enough time for her broken heart to heal. And time had run out...

She switched her eyes back to Rosemary, feeling as well as seeing the strength and maternal power that resonated from the core of this amazing person; a woman who seemed so in tune with human nature. She had cherished her companionship. She was the closest person Eleanor had known to a mother since her own had tragically passed away.

Rosemary frowned. She was still pondering over Eleanor's dilemma; *where to move the caravan...* Rolling hills sailed through her mind, memories of an idyllic village.

"I've got it!" she gasped. "What about Aldwyck where my sister lives? It's tucked right away in the countryside."

"Of course!" Alison piped up. "How could we forget Auntie Marilyn?" She threw her mother a conspiratorial smile. "Mum's right and it's not too far away. We could come and visit you."

"It's about twenty miles from London," Rosemary kept enthusing, "a county called Kent. It's so beautiful, Eleanor, you will love it!"

Even Luke was nodding. "We went there one Christmas... Isn't there some great big country house there too? The owner's some upper class gent. But he was nice. He let us walk around the gardens and we had a picnic..."

"James Barton-Wells," Rosemary finished for him.

Closing her eyes, she could picture the village clearly - never to forget this kind-hearted man who lived on the periphery. He owned a substantial amount of the land there.

"He's always shown sympathy to travelling folk," she mused. "Furthermore, he allows one of his fields to be used as a temporary site. Why don't we tow the caravan over that way?"

"And you say it's a fair distance from London," Eleanor pressed.

"Yes," Rosemary muttered. "A good half hour journey, which should put enough distance between you and your enemies. I'm going to phone my sister right now..."

Straightaway, Eleanor sensed an aura of mutual relief. They could hear the murmur of Rosemary's voice from the hallway.

From her position on the sofa, Alison shifted slightly, wriggling up against Eleanor.

"Let me give Eli a cuddle?" she whispered.

Eleanor heard the break in her voice. Tears glistened in her silver grey eyes as she slipped the sleeping bundle into her arms.

"Don't be sad," she counselled her softly. "We'll stay in touch, I promise! I want to be there for *you* when you get your big break as an actress."

A smile touched Alison's lips despite the tear rolling from her eye.

"I'm gonna miss you too," Joshua added with a tiny grin, "and what about Holland? You still thinking 'bout doing that trip? I wanna come with you..."

"And me," Luke added possessively.

This was something they had decided in the wake of the press conference; a spontaneous jaunt to Nijmegen in their old camper van. Furnished with Joshua's guitar and Jake's song lyrics, this would be a chance to reconnect with Jordaan. Perhaps they would finally get to meet Andries too, Jake's fellow musician and friend.

"You bet!" Eleanor smiled at them. "It's what we said we'd do isn't it?"

III

By the time the sun rose next morning, Eleanor had been awake for some time. Settling herself down in the kitchen, she found herself gazing across the garden as the first light of dawn radiated a violet hue into the sky. It gradually lightened to blue. The caravan in all its detail began to reveal itself, anchored in a sea of grass.

Two hours later, she stepped outside where the heavy rain had drenched the ground. It wafted a lush scent into the air.

Assisted by Rosemary and Alison, they gave the caravan a clean. To her spiralling delight, there was a certain newness about it. It was already equipped with cooking equipment and lanterns. Rosemary had added bed linen and towels; a box of candles to make it more homely. Eleanor's new 'home' also contained a gas bottle for the stove and fire, chemicals for the toilet... All that was needed was to hook it up to an electric supply and she would be completely self-sufficient.

Wandering upstairs to pack, she felt a surge of remorse.

If only she could have slept a little better on her final night yet an unshakable fear had gripped her, filling her with an overwhelming urge to protect her son. Torn from her bed on numerous occasions, she could not resist fussing over him. It took one glance at his flawless face to bring back the memories; from the vicious-looking knife Theakston wielded, to the disturbing sight of his forearm with its trail of cigarette burns... Conscious of Elijah's baby soft skin, just thinking about it made her shiver.

She wondered whether to mention the scars to Rosemary. There was no question, Dominic must have been damaged in some way but she pushed the thought aside. Regardless of the torment he may have suffered in his life, he had no right to threaten people the way he did; whatever else life threw at her, she would never turn out like him.

No sooner had they finished breakfast, they prepared to make a move. Rosemary's neighbour called round to help the boys shift the caravan. It took lashings of grease to loosen the wheels but with a considerable amount of manpower, they managed to coax it out of the earth.

The whole family were braced to accompany her. They had decided to make a day of it; to spend some time exploring the village and visit the idyllic country pub where they might even get to meet some of the locals. But Eleanor had one final journey to complete before her departure. She wanted to lay some flowers on Jake's memorial.

This time, she would be accompanied by Luke and of course, Elijah.

"This might be my last chance," she whispered to Rosemary. "I daren't come back to London, not for a while... You will keep an eye on it for me, won't you?"

"You know I will," Rosemary soothed her, taking her face in her palms. "But for today, stick with Luke. You can't risk being alone... not after what happened yesterday."

The others lingered in the road where a spreading pool of sunshine warmed the pavements.

Only Eleanor hesitated. Hankering to spend her last precious moments in the house alone, she absorbed the eclectic colours and contents; the blend of furniture that didn't quite match and the polished gleam of floorboards. Closing her eyes, she breathed deeply, drawing in the fragrance of sandalwood and rose petals. All she could picture was a mantle of candlelight; memories of the first magical moment when she and Jake had wandered inside... She clung to the vision for a few more seconds, then glided out through the door.

Rosemary was clambering into the passenger seat of her neighbour's Land Rover. Eleanor had only just learned that his name was Roger; a bull of a man with a dark beard, he smiled and winked at her. Alison and Joshua had already commandeered the back seat.

The plan was to meet up at a service station, on the periphery a town called Rosebrook.

Luke meanwhile, lounged against his red mini. Second-hand but polished to a brilliant gleam, this little motor car had cost him almost a years' wages yet it was his pride and joy. Small and nippy enough to weave through the busy streets of East London, it took only a few minutes to reach Commercial Road.

Eleanor did not look back. Nor did she notice the black London cab which had immediately started tailing them. She closed her mind as the familiar sights flashed past; trying not to think too hard about leaving Forest Haven and the delightful life she had led there.

Craving the tranquillity of the park, she had already spotted the outer railings encircling banks of laurel bushes. Pointing to a tiny wrought iron gate that led to the garden of remembrance, she asked Luke, if he could park as near to it as possible.

"D'you want me to come with you?" he suggested.

"Yes please," Eleanor smiled gratefully.

Safe inside the enclosure of the park, she found herself glancing across the lawns. Clusters of people strolled in the distance, bringing a wave of desolation. She clutched Elijah to her breast, taking her first cautious steps towards the garden.

With eyes darting in every direction, searching for enemies, even Luke was hit with a sense of menace as he lingered by her side. He had seen the taxi, parked a few cars back from his own car but thought nothing of it.

Once inside the garden, Eleanor crept up to the spot where Jake's memorial lay. Wasting no time, she dropped to her knees and settled Elijah into her lap, easing back the folds of his blanket. She leaned towards the stone. It shone almost as green as the flecks materialising in her son's eyes.

Elijah stretched out his hand. His little fingers grazed the surface and he was gurgling happily to himself as if the polished coolness of the stone soothed him.

Luke lowered himself onto a bench, watching.

It seemed heart breaking to imagine that this child would never know his father.

"A little piece of Daddy's spirit lives on," Eleanor whispered, moving her face close.

Sweeping a strand of hair from his forehead, she coiled it around her fingertip; it possessed the lightness of a feather. Eleanor breathed deeply, hand trembling, as she placed a posy of white carnations on top of the stone. Her departing words fluttered on the edge of her lips...

"Jake, my love, I have to leave now... But I swear that one day, I will find out the truth. I'll discover the real reason they killed you and I swear to you that those responsible will pay. Elijah and I have to go away for a while but I want you to know, I still love you and always will..."

Even from a distance, he could see her lips moving. Every so often, a beautiful smile lit up her face as she gently bounced the child in her lap. The tiny creature was stretching, reaching, clearly fascinated by whatever lay hidden in the shrubs.

From the other side of the railings, Dominic watched without expression. He was slumped in the back of an old Hackney Carriage; the car that had been tailing them, courtesy of a local taxi driver on his payroll. Any other vehicle would be suspicious. Braced on the other side of the seat, Dan Levy fumed in silence but of course, they had to follow her.

"What's in there?" Dominic muttered softly.

"Garden of Remembrance," Dan snapped. "'Spect she set up some sort of shrine."

He nodded, unable to take his eyes off her as she lowered the flowers to the ground. A peculiar feeling swamped his senses which he couldn't define. *To think of the weeks they had spent, scouring the streets looking for her - the fantasies of what he would do to her on the day they found her.* That day had arisen yesterday where it had taken a split second to realise those feelings were not yet relinquished. Something felt wrong, it shouldn't have ended like this.

So he had done what was expected of him; played havoc with her emotions and driven home a threat so nasty, she had no choice other than to flee from London. According to his paymasters, this girl had become a *serious liability*. With echoes of Jake's murder resonating, never was it more essential to get her away from that family; intelligent people who had raised too many questions...

301

Dominic sighed, flipping open his cigarette tin. He hadn't failed to acknowledge the mature looking, dark-haired boy who accompanied her.

"That's the Merriman boy, ain't it?" Dan murmured intuitively.

"Yeah," Dominic sighed, lighting a joint.

Not one to usually smoke weed in the daytime, he needed a buzz. Eleanor moved away from the spot and lay the small wriggling infant down on the grass. Dominic pulled deeply on his smoke, a sense of dismay dimming his euphoria...

"What's up, Dominic?" Dan grunted, interrupting his thoughts again. He must have observed the slight tremor in his hand. "You seem pissed off..."

"I fucking am pissed off," he retorted icily. "D'you honestly think I wanna be here? Trouble is, no one trusts her, so we have to sweat this out. Promised that prick, Whaley!"

Dan betrayed a smirk. "Been fun to see the bastard squirm! Shame 'e didn't 'ave the balls to sort it out 'imself though... Did you mean what you said about hurting the little 'un?"

Dominic's eyes narrowed as the rage inside him soared.

"For fuck's sake, Dan," he snarled. "It was fucking Whaley's idea to threaten her kid, not me!"

His head was swimming, releasing a torrent of thoughts and emotions. In truth, he took no pleasure in voicing such threats any more and for this reason he faced another dilemma. Renowned to be *one of the hardest men in London, employed to hurt people*, the last thing he needed was for his clients to think he was full of shit! So he went with the flow.

That aside, why was he even bothered? Organised crime was his trade. He had netted a small fortune. Next week, he was moving into a new house; an upmarket terrace with bow fronted windows. He had even considered asking his girlfriend, Rosa, to move in with him, having finally met a woman he wanted to spend more than a night with. *Like it or not, Dominic sensed something changing in him; some secret part of him locked away by years of gangland violence... and it was finally beginning to unravel itself.*

Unfortunately, it did nothing to alleviate the insufferable situation he found himself in now. Dominic's lips tightened. At the end of the day, Eleanor Chapman had unashamedly named him as Jansen's killer. A large part of him prayed his ultimatum would work. She would stay away from London and he would never have to see her face again. He exhaled slowly, the car choked with the fragrance of grass. Dan opened a window.

Eleanor had risen to her feet, snuggling the child against her bosom. She tiptoed onto the path to the gate, the Merriman boy anchored to her side.

With her back turned, he could see the baby's face, his delicate features, the subtle sheen of auburn in his hair. It hit him like a blow; the shocking realisation, he was staring at *Jake's son*. In that final chilling second, the infant reached across Eleanor's shoulder, his tiny hand stretching towards him... Dominic froze, staring directly into the baby's eyes. *Who was he kidding?* There was no mistaking this entire sequence of events would have far reaching consequences and if an invisible thread could stretch across the decades, it was created in that instant.

He tore his eyes away with a shudder.

"What now?" Dan muttered, clearing his throat. "Ow much longer 'ave we gotta sit this out?"

"We have to be absolutely sure they leave London," Dominic snapped, chucking his joint butt out of the car window.

Luke took the road known as the South Circular, unaware of the taxi still tailing them in the distance. It was a vast road which drew them right underneath the Thames via the Blackwell Tunnel. They joined the road which eventually funnelled them out of London towards Kent.

Eleanor stared ahead as miles of verdant countryside began to open out before them; the roads becoming narrower, the traffic thinning out at last. The impact of so much open space was beginning to overwhelm her.

Braced in the passenger seat, she turned her head, unable to resist a last glimpse of London before it faded into oblivion.

It lurked hazily in the background; masses of houses in their tightly packed rows, chimneys of factories and warehouses which symbolised the Docklands. Silhouettes of cranes soared in the sky like sentinels, watching them. Yet there was something quite murky about it. How much this perception arose from the menace that had tailed her, she was unsure. Struck with an impression of darkness, she recalled the streets of the East End, cluttered with half demolished buildings - the lingering threat of violence hidden in every shadow. She wasn't just letting go of the City but the memories.

Unable to shake off this perpetual haunted feeling, Eleanor swivelled her head back around.

Her heart thumped painfully as the car surged onwards, everything she had suffered spooling through her mind like a tape. London was a place where she had said goodbye to her father. She had fallen in love with Jake, the most incredible person she had ever met and would have happily spent the rest of her days with him....

With gritted teeth, she remembered Inspector Hargreaves; the corrupt police officer who had abused his power to detain and later, frame him - the sinister Councillor Whaley, whose lies and deceit had destroyed their final chance of survival together.

Finally, she recalled the press conference, having vowed to make one last stand against her enemies; an event that had brought her face to face with a mysterious, blonde politician, one whose name she had never discovered. He was just the sort of man Jake always imagined to be behind the conspiracy. To think, how very close to the truth they had veered, that night... But time had run out. The revelations of the press conference had unleashed the truly intimidating power of Dominic Theakston, their hired thug. How could she ever forget the horrific threats that had forced this departure? Staring fixedly ahead, Eleanor chose not to look back any more.

No, London was a city full of dark memories, a place she would forever associate with violence and fear. She was glad to see the back of it.

The tapestry of countryside unravelling brought a sense of calm. In every direction, she could see fields of arable farmland which seemed to stretch for miles. The rolling hills in the distance were smothered in woodland and dotted with clustered of houses.

Her racing heart gradually slowed itself as she turned to Luke... "It's so beautiful out here," she murmured. "I can't believe all this was on our doorstep!"

Swerving into the service station at 12:00 noon, they were delighted to reconvene with Rosemary and the others. They seemed excited, if not a little furtive in their knowledge of what was to come. Continuing the journey through the little town of Rosebrook, they finally turned into a country road; one signposted to the village, about to become Eleanor's new home.

No sooner had they crossed the threshold into Aldwyck, she was stirred by a sense of fortune. Despite the past, she had to count her blessings. *How lucky she was, to have met the Merrimans.* Not only had they loved and accepted her, but secured her protection right up to the day she had safely delivered her beautiful son, Elijah, into the world. She had discovered a reason to carry on living. And now they had brought her to this idyllic village. It felt safe and tranquil in a way that reminded her of Forest Haven but without the enclosure of the City.

A row of shops lined the cobbled pavements. A little further in, nestled a village green surrounded by chocolate box cottages; faded bricks, walls smothered in ivy and climbing roses, exposed oak beams... Eleanor felt the touch of a smile. Directly opposite, crouched a delightful country pub, the 'Olde House at Home.' Its beauty was enhanced by a display of wooden tubs and barrels, overspilling with summer flowers. There were plenty of tables and chairs outside where some of the villagers had already congregated.

Eleanor inhaled deeply, so enraptured by her first sight of the village, she felt as if her heart could burst. She gazed down at Elijah, dozing peacefully in her arms. The clean country air had brought a bloom to his cheeks and suddenly, she didn't feel afraid any more.

As they drew deeper into the village, she noticed a brook trickling under a mossy stone bridge; a lovely church constructed in flint and stone. Seconds later, the Land Rover pulled into the side of the road. Eleanor caught a glimpse of ornamental stone gate posts. They appeared to be flanking a set of wrought iron gates, the entrance to Westbourne House...

She felt the breath catch in her throat as Luke eased his car to a halt.

"This is it!" he announced. "This is where Mr James Barton-Wells lives!"

"Oh, Luke," Eleanor whispered. She felt a grip of anxiety. "Are you sure he'll want to help someone like me? Didn't you say he was upper class?"

"He is," Luke smiled, "but he's kind! See that field opposite? That's where Mum said we can park the caravan. Auntie Marilyn and her husband live in the farmhouse next door, so stop worrying."

She bit her lip as he opened the car door. Clutching Elijah, she eased herself carefully out of her seat. Yet only now, did the full power of her emotions rush to the surface. *There was no turning back, she was here to stay.*

Tears swam before her eyes as she drifted towards Rosemary. Hovering by the gateposts with Alison, she smiled across, arms outstretched to beckon them. Joshua in the meantime, pressed his youthful face right up against the gates to peer through the bars. A long drive bordered with beech and horse chestnut trees led to an exquisite country estate; a building whose symmetry gave an impression of magnificence even from a distance.

Eleanor followed his gaze, absorbing the sight for herself.

She could just about distinguish the figure of a man striding down the driveway. Tall and of wiry stature, he wore a tweed jacket, a mane of thick hair framing haughty features. Observing the powerful rhythm of his stride, she was reminded a little of her father.

Elijah rested peacefully in her arms and as she gazed at his face, she was delighted to see his eyes wide open. He too, seemed mesmerised by the sweetness of their surroundings...

And she clung to that moment, knowing she had entered a new era; a life that would be so very different to anything she had ever known. Her eyes were drawn to the ring on her engagement finger where the two stones of golden amber and green tourmaline trapped the sunlight in their colours. She could feel the cool stone of Jake's pendant as it rested against her chest - the warmth of their baby son as she cradled him in her arms.

"It's just you and me now, my darling," Eleanor whispered, kissing the top of his head, "and we're going to live in a beautiful village. Your daddy, Jake, would have loved it here..."

With her words trailing off, they continued to run silently inside her head like a prayer:

I'll never forget you, Jake. Elijah and I will find others like us... and together we will create a society where everyone will be able to live in safety.

This is not the End
This is only the Beginning

'SAME FACE DIFFERENT PLACE - Book 2 - Visions'
available in kindle and paperback.

Printed in Great Britain
by Amazon